Rachel Neumeier

DEDICATION

This novel is dedicated to Little Fuzzy – first brought to life by H Beam Piper, beautifully envisioned by Michael Whelan, reinterpreted by William Turing and Ardath Mayhar, then later by John Scalzi and Wolfgang Diehr.

Little Fuzzy snagged my imagination too.

This novel is therefore for Little Fuzzy, and for everyone who has ever enjoyed stories of Little Fuzzy and his kin.

CONTENTS

ACKNOWLEDGMENTS

Many thanks to Craig Neumeier, Mike and Linda Schiffer, Kim Aippersbach, and Deb Boyken for editorial comments; and to Dolores Neumeier, Linda Schiffer (again!) and Hanneke Nieuwenhuijzen for proofreading.

1

Twelve Disks and forty Blades, right here in this ordinary juncture system—right *here,* in this utterly unimportant, empty system between living worlds, at the near edge of Ka' Taand space, where no serious danger ever came.

Twelve Disks were too many, a lot too many—*forty* Blades were a whole lot worse—and worst of all, that enemy formation had come raking through the outer-system slide only after *Nkaastu* was already *far* too close to shear off, mask up, and hide.

For that first stretched instant, while the computers resolved inputs and painted increasingly horrifying images in the display, everyone on the bridge, including Daamon himself, stood frozen in shock.

"Daamon!" Paaol said urgently, first to recover. "Give me a hundredth chime, I'll get the heart-Disk spotted and get you a firing solution!" He had been lounging back, his eyes half closed, bored and probably half asleep, letting his main-crew partner, Aanhk, support most of his weight with her left arms. The blazing icons in the display had snapped him to attention; now he was on his toes, leaning forward, almost vibrating with eagerness, skimming fingertips across the console he shared with Aanhk, not waiting for her to drop the console to comfortable uman height.

Paaol had to know this was disaster, obviously everyone understood it was disaster. But that was Paaol, ready to leap into even the most horrifically unequal fight, convinced they'd win or—in this case—ready to die trying. That wasn't an attitude Daamon had ever thought he'd need on *Nkaastu*. But, gods beloved and forsaken, he was grateful for it now, especially as Paaol's urgency broke him out of that shameful heartbeat of paralysis.

Tightening his grip on his cane, Daamon took the instant necessary to strike the battlecommand signal hard with the heel of his right hand, taking priority command of the ship and summoning the rest of the battlecrew. The emergency lights across the high ceiling of the bridge flared to life, bright purple and crimson, warning tones ringing with the slowly gathering resonance that signaled the emergency transfer of command. Across the bridge, all the primary consoles automatically dropped to uman height, leaving secondaries for the turun crew.

Beside Daamon, *Nkaastu's* captain, Kuotaan, had stiffened into a defensive pose, leaning forward, gripping the railing with one lower hand, setting her other lower hand on Daamon's back in support as she ran her own swift calculations of possibility and risk on their shared console with both upper hands. All the turun across the wide bridge were responding to imminent threat in the same way, opening their golden eyes wide, leaning forward, bracing their four powerful legs, gripping the crash railings, supporting their uman partners. That was how nturun responded to a threat: by bracing to defend. The males, the uturun, were more than aggressive enough to face any enemy, but uturun could not work together and were never khand—crew—only allied passengers. Flexible, fast-moving, adaptable, and above all *cooperative* aggression was the entire purpose of the uman battlecrew.

Daamon had not expected to need any of those qualities *here.*

Uut should never be here, not along the near edge of Ka' Taand space. Definitely not anywhere along the simple run from the heart-star of Gaatuu to long-settled Hanaa, through this empty juncture system to the settlements at newly discovered Aam and back again.

Rival matrilines might attempt half- or near-piracy, yes. True pirates had become a significant threat, yes. That threat was excitement enough for a man who'd nearly died—twice—in the fighting along the far edge. *That* was where a person expected to encounter uut, Blades leading Disks as they probed for an unguarded opening through the complex geometry of the slides that wove space together into a complex, twisted lacework of junctures. Out *there,* distant from home and hearth and family, a ship might run into any gods-be-forsaken disaster. Not *here.*

But here they were: twelve Disks blazing red in the display, cutting through the outer reaches of the juncture system straight toward *Nkaastu,* every one of them larger and more heavily armed than a small half-fighter tradeship. Worse, those viciously fast Blades were so small, they were much harder for targeting to acquire, still showing mostly as white flickers of extrapolated positions, only a handful of the closest burning steadily in the display.

No blue or green anywhere. No full-fighters passing through the juncture who might have better matched this level of threat, which was going to lead to disaster. But at least no tradeships to fall helpless prey to the uut.

Fall prey to the uut *first.* Everyone at Hanaa was in deadly peril now. They just *thought* they were safe, exactly as Daamon had thought they were safe until this moment.

"Got it!" cried Paaol, and then shook his head in frustration, feather clips swinging in his long hair. "No—sorry, that's not the heart-disk, forsaken uut are playing hard to tag. But I'll get it, Daamon, don't worry!"

"Four thousand worries, that's not one," Daamon promised Paaol, with perfect sincerity. He'd bent his own attention to throwing *Nkaastu* onto a different course, one that would skate them at an angle away from the uut, delay engagement, but keep *Nkaastu* between the uut and the Hanaa slide. If even one Blade got through to Hanaa, then got away again, that might be worse than half-disaster or near-disaster. That might be *absolute* disaster.

There was no way a single half-fighter could take out a formation like this. But whittle the numbers down to something whoever was at Hanaa might handle ... maybe. *If* the beloved gods were merciful.

"Got—no, gods be forsaken, who's taught the uut to scramble their patterns like that?" Paaol sounded seriously offended rather than upset or afraid. Battle-keen even for an uman, Paaol had his saaom tournament feathers coated in protective lacquer and wore them all the time. His partner Aanhk, alone among the primary crew, wore three clips of her own, the feathers swinging from rings through the edge of one pierced ear, showing her pride in her battlecrew partner.

Daamon left them both to sort out priorities for the computers. He was running different scenarios as fast as he could, modeling tactics. No great options, no good options, no mediocre options ... he set interdicting the Hanaa slide as first tactical priority and disabled every other possible priority, including *Nkaastu's* own survival, and that finally did the job. In a sense. Daamon looked up at Kuotaan, looming beside him.

Matriline before every other consideration, that was ever and always the nturun priority. But Kuotaan had been out there too, on the far edge. She, along with Daamon, had faced the uut during those very first battles, when the Ka' Taand had suddenly discovered they were in a war they had not expected, fighting an enemy they did not know. Both of them junior, both of them painfully inexperienced, neither of them expecting to take command. But their primary captain had fallen, and half a chime later their secondary captain, so Kuotaan, youngest and least experienced of the captains, had shouldered the burden of command horrifyingly alone. Then word came echoing from ship to ship that uman crew might do best against the uut, and Kuotaan had—personally, without support from secondary commanders—risked everything to throw battlecommand to a very young uman crewmember whose own uman seniors were dead.

She'd been desperate. But she'd been right. Daamon had gotten their ship out of that mad, desperate, bloody series of disasters mostly because the beloved gods had been merciful and the main fighting had passed on and left them on the periphery, but partly because he'd made decisions that were just barely fast enough and good enough, tied their ship into a staggering, cooperative defense with a handful of other unarmed and half-armed tradeships. That defense had served to get most of them back through to the heart-stars of familiar space.

Daamon remembered vividly the long, limping nightmare journey through one juncture system after another, the nuclear flares behind them as, all along the far edge, slide after slide was deliberately destabilized to prevent the uut from following them toward the heart-stars. He remembered rather less clearly the long recuperation afterward. He had returned home. Everything had been the same. Nothing had been the same. Every time he looked at the sky, every time he closed his eyes, Daamon had seen again the fire running through the dark, intricate lacework of the far edge, the bloody coruscation of the destabilized slides that warned of monsters waiting out there in the dark.

Two years later, the Aanuku matriline had sent an offer of alliance to Kaamharaa, and a separate specific offer to Daamon. A new settlement at Aam; a routine, easy run out from Gaatuu and back again. They needed battlecrews, but not for the full-fighters that guarded against uut incursions along the far edge, not even for the half-fighters that escorted big tradeships. For half-fighter tradeships, meant to face ordinary threats. Kuotaan wanted him. Would he come?

Daamon had not exactly thought he would return to space. But in all that year, he had not managed to find or make a real place for himself within his sep' family. The offer of alliance was a good one: good for Kaamharaa, who could build upon his already solid reputation for complex trade negotiation. Good for Daamon, who, with that offer in hand, had realized at once that he did not want to face the uut again, but also that he did want to return to space. Good for their family because the offered alliance would also pull the matriline of Guuan, from which Kaamharaa's uman family had come, into alliance with the rising matriline of Aanuku.

He had said yes.

Kuotaan had trusted his judgment then. Now, nine years on, having faced together a good many pirates and near-pirates and occasional trade agreements gone seriously wrong, they each had confidence in the other.

Daamon had better not be wrong. But he wasn't wrong. The priority *had* to be keeping the uut away from Hanaa, gateway to the heart-stars and the entirety of familiar space.

"Yes," agreed his captain, her voice a low rumble. "Nda Daamon, we approve." She inclined her head to look down at him from her one good eye. She also tapped the console, formally accepting the priorities as he had set them.

Daamon acknowledged with a nod and locked in Hanaa's protection as the only priority.

A heartbeat later, Kuotaan's secondary captain, Tuutka, slammed onto the bridge to take her place beside and behind Kuotaan. Daamon hardly noticed. All his attention had gone back to the displays.

Aanhk, Paaol's partner, threw a look over her upper shoulder toward Daamon. She'd followed that reorientation of priorities, but she didn't say a word, only braced Paaol with a lower hand against his back as he rapidly figured priorities and firing solutions. Left to himself, Paaol might move too fast and commit too early, but Aanhk would keep him from running too far ahead of the action.

Daamon steadied himself with one hand on his cane, glad now for every moment he'd spent studying the maneuvers and mistakes of real battles, those early disastrous battles he'd been caught up in and those barely less desperate that had taken place afterward.

He was glad as well for every saaom tournament he'd entered since taking his place as battlecommander of *Nkaastu,* glad that his sep' brother Paaol had practically submerged himself in the games and dragged the rest of them up the rankings with him. Saaom was deadly serious practice for battlecrews, and while mostly that meant the battlecrews of full-fighters, not half-fighters and certainly not half-fighter tradeships, Paaol ranked right up among the top saaom reputationists. Daamon thanked the beloved gods for that.

He was even grateful for every single pirate they'd ever faced, even the occasional sad, grim encounter with uman pirates who had rejected every possible civilized tenet of the Ka' Taand. He certainly hadn't expected ever to be grateful for pirates, but those sharp, vicious battles had provided crucial real experience for himself and his battlecrew.

Their situation here was terrible. But Daamon thought they might yet manage to do something useful with the handful of dice the beloved and forsaken gods had thrown their way. Tactical options tumbled through his mind as the tactical displays changed and changed again. Mostly not very good options.

Even as he watched the tank, the computers reordered the display, updating the positions of the icons. The Disks had taken on an attack formation, pairs of Blades curving away from the main Disk formation to wait their chance for independent runs toward *Nkaastu*. Worse, most of the Blades, all but eight, had already slashed away along the line of *Nkaastu's* original course.

Saraa arrived, out of breath and panting, throwing herself toward her station, letting her partner Tsumon catch her and swing her into position. "A bit of a mess," was her comment as she assessed the situation. "I expect you want every option we can develop." She was speaking to Daamon, not her partner, so her tone was cool.

"As fast as you can work them out," he confirmed. "Priority every option that takes out a good number of that formation. The Disks, not the Blades."

Genru, a decade older than anyone else in the battlecrew, came onto the bridge hardly a twentieth chime behind Saraa. He took in the displays with one appalled glance, but made no comment as he settled in beside his partner Suumat. Those two were a great deal alike, though Suumat was turun and u Aanuku; Gen was uman and u Guuan. They were both gifted with signals work, but more important, they were both calm and unruffled in every situation. That was a valuable counterpoint set against Paaol's volatility and aggression on the other side of the bridge.

That was the full battlecrew at last, and Daamon tried not to waste time wishing he stood on the bridge of a full-fighter, with at least twice the battlecrew and a minimum of four times the firepower. He definitely did not let himself wish some other battlecommander stood right here on this bridge with *this* battlecrew—someone more aggressive, someone *eager*. Someone who hadn't tucked himself away on a half-fighter tradeship that flew nearly safe routes on the near edge because saaom was one thing, near-pirates were a second thing, full-pirates were a third thing, but he had not wanted ever to face real battle again.

Daamon took a breath, let it out, and shoved all that stupidity out of his head, hard.

"Leftmost Disk!" Paaol called, setting the one he meant as a double-priority for targeting, painting it a much brighter red in the display.

"Huh." Genru raised his eyebrows. "I guess you're sure."

Paaol made a scornful sound. "I'm sure, all right—I've got it now! That's the heart-Disk, I'm telling you."

That was definitely not the usual position for a heart-Disk, and Daamon hadn't picked that one out himself, but Paaol was the best of them all, so fine, leftmost Disk. He began to calculate an intercept solution between the formation and the Hanaa slide that would give *Nkaastu* a reasonable shot at that specific Disk, then more sensibly shunted his half-completed solution to Saraa's console.

"Check the priorities," he told her.

"Teach your grandmother," Saraa answered coolly.

Even under the circumstances, Daamon had to smile at the rebuke. She didn't actually mean *Stay out of my business*. She meant, *I've got this*.

Saraa was a viciously clever battle navigator. She wasn't like Paaol, running on instinct and sheer ferocity. No, Saraa's mother was the north wind. Nothing could knock her off fast, steady assessment of upcoming possibilities. The computers handled the instant-by-instant maneuvers, of course—but Saraa would set upcoming battlefield priorities and present Daamon with plausible choices for the tactical goals he handed her.

Genru said over his shoulder to Daamon, "Gods beloved and forsaken, what's this big a formation doing on the *near* edge? What are *any* uut doing on the near edge? We can't stop this many, Daamon!"

"You know you love a challenge," Daamon answered. Genru told him in pithy uman cant what he could do with his challenges. Like anyone sensible, like Daamon himself, Gen preferred overwhelming superiority rather than any kind of challenge.

Paaol, who *did* love a challenge, said, "Who cares why they're here? We'll turn 'em into stripped particles, Gen! Think of the glory accents we'll win from this!"

His show of confidence wasn't an act. Paaol really did feel that confident. Daamon wished his sep' brother's delight in battle was based on realistic odds. But it wasn't Paaol's job to come up with a brilliant strategy that would let *Nkaastu* take out a good proportion of those uut fighters by herself. That was *his* job.

"Saraa?" he asked.

"Disks are shedding vee, angling for an intercept. Forget the thirty-two Blades, they're way out of reach, they're going through and we can't stop them, but we can get in front of the rest of the formation if you want to do that. I don't think it'd be great for *Nkaastu*, but looking at the priorities you've got locked in, I guess that's all right with you." She paused. Then she said crisply, "Okay, here we go, we can get in front and cut them off from the slide in two point two one chime-down. Or we can cut and run, then come around behind them and try to pick off the ones in the rear. Or something else if you've got a brilliant idea I haven't thought of. We need a decision within point zero nine."

All that with perfect calm. Daamon was glad of every drop of glacier melt in her veins. He said, "Assume the intercept, options for the Disks, priority the heart-Disk," and let her alone to figure that.

The swarm of Blades that had already gotten past them, cutting toward the Hanaa slide, were a serious threat to everything in Hanaa system. But, depending on who was flying what on the other side of that slide, maybe thirty-two wouldn't be too many. If his own people played this right, if *Nkaastu* managed to cut through the rest of this formation hard enough, then whatever full-fighters and half-fighters might be at Hanaa right now *might* be able to finish those thirty-two Blades plus however much of the rest of this formation got through.

They *had* to do that. Because some Blades carried worldbreakers. That was something the people of the Ka' Taand had learned on the far side. Not all Blades carried those, but some. You never knew which. If the wrong Blade got through to Hanaa, the whole world might be lost, burned off like Nguaa at the very beginning. That memory cracked open, threatening to begin a terrible cascade of memories.

Daamon shoved memory away and firmly shut that door, shut every door between this present and that past. He couldn't afford the distraction. Because even worse than Nguaa, even worse than burning *one* world, if just a single Blade got away again, carrying word back about the route it had followed to find Hanaa, a lot more uut would surely turn up, and soon. And if uut swarms got through Hanaa system into the actual heart-stars of the Ka' Taand ... Daamon cut that thought off hard. That kind of terror was just too paralyzing.

Fears that cut closer to home were bad enough—fears about what losing *Nkaastu* would mean. Kaamharaa himself was on this ship, one of the first and few turun males to establish residence on an allied matrilineal ship. Daamon's own little sister Taya was on this ship. He could hardly bear to think of losing either of them, far less both.

If Kaamharaa died, their sep' family would almost certainly shatter and dissolve. Worse, every tentative attempt to bring individual uturun into permanent alliance with major matrilines, an effort supported by every sep' uman in the Suund but only a few turun matriarchs, might shatter as well. The hard-won progress uman people had made toward pulling adult turun males into broader society might very well begin to fail, setting the whole effort back—who knew—a hundred years, two hundred, more than that.

All that was true, but at the moment Daamon cared less about that than the risk to his own and Kaamharaa's family—to Taya and Paaol, who also belonged to sepu Kaamharaa; and beyond them, to his own battlecrew; and to his captain and the main crew of *Nkaastu*.

No choice but forward. He shoved all that aside too, because at the moment, he could not afford to care about family any more than ship.

"Paaol," he said. "Defer the heart-Disk, set immediate priority on the central Disk, range that one as loud as you can, let's persuade them we missed the real heart of their formation. Saraa, take the intercept, get us in front of the main formation."

The eight Blades that hadn't headed straight for the in-system slide were directly in front of the formation of much larger Disks. No surprise there, that was just how uut liked to arrange formations. Daamon went on. "I'll try to give the word in time for it, but if I don't, call it yourself, got that, Saraa? Get us right in front of the Blades, *right* in front, point zero zero in front of the Blades if you can manage it. Gen, assume they'll try to target us with energy weapons."

Probable. Missiles fitted with insystem drives were higher-vee once they got moving, but much slower to target extremely close enemies; Blades usually relied on energy weapons for short-distance battle and saved their missiles for use against stations and worlds and other big, stationary targets. Daamon added, "Saraa, set up a skip-path that'll blink us out of their way the instant the Blades fire, but drop us *right* back again behind them, in front of the Disks. Paaol, range the Blades and the central Disk, but the instant the Blades are past us—"

"Got it, good plan," said Paaol, with a satisfied little lift of his head; he loved risk and riding the knife's edge of disaster. Paaol would have done just fine out on the far edge, battlecrew on a full-fighter, working to keep uut out of a handful of truly crucial juncture systems that linked important settlements. He'd only joined *Nkaastu* because Daamon was already battlecommander and Paaol knew he'd be able to join the battlecrew right away—and a little because he didn't want to leave Kaamharaa.

"Oh, yeah, *great* plan," said Saraa, but her hands flew over her console, setting up the break he'd asked for and, knowing her, probably three more for good measure.

Daamon said, "If we cut down the number of Disks, whoever's at Hanaa can handle the rest of them, plus the Blades." They would have to.

"Maybe. *If*," said Saraa.

Paaol ranged the uut ships Daamon had specified; the whole hull rang with his marks. The formation of Disks cut away to evade the attack that ought to have followed, then tightened their angles to a sharper, more direct course when no attack was forthcoming after all.

"They must think we're fools," said Paaol, grinning tightly. "Or empty and trying to slow them down with a bluff. They're in range, Daamon. Fire incoming—"

"Break to random walk," said Saraa.

There was no sense of movement; there never was any sense of motion aboard ship, of course. Only the tank display showed *Nkaastu's* change of position and course as they shifted from a straight course to a random walk, sharp shifts in vector, acceleration, velocity—very difficult to target, though sheer bad luck could still drop them directly in front of enemy fire. But random walking was still the best tactic for a smaller ship, less well armed and a lot less heavily shielded than a full-fighter. They should be much harder to target now, which should buy them time to set up and execute a skip course.

The insystem drive made one or two peculiar maneuvers possible, as well as bringing whole systems within convenient reach. From a near-star slide to the far reaches of a system took chimes or days, not months or years. That was important for tradeships and matrilineal envoys. But the capacity for skip-courses and slip-courses was the part that mattered to a battlecommander. The Blades' first attack missed as *Nkaastu's* course and velocity flickered and stuttered, random and therefore comprehensively unpredictable. A pause drew out as Daamon waited for the true uut heart-Disk to come within range.

This was one of those moments that occurs during battle, when everything was set and there was nothing to do until the chime rang down. Daamon glanced up at his captain, whose ship he was planning to risk and most likely sacrifice. Kuotaan angled her head to gaze down at him, her single golden eye meeting his, the white seams of the scars across the other side of her face a reminder of horror.

She knew what he was doing. Nturun would never, could never, subordinate the needs of their own matrilines to any broader priority. As the saying went, it was nturun who made the matrilines, but it was uman who made the Ka' Taand—the Karuuka Saahu Taand, the great civil society of familiar space, the accord that kept the heart-stars from breaking into four hundred competing polities. Kuotaan would never deliberately sacrifice *Nkaastu*.

But she wouldn't stop him from doing it. Even though she saw it coming.

He said to her, quietly, "Tsaa Kuotaan, I thank the beloved gods I was blessed to fly with so diligent and meticulous a captain." There was no time for her to answer. In lieu of further words, he set a hand on her muscled lower shoulder while he turned his attention back to the Disks.

"In-and-out in point zero four," Saraa said coolly from her station. She shunted the finished maneuver to Genru to carry out so that she could turn her own attention to predicting what sort of maneuvers they might need next.

The eight Blades flashed through the tank display, glittering white. The slower Disks came inexorably onward, glowing a dull red—the color dull because they were hardly bothering with defensive countermeasures. They thought *Nkaastu* had targeted the wrong Disk. They were perfectly ready to let *Nkaastu* focus on that one, take the opening that mistake gave them to swat the half-fighter tradeship and follow the Blade swarm in-system.

"Ready to engage," Daamon said to Paaol, not a question.

"Ready, holding ready," Paaol said tensely, poised over his console. Aanhk rumbled in wordless encouragement and set one of her big lower hands on Paaol's shoulder in support and encouragement.

"Mark, point zero zero two," said Genru.

"Saraa," said Daamon.

"In and out," she answered in a crisp tone, and the skip-jolt came, sharp and sideways, out and instantly back into normal space, with the eight Blades past *Nkaastu* and the Disks much closer. But now six of the eight Disks couldn't fire on *Nkaastu* without risking their own Blades, and the other two were far enough away they could be evaded. Paaol, grinning tightly, had already triggered his firing solution against the Disks.

They did not take out all twelve. There had never been any hope of that. But Daamon had the satisfaction of watching the glittering icon that represented the heart-Disk disintegrate into dusty sparkles in the tank display, and three of the Disks closest to it as well. Targeting failed with the Disks farther from the heart-Disk; those had been painted with a lower priority and the uut had good confounders. Better than a turun ship, especially at close range.

It wasn't true, as Daamon knew very well, that taking out the heart-Disk would leave a formation helpless. But generally uut tactics afterward were simplistic. Only the heart-Disks were actually flown by living uut; that was the theory. The others might be controlled by automated routines or by mechanisms; even after eleven years of battle, no one really knew. They knew that weirdly acellular biological debris was recovered with some Disk remnants, but not all, so it seemed reasonable that uut crew were aboard only some Disks, not all.

Destroying the heart-Disk did not create enough confusion this time. Return fire raked *Nkaastu* all down one side as a Disk found a firing solution that nearly worked. Saraa almost but not quite got *Nkaastu* clear, the ship staggering as the primary gravitics failed and the secondary gravitics took the load. Kuotaan supported Daamon and kept him from sprawling, as all across the bridge turun supported uman battlecrew.

"Random walk!" said Daamon.

Saraa said tersely, "Can't, we've lost half our ventral propulsion and lateral's not so great either, too many crossconnections down, I'm faking it by hand."

They all knew neither uman nor turun could generate a true random walk, and the remaining uut ships wouldn't be fooled long; the moment their computers spotted the inevitable pattern Saraa put into her evasion, *Nkaastu* would be gone.

"Gods be beneficient," said Genru, from his tone a fervent prayer rather than an exclamation.

Daamon agreed, though silently. He'd believed *Nkaastu* could at the very least take out several more Disks; now he feared that might not be possible. He should have done better than this, he had needed to do better, he was *furious* at his inability to do better. But he said, absolutely deadpan, "I'll be embarrassed for us all if we can't take out more than three Disks after striking the heart-Disk. Saraa, options?"

"I don't think there's any course that'd set us up to take out more than one at a time. Anything I can see, we'd be setting ourselves up for return fire." She didn't need to say that Nkaastu couldn't handle another hit like the last one. She said instead, "But since, looking at your priorities, we're apparently *willing* to take return fire, maybe that's okay. I'm shooting everyone a course; see what you think."

"I like it!" Paaol exclaimed almost at once. "Daamon, we can do this! We should do it!"

"Yes, this is why no one asks for your opinion in actual battles," Daamon told him. The attack run Saraa had suggested did not look very survivable, but taking it might give them a chance to take out several more Disks—up to four, if Paaol gamed out targeting just right.

Paaol ignored Daamon's comment. "We should do it! I've got firing solutions, Daamon!"

Destroying eight Disks out of this formation might make all the difference at Hanaa. Against that—against that, his own stabbing fear and grief for himself, for them all, could not be allowed to make the decision for him.

He didn't look up at Kuotaan. This was exactly the kind of decision an uman battlecommander was supposed to make. He took a breath and said, trying to keep his voice steady, "On my mark, do it. Saraa, give us a good kick a thousandth chime after we fire. Gen, throw everything into taking us dark the second after Saraa kicks us out of the way of return fire. Ditch accel, weapons, shields, everything but basic gravitics. We'll run dark as long as we can, see if inertial drift carries us clear."

Pouring every bit of available power into darkmasking was the only tactic he could think of that might give them a chance to survive the inevitable counterattack. Not a great chance, especially since every bit of power they could divert would still only hold the darkmask for a chime or so. But it was still the only chance he could see. Maybe every single uut ship would head out instead of sitting right here to wait for *Nkaastu's* mask to fail. Not likely, but he could hope.

Saraa's hands flicked across her console, preparing to implement the course the instant Daamon gave the order. Paaol had already programmed the firing solution and hovered over his console, ready to adjust priorities on the fly if necessary. Genru looked at Daamon, signaling his readiness for the maneuver.

Daamon drew breath to say *Mark!* —

—and at that moment, something new came through the Aam slide. Something big, flashing sharply into the display with the brilliance that meant *powerful energy signature*, and the lavender that meant *unidentified*.

"Unknown ship's fired!" Paaol cried, almost before the stranger had cleared the slide. For once he sounded rattled. In the display, every single remaining Disk and Blade flared and dissolved, one after another, so fast it was hard to say which had gone first and which last.

Genru said, obviously equally shocked, "Beneficent gods, did you see that? Whoever they are, they must've painted juncture space for uut *before* they were all the way out, did you see, they had solutions before they were all the way out of the slide!"

"As they solved for the uut and not us, we have no complaint," rumbled Suumat. She had wrapped her lower left arm around Genru's shoulders, steadying him through his first instinctive recoil at the newcomer's blazing display of violent efficiency.

All the turun crew were rumbling deep in their chests, the sound at once reassurance for their own people and warning for any enemy. Kuotaan was rumbling too. It did help. Every uman knew that sound meant *safety*. Even a battlecommander whose actual job involved protecting the people of his ship—or, if necessary, spending their lives to protect others—felt that deep promise of safety, of protection, right in his bones.

Daamon drew a breath, let it out, patted Kuotaan's lower shoulder, and demanded, "Gen, what *is* that? Do we have that in records *anywhere?*"

"First pass search isn't kicking up anything—"

"We're being ranged!" said Paaol.

"Don't range them back!" Daamon ordered. "Paint them if you can, but *very, very quietly*. Kill our accel, keep our relative vee just as it is. Saraa, lay out every course you can think of that we might need. Gen, can you get us a visual signature?"

"Suumat?" Genru said to his partner.

Even during combat, primary crew were allowed to assist battlecrew if requested, and Suumat had obviously already been working to sort out incoming signals. "Yes," she rumbled. "Visual!" She loaded her images into the display.

It was black and silver, that stranger, with sharp, raking lines and a narrow prow and lights flaming crimson and gold along its flanks. It was huge; Suumat had tagged the icon with an image of *Nkaastu* for comparison, and this new ship was at least eight times the size. More. Daamon shook his head, comparing chunky *Nkaastu* to that monster. Twelve times bigger. At least.

"That's designed for atmosphere," Genru said softly. "Who builds something that big for atmosphere?"

"Who builds something that *vicious* for atmosphere?" muttered Saraa. "Did you see it take out *all those uut* practically *all at once?*" She was throwing courses into her console, mostly different options that would get them away from this strange ship and back toward the Hanaa slide.

"Yeah, you think maybe we blinked and missed it?" said Paaol. "Daamon, you know what I think, I think that monster *chased* those uut through the Aam slide, that's why it had solutions so fast. Who goes hunting uut with just a single solitary ship?"

Who was definitely the question. Daamon asked, "Tsaa Kuotaan?"

"That is no people we know," Kuotaan stated, her deep voice rolling out with slow assurance. "That is nothing built by the Ka' Taand. We have no record of any such ship. That is some foreigner."

Daamon gestured acknowledgment. He asked, mostly for courtesy, "Captain, do you want command?"

Kuotaan flicked an upper hand in a gesture of negation. She answered, still in the nturun plural. "We do not. This assuredly remains your command, Nda Daamon."

Daamon nodded and turned briskly to his battlecrew. "Saraa, forget subtlety. Lay in a course that will take us back to the Hanaa slide at our best possible accel, but just hold onto that for now."

Saraa nodded, but warned him, "Even if that ship out there lets us go, there's no way we can catch up to those Blades."

"Give me a course that'll make the best possible try at it. I also want a slow course toward the stranger, minimal accel, but hold that, too. For now keep us just as we are. Paaol, quick, what would you think if you were them and we picked up just a little accel on an approach course? Would that look aggressive to you? If we head back toward the slide, would you think we were trying to run away, and if you did, what would you do about it?"

Paaol gave him a look. "Gods be beneficent, *I* should know?"

"Gut feeling. Give it a try."

Paaol raked a hand through his hair, stroked the brilliant feathers that gleamed in the accent clips, and shrugged. "I wouldn't head toward them. If we slowly add accel toward the Hanaa slide, that couldn't be taken as an attack, at least I don't see how, so nobody over there ought to take it as a reason to turn us into stripped particles, unless they want to do that anyway. If I were them and I wanted us to stop, I'd shoot across our path with an energy weapon."

Daamon nodded. That sounded right to him, and if Paaol, the most aggressive uman on the battlecrew, thought a slow retreat shouldn't prompt attack, that might be good. But he knew uman instincts might not predict this stranger's reactions. They all knew that.

"I've got a solution," Paaol added. "But I wouldn't use it if I were you, because if we don't look like a threat over there, I sure don't want to change anybody's mind."

"Absolutely do not fire on that ship, no." Daamon scrubbed his palms across his face. "Those thirty-odd Blades that cut off first, they'll certainly get through to Hanaa." They were out of scan range by this time. Possibly they'd already found the slide. If there weren't enough full- or half-fighters currently in that system, then the world itself must be in deadly danger. And here was this foreign ship, hunting uut, and here was *Nkaastu*, perfectly placed to show it exactly where the Hanaa slide lay and lead it through. Obviously this stranger would have no difficulty at all dealing with even a fairly sizeable Blade swarm like that one. What this ship might do on its own account once these strangers saw they'd come to a green and glowing world ... Daamon had no idea. No way to guess.

But they had no need to guess about what those Blades would do, or try to do. Daamon realized he was gripping the head of his cane so hard his fingers hurt, and deliberately eased that grip. He said to Genru, "Can you ping them?"

Gen shrugged. "I *can*, sure. Whether they'll answer, that's a different question. Who knows if they're in the mood for a chat?"

"Yeah," said Daamon. "Saraa, give us just a touch of accel back toward the Hanaa slide. Roll us to point our main weapons away from that ship. No, you know what? Roll us to show them our damaged flank." That ought to be taken as acknowledgement that they knew the other ship was much stronger. It might even be taken as a request for help. *He* would take it that way. He added, "Gen, ping them, just one quiet little ping, we'll hope they can tell a courtesy when they hear one. I sure hope you can make sense of any signal they broadcast—"

"We've got one," he said, mirroring the signal to Daamon's console. "Not a ping, and I don't think it's broadcast—I think it's a directional signal, meant just for us. Oh, it's binary. That's good. How complicated can a binary signal be?"

"So they want to talk," Daamon said confidently, as though he were certain this was a good thing. "That's hopeful."

"Them not firing, that's what *I* find hopeful," Paaol said.

Genru, ignoring Paaol, said, "Saraa, I'm mirroring you what I'm getting. Look at the variation in intervals. I'm not sure this is binary after all."

"Huh," said Saraa. She turned to Tsumon. "Look at this signal, Tsu', and see if you can help me figure it out faster than Gen, right?"

"Suumat, help!" Genru exclaimed, and bent over his console.

Daamon privately bet on Saraa and Tsumon; Gen was the signals expert and he worked well with Suumat, but Saraa and Tsumon had grown up together, half-sisters, with the advantage of close familiarity. He left both teams alone to work on the problem, studying the foreigner. They had set a parallel course. Matched acceleration, maintaining distance and orientation. That didn't seem like an aggressive move. He glanced up. "Tsaa Kuotaan, how would a turun interpret all these events?"

His captain gazed at the visual display of the foreign ship, cupping one of her upper hands and then the other in a gesture of turning over alternatives. She said at last, "It is our feeling that no turun could mistake our actions for either challenge or hostility. Any turun would understand a slow retreat, turning our wounded flank toward them, as the gesture of a subordinate entity. We believe that this is also your uman perception, yes? This was your intention to convey."

Daamon opened a hand in assent.

"To our eyes, the response of this foreigner signifies a like understanding," stated Kuotaan. "We see their act in following and paralleling our course as an act of dominance, directed toward an entity they believe is inferior."

At Kuotaan's side, Tuutka inclined her head and added, "Though these actions are not necessarily hostile, we yet wonder if they believe that they may claim this territory and intend to escort us away from the region they claim."

Daamon thought about this. "You don't read their parallel course as curiosity?"

"Curiosity," Kuotaan rumbled. She and Tuutka exchanged a glance. "Curiosity," Kuotaan repeated. "Perhaps. We had not considered that possibility. Interesting. Perhaps it may be so."

Daamon studied the narrow, elegant foreign ship. Dominance, aggression, maybe hostility. How would one distinguish any or all of that from curiosity? Or from some other unknown, unknowable, alien motivation? "Paaol, time to intersect the Hanaa slide at our current acceleration?"

"Uh—" Paaol worked it out, not quite as fast as Saraa would have. "Two point six two."

That seemed a long time, under the circumstances. Daamon added a touch more accel. Then a little more.

"Got it!" said Saraa, and a hairsbreadth behind, Genru snapped, "We have it!" They looked at each other, Saraa with an ironic quirk to her eyebrows and Gen with a mute shrug that conceded the contest.

"So, we can ping the foreigner now, and talk to them if they answer. Want me to do it?" Gen looked at Daamon, expectant, waiting, his hand hovered over the glowing enamels of the primary signals console.

Daamon took a deep breath and looked around the long smooth arc of the bridge and its stations. The stations, rising in parallel curves, were sized to the primary turun crew. Yet the uman battlecrew did not look out of place. Small relative to the high arches of the stations, yes, but not out of place. That impression might have been created by the supportive attitudes of their turun partners. The walls and consoles glowed, turquoise and dark loam-brown, pearl and sea-green, translucent taupe and dawn-pink; the soft hues reflecting from the polished turun hide and glowing against the softer and more variable colors of uman skin. The emergency lights still glimmered in a delicate tracery of violet-lit black. Even those were beautiful. The image of the foreign ship rode in the display, all raking lines and aggressive angles. It, too, was beautiful, in the way that the great predators that hunted the oceans of Gaatuu were beautiful.

Daamon opened one hand and then the other. "Saraa, can we pick up a random walk yet?"

"Not yet. I can set up a series of skip-courses in case we detect incoming fire, try to duck if they get mad." She was doing that without waiting for his assent.

Daamon tipped his chin up anyway. "Set an automatic trigger. Signal Gen when you've got that set up. Gen, when you get the signal, send your ping."

"Right," Gen agreed, tense but steady, and a moment later sent the signal: one ping whispering softly out through silent space to the other ship, which might respond with curiosity or hostility or maybe some other unguessable alien reaction. Daamon laid his hands gently on the face of his console, waiting.

"They're responding," murmured Gen. "We *should* have visual and sound, if we got the translation close enough the computers can fill in the gaps. I'm fairly certain they're trying to give us a real-time feed from their ship. I'm answering with our standard real-time bridge feed. I think that's best, don't you?" He glanced at Daamon, who nodded, hoping they weren't making a terrible mistake, but what else was there to do but try to talk to this powerful stranger?

"Right," said Gen. "I'm feeding their signal directly into our display ... now." He stroked his console, and the image of the foreign ship flickered out. For a moment that stretched out painfully, the display was blank.

Then the display flickered again. Figures began to take shape in the main display tank, dissolved, and half-formed once more as the translation algorithms tried to resolve the foreign signal into familiar parameters. Suumat, her golden eyes narrowing with annoyance, reached down past Genru and made a tiny adjustment. The signal resolved, and the display hardened and clarified.

For a long, long moment everyone just stared at the images in the display.

That was, Daamon assumed, the bridge of the foreign ship. It had the look of a control center, though the space seemed small for a bridge, and the square, blocky shape of the room was all wrong, and the consoles were set into individual narrow pedestals rather than along smooth curves, and the whole space was too bright and too stark, all naked metal relieved only by narrow slashes of matte black and crimson. It was very different from flowing Ka' Taand design. But that was not why everyone stood so still for so long, just staring. That was because of the people on that foreign bridge, who stared back in what Daamon could only assume was equal shock.

"But they are uman," Kuotaan said, her voice so deep the whole bridge seemed to hum with it. The foreigners all twitched at the sound of her voice, staring at her from their individual stations. She did not notice, having turned to look down at Daamon.

Daamon could only open his hands in astonished agreement. It was hard to imagine a lot of uman choosing to dress like that, everyone alike in dull black with little crimson flashes; everyone with hair cropped short just the same and with expressions rapidly becoming just the same, blank and stiff and closed, as they recovered from their surprise. Daamon wondered what these people could possibly think when they looked at him and his battlecrew. Maybe they were shocked at the free use of color, at Saraa's sweeping pearl-and-turquoise waterfall robes, at his own layers of brown and taupe, at the clips of feathers Paaol wore in his long hair or the sea-colored embroidery up the left side of Genru's vest.

What kind of people would dress all the same, cut their hair all the same, sit all the same, one at each station, but all so stiff and straight? What kind of people would design a ship interior like that, all square corners and naked metal?

The kind of people who would hunt an uut formation in a single ship, drive the formation through a slide, come through the slide with firing solutions already prepared, and destroy the uut with blinding efficiency. Daamon's mouth had gone dry. Yet these were ... "Cousins," he said aloud. "These are our cousins. We always knew they were out there somewhere."

"Yes ..." Paaol didn't sound like he much cared for the idea of long-lost cousins. "They don't look happy."

"They look," said Saraa succinctly, "like they've never been happy a day in their lives."

This was true. It was those stiff, unsmiling, blank expressions. All the same, on the women and men alike. These cousins looked starkly, harshly *foreign*. He thought the broad man in the center of the room was probably the battlecommander, or possibly the captain—no, with an entirely uman crew, probably they wouldn't make that distinction. Gods be forsaken, imagine being responsible for *everything, all the time*. Without thinking, Daamon reached out to lay his hand on Kuotaan's lower shoulder. Perhaps guessing his thoughts, she looked down at him, gripping his arm with her nearest upper hand.

Both Paaol and Genru hissed between their teeth. "Did you see that?" Genru asked in a low voice. "The way they flinched?"

No one could have missed it. Every single foreigner had flinched and stiffened at that simple gesture. Every eye was on Kuotaan, on Daamon. Every one of those people looked quickly over their shoulders at their own commander, plainly to gauge his reaction. The broad man had also stiffened, his expression hard and closed, but he made a swift, chopping, palm-down gesture and said something short and sharp, and somehow the common attitude of his people eased, just perceptibly. Daamon stood still, not knowing whether he should draw back from Kuotaan or stay exactly where he was.

Kuotaan patted Daamon's arm gently, watching the foreigners with careful attention, concern evident in her wide eye and tucked head. Then she settled back, taking on the compact, slightly crouched stance of a turun trying not to frighten a pet animal. "That is an alarming response," she stated. "Nda Daamon, do you also find this response alarming? It is our belief that these persons are fearful, and that fearful persons may act with unfortunate haste."

"Tsaa Kuotaan, they don't know you," Daamon said. "It's true you are ... very large. Any uman who didn't know you might well be frightened. I will ask all turun here to be still and think before moving."

"Yes," said Kuotaan, reinforcing that command, which technically she shouldn't have done, but Daamon appreciated it, since he could not legally issue orders to primary crew save in battle conditions. Whatever this was, they must all surely hope it was not actually battle.

One of the foreigners, not the commander, said something. His voice sounded a little shaky. The commander answered, his tone curt.

"Is that ... cant?" Genru said, his voice low and cautious. "Do we have anyone on *Nkaastu* who actually *speaks* cant?"

"Kaamharaa," Daamon and Paaol said together, glanced at each other, and paused. "Feed this signal to Kaamharaa's quarters," Daamon ordered. He could call Kaamharaa to the bridge ... but the nturun crew wouldn't like it; the bridge was no place for an uturun. Beyond that, if these cousin uman were alarmed by nturun, he could just imagine their reaction to a male, three times as large, with much more impressive tusks thrusting up from his powerful lower jaw. He said instead, "Link Kaamharaa's com directly to the bridge feed, advise him to split his display so he can see and hear us as well as them. Saraa, how long do you calculate it will be before that Blade swarm gets through to Hanaa?"

Saraa glanced swiftly at her console and answered, "Point two one, but what do you think these *cousins* will do if *we* try to enter the slide? If they follow us—" she stopped, shrugging, meaning who knew what these foreign cousins might do, faced with an entire world filled with alarming turun.

"I know," Daamon said. "Your advice?" He looked around the bridge, meeting the eyes of turun crew as well as uman battlecrew. "All of you, everyone here. We don't know these people, but we know the uut. I want to lead this ship to Hanaa, if these cousins will follow us. I don't think they'll fire on us as long as we don't fire on them. I think that's a risk worth taking for the hope they'll fire on the uut, not us, not our people. Anyone disagree?"

Deep, doubtful rumbles. But Tuutka, as secondary captain used to being asked for her advice, swept up two of her great hands in a smooth gesture and declared, "Let uman judge what uman will do. Those Blades present a dire threat to our Aanuku holdings at Hanaa. Should a Blade escape to lead its people here, plainly that presents a threat to Aanuku entire." A slight pause, and then she added, surprisingly, "Also a threat to the heart-stars and the whole of the Ka' Taand."

"Yes," Daamon agreed, quick and intense.

"Yes," Tuutka rumbled. "I would trust *any* uman people, foreign or otherwise, before I would hope that whatever ships currently reside at Hanaa may successfully guard that system or familiar space against so many Blades."

Kuotaan gestured agreement at once. "We agree, Nda Daamon. All of us here assuredly agree." She used the pronoun that meant all the nturun present.

"Of *course* we should lead our cousins through the slide!" Paaol declared, barely waiting for their captain to finish speaking. "I can't *wait* to see everyone's reactions when this ship takes out those uut! They won't fire on us, why would they fire on us? We can't touch them, a ship like that? Gen, tell him!"

"Your sep' brother is an idiot," Genru told Daamon. "But I think he's right this time."

"I think you're all wild optimists," Saraa said. "This isn't a gods-be-forsaken romance-adventure story, and even if we could talk to these ... these cousins, we can't invoke some handy literary device that'll make them follow our lead just because we say we have special awareness of the field of battle or the stakes." She paused. Then she shrugged and added, "But I don't think you're wrong. I agree with Tsaa Kuotaan."

"She agrees with *me,* Daamon!" Paaol said instantly. "So do you! You know you do! This would make a *great* romance-adventure!"

Saraa rolled her eyes, but she said, "Fine, sure, *this one time* I also agree with your idiot sep' brother."

Daamon nodded. He hadn't thought of romance-adventure novels or the various literary tropes that ensured happy endings in those novels. Plus, honestly, some degree of optimism did seem to be actually warranted. Looking into the display, he met the gaze of the foreign commander. The man stared back. His expression was hard to read, but his gaze was steady. His eyes were dark brown, a surprisingly dark color in a light-skinned face; lighter than most uman people Daamon had ever met. Some u Kaoluun uman had paler coloring, as everyone knew since Siiv u Kaoluun was the seniormost battlecommander in the entire Ka' Taand. But the u Kaoluun people had light-colored eyes, grey or blue or light golden-brown, to go with their light-colored skin. And they usually had lighter-colored hair.

This man's short-cropped hair was a brown that was nearly black, not yet greying although he did not seem young. His jaw was set, his shoulders straight, his posture upright and stiff. He stood out in the middle of his bridge, all the stations oriented so that he could see them with a turn of his head. But he did not turn his head. He stared steadily at Daamon. But was that curiosity, or suspicion? Was he thinking, *Ah, here are our cousins, lost to us so long ago?* Or was he thinking, *Here are enemies who might understand us?*

Daamon took a deep breath. Then he stepped away from Kuotaan and the station he shared with her, out to the middle of the turun bridge. *See me*, he meant to convey to the other man. *I, like you, command.*

The foreign commander did not move, but his eyes narrowed.

Daamon did not look away from him. He took one more step forward, then one more, careful of his balance—this would not be a good time for his bad leg to give way. He needed one hand for his cane, but he held out the other, open, palm down, in a one-handed uman version of a turun gesture that mean something like *Let us be friends* and something like *I won't challenge you; you can be leader*. He had not learned that gesture from Kaamharaa. It was not the sort of gesture an adult male turun would make to anyone. But uman people of both sexes used nturun gestures if they grew up within matrilines, and sep' uman picked them up that way. Daamon tried to guess how such a gesture might look to someone who knew nothing at all of turun society. He hoped it looked peaceful. He thought it would not, at least, look aggressive.

He said slowly and carefully, making every word distinct and clear as though that might help the foreign commander understand him, "The Blades went through the slide. Thirty-two Blades. We must go after them. We must go now." He thought of every romance-adventure novel he'd ever read and added, his tone a little dry, "I'd invoke priority overrule if you could understand me, and if that were more than a plot device. But I hope you understand that I've got reason to want you to follow us. This is important. Please do not fire when we move. Please follow and assist." Daamon slowly lowered his hand to his sides, and added, "Okay?" which was one of the few cant words everyone knew.

The commander's dark eyes narrowed again. He said something, as slowly and carefully as Daamon had, in a language that sounded half familiar. Cant, or the language that had devolved into cant, Daamon assumed; he did not understand a single word. Daamon opened one hand, deliberately, not looking away from the foreign commander. He said, "Saraa, step up our vee. Increase accel by a fifth every twentieth chime until we're moving at our top acceleration."

"Right," she said coolly. "If they *do* fire?"

"That's why you've set automatic skips, yes? Skip us toward the slide if you can. We won't fire back, Paaol, understand? No matter what happens. Kaamharaa?"

"Yes," answered Kaamharaa's deep, deep voice on the blue within-ship channel. "I am attempting to elucidate the words of your relative, Daamon, but, as I am certain you have observed, this language is not cant, although obviously related, and the enunciation of certain phonemes has plainly diverged to a considerable degree—"

"Yes," Daamon said, cutting into this threatened monologue. "Please keep me informed as to your efforts and, I hope, your success. How do you say, 'Please don't shoot us,' in cant?"

"Indeed, you will recall that in their extremity your ancestors did not retain any form of ranged weapon, so that the concept of 'shooting' was—"

"Anything that will serve," Daamon interrupted. "Quickly, if you please; speed is more important just now than precision."

Kaamharaa hummed over the connection for a moment, the deep purring hum that meant he was thinking. Daamon braced himself with his cane and pretended not to be impatient. *Nkaastu* had picked up a fair vee now, and though the foreign uman ship had continued to match their course and vee, their commander had not ordered his people to fire. Surely that was a good sign. If Kaamharaa couldn't help, which was starting to seem infuriatingly likely, maybe the foreign uman commander would hold his hand anyway—

Without looking away from Daamon's face, the commander of the other ship said something, a few words only, short and sharp.

"They're ranging us!" Paaol said urgently.

Daamon's gut clenched. He took a step toward the display. The foreign commander held up one hand, a sharp, forbidding gesture, and spoke again.

"They might want us to come about and hold still," Saraa said. She threw courses his way, lighting them up in order of priority, but she added, "Might be a good idea to do that." She sounded perfectly calm.

"Hold our course steady unless they actually fire," Daamon ordered, trying to sound as calm. He tagged one of her options, setting that course to trigger if the computers detected the kind of power bloom that might signal incoming fire. But he said, "We *need* them to clean up the Blades that got through to Hanaa. We need them to do it fast. They won't fire on us. We wouldn't, in their place." He thought he was right, but he added with some intensity, "Kaamharaa, now would be a timely moment for your assistance."

"Yes, yes, Daamon," rumbled Kaamharaa's unseen voice. He pronounced, slowly and carefully, a series of phrases. Daamon recognized only three words, and 'yes', 'no,' and 'okay' were a little light on meaning in the mysterious context Kaamharaa gave them.

"That's a lot more than 'Don't shoot,'" said Daamon, but he could see that the cant phrases, even pronounced in Kaamharaa's deep, deep voice, had had an effect on the uman foreigners. The line of the commander's mouth had thinned, but he also tilted his head in an attitude that suggested concentration more than anger. Maybe the threat had been a bluff anyway. Daamon thought it had probably been a bluff. Though he would just as soon not have been forced to test it.

"We can't make the Hanaa slide, even at our very best accel, for another one point six five chimes," Saraa said. "I can't do better. That swarm is going to get through more than a full chime in front of us—*if* we keep moving and no one shoots us out of space."

The foreign ship did not fire. The foreign commander continued to study Daamon and *Nkaastu's* bridge crew and battlecrew.

"Hold this course. Take our accel up as high as you can." Daamon didn't look away from the foreign commander. One and a half chimes was going to seem like ... quite a long time, probably, if none of them could relax. He said, "Kaamharaa, ask them again not to shoot. Ask them to be patient. I don't suppose cant has any useful way to talk about *slides* and *uut* and *no, this is really urgent, I swear before the beloved gods.*"

"I shall attempt it," Kaamharaa's deep voice assured him.

"You really think we'll be glad these cousins of ours followed us home?" Genru asked. "*If* they do. There won't be anything in Hanaa's system that can begin to touch that ship, I bet."

Daamon didn't have an answer for him. He said to Kuotaan, "I hope we will be very glad to see these people come into Hanaa space. But we can't know for certain what they'll do. This is not exactly a battle decision."

Kuotaan looked around the bridge, meeting every nturun's gaze, collecting opinions from one and then another, ending with Tuutka. Gathering or creating unanimity of opinion was very much an nturun thing; an uman couldn't really perceive it, far less participate. Daamon held his breath. But finally Kuotaan turned her broad face down toward Daamon again. "We are willing to declare that this is a battle decision," she told him. "We do declare so. In either case, we agree with your decision. We would far rather see your-and-our cousins enter Hanaa space behind the uut than see the uut go through alone."

She had used the pronoun that indicated closer-and-farther kinship, but definitely recognized kinship. That alone made her decision clear. Daamon, too, glanced around at the other nturun. None of them made any suggestion that she disagreed with

Kuotaan. They probably wouldn't speak up even if they did disagree. Nturun unanimity was a wonderful thing, if it happened to be on your side.

Daamon bowed slightly, a comprehensive gesture that took in all the turun bridge crew. He said, "Hanaa. And we'll just see."

An endless time crept past. Finally Saraa said, "Point zero four. Point zero three. Point zero two. Brace for slide."

Nkaastu twisted inside out and back again. Kuotaan reached over the arch of her console and caught Daamon when he staggered—he hadn't realized he was so tired, but that last chime had seemed to pass very slowly indeed. Even though practically nothing had happened. Slow rumbling cant from Kaamharaa, occasional baffling responses from the cousins, but by that time everyone on both ships had apparently accepted that they were going through the slide.

Kuotaan steadied Daamon until he caught his balance. He gripped her forearm in thanks and studied the display. Someone had already set it to show Hanaa—Suumat, always the nturun most ready to quietly skirt legality and assist battlecrew without waiting for a direct order. Hanaa was a beautiful green world swirled with white and streaked with golden tan. Though not large, Hanaa was a jewel set within familiar space. Its population was small, but lights spangled the night-side of the world. Hanaa had two worldlets in orbit, but fortunately neither was visible at the moment, both on the other side of the planet, out of the way of any kind of attack, so that was a little better than it might have been.

On the near side, Genru grimly painted a glitter of tiny ships, green for Ka' Taand tradeships, white for the uut Blades. Seventeen Blades, maybe twice that number of tradeships. It was immediately obvious that the tradeships barely counted as a distraction for the uut. Given the disappearance of the rest of the swarm, Daamon was sure at least a couple of half-fighters had been in Hanaa's near-orbit very recently, maybe a full-fighter. They were gone now. No blue-green or blue icons anywhere in the display.

Those remaining Blades were certainly going to get past those tradeships within another half-chime. They'd probably only paused to give themselves the pleasure of tearing the tradeships out of the sky. Two more of the turun ships dissolved from the display as he watched.

Saraa said calmly, "We'll be in range in point four two, point four one—"

"Range 'em," Daamon said curtly to Paaol.

"Yes," Paaol said, just as curt, and added, "They've spotted us."

"Bet they're wondering," said Genru. "Can't seem real likely we took out the rest of their formation all by ourselves."

Daamon tipped his chin up in acknowledgment and agreement. "If I were them, I'd break away from those tradeships and either press straight toward Hanaa or come back up to see what we are—"

Paaol slapped his console. "Both! Ten pressing down, seven on approach—oh, whoops, worse, I think at least two of the seven are planning to cut around us and get back through the slide! You *know* they're going to try to get back and tell their swarm all about us, Daamon!"

Daamon signed grim agreement. The worst of all possible scenarios, because *Nkaastu* obviously had to stop those two, all seven of these Blades if they could, and that meant they couldn't get in toward the settlements nearly fast enough to stop the other ten from doing anything they wanted to Hanaa. Some of the tradeships, the small ones with uman captains, were flinging themselves into intercept courses, the only thing they could do. That was a brave and useless sacrifice because the best they could do was momentarily slow the Blades. Unless someone appeared at the last moment to protect Hanaa and redeem their sacrifice—

"*There* they are!" Paaol said fiercely. "Through the slide and on our tail!"

There they were indeed, their cousins on that long ship with its narrow raking lines, the icon painted blue as well as lavender in the display because now it was only half unknown. Daamon let out his breath and said, "Keep an eye on those two Blades, but get us out of our cousins' way and let them go." Then he watched to see what their foreign cousins would do, faced with those Blades and that clutter of turun tradeships, and with Hanaa, open and defenseless, lying there in the light of its golden sun.

What that ship did was instantly engage with the seven closer Blades and simultaneously send a rapid pulse of tiny lavender dots—some kind of unidentified attack—toward the ten Blades farther away.

Daamon breathed out, slowly, as the two Blades that had tried to get back through the slide dissolved into a scattering of sparks in the display. The other five closer Blades shattered into sparks a tenth-chime later, but the more distant ten darted away, evading attack, giving up their own run toward Hanaa, slashing back toward the foreigner.

"Engage the nearest the instant it's in range," Daamon snapped, unwilling to let these new cousins, however deadly, do *all* the fighting.

"Ranging the nearest Blade," agreed Paaol. "Got it, solution working ... got a solution, firing!"

The targeted Blade responded to *Nkaastu's* fire by abandoning its run toward the foreign ship, cutting away from its fellows to engage *Nkaastu*. Without waiting for orders, Saraa spun *Nkaastu* into evasion, ignoring Paaol's curses as his firing solutions became abruptly much more complicated. "Like we should hold course and wait for 'em!" Saraa said scornfully.

Their pursuer dissolved suddenly into a shower of sparks across the display. The lavender foreigner flashed triumphantly through the glitter of destruction and then stuttered as it began shedding vee, opening up its course options within the system.

"Think we should try to get ourselves between that ship and our tradeships?" Saraa said, in a tone that made it clear she thought Daamon ought to have given that order already.

She was right. He opened a hand in agreement. "Kick our accel, get us there at our very best vee. But, beloved gods, keep our course open, obvious, and out of their way."

"Yeah, I think that's right, let's not look sneaky," Saraa agreed. "Think they'll believe those tradeships are harmless?"

Above Daamon, Kuotaan made a low, wordless sound in her upper chest and then said, "They *are* harmless."

"They saved Hanaa, getting in the uut's way," Daamon said. "Courageous and admirable, but let's not tempt the forsaken gods by letting them get in our cousins' way. Suumat, if our captain wishes, you might take a moment to hail those tradeships and pass on the word about these uman cousins; let's avoid any gods-be-forsaken misunderstandings. Saraa, get us—right, like that," he added, seeing their altered course paint itself across the display, ending with *Nkaastu* taking station between their foreign cousins and the turun tradeships.

"Not that we can even slow 'em down, if there are any *misunderstandings*," Genru said.

"We can, though." Daamon paced, four steps one way and then back, trying to sort out his thoughts, not wanting to get too far from his console. "They're cousins," he said at last. "They're uman. We *do* understand each other, at least a little." He paused. Then he said, more quietly, "Ping our cousins. Just one very soft ping. And if they send us a feed—which I think they will—accept it and reciprocate. Right?"

“Right,” said Genru. “And they are. Incoming feed.” His hands moved over his console, switching the display to a reciprocal real-time feed.

2

Lem Gerstner stood with his hands relaxed at his sides, his back straight in a casual at-ease stance calculated to demonstrate his confidence that everything was perfectly fine. Brand-new space-faring alien societies notwithstanding. Even if they were plainly not new at all, to someone.

No guessing which lost colony had generated this ... situation. There had been dozens of colonies once, and nearly all of them had been lost the moment Earth had been forced to slam shut every flashpoint, abandoning everyone outside Sol system.

So far as he knew, no other colony had let itself be *absorbed* into the society of *an alien species*. Though maybe this kind of thing had happened to all sorts of colonies. Possibly various task forces would be tripping over giant four-armed pig-tusked troll-faced centaurs everywhere they turned, now that they had at last pursued the Enemy out of the Shallows around Imperial Republic space and into the unknown Deep. But whatever anyone had expected to find out here in the Deep, *nobody* could have expected to run into butt-ugly four-armed aliens who shared their ships with real honest-to-God human people.

But, ugly as they were, those centauroid aliens seemed to be enemies with *the* Enemy. That argued in their favor. The people on that tubby little ship seemed to be treated as equals. Even superiors. That man in the brown robes had been in command; there was no chance Gerstner could have been mistaken about that. The *humans* had been running the boards on that bizarre rainbow-glowing bridge, not the centaurs. But then why had every person had a centaur standing over him? Or her; one of them had been a woman.

The way that other commander had reached out so casually to touch that alien's arm; actually touch it, like it was a friend or companion instead of some kind of monster. And it had touched him in return. Gerstner's skin crawled, thinking of that. But the man had not seemed to mind. Had, in fact, seemed to take that gut-wrenching gesture for granted.

Plainly those people didn't remember much of any human language. *Okay,* tossed right in with alien babble. That was almost funny. Except nothing about this business was funny. What kind of people would join an alien society, let their own identity be subsumed so completely they forgot their own language? In the end, the voice that had come out with a few English words and phrases had definitely not been human. Its accent had been indescribable and its heavy resonance unbelievable, but several words and phrases had been recognizable, if a man listened hard enough. *Friends, all friends, yes. We you not fight no.*

Alien or machine-generated, either way, Gerstner could well believe that those people, human *and* alien, did not want to fight. Obviously that ship could not begin to match *Vengeful.* Obviously it had been about to lose its brutally one-sided battle with that Enemy formation. *Vengeful* had saved that ship. They must know it.

Vengeful had also almost certainly saved the world in this system from a violent, fiery death. Enemy arrowpoints carried worldbusters. That other commander had led *Vengeful* here deliberately. Gerstner had no doubt about that at all. That had been ... well, that had been quite daring, in fact. A gamble on a stranger's goodwill. Which had paid off handsomely. But what this contact might mean for *Vengeful*, or the rest of Task Force Aleph, or for the Imperial Republic as a whole, he had no idea.

The rest of the task force ought to have just about finished up a proper survey of systems G67 and G68 while *Vengeful* chased down the little Enemy formation that'd turned up. A far-ranging scouting formation, not much doubt about that, though that had been a lot of arrowpoints for a scouting force. Regardless, crucial to nip a scouting force off quick before it could get away and then come back with all its friends from its mothership.

So he'd pressed the Enemy formation hard, straight through two unmapped flashpoint junctions. That had been a gamble. Right through a system with at least one living world, plenty of signatures saying *people live here.* That had been unexpected and exciting, a real feather in the cap for Aleph, finding a long-lost but apparently thriving human colony out here in the Deep. So, push the Enemy hard, make damn sure none of the arrowpoints made a try at that world, follow them close and blind—that had been a little *too* exciting. And now *this*.

A system with a very nice living world and a whole lot of signals indicating high tech everywhere. Long settled. Lots of settlements. Obviously part of a larger polity connected to the living system they'd cut through, surely home to that little ship that wasn't an Enemy ship. This *definitely* wasn't any ordinary lost colony.

Gerstner wondered whether giant troll-centaurs and actual people lived commingled everywhere in this system, this whole society. It seemed possible, even likely, since the first ship they'd met was like that.

Vengeful had saved them all, whoever they were. But obviously nothing in this system could begin to match a dreadnought. What must they be feeling, the people here, aliens or humans or both? They must be ... terrified, worried, desperate? Or grateful, appreciating that *Vengeful* had saved their world and trusting human people to be *friends*? Or all of the above?

"Sir," said Maxson suddenly, waited for Gerstner's nod, and went on, "The original ship's just now sent us a pulse. I think they want to, uh, reestablish communication."

The lieutenant's voice was a little stifled. Keith Maxson was exactly the sort of man who would most enjoy this ... ambiguous situation. Gerstner clasped his hands gently behind his back, gazing thoughtfully at the main screen. The fast little Enemy arrowpoints had been destroyed; the alien ships had arranged themselves pointedly between *Vengeful* and the living world. The original ship had taken up station between *Vengeful* and those other ships. That was reassuring, in a way. It was at least *understandable*.

He said, "Very good, Lieutenant. Let's answer that hail and see what our friends have to say."

This time it took hardly a moment to establish a mutual connection. Maxson lifted a warning hand as soon as the connection had been made. All across the bridge, attitudes tightened. This time, prepared, no one actually swore out loud or flinched, though Gerstner heard more than one indrawn breath.

It was such a very alien bridge, and the aliens were so very alien. And the people so very normal. Though they, too, looked incredibly foreign. So informal and colorful and *civilian*. All those loose, floating fabrics, no two outfits the same. One of the men wore *feathers* in his hair. His *long* hair. That man could not have looked less like a soldier if he'd specifically set out to design a civilian outfit. It wasn't just the feathers. It was something about his whole attitude. An attitude shared by all those people. Not exactly flamboyant, but ... no, maybe gaudy wasn't fair, either.

Nevertheless, that other commander, the man in brown, met Gerstner's eyes with the kind of frank, steady courage that seemed appropriate in a commanding officer. The cane might imply he had seen battle, violence at close quarters, and survived.

The alien that stood behind that commander was huge. If it didn't mass close to a ton, Gerstner would be astonished. It was even uglier than he'd remembered, too. Its harsh, weirdly human face looked as though it had been hacked out of granite by a sculptor used to carving gargoyles on cathedral walls. Gerstner's eye wanted to interpret that craggy face as male, but who knew.

Short, blunt tusks projected upward from the alien's lower jaw. That caught the eye. There was something strange about the joints or the musculature. No wonder, four arms, lots of joints had to be fitted into that massive torso above the ... other torso. Ordinary anatomical terms didn't stretch to cover anatomy like this. Its hide was a shiny dark mahogany, appearing more like polished wood than skin. Its presence—the presence of *all* those aliens on that bridge was just enormously disturbing.

The human commander didn't seem to mind the giant alien standing close behind him. He didn't seem concerned at all, or not about that. He stood with one hand resting on the smooth rainbow-colored arch that must contain some sort of control board, the other hand gripping the polished head of his cane. He stood straight, his head up, but his posture completely lacked the military precision Gerstner might have expected in the commander of a ship, even a civilian ship. All his attention was plainly focused on Gerstner. He held out one hand, palm down, in a deliberate, careful gesture that was plainly meant to convey ... something. It did not look like an aggressive gesture. Other than that, Gerstner couldn't even guess. Maybe he was saying *thank you*. Or *please don't hurt us*. Or *take us to your leader*.

That last one sounded like a fine idea, actually. Gerstner would be *more* than happy to hand this unexpected, bizarre complication off to Commodore Marchetta, let the commodore explain all about troll-centaurs and long-lost humans to Viceroy Modhwadiya and Witness Falconer, let the three of them hash out who ought to handle the next steps of ... not quite a *first* contact problem, was it? But it was sure as hell *something*.

Well, every kind of problem these ... people ... presented was way, way above Gerstner's pay grade, and he was damned glad of that. Getting these people—aliens, humans, that little ship, the whole lot of them—back to the task force in one piece, preferably undamaged, preferably not too upset, that much was right smack dab in the middle of Gerstner's pay grade.

Moving just as deliberately as the person on that weird alien bridge, he lifted his own hand. And beckoned, the crook of a finger: *Come. Come here.* He doubted the gesture carried any intrinsic meaning, so he said it out loud as well, enunciating each word carefully: "You. Come." And repeated it, "Come." Then he added, "Lieutenant Vaughn. Take us back to the flashpoint. Gently. One quarter slow. Lieutenant Maxson, track our little buddy here. I want to know what that ship does half a second *before* she does it, understand? Grigson, we see a power bloom over there that looks the least little bit like their weapons systems coming up, I want bracketing fire, but out a good long way. Shake 'em up, yes, but I don't want to crack an eggshell in their galley, if they have a galley. Or eggs. Clear?"

A low chorus of acknowledgment.

Gerstner turned once more to look again directly at the other commander on-screen. "Come," he repeated.

As he had half expected, that deep, deep alien voice spoke. It rumbled through his bones even over the link. It didn't sound like language at all; it was so deep and rolled so smoothly that it sounded like thunder or machinery, except in some way it also sounded plainly biological. Despite the absence of anything a man could hear as identifiable words, Gerstner assumed it was one of those pig-tusked centaurs translating his command.

Though it sounded like far more than a one-word translation. How many ways could one say *Come?* Maybe the alien was explaining the uncertainty of translation, or appending its own opinion. At some length.

The human commander on the alien ship turned his head to the side and said something, not in English, but in that other language. A little like Gujarati, which was the only other language

Gerstner knew by ear, though he spoke only a few words of it himself. This alien language sounded far less peculiar in a human mouth than it did when the aliens spoke it themselves. It almost sounded like a reasonable language.

One of the other men spoke up, and the woman, speaking over each other and over the commander.

Reese Kennon stepped up to the command dais and gave Gerstner a sideways look, communicating just with that glance, *Undisciplined bastards, aren't they, sir?*

Gerstner lifted his eyebrows fractionally: *They're not Fleet officers, Exec.*

Reese tilted his head in answer: *Really, sir?*

Gerstner let the corners of his mouth twitch upward in appreciation of his executive officer's peculiar sense of humor.

The people on the alien ship were still arguing. Or discussing, or debating, or reciting poetry, or whatever. Twice, one of the centaurs spoke. Their voices were certainly ... unmistakable.

"Sir," Lieutenant Maxson said. "That ship is moving." A tiny pause, and then he added, his tone tight with suppressed excitement, "It's matching our trajectory, sir. They're following us."

"Splendid!" murmured Reese. "If they follow us home, do you suppose Daddy will let us keep them?"

Naturally Reese was looking forward to presenting this startling find to Commodore Marchetta. Also to watching the commodore turn around and present it, them, this whole situation, to Viceroy Gopaal Modhwadiya, and most *particularly* Imperial Witness Ronsard Falconer.

Modhwadiya, one of the viceroys shortlisted for the Imperial Throne when Emperor Elliston stepped down, was strongly aligned with the expansionist Outlook party. Every political fracture line within the Imperial Republic yawned wider as the date for the succession approached, and while the emperor couldn't simply designate an heir, his stated preference would carry a great deal of weight when the vote came around. Naturally Elliston was watching Modhwadiya very closely, particularly watching how the viceroy handled crisis or disaster. Thus, Witness Falconer.

Falconer was nobody's fool; that was the general opinion. The man was widely reputed to think sideways from everyone else. But, as much as he favored any faction, Falconer was inclined toward the Home Party, and therefore toward the notion that if humanity just stopped looking out at the Deep, the Enemy would stop staring back. Stay to the Shallows, reduce humanity's imprint in space, avoid drawing notice, and the Enemy would understand humanity meant neither rivalry nor enmity and would never again come raking into human space, burning everything they found.

That, Gerstner had long ago decided, was an attitude born out of fear, which was reasonable; plus the notion that if you didn't want trouble, trouble wouldn't come find you, which was damned wishful thinking. But that attitude was powerfully seductive.

Falconer would quite possibly spontaneously combust in the most spectacular manner the moment he saw these giant centauroid aliens.

Reese Kennon enjoyed lighting off fireworks, and skimmed through any resulting explosions with perfect aplomb. Gerstner suspected that Reese would someday be the kind of captain people called *lucky*—the kind who took wild chances and pulled them off. Wild chances were plainly embedded all through this situation.

Out loud, Gerstner said, "Very good, Lieutenant." Then he added more quietly to his Exec. "I can hardly imagine a better location for a ... not quite first-contact ... than a random junction system well out from the Shallows, currently occupied by a whole lot of human firepower and nothing else. I also can't think of a better man to hand this situation off to than Modhwadiya. I don't believe we've ever seen the viceroy startled. This should do it, I imagine."

"Yes, sir. Granted that's all true, and I'm sure the viceroy will be thrilled when we drop this little ship in his lap. Falconer, maybe not."

"Thrilled or not, you and I both know he'll expect to be handed every kind of peculiar situation. Not likely we'll trip over anything more peculiar than this."

"Yes, sir. I suppose you saw their ... tusks, sir."

"Certainly one of the more startling details, Exec."

On the screen, the foreign commander of that little ship held up a hand, and everyone else fell silent—the first truly unmistakable gesture of command Gerstner had observed. The man said something to the woman, glanced around and said something else, and finally turned to speak to the alien beside him. It bent its massive head and answered, its voice a deep rumble, its rolling words blurring together, utterly inhuman. Then it spoke again, lifted one of its four hands and gripped the man's arm. All across the bridge, shoulders twitched. Gerstner suppressed a twitch of his own.

Over at Ops, Samuel Lockwood rubbed his hands on his trousers, as though imagining a little too vividly what it might be like to touch one of those troll-faced centaurs, or be touched by one. He was sweating. Gerstner made note of that: if someone must interact with those ... creatures, Lockwood was probably not the best choice among his officers.

That was unfortunate. The man was on Falconer's personal staff, just as Sun Grigson was on Modhwadiya's. Each man would expect his own agent to be made privy to important information and decisions. Ordinarily, Gerstner didn't particularly object to that. Lockwood was solid enough on Ops, and Grigson was truly gifted on Weapons, and both of them took orders with hardly more than the faintest impression that once they stepped off his deck, they answered to a higher authority. There had been times during Imperial Republic history when political officers might be a good deal more chancy. But Elliston was a decent emperor, better than decent, and the whole business was a good deal less fraught than it had been in the past.

But just at this moment, the look on Lockwood's face ... given a free hand, Gerstner would have preferred to keep the man far away from a first contact situation. Keith Maxson would almost certainly do better than either political officer, if Gerstner were fully capable of assigning personnel as he wished.

Though he tracked his own people, most of Gerstner's attention was actually bent toward watching the commander on that other ship. He expected more than that ship moving. He expected an official answer. He was determined to understand it.

The other commander seemed equally determined to be understood. Turning back to face Gerstner, he brought one hand to his chest and said carefully, accented but unmistakable, "I." Then he made a broad gesture around the smooth, strange space of the alien bridge and said, "We." Finally he cupped his hand and nodded toward Gerstner. "Come," he said. "Yes."

"Sir, they're picking up a touch of acceleration," put in Maxson. "If they keep that up, they'll intersect the flashpoint barely twenty minutes after we hit it."

"Very good," Gerstner acknowledged. And said to the other commander, "Yes. Good. Come."

"I'm sure we shall all look forward to debating philosophy and exchanging epic poetry in our common vocabulary of a dozen or so monosyllabic words," Reese murmured.

Gerstner gave him a look, with the slightest jerk of his head, and his executive officer let his breath out, returned a faintly apologetic nod, and moved away to his own station.

"Hold our course and acceleration," Gerstner told Annette Vaughn, and added to Keith Maxson, "Inform me at once if that ship alters her own course or acceleration." Then he went on, "Weapons One, Weapons Two, track our little friend back there, but I want your attention ahead of us. We came through a living system, who knows who might've followed along? If that junction system where we met this little ship isn't empty now, I want to see whoever it is before they see us and I want solutions right quick. But don't fire until I give the order, got that?"

Murmured acknowledgements. Gerstner nodded. He did not think the other ship would alter her movements in any particular. He thought she would come, exactly as he had ordered. She was damaged, but obviously she was flash-capable; she was crewed by aliens, but plainly they were able to comprehend very simple spoken English. Her commander, however strange, appeared to be a man with good sense and considerable courage. If *Vengeful* met that little ship's friends in the junction or in the system on the other side, he thought there was a good chance the commander on that little ship over there would talk down any hotheads on that side. Gerstner did not intend to spark off a problem with a brand-new weird human-alien civilization. That was definitely not the kind of problem he intended to drop on Commodore Marchetta, or Viceroy Modhwadiya, or Witness Falconer, or anyone else. Not if he could help it.

So. Out of this unfamiliar system and through the flashpoint, and through the juncture system and the inhabited system beyond that, carefully staying clear of the settled world, and out again, following the flashpoint web, and then Gerstner could turn these exceedingly peculiar ex-colonists and their aliens over to Marchetta. Then he could append his personal report, step back into his own proper place within the task force, and ... who knew what would come of all this? Allies, possibly. Allies at last, against the Enemy. That seemed possible.

Or, if anybody handled this situation badly, everything could go wrong and humanity could acquire a brand-new Enemy.

But right now, Gerstner was the one juggling ... exceedingly fragile eggs, possibly. He hoped the situation wasn't actually quite that fragile.

If the Imperial Republic could make common cause with this strange, blended civilization they'd met ... or if they failed, and suddenly faced a different enemy on a different flank of the Shallows ... no way to guess what might come of this contact, not yet. But either way, the entire momentum of the long and endless war against the Enemy was going to shift, one direction or the other. He could feel it.

3

Back toward the slide, then, with no delay. That the cousins swiftly withdrew from Hanaa space seemed good, overall. That might be tacit acknowledgement that this was not their territory. Though not wanting to linger and look around, approach officials, receive a diplomatic approach … that suggested possible urgency. Maybe a need to withdraw and return to their own people. Perhaps this ship was part of a larger battlegroup—that would make every kind of sense—and was expected back in short order. Or maybe this ship was actually needed to face a larger uut offensive. That wouldn't be good. Though in that case, they probably wouldn't have delayed to listen to Daamon or follow *Nkaastu* through to Hanaa.

Or maybe they would have; who could guess?

That they wanted *Nkaastu* to accompany them into space where they had allies and *Nkaastu* would be alone … terrifying, yes, but not *that* terrifying. Daamon thought he understood that demand. The other ship was so powerful. Its commander knew he outmatched everything in Hanaa space; he could hardly fail to know it. Curiosity, then, and the arrogance of strength. That demand felt, in fact, rather like usuonn—the masculine attitude that combined casual arrogance with good will.

Daamon was fairly certain about the arrogance. The good will remained largely a hope. But the other ship had destroyed those uut, protecting Hanaa without hesitation. That was surely grounds for a certain degree of hope.

"Opinions?" he asked, glancing around at the rest of the battlecrew. "Options?"

Genru answered first, his tone as mild as ever. "I vote we do exactly what he told us to do, Daamon. We want to know a lot more about those people, so let's cooperate and find out where he wants to take us and why."

A quiet kind of courage there, well suited to negotiation. In the whirlwind of battle, Daamon would want Paaol up front. In the ebb and flow of negotiation with someone unknown, a potential ally, he'd want Gen.

"Yes, let's!" Paaol was actively enthusiastic. "I've *got* to see more of that ship, Daamon! If we're lucky, they'll let us get a look at their weapons systems from the inside. Do you think they'd mind if some of us took a good look at their weapons?"

"Let's not be pushy," Saraa said. The word she used was utaraan, the sort of juvenile cheek typical from adolescent male turun. That would get a youngster knocked back hard, first by his older female relatives within the matriline and then, once he'd left his mother's matriline, by older, stronger males in whatever reserve he'd entered. Saraa meant to emphasize that *Nkaastu* couldn't begin to challenge that foreign ship. Paaol rolled his eyes, but he didn't argue. Everyone knew that was true.

Daamon made the only realistic decision. "Gen, put us on a course that complies with their request. Saraa, set up some options. I'd like a good handful of slip-courses ready to deploy the instant we clear the slide. I doubt we're stopping in that junction, so hold those courses ready every time we approach any slide; be ready to throw *Nkaastu* back and out of trouble before we even know what kind of trouble it is." As it wasn't entirely legal for him to issue orders to the primary crew, he went on, speaking formally now. "Tsaa Kuotaan, captain, if I may make an irregular request, I would appreciate, in this unusual situation, the efforts of turun khand to assist with refining all scans and signals."

"Kha Suumat may assist," rumbled the captain. She added, "Also Kha Aanhk," because nturun hated doing anything alone and Tsumon was already discreetly involved in helping Saraa set up a wide variety of potential battle maneuvers. Suumat and Aanhk mirrored each other's console displays and began to refine the foreign signaling protocols. Daamon mirrored that to a side-display on his own console, just to keep half an eye on their progress.

Saraa slapped her console lightly to get Daamon's attention. "That ship'll hit the junction slide in point one seven," she said. "We'll go in at point two five, assuming no change to our accel. I'm setting the default as straight in and straight out, with a random slip-course to trigger automatically if we read energy discharge as we come through."

"Good." Daamon agreed with all that. "Let's hope the beloved gods are merciful and we don't find any more surprises."

"The other ship's through the slide," Genru said, his voice just a little tense.

Saraa nodded. "So are we, in point one eight chime-down." She paused, watching the count. Finally, she said, "Point zero six. Point zero four. Point zero two ... here we go ..."

Space twisted inside out and straightened itself out again, and there they were, exactly as before, coasting through this perfectly boring and ordinary juncture that possessed nothing at all of interest, save the insystem Hanaa slide here and the Aam slide way out in the empty reaches of the system. The debris from the earlier battle was by now too cold to show on any scan. Nor was there any sign of other uut formations, thankfully. Only the uman ship, point zero eight chime-up in front of *Nkaastu*, having added a touch of accel since they'd come through the slide. Gliding out toward the Aam slide. Nothing exciting. Nothing remotely urgent.

Now, finally, there was time to breathe. The cousins' ship was heading straight for the Aam slide, but the transit through the juncture would take four chimes plus at their current accel.

"On the whole, considering what we may find," Kuotaan said to him, "we are pleased that we will make the transit to Aam in company with your-and-our cousins rather than alone. We have every good hope that we will find everything in order at Aam, as we believe the defenses there may well have guarded the system effectively until your-and-our cousins drove away any uut formations that came upon them. Nda Daamon, may we ask whether you anticipate finding any other situation? This seems unlikely to us. To us, it seems most likely that the foreign uman ship would not have come through the Aam slide into this juncture unless they had first cleared Aam space."

Daamon tipped his chin up. "I agree, unless that ship's allies took on that task, freeing it to pursue the uut formation we met. In that case, the close kin of these cousins may have approached the settlements at Aam, one hopes without incident." He winced, thinking of the orbital defenses in that system, of possible mistakes as well as the kind of tragedy that might have occurred if those defenses had been overwhelmed. He asked, "Does anyone have any idea what ships might have been at Aam when the uut and our cousins came through the system?"

Genru turned at once. "Daamon, Siiv u Kaoluun was at Aam, with *Sepuuk*. You remember that! It was in the newsfeed when we came through Hanaa the first time."

Daamon had actually forgotten this. He certainly remembered it now. Siiv u Kaoluun sep' Upuonnu, whose captain was Tnakaa u Kaoluun. *Sepuuk* was a full-fighter, head of a battlegroup—head of the *first* battlegroup. Tnakaa had been the very first turun captain to trade command off to an uman, during the long, terrible year on the far edge of familiar space, when the Ka' Taand had lost so much territory and so many settlements to the first wave of uut attacks. Tnakaa had passed command to Siiv, who had put together a battlecrew for his own ship, then forged a battlegroup from every armed ship in range of his urgent appeals. Then Siiv had led the effort to drive the uut back, giving the rest of them, staggering and limping and half-crippled as they were, time to get out of the far edge. Giving the whole Ka' Taand time to interdict as many as they could of the slides through which that attack had come.

Daamon had not known anything about that at the time; only that something had pulled the main battle away somewhere else, providing an opportunity for Daamon himself and so many others to claw their way back toward familiar space.

Later, it had been Siiv who laid out methods by which turun ships and battlegroups might successfully outfight uut formations—even whole swarms, if the swarm wasn't too enormous. He had laid down standards for selecting and training battlecrew and, with his captain, designed formal rules for yielding and taking back command. By then, Daamon had had a much clearer idea of what, and who, had made that chance for the rest of them. He had watched all the commentaries afterward, studied all the image captures, finding a strange reassurance in fitting his own bloody, chaotic memories into a framework that made some kind of sense. He'd understood right through to his fingertips what Siiv had done, what Siiv's captain Tnakaa u Kaoluun had helped Siiv do.

Even now, nearly all the standards and rules Siiv and Tnakaa had designed were still in place, used throughout the Ka' Taand by the full-fighters and near-fighters that continually patrolled the remnants of the far edge, preventing uut incursion through the slides that were so entirely stable that no effort could get those slides closed.

Daamon could guess why *Sepuuk's* battlegroup might be out here on the near edge. Pirates and near-pirates had become more troublesome recently, a problem for every matriline with resources invested along this edge of familiar space. Many matrilines had pulled up half-fighter tradeships for these important trading runs for that reason. But Kaoluun, with three times as many full-fighters as any other matriline, belonging to a clan with many other matrilines that emphasized full-fighters, had probably decided to deal with the piracy problem a lot more decisively.

Either way, if *Sepuuk* and its battlegroup had been at Aam, well, that was a huge relief. Daamon could hardly imagine anything but a full swarm, an enormous swarm, of uut getting past that battlegroup to the settlements. If the cousins had been driving the uut ahead of them, then very likely the settlements were actually all right. This was a *tremendous* relief.

On the other hand, if *Sepuuk* were there right now, Daamon could all too easily imagine a completely different kind of disaster. If any big foreign ship approached the settlements, Siiv wouldn't wait for that ship to get within range of the orbital defenses. No, he would certainly take his battlegroup and move to interdict that approach. If fire were exchanged ... he took a breath.

"If the beloved gods are merciful, our cousins might simply have passed through Aam in pursuit of the uut, and will now head out to some slide in the far reaches of the system, not in toward the settlements," he said. "If we pick up any signs of battle near the settlements, battle past or present ... we'll think fast, I suppose. If this ship attempts to head toward Aam, and everything looks otherwise normal, we'll want a course that puts us ahead of them, squarely in their way, as fast as possible." And what they'd do after they got themselves in that position, he had no idea. Think fast, no doubt.

"I can plot that now, more or less, and I'll priority it," Saraa promised him. "Our cousins will just touch the Aam slide in three point eight chime-down. After they enter the slide, we'll have point four one to set up our own nav solutions before we go in. I'm planning a smooth approach, no change in relative vee, bring us out in the same relative position. Last chance to let me know if that's not what you want."

She knew it was what he wanted, of course. Daamon nodded. He was still thinking about Siiv, and turun fighters, and uut formations where they didn't belong, and distant uman cousins who didn't know the first thing about turun.

"Let's game it out," he said. "Just like a tactical exercise in saaom." It wasn't exactly like any tactical exercise that he could quite imagine would ever come up in saaom, but he went on. "We have to interdict our cousins from approaching Aam, or the other way around, stop *Sepuuk* and that whole battlegroup from approaching our cousins, how can we do that? Worst case: if we go through and find our cousins or their close kin already fighting *Sepuuk's* battlegroup, what then? Since that's maybe the worst case, let's think about that."

"That's not the *worst* case," Paaol objected. "The *worst* case—"

"Whatever *moderately realistic* scenarios in which *Nkaastu* could possibly be of some use, game them out. We have ..." He glanced at the console ... "Three point seven four chime-down to run scenarios. Let's run some. Wild is fine. *Whatever* we find at Aam, I want to have thought of something similar before we get there."

Saraa acknowledged with a casual lift of her hand and Paaol with an aggressive toss of his head. Daamon left them to it, with Genru to take all signals and monitor the cousins' ship and the whole system for anything unexpected. He began to replay the two exchanges with the other commander, trying to wring every bit of meaning out of those recordings. He knew Kaamharaa would be doing the same from his isolated territory within *Nkaastu*.

As a linguist and a skilled trade-negotiator, Kaamharaa might well see plenty in those recordings that escaped Daamon himself. Plus, as Kaamharaa had worked for many years with Daamon's full-mother, an expert in the field of political interactions among the twelve thousand matrilines and handful of independent uman families that made up the four thousand clans of the Ka' Taand, Kaamharaa might also be able to propose arguments that would make even Kaoluun matriarchs stop and think.

Daamon sent a formal query to Kaamharaa, providing the legal justification any uturun needed before he could provide advice to the nturun captain and uman battlecommander of a matrilineal ship. That was one of the important rules that governed the physical presence of an uturun aboard a matrilineal ship—and all ships were matrilineal, barring a very few that were crewed solely by uman.

By arranging for Kaamharaa to establish a personal territory aboard *Nkaastu*, Daamon's mother had established their personal sep' family within the broader political authority of the Aanuku matriline while also increasing the financial status and political influence of Aanuku within the Suund, the gathering that governed the Ka' Taand.

Now, it would just be amazingly useful if Kaamharaa's linguistic interest and acumen in negotiation permitted *Nkaastu* to forge any kind of alliance between these newly discovered, or re-discovered, cousins and the matriline of Aanuku, maybe even with all the associated matrilines within the whole broader clan to which Aanuku belonged. Maybe even an alliance between the cousins' civilization and the whole of the Ka' Taand ... Daamon was probably running too far ahead of himself.

First, make sure no horrifying disaster occurred at Aam.

Aam was—had been—one of the outermost worlds of the near edge. The Ka' Taand had only recently found it while exploring, cautiously, to see if they could expand in a direction less subject to danger from the uut. Almost at once this hope had been rewarded by the discovery of Aam. The settlements in that system mostly surrounded a jewel of a world with a very useful asteroid belt. Immediately, various ambitious matrilines and allied uturun reputationists had begun studying the biosphere, acquiring land and orbital rights for worldlets or stations.

But if the peculiar and contorted lacework the slides wove through ordinary space meant that Aam turned out to be unexpectedly part of the *far* edge, fully *half* the important heart-stars of the whole Ka' Taand would suddenly find themselves just a juncture away from possible uut invasion. Daamon couldn't imagine any possible decision other than interdicting the Aam slide as fast as possible. That was a good slide, stable as anyone could wish, but almost certainly not so stable that a determined effort couldn't send it into wild unpredictability, close it to every kind of transit for forty years, a hundred, more than that.

The Suund, famously cautious, would surely make that choice. That would be potentially ruinous for Aanuku and bad for sep' Kaamharaa. That decision would also probably shut down any chance of contact with these astounding cousins with their giant ships and amazing weaponry. The Suund probably wouldn't mind that. But personal curiosity aside, an uman battlecommander had to ask, what if the uut got into familiar space *later,* from a *different* direction, equally unexpected, equally disastrous?

Daamon could definitely see all kinds of reasons they urgently needed to establish contact with these powerful cousins.

Time crept past. Daamon kept an eye on the scenarios his battlecrew threw out, occasionally tweaking one himself. He doubted *Nkaastu* would actually wind up having to try to fight the cousins' ship ... but if they had to do it, some of these ideas were only moderately crazy rather than absolutely suicidal.

Finally Saraa announced, "They're in the slide. So are we in point zero five ... point zero three ... point zero one ... Brace for slide."

Space twisted, and untwisted, and there was Aam. Quite close. Aam was the fourth planet out from the star, and this slide rode near the planet in a stable orbit, close enough to Aam for *Nkaastu* to pick up the world and associated settlements almost at once.

Daamon leaned forward. Genru was throwing images into the display as fast as the computers could gather them: Aam itself in shades of green; the big worldlet polity of Taaraaku Suul Aam, generally called Ta' Aam, visible on this side of the planet; a handful of blue defense stations, a whorl of blue and green turun ships in its close space. The brightest blue would be *Sepuuk* and its battlegroup, and yes, the battlegroup had plainly moved to interdict the settlements. Tradeships, dimmer green, heading around the world, getting out of the way in case there should be trouble. A few half-fighters and a scattering of half-fighter tradeships very much like *Nkaastu*, icons midway between green and blue, shifting courses to support the battlegroup of full-fighters.

Much closer, the cousins' ship blazed lavender and blue, the most brilliant ship in the display. It was *not* heading toward Aam.

Nothing else lavender was perceptible in the displays. That seemed ... simpler, at least.

The full-fighters near the settlements had *not* headed out to intercept the cousins' ship; having deployed to protect the settlements, they were now holding back, not coming out to force a confrontation.

Thank the beloved gods, none of the more exciting scenarios would be relevant. Daamon breathed out, a slow exhalation.

"Outbound," Saraa announced. Obviously she'd been worried too, or she wouldn't have bothered saying something they could all see perfectly well for themselves. She went on, "How far out is a question, but out for sure. Obviously there *is* another slide in the cold reaches of the system."

Daamon gestured acknowledgment. "Keep us as we are relative to that ship. Kuotaan—" he cut that off and started over, much more formally, with the proper little bow. "Tsaa Kuotaan, Captain, we could head in toward the settlements and trust *Sepuuk* and the battlegroup could cover us if our cousins take exception. But somebody needs to speak with our cousins and make an attempt to understand them. I think we should do that, especially as Kaamharaa is an entirely suitable choice of advisor for this approach to possible allies. Sep' Kaamharaa would entirely support your personal involvement and Aanuku's involvement in any negotiations that may take place. But I understand that a matriline as powerful as Kaoluun might declare Aanuku presumptuous for taking on negotiation with these near-unknown people and might particularly declare a captain not yet a matriarch presumptuous for taking that on herself. This is most properly your decision."

Saraa u Aanuku said, "Kaoluun's pushy, but we're already involved. Pretty sure we'd get unanimity on that among u Aanuku."

Kuotaan moved two hands in a gesture of half-agreement. If she actually disagreed, she would probably have said so already. If Tuutka disagreed, she would probably already have communicated that to the primary captain in some subtle way an uman couldn't perceive. But they could both see all the same options he could. He wasn't surprised at all when Kuotaan rumbled, equally formal, "Nda Daamon, we consider that we have already taken the first steps toward association with your-and-our cousins, on behalf of Aanuku and of the Ka' Taand. We concur that we are currently in the best position to consider further steps. Further, if we do not go with these cousins of yours-and-ours, we suspect we might be required to cede command to you again very shortly. Taking command ourselves therefore seems a foolish and unnecessary risk. We will communicate all these decisive opinions to the matriarchs of both Aanuku and Kaoluun should questions arise. By all means continue. Command remains yours."

Daamon gestured formal agreement and acceptance. "Keep us as we are," he told Saraa. "Gen, put together a transmission, the relevant part of our log and send it to *Sepuuk*. Send it broadly and tag it as open information, available without cost to anyone. Tsaa Kuotaan, I maintain free release of this information is a battle decision, despite the loss of potential profit."

"We concur," Kuotaan rumbled.

"Thank you, Captain. Paaol, work up your best guesses about our cousins' battle capabilities and append that to the transmission." That might prevent the most dire sort of misunderstanding later. He hoped any actual understanding would be ... not dire.

Everyone signaled acceptance, but Saraa turned to lean on her console, regarding Daamon narrowly. "So Aam's fine, and with Siiv's battlegroup there I bet it's in a lot less danger than we are. If we're heading for a wayout slide—and we obviously are—it'll probably be chimes before we get anywhere. Maybe more than a day; who knows? You came on how many chimes ago? It's time for you to take a break. I can perfectly well keep one hand and half an eye on the consoles. You—" she made a little shooing gesture. "Go."

Daamon nodded. She was right. And it was just as well: he knew without having to check that repair crews must already be hard at work on *Nkaastu's* damage, spinning new circuitry and fabricating hull panels and whatever else needed to be done. *Nkaastu* had good repair teams. If this outbound leg of their journey took long enough, they'd not only get *Nkaastu* as close to full-function as any internal repairs could, but polish out any scratches and buff the hull to a fine finish.

And that, too, might matter. Battle scars were no shame to a fighter, that was so, but still, he hardly wanted to trail after the stranger looking like some poor relation come visiting the wealthy family of her ancestral matriline.

Yes, the longer it took to reach the outer slide, the better.

"I want to talk to Kaamharaa anyway," he agreed. "Gen, take the next four chimes. Saraa, the four after that. Paaol, you came on with me; you're off now. Stay off for the full eight."

From childhood, Paaol had been so intense; he'd wear himself out and hardly notice until he actually collapsed. He looked like he was going to protest now, but Aanhk, who had been resting two of her big hands on his shoulders, gave him a little shake and a wordless rumble, and Paaol shrugged in reluctant agreement.

"Good," said Daamon. "Whoever's on the bridge, keep track of the repairs, right? Mirror all those reports to every battlecrew console. Anything changes with our cousins' ship, or when we spot the slide, whistle." He hesitated, but if he'd missed anything important, he couldn't think of it now. And Saraa was nodding. He nodded too and said, "Very well, then. Kuotaan?"

She set one enormous hand on his shoulder, tilting her head to look down at him. "We approve all our battlecommander's decisions. We will direct primary crew to monitor events carefully and yield to battlecrew on request."

"Thank you, Captain." Daamon patted Kuotaan's muscled lower shoulder, gave everyone else a slight bow, and went out, careful of his bad leg on the angled floors of the corridors.

***

Kaamharaa's quarters aboard *Nkaastu* were immense by shipboard standards: seven chambers in a row like beads strung on a necklace, not one of the rooms less than twelve strides across. Turun strides, not uman. Uturun strides, even longer than female nturun: they were big rooms. Thick rugs and rich draperies in comfortable worldtones, blues and browns, dusty greens and tawny golds. Vaulted ceilings so high that even Kaamharaa could stand up straight without having to think of ducking his head. Potted timhk against the walls, soft green foliage falling in waves over amber branches, and in the center of the reception chamber, a single graceful ndao nearly as tall as if it had grown in the true earth of Gaatuu, its fragrant golden fruits nestled amid black-green leaves. Kaamharaa loved luxury, and could afford to indulge his tastes even here aboard ship. And, of course, since he never left these rooms while *Nkaastu* was underway, it was only right they should be beautiful and comfortable.

The screened reception chamber was deserted, not astonishing under the circumstances, although often enough the children would be playing hide-and-find around the timhk and screens. Daamon strode across the room, touched the ndao's polished trunk for luck, stepped past the ornate enameled screen that protected everyone's sensibilities should Kuotaan or any other nturun discover an urgent necessity to speak directly to Kaamharaa, and entered the lounging chamber.

On any ordinary day, most of the household would likely be right here. Nkan, Paaol's mate, and Mattu, seniormost of the sepu family aboard *Nkaastu,* would be competing to work out the best tradeship options for future trading runs. Mattu's mate Karuu would be tinkering with code; the children would be playing tank games or studying. Quiet Vaeh, eldest daughter of Mattu and Karuu, would be reading, either an uman-authored romance-adventure or a turun-authored finance-adventure, probably reading particularly entertaining passages out loud. Kaamharaa himself would probably be trying once again to beat Daamon's sister Taya at saaom, and Pehha, Mattu and Karuu's youngest daughter, would be watching over Taya's shoulder, offering wry commentary.

This was the largest room in Kaamharaa's suite, twice the size of even the sleeping chamber; it was the only room where everyone in the household could spread out comfortably. But at the moment,

Nkan and Mattu would be with their damage repair team; Vaeh would be at her emergency station; Karuu would have taken Pehha and Vaeh's two children back to the sleeping chamber to keep them out of the way. And, of course, Taya would be with Kaamharaa, and Kaamharaa would be ... Daamon skirted the central pool and swept aside the beaded curtain that separated the lounging room from the high-ceilinged solar.

The solar wasn't *really* a solar, of course. But the illusion of tinted skylight and bright sun beyond was astonishingly persuasive, and the white-blue ceiling and gold-toned draperies, the rugs just the color of the tawny and emerald grasses of Gaatuu's savannah, all added to the effect, until the whole room seemed to glow with natural sunlight and Daamon almost imagined that he could smell the hot earth and whispering grasses.

This, of course, was the room to which Kaamharaa had retreated, as naturally as a flower turning toward the sun. Kaamharaa had been born in the city of Ndask, which spread out for a great distance along both banks of the Tuaam River at the edge of the savannah. After leaving the matriline of his birth, he had spent his youth in the wide reaches of the savannah reservation set aside for young males. Naturally he still longed, particularly when upset or angry, for wide spaces and hot sun. Or at least the illusion of distance and sunlight.

Daamon, too, had been born near Ndask, though several tens of years later, long after Kaamharaa had established his reputation and the beginnings of his wealth and had been able at last to secure a territory in the male reserve, build a homestead, and apply for an uman family to join him in a proper household. Daamon's mother had been one of the first uman women to join Kaamharaa, when the uman part of the household had comprised only herself and her brother, her mate and her brother's mate. Two young uman couples, all u Guuan, city-bred, raised in the matriline amid a crowd of nturun cousins and aunts and sisters. Daamon imagined it had taken courage to step away from the bustle of Guuan and the city. Courage to gamble on the growing reputation of then-young Kaamharaa, and his willingness to pay four honor fees to Guuan for the privilege of bringing uman couples into his household in the hope they would find themselves compatible and forge a permanent family.

Fortunately for Daamon, his mother and his father and his second-parents had all proven to love living under a sky that stretched out into the peaceful distance, the wind through the dry summer grasses, the warm scent of the earth after the season turned and the rains came, the cry of the tgaan floating through the dusk and the whistle of the nnagu at dawn.

As a young man, Daamon had been glad to go to space; he'd wanted to explore, to find new worlds for the Ka' Taand, to build Kaamharaa's reputation by building his own ... he'd had no idea. None of them had, before the uut had slashed into the far edge and begun devastating the worlds there.

Now, though he loved *Nkaastu,* he sometimes missed the wide savannah with an ache that was almost physical. Lately, for the first time in the years since he'd left the care of the surgeons and stepped on board *Nkaastu,* Daamon had found himself wondering whether a woman—whether Saraa u Aanuku, specifically—might possibly consider leaving crowded Aanuku for the peace of an uturun homestead.

Probably not. Probably, if she wanted to take a mate, she'd choose someone from Aanuku. He'd definitely had that impression. She would probably find the restricted and rural life of a solitary uturun's household unbearably tedious compared to a bustling urban line-house. But she might like a sep' household if she visited long enough to feel the difference. And after all, Kaamharaa was allied to Aanuku, so joining his household wouldn't mean separating herself entirely from her sisters and cousins.

He'd never actually *asked* her. Maybe he should. If they all lived through the current crisis, if these peculiar cousins of theirs proved to be allies, even friends, rather than a very unfortunate new sort of enemy ... if, in a month or a year, they were all in a decent position to offer and accept invitations ... particularly if Daamon himself had added one or another glory-accent to his own reputation ... then maybe he would.

But not today.

Kaamharaa was bent over the console set into the solar's wall, Taya tucked into the curve of his left arms where she, too, could have a clear view of the display. The console was replaying the exchange with the strangers, every captured word and gesture. Both of them were too intent to pay attention to Daamon's entrance—a good sign, as that was exactly where he wanted their attention. He eased himself down on a nearby cushion and waited.

When the recording ended, Daamon observed, "They shorten their vowels, don't they?"

"They shorten everything!" Taya exclaimed, not looking up. "They shorten their gestures, too, they cut everything up in sharp little bits, it's very strange. But they don't do or say nearly enough on these recordings. It's hard to get a feel for them." She touched the console, sending the recording back to the beginning.

"However, even with this small sample, one begins to develop an appreciation of how far your people have adapted your manner to accommodate turun preferences," rumbled Kaamharaa. He turned his massive head. "I fear I may not be able to develop a proper appreciation for your cousins' artistic taste, however."

Daamon couldn't help but smile. But he only said, "Kaamharaa, I need you to teach me cant."

"This is not precisely cant, of course, though the similarities—"

Taya interrupted cheerfully. "I already know some cant, a lot more than you do, big brother. Kaamharaa can teach me to speak it better. *You* can concentrate on weaving an alliance that'll send every uut in the galaxy to the forsaken gods' hell. Kuotaan *is* planning to make an alliance with our new cousins, isn't she? She'd better! If she's not, you have to tell her this is all part of fighting the uut. Which it is! We *need* these people. Did you *see* how they took out all those uut ships? Like lightning striking so many little gnats!"

Gnats was overstating the situation, and obviously Daamon could hardly trample the captain's prerogatives. But he gestured agreement to the important part of this suggestion. "Kaamharaa *can* teach you cant. That's a good idea." It was an immense relief, in fact, when he had so much else to claim his attention. Taya was quick with languages, having played linguists' games with Kaamharaa since she could barely toddle. It was an *excellent* idea, and never mind that she had barely taken her autonomy exams.

"Don't sound so surprised, big brother. I have lots of good ideas."

"*Occasionally* you might have *one*."

"Lots," she insisted, tossing her head in an arrogant gesture she'd picked up from Kaamharaa. Daamon suppressed a grin, but she went on, quick and urgent. "Listen, Daamon, did you see how they all dress alike, in that terrible drab black? We should run up some clothing like that, kind of the same style. Not black of course, surely we needn't be *quite* as gloomy, but enough like theirs so they'll feel we're more familiar. Like shaving your head when you visit Suuarot, you know, to show respect and set the dedicats at ease. Don't you think that's a good idea too?"

Actually, it was.

Before Daamon could say so, his sister rattled on, "We could use lots of red! It's the only color they wear, did you notice? Doesn't that seem strange? Maybe they're all partly color blind and can't see blues and yellows! Maybe our ancestors evolved color vision after they were abandoned. Wouldn't that be lucky for us? Imagine going through life unable to see any color besides red!"

Daamon doubted this. "Our ancestors separated from theirs a long time ago, but probably not that long. Besides, if red is a special color to our cousins, do you truly think we should take it up ourselves?"

Taya blinked. "You're smart, too," she conceded. "Okay, not red. Which is great! Because that means we definitely shouldn't wear black either." She looked him up and down. "Browns and blues," she said decisively. "You look good in browns and blues. Those people should respect you, even if their ship is huge and has all those sharp edges and strikes down dozens of uut at a time like flash lightning. I'll run up some clothing kind of like theirs, but not exactly, just enough to make them feel we're familiar and respectful."

"Vaeh can do it. Or Pehha. *You* practice cant." Daamon finally found a chance to address Kaamharaa again. "Can you make out much of their language? How close is it to cant, can you tell?"

Kaamharaa, who had been lying couchant on the floor so that he and Taya could both watch the recordings more or less comfortably from a display set only uman-high, had now rolled his lower body to one hip in a more relaxed pose. He answered in his deep voice. "It would be far easier to extrapolate from the true, sophisticated language to the degenerate form rather than the reverse. Nevertheless, I do believe that the remnants of the original language preserved within uman cant should allow us to establish communication relatively swiftly and easily with these cousins of yours, though no doubt with a limited and primitive vocabulary at first. Unlikely as we may be to discover any urgent need for terms such as *club* or *dig* or *leaf shelter*, other terms, such as *danger* and *home* and *us together,* may prove of great use. I shall teach such useful words to Taya. She will learn quickly."

Daamon waited patiently through this leisurely discourse. He certainly agreed that *us together* would be a useful phrase. Especially connected not merely to *danger* but also to *uut*. When Kaamharaa rumbled to a halt, he nodded and said, "Good. That will be an immense help, I expect. I'd like to hear every tentative conclusion you and Taya can develop regarding our cousins. Their attitudes, their motivations, their inclinations." He lifted one hand. "I understand the inherently unreliable nature of every conclusion. Nevertheless. Please put together a concise report."

"I will tag every statement and assertion with the degree of reliability I feel it deserves," Kaamharaa stated. "Those tags will also be unreliable, Daamon, as I am confident you are aware."

Daamon had to smile. "Acutely, I assure you. I know you don't like working under a tight deadline, but I would ask that you take no more than three chimes to develop your initial conclusions."

To any crewmember, Daamon could have made that an order. He couldn't possibly give orders to Kaamharaa. But Kaamharaa might take the three chimes as a reasonably hard limit, rather than a mere suggestion. He had been one of the very first uturun to establish a secondary territory within an nturun ship, and he was therefore far more accustomed than most to pretending he took hierarchical ranks seriously. He inclined his massive head in acknowledgement.

"Good. Thank you. Now, we're heading out toward a distant slide, probably, and at current vee it may be quite a few chimes before we get to it. Battlecrew is staying on scant-duty, one on the bridge at a time. I need to rest. Whoever's on will give a whistle if anything changes or when they spot the slide."

Taya nodded. "If you're off, I'm sure Mattu and Karuu won't mind if you borrow their room. Karuu's got the children in the sleeping chamber, so that's not exactly restful."

"Those cushions will be fine. You won't bother me." The deep tones of Kaamharaa's voice and the light, quick voice of his sister were actually just what Daamon needed to ease into rest. He leaned his cane against the wall, lifted his bad leg up onto the cushions, and lay down. And closed his eyes. He doubted he'd actually sleep. But he could rest. If anything unexpected happened, Saraa would handle it. When she sent down her whistle, he'd be ready to go back up to the bridge and face whatever was waiting on the other side of that unknown slide.

***

The whistle from the bridge woke him, a sweet series of tones that ranged from low-pitched toward high and eased Daamon out of sleep without any sense of urgency, so that even before he was quite awake, he knew that nothing unexpected had happened while he slept.

Relieved, feeling almost rested, Daamon sat up. Taya jumped to her feet and handed him a cup of hot tsuaeh. The sweetly acerbic sting was just what he needed to wake himself up.

"It's nearly twenty-eight. You slept for almost eight chimes. You ought to eat something, but I know you won't," Taya told him, and dropped a couple of methk bars into the pocket of his outer robe. She added a handful of words that sounded choppy, at once half familiar and quite incomprehensible.

"You've been studying," Daamon observed.

"I said *you-us be careful, watch out where you put your feet.*"

"You said *foots,*" Kaamharaa corrected, repeated the word in Uom and uman cant both. "That was a mistake. *Feet* is the plural."

Taya rolled her eyes. "That's a stupid plural. I bet the real language doesn't have such stupid plurals."

"It was a good job either way," Daamon assured her. He hadn't understood a word of it and was grateful he didn't have to.

"Your sister has proved a most apt pupil, as always," Kaamharaa stated, "I have routed my initial observations and conclusions to your console, tagged with an urgent stamp. Where Taya and I disagree, her hypotheses are presented in parallel with mine."

Daamon opened one hand to acknowledge this. "Thank you, Kaamharaa."

"It was indeed my pleasure. This encounter offers a most exciting and unusual opportunity for both linguistic analysis and tradecraft, as well as perhaps delightfully complicated political maneuvering." Kaamharaa heaved himself to his feet, a complicated rocking motion that involved front and rear in alternation and ended with a heavy, solid thump as he settled his weight on all four powerful legs. Then, fully upright, he inclined his head to gaze down at Daamon from his towering height. He said, in rather magnificent tones, "You must arrange matters so as to guarantee your sister's safety, Daamon. I have complete confidence that you will do so. And the safety of all our household. And all *Nkaastu*, to be sure, and Aanuku beyond *Nkaastu,* and the broader Ka' Taand," he added, but without making such a business of this addendum.

Daamon smiled. Kaamharaa enjoyed grand pronouncements, but he was perfectly serious about this one. An uman might think wide and broad, but turun focused mainly on family. To a reputable, established uturun such as Kaamharaa, the security of the Ka' Taand was distantly important, the wellbeing of the allied Aanuku matriline certainly desirable, but paramount above all was the safety of his own household.

Daamon hadn't the least desire to argue with those priorities unless he had absolutely no choice. He patted the uturun's lower shoulder, which was as high as he could comfortably reach, and said sincerely, "That's my firm intention, I assure you."

"Good," said Kaamharaa. He lifted Daamon to his feet, gently, mindful of Daamon's bad leg and his own immense strength. "Good. I value the warmth of your regard, Daamon, and in this exigency I shall trust to your cunning and audacity. You may be certain that I shall do anything in my power to assist you or Tsaa Kuotaan. You may assure Tsaa Kuotaan of this, also."

Daamon tipped his chin up, opening a hand in acknowledgement and assent.

"Be careful! Be clever! Be correct!" ordered Taya, peeking around Kaamharaa's lower chest. *That* was a line from a favorite romance-adventure Kaamharaa had read to them both when they had been children back on Gaatuu, running half wild through the savannah surrounding Kaamharaa's house. Taya had loved uman-authored romance-adventure stories much better than turun-authored finance-adventures, and that line had been a joke with her when she'd been a child.

But then they'd grown up, and the uut had suddenly sliced into the lacework of the far edge of Ka' Taand space, and the cascade of ruin and disaster had sent shockwaves radiating through Ka' Taand space ... and Daamon had turned away from the far edge and become battlecommander of *Nkaastu*. Now it wasn't a joke at all, however lightly mocking Taya's tone.

Daamon opened a hand to his sister, too, and then put his back to her, to Kaamharaa and to his whole close family, heading back up to the bridge and battlecommand.

***

The moment he arrived on the bridge, a single swift glance at the tank display showed Daamon that *Nkaastu* was still nearly three tenth-chimes from the slide. The stranger's long, sleek, predatory ship must have gone through already, as its brilliant lavender and blue icon was not in evidence—yes, a glance at the command console showed the timestamp of its passage through the slide.

A second, more comprehensive glance took in the repair reports: lateral propulsion creeping back toward optimal function, ventral coming along nearly as well. Hull integrity not yet perfect, but in the region of ninety percent. The repair teams were certainly doing fine work, and grant the favor of the beloved gods that they needn't scramble that hard any time in the near future.

He also noted that a drone trailed them, way back, painted in dim blue. *Sepuuk*—or some ship—had been quick, getting that on its way fast enough to keep up. Genru had already set a directional pulse to help the drone keep track of *Nkaastu*, so there was nothing to do there. All right, so, all this was fairly reassuring. No immediate crisis, at least.

Kuotaan, of course, stood four-set and solid in her place. She tipped her head toward Daamon, permission for him to resume his place. He stepped to her side, accepting the assistance of the lower hand she set under his elbow. "Kaamharaa is teaching my sister uman cant," he told the captain. "Taya is quick to learn, and though cant is, we assume, very much changed from the true language, we hope this will prove useful."

"Indeed," Kuotaan agreed, and lowered the command console in tacit approval for him to resume battlecommand.

Daamon touched her lower shoulder in appreciation, logged the transfer of command, leaned on his cane, and studied the updating reports as they came in. Every report having to do with the cousins was tagged all over with high measures of uncertainty. Of course. But here was Kaamharaa's initial report, interesting despite the many tags. Kaamharaa seemed to have gained an impression of the cousins and of their commander that half-agreed with Daamon's own feeling. Or maybe this was closer to a near-agreement. Aggression and goodwill, but Kaamharaa read the first as more certain and tagged the second as highly uncertain. Taya reversed those tags. Both added curiosity as a near-certain motivation, but only Kaamharaa suggested the other commander might desire to turn important decisions over to a matriarch or other leadership figure. Taya suggested an alternate interpretation of seeking-safety-with-kin, a far more important motivation for nturun and uman than uturun.

Looking up from the report, Daamon glanced around the bridge. Saraa and Genru were at their stations with their turun partners Tsumon and Suumat, though Aanhk still held her station alone, Paaol not yet having returned—ah, here he came. Patting his partner's lower shoulder, Paaol resumed his place before their common console as Aanhk ruffled his hair in return, a familiarity not quite proper on the bridge and on duty. Daamon and Kuotaan both pretended not to notice. Daamon pulled the conclusions from Kaamharaa's report and mirrored that to every bridge console.

"No further communication before they went through," Saraa told him, her long fingers shifting across the console's enamels as she glanced over the report. "I expect they'll be waiting for us at the other side of the slide. I vote with Kaamharaa: I bet they're heading straight for the nearest ranking matriarch."

"And for half a hundred of their closest kin, probably," Genru put in. "I vote with both Kaamharaa and Taya: I'm betting our cousins probably want to get a high matriarch involved *and* get their own close-kin at their backs."

Saraa snorted. "If they have half a hundred more ships on the other side, they'd have come exploring this way a lot earlier—"

"Not if they needed the uut to show them the wayout slide," Paaol argued.

Genru shook his head. "No, if the uut already knew about the slide, they'd have hit Aam *way* before now—"

"The uut probably just discovered this slide, probably they were just setting up for a raid and tagged our cousins by mistake—"

"Point one zero," cut in Saraa. "I'll take us in on the same trajectory as our cousins' ship, Daamon, unless you want something else." She put a slight, ironic accent on 'cousins,' making it clear she was reserving her opinion of the uman strangers.

Daamon gestured agreement to Saraa, meaning it to cover both the voiced query and the unvoiced doubt. By common agreement, they all let the discussion die in the knowledge that very soon they were all going to leap into the unknown reaches of the universe and for good or ill find out what was there. Whether the beloved or forsaken gods would govern the chance, no one could yet guess.

Nevertheless, all Daamon actually said was, "A little distance between our cousins' space and ours wouldn't necessarily be a bad thing, and a lot of distance between uut space and ours is ardently to be desired. We can at least hope the gods so arranged the universe."

"We'll find out," said Saraa, neither agreeing nor disagreeing. "Slide in point zero three. Brace for slide."

"Beloved gods, bless our endeavors," Daamon murmured.

Kuotaan seconded this with an *avert* gesture against the forsaken gods and quietly signaled primary crew to stand ready to support Daamon's battlecrew.

"Point zero two nine. Point two eight. Brace, brace." The ship twisted inside out and back again, and yet again they were elsewhere, this time somewhere entirely unknown, passing through the wayout slide into yet another bubble in the lacework stitched together by slides and other, more violent, wormholes.

Computers scrambled first to make sense of radiation signatures, and then to sort through the violent, sleeting radiation of a nearby star. Genru called out, "No ships other than our cousins' anywhere nearby as far as I can tell, though we're so near the system primary I could probably miss thirteen worldlets and a parade of dedicats with bells on. They're taking a tight course around the star, not heading out." He threw the other ship's course into the display, lit up in braided blue and lavender.

"No incoming fire, no trouble," Paaol added, and sat back, looking mildly disgruntled at the lack of immediate excitement.

Daamon couldn't see anything exciting anywhere either, but unlike Paaol, was far from unhappy about that. They'd sure come through a slide uncomfortably close to a star, and just as well they'd recovered nearly complete hull integrity before they found themselves riding this kind of solar flux. It was a rough ride for *Nkaastu*, but Saraa had thrown into the display the course the cousins' ship was tracing, and Daamon suspected they wouldn't be in this system long. "Tight arc," he said out loud.

"I'm extrapolating their course and trying to find the next slide," Saraa agreed. "I don't have it yet, but it's close or we'd be heading out, not around."

"Here," rumbled Saraa's partner Tsumon. She highlighted the route they were following and pointed out the area where a drop in perceptible solar radiation indicated the presence of a second near-star slide.

"Certainly an uncomfortable juncture," Kuotaan declared. "Difficult to scan properly. If you agree, Battlecommander, let us drop a drone to mark the path."

Daamon tipped his chin up in agreement. "Two drones, let's mark each slide, we don't want to lose anyone tracking us. Suumat, if you don't mind, you might pick up the course details from Saraa and see to programming the drones." No question that *Sepuuk* and probably others would be tracking them.

"One point two chime-down," Saraa said, finishing her own calculations. "These two slides are so close together, I bet their orbital dynamics are tremendously unstable, and they're so near the primary, that'll make it worse. I'm sending you a compensation package, Suumat, take a look and see if you want to integrate it with whatever you're putting together."

Suumat rumbled wordless agreement. Turun were almost always happy to consult and take advice; it was one of the reasons turun crew worked so easily with battlecrew, as long as captain and battlecommander were both willing to let that happen. Daamon added, "Add a suggestion for anyone following to pick up the drones, not leave them sitting right by those slides, ready to be scanned. Last thing we want is to mark the slides for the uut, if they haven't already got them."

Murmurs of agreement, followed by a long, tense pause. Tenth and then quarter chimes crept past. Finally Saraa said, "Here we go again. Point zero three chime-down." Her hands moved across her console. "Point zero two nine. Point zero two seven." And yet again they were elsewhere.

And ... nothing. The new system was, to a first glance and a second, utterly normal and ordinary, offering nothing of either threat or promise. Except the stranger's deadly ship; that had added a touch more accel and so had gained a little more distance from *Nkaastu*, but it was still moving smoothly through space, no sign of trouble anywhere. No other lavender icons lit up in the display—no red or white, either. Only the single ship that had led them to this place, and *Nkaastu* itself, and a completely vacant system. That was fine, definitely better than so many other possibilities, but Daamon couldn't help but feel disappointed. Since they were going *somewhere*, he would just as soon get there and see what they faced.

Way, way out this time: nothing interesting anywhere, so far as the sensors could tell or the computers could calculate. A completely boring system except for the slide they'd just come through and somewhere, presumably, another slide that led somewhere back toward the cousins' familiar space. That faint blue speck must be the system primary, though it was so distant sensors barely tagged it. Ah, and scans picked up a cold giant, way out from the primary. But, yes, at the moment, this system seemed to offer largely empty space. Any rocky planets were too far away for the sensors to paint them in the display. Right now, the system looked entirely boring.

The cousins' ship had set a course toward nothing obvious. Another slide, undoubtedly. Well, that was fine.

"The cousins are heading out, not in," Saraa announced. The other ship's course traced itself across the display, a line of delicate lavender through the tank. "I'm guessing we've got another slide out here, since there sure doesn't seem to be anything else they could be heading toward."

Daamon tipped his chin up. Nothing else immediately made sense. This system might well be a useful junction because two wayout slides implied at least a couple near the star. Pity *Nkaastu* was a half-fighter tradeship instead of an explorer or half-explorer. He'd have given a lot for that kind of sensor suite.

"Ah," said Tsumon from her place beside Saraa. "There is the next slide, we believe. Unusual, to find two so close together. Yet here it is."

Tsumon's projected course for the other ship intersected her postulated slide, which she'd painted lavender and pale pink for unknown and possibly dangerous. Daamon checked Tsumon's numbers and observed, "Well, that's not far at all." He ran a finger across his console, calculating the distance.

Saraa hummed a surprised note, beating him to the finished calculation. "Definitely not far at all," she agreed. "One point nine six. Not quite time for anybody to take a nap. Too bad, since I'm thinking it was my turn." Her tone didn't match her complaint, though. She was already tapping her console, sending an echoing alert through *Nkaastu* so that everyone would know another slide was fast approaching. One point nine was far from immediate, but it was starting to flirt around the edges of imminent.

"A potentially useful but also potentially dangerous system, if slides prove to be scattered thickly through its outer reaches," observed Kuotaan. "Nda Daamon, let us deploy a handful of drones in the hope that we may eventually elucidate the positions of other slides here." The captain did this herself without waiting for his agreement, though of course he gave it with a little tip of his chin. Obviously exploratory drones were a good idea.

Checking the repair reports again, Daamon tapped back accel just a fingerwidth, and a fingerwidth more, to help the repair teams complete their work in time.

"Oh, fine, now it's two point three," Saraa said. She leaned back, stretching. "Anybody got a methk bar?"

Daamon gave her one, then passed out the rest to everyone else on the bridge, keeping one for himself, though he was too tense to feel hungry. He pretended calm confidence. "Saraa, take a break. One chime. Get something better than a methk bar and relax. Tsumon, with Tsaa Kuotaan's approval, rotate off as well for the same interval. Suumat, if you'd please take that station for the next chime."

"We agree," Kuotaan declared. "We have no objection."

"You're sure?" Saraa glanced from Daamon to Kuotaan and nodded. "Fine, great, one chime. Suu— thanks, yeah, you've got it." Saraa stretched, yawning. Tsumon put a lower arm around her shoulders, and they went out together as Suumat picked up navigation functions.

Kuotaan was probably no more relaxed than Daamon felt, but she accepted the methk bar he gave her with a small nod even though it was uman-sized rather than the much bigger kind made for turun. She added, "We would be as pleased to find many empty systems between your-and-our cousins and familiar space. The uut came from this direction too."

She wasn't wrong, but Daamon still hated the waiting. All his earlier doubts crowded back. All the risks he'd urged upon Kuotaan—what if his advice had been wrong, all his hopes and opinions mistaken? What if he should have advised every kind of caution—or fled for Aam and thrown the whole problem to Siiv u Kaoluun and Tnakaa u Kaoluun?

Yes, true, Daamon was the man who'd established the barest beginning of a conversation with that foreign commander. And yes, he was sep' Kaamharaa, and Kaamharaa was surely one of the best possible advisors for this kind of unexpected and deeply fraught conversation, his reputation far more in line with this kind of task than Upuonnu, the most prestigious male allied to Kaoluun. Upuonnu might have one of the brightest reputations of any uturun, but his specialties lay in engineering, particularly aeronautics and ship construction, not in negotiation and tradecraft.

Also, if pressed, Daamon would have to admit he trusted Kuotaan and the Aanuku matriarchs more than Tnakaa u Kaoluun and the Kaoluun matriarchs. For unceasing vigilance and battle, Kaoluun, absolutely. But for negotiation and possible alliance, surely a tradeship captain was a better choice. Even if Kuotaan's battlecommander was nothing like as experienced and brilliant as Siiv, and her ship nothing like as well armed as *Sepuuk*.

Pretending he wasn't at all tense helped, somewhat. Daamon bit off a piece of his methk bar. The sweet pressed grain and fruit settled his stomach. He ate the rest, slowly, leaning his weight against Kuotaan's shoulder, letting her support him with a comfortable lower arm around his waist so he needn't have any weight at all on his bad leg. Tenth chimes trickled past. Paaol, never a patient man, tapped the uman-level primary console and ran firing solutions based on all sorts of wildly improbable scenarios.

Saraa and Tsumon arrived together a tenth-chime before they were due; both of them reclaimed their shared console from Suumat without comment on any side. Saraa frowned at the display and began a countdown.

"Point two," she said at last, though they'd all been watching the same display and knew the count. "Our cousins are through the slide. We're going after them in ... point one four." A pause, and then, "Point one. Point zero six."

Paaol ran a check on the weapons systems, which were already up and ready.

"Brace, brace," Saraa announced, and they were ... in, and through.

This system was far from empty.

Daamon took half a step without thinking, catching himself against the rainbow arc of the console as too much of his weight came onto his bad leg. Tsumon exclaimed, her deep turun voice punctuated by uman soprano as Saraa made a short, unconsidered sound of dismay. Paaol hit his console, grinning fiercely as Aanhk, beside him, forgot shipboard manners enough to swear by every forsaken god Daamon knew; Genru's partner Suumat contributed a handful he'd never heard of. Icons proliferated in the tank display as the computers sorted out the wild bursts of signals: blazing lavender surrounded by the slashing white of Blades and *a lot more* red, burning everywhere, *far* too much red. The computers, convinced by data Daamon hadn't yet had time to sort out, started painting everything in every direction red red red.

Daamon cried, "Saraa!"

Before the word was out, she slammed *Nkaastu* back through the slide in a twisting, awkward double-skip maneuver that made the whole ship ring like a bell as the gravitics adjusted and adjusted again.

"Tank display!" Daamon ordered. "Gen, pull up the display capture and let's have a look at what we actually saw in that forsaken system. Paaol, keep an eye on the slide—if anything comes through after us, we'd better spot it before it spots us. Don't wait for orders, shoot anything red or white. Saraa, pick up vee." Slow was dead if something fast came after them. He added, "Set us on a course that'll loop us around and give us choices. We don't know what we'll be doing, so options, please."

"Right, right, on it," muttered Genru, and Saraa nudged Tsumon.

A second later, the captured image built itself in the tank: a central star, yellow-white, neither large nor small; and close at hand a cool blaze of lavender, multiple stationary icons mostly in close formation, surrounded by darting sparks of red and white. Oh, yes, those lavender ships were in very serious trouble. Daamon couldn't even *count* the red icons of uut Disks, and the white icons of Blades flashed and wheeled *everywhere*.

Worse, submerged within the swarms of red and white, four great round icons, immense and red and terrifying.

For nearly a tenth chime, no one spoke.

Genru said at last, "Gods be forsaken, those four ... things. Base ships, maybe. Way too big to be fighters. Base-ships or stations, and I'm betting on the former because all those fighters have to've come from somewhere, and anyway, who'd put four stations there?"

Daamon shook his head, not disagreeing, but awed. "Can you give us a scale?"

"Uh ... bigger than Ehnuuk? I know!" Genru said defensively. "That's my best estimate!"

Ehnuuk was one of the larger turun stations that orbited Gaatuu. Daamon had never dreamed a ship that big was even *possible*. Not even in his *nightmares* had he ever imagined the uut might have ships like that. And that was on top of the giant swarm of ordinary fighters.

Suumat lifted one dappled hind leg and stamped gently, requesting his attention. "One-tenth greater diameter than Ehnuuk," she stated.

Daamon opened a hand in acknowledgment. They'd never seen anything like this on the far edge. He certainly wished they weren't seeing it now.

"The lavender ships are big, too; some of them are very large," Tsumon offered. "Perhaps, if I may offer an opinion, they may not be lost too quickly."

Daamon shrugged with one hand, not wanting to hold out false hope. "That many uut, I guess they're not going to hold for long."

"Yeah, we got here just in time to watch our cousins get torn down," Genru said, his tone grim.

But Paaol, who had been bending over his console, suddenly pivoted to face the rest of the battlecrew. "Yes, *maybe*, but you know what *I* think? I think maybe it's not as uneven as it looks. Look at this!" Spinning back to his console, he scattered dozens of sharply angled planes between and among the icons representing the cousins' ships. "Look, they've *got* to have shields overlapping pretty much like this or they wouldn't be holding that kind of formation at all. I think they've got themselves into a solid defensive arrangement. I mean, look at this part here." Paaol played back a brief section of the recording. "You can see the uut fighters trying to break through. But our cousins are holding! Except a few of their ships, these right here, are more exposed, and *our* ship, they're *totally* exposed, so that's not great, we should go help them quick before it's too late!"

Once Paaol had laid it out, Daamon could see all that for himself. He turned decisively to Kuotaan. "Tsaa Kuotaan, Captain, we have to go back through the slide. Those are our cousins. Also, if the uut win here, very soon they'll come against Aam. There are so many! And the slides are so close together in this juncture; they'll certainly find the way. We need to see what happens there, and if we can help, we need to do it. That ship, *our* ship—" he gave it the same inflection Paaol had, the familiar inflection, for someone known if not necessarily allied. "We know each other, a little. We don't know any others of those people, they don't know us, we *need* that ship."

"We are merely a half-fighter tradeship," Kuotaan reminded him. "This is true battle against great odds." She was not exactly refusing permission, not even exactly even arguing against his proposal. She couldn't; this was definitely a situation when the battlecommander held priority. But she wasn't happy, and she wasn't wrong.

"Yes," Daamon acknowledged, with a gesture conceding that everything she said—everything she'd meant—was true. "I won't forget our limits, Captain. Suumat, if you don't mind, please dump that display capture to another drone and send it back the way we came. Saraa, take us back through that slide, but set us up for a fast sideslip and a random walk even before we're all the way out, you know somebody's got to be targeting the slide. Paaol, throw out covering fire before the displays clear, don't wait for good resolution, but don't shoot at anything lavender!"

"Right," Paaol said, posed tensely over his console.

"Brace, brace," added Saraa almost at once, and *Nkaastu* slid sideways, the tank display swirling and clearing and filling once more. Someone might have been targeting the area near the slide, but no one fired at *Nkaastu* or else incoming fire missed, because no alarms rang through the bridge; Daamon checked the fast course Saraa had set up. Wildly variable accel and a sharp jinking random-walk course that would eventually bring them back to the slide and in the meantime made them hard to target. Though so far as Daamon could tell, everyone on both sides was too busy with other enemies to go after a turun half-fighter tradeship just at the moment.

"*That's* our friend," Genru said, painting one nearby icon blue as well as lavender. "*Look* at those forsaken uut, eighty at least, maybe more than that!" He lit up the red and white sparks that had deserted the farther battle to close a vicious net around the half-familiar icon. Already the display showed a generous dusting of debris near at hand, mostly lavender punctuated by bursts of red and occasional white. However deadly that lavender-blue ship might be, it was plainly staggering under this unexpected onslaught—surely unexpected, surely they wouldn't have led *Nkaastu* into this maelstrom on purpose and without warning—

"Heart-Disk," Daamon snapped as the swirl of icons took on a recognizable pattern. He lit it up in the display, a single Disk toward the edge of the cloud around the cousins' ship. It was hanging back, yet exerting clear control over many others, like the central star in a system cluttered with orbital complexities.

"No—I mean yes, but this one, too." Paaol highlighted another Disk on the other side of the attacking cluster. "Forsaken gods, and this one!" He tagged another.

Even with the highlighting, the third Disk didn't stand out to Daamon's eye, but he trusted his sep' brother's eye more than his own. He nodded and ordered, "Range just those, set priorities. I don't think our cousins have the heart-Disks spotted, Paaol, do you agree?"

"They don't!" Paaol answered immediately. "Looks to me like they're prioritizing the Blades when they should be going after the Disks, and when they do target the Disks, they're just hitting the nearest and the ones making immediate attacks. I think they're letting their computers do all the targeting and set most of the priorities, and that's going to cost them in maybe another tenth chime-down."

The lack of effective targeting was already costing the other ship, judging by the lavender sparkle of damage surrounding it, signaling debris or lost atmosphere or both. Daamon's instant impression was that the cousins simply did not know how to unfocus the gaze and find the heart-Disks, at least not when they were so seriously outnumbered.

"I've got every one of *Nkaastu's* confounders ready to disperse," Saraa said calmly. "The uut aren't prioritizing us, look at their pattern. If we go in on a repeated snap-course with pseudo-random variation, I bet we can get right in among them before they figure we've got their heart-Disks prioritied. Not more than once, not even with every beloved god in the whole pantheon hovering over us, but I bet we can make *one* attack run and still get clear."

For all his respect for Saraa's skill and confidence, Daamon wasn't nearly as certain as she sounded. Making it into the middle of the swarming uut, yes, they could do that. Out might be another matter. But if they didn't haul their cousins' ship out of the storm, it was surely going to be destroyed. If they *could* get it clear, then *Nkaastu* wouldn't be on its own.

All this went through Daamon's mind in a fast blink of time. He spared a single glance up at Kuotaan's heavy-jawed face. Her one golden eye met his. Then, though she wasn't supposed to have an opinion in anything concerning battle, she deliberately tipped up her chin.

Audacity was a quality praised in uturun, not nturun, but Daamon set a hand on Kuotaan's lower shoulder in gratitude for her support. Then he said crisply, "Saraa, get us an in-and-out course that will bring us out *here*, then let us get over *here*, preferably without losing *Nkaastu* anywhere in the middle." He highlighted the positions he meant. If *Nkaastu* could take those positions, then they'd have a chance to take out all three heart-Disks—if all three followed the courses Daamon felt they would. "Gen, we may not be able to get out after we do this, not by ourselves, but what we *can* do, is close up tight against our cousins' ship, so get on our signals, make sure they know who we are."

He didn't have to explain what he wanted in more detail than that. They knew. That wasn't from defending *Nkaastu* against pirates and near-pirates; that was from saaom, which in the past decade had specifically and strongly emphasized tactics useful against uut. Paaol knew to double-priority the heart-Disks and ignore every other Disk in the swarm; Saraa knew to set up half a handful of courses back out of the swarm, making her best and most intuitive guesses about uut responses and movements and reactions. She also knew, it was obvious, that she'd better be quick off the mark with the confounders and sharp in getting *Nkaastu* tucked up against the cousins' ship at the end. Daamon could tell from the barest glance at his own console that Genru was already setting up a series of don't-shoot-us pings and messages.

Daamon took one more breath, let it out, and ordered, "All right, go!"

4

Gerstner was acutely aware that his recent distraction and his pitiful lack of imagination might very well get his ship killed.

He'd been thinking about Viceroy Modhwadiya's reaction to those damned troll-centaurs. He'd been thinking about Witness Falconer's reaction to the humans on that alien ship, the way they cozied up to the aliens. What he hadn't been thinking about was the possibility that *Vengeful* might come through that last flashpoint and discover that the *entire task force* had been engulfed by *all the Enemy fighters in the entire God-damned galaxy.*

He'd brought *Vengeful* through that last flashpoint as though he hadn't a care in the world, exactly as if they'd been on easy duty in the Shallows, not out in the Deep where any damn thing could happen. His own carelessness enraged him, though he held the rage in the back of his mind, buried it, so he could face *this* moment, deal with *this* crisis.

The task force was holding. They'd obviously had enough warning for most of the ships to tuck themselves into a tight defensive formation that could hold for a good long time. Days at least, maybe four days, five. They'd better hold out. Losing the whole God-damned task force was bad, losing an Imperial Witness might arguably be almost as bad, but losing Viceroy Modhwadiya would set a whole bunch of political dominoes falling that a plain Fleet captain couldn't even imagine.

Nothing Gerstner could do about that, and if it happened it'd be Fleet's problem anyway; he had enough to deal with right here. Cut off from the flashpoint, cut off from the task force, ugly damn situation and not getting better.

Plus the little alien ship. He'd led that ship right into this mess. From their point of view, he'd led them straight into epic disaster. That could not be good. It might, depending on the resources and inclinations of those aliens, be *another* disaster. And his fault all the way.

Nothing he could do about that either.

He had his eye on *Implacable* and *Retribution*. Those two were closer to *Vengeful* than the rest. They'd been caught too far from the bulk of the task force to lock into the same defensive formation, so they were trying to guard each other's flanks. Two dreadnoughts were not enough for proper overlapping shields and confounders, but where two could draw just a line, three could set up a proper plane, not as good as a solid, but a whole damn lot better than a line. That was something Gerstner might be able to do something about—if he could get *Vengeful* linked in with those two, they'd *all* be better off. In some ways, at least.

If he couldn't, the Enemy were going to eat all three ships for lunch, probably.

"Swarm this thick, there's got to be more than one mothership involved," his Exec observed. Reese Kennon sounded relaxed, confident, almost amused when he added, just loud enough to be heard clearly across the width of the bridge, "Which, if I recall correctly, the Intelligence people insisted couldn't happen. One mothership per swarm, that's supposed to be the rule." He raised his voice slightly, addressing Maxson at Signals First. "Let's get proper scans all round, shall we, Lieutenant Maxson. Always nice to remind the staffers over in Intelligence that there's still more in the heavens than they've dreamt of in their philosophy."

Even under these circumstances, that got a little reaction, a little straightening of spines all around the bridge, as everyone bought the idea that they were going to survive long enough to throw this dire situation back in the faces of the Intelligence staffers.

But the direct look Reese gave Gerstner was anything but amused. He said, much more quietly, "If we lock in with

Retribution and *Implacable*, we'll be safer—for a while—but stuck." There was an edge to that, which Gerstner had no trouble reading. *You're the captain—you'd better have a plan to get us out of this.* Which meant Reese himself was clean out of ideas except maybe one or two crazy ones in the back of his mind. Some of those might match the crazy notions Gerstner was turning over himself.

Reese was right about the mothership, or motherships. Never mind that neither Signals nor Ops had located more than one yet, right at this moment the system was so busy they might perfectly well miss a mothership the size of Pallas Athene unless it strolled right up and patted *Vengeful* on the nose. Which would almost not surprise Gerstner, at this point.

Reese was right again about the long-term problems they'd be buying if they linked up with the other two dreadnoughts. Almost right. Three ships locked into a triangle could maneuver as a unit with reasonable facility. The kind of lattice the rest of the task force had slotted together would maneuver about as well as a derelict scow with half its engines crippled and the other half seized up entirely, but a smaller number of ships might manage something. If they were desperate enough and lucky enough and felt like taking one or two Godawful chances, they might be able to flash all three dreadnoughts simultaneously, get back into the previous system, then come up with step two of a brilliant plan, such as maybe pulling an alliance together in a tearing rush and getting back here to rescue the larger part of the task force.

If they were unlucky, somebody on one or another of those three ships would get a hair out of position, screw up the flash, explode and take the other two ships out as well, plus destabilize the hell out of that flashpoint for a good long time.

Which would be bad, but slamming that flashpoint closed would at least keep the Enemy away from the systems of—whoever the hell they were—potential allies, at least human, at least some of them, and that wasn't the outcome Gerstner wanted, it was damn little to save out of this mess, but it was *something*.

He said, deliberately calm, "Lieutenant Vaughn, set a course that'll slot *Vengeful* into a common defense triangle with *Retribution* and *Implacable*. Signals First, get a channel and tell 'em the second we get ourselves locked together, I want both their Nav boards slaved to ours."

"Oh, that's optimistic," Reese said, but very much under his breath.

Gerstner ignored him. "Lieutenant Grigson, while we're working on that, get that damned cluster of saucers away from *Implacable*." He set the tag himself to make sure she saw the cluster he meant; Grigson was good, but a political appointee, not an officer who'd ever come in out of the Deep after a long run; he didn't trust her to spot the danger. Those particular saucers were maneuvering, not to destroy *Implacable*, but to tear her open so the Enemy could seize prisoners ... they did that sometimes, if they could. The mystery of what they wanted with prisoners was an interesting puzzle for the Intelligence types, but a plain nightmare for everyone else in Fleet.

Once the saucers were tagged, he left that for Grigson and went on. "Weapons Two, make a hole for Lieutenant Vaughn, and kindly target those arrowpoints on *Retribution's* flank." The images from Ops might be a damned confusing mess, but *Retribution* was getting the worst of it and obviously needed help—

The screen replaced *Retribution* with a spreading cloud of muted light. Gerstner bit back a curse. A hiss of dismay ran around the bridge, and Annette Vaughn simultaneously shot a new course to Gerstner's command screen and slammed *Vengeful* into that course, as tying *Vengeful* into *Implacable's* defensive envelope suddenly became far less useful and much more difficult. Despite

Vaughn's efforts, an endless supply of Enemy fighters mobbed both surviving dreadnoughts—

The tubby little alien ship darted into the midst of the swarming Enemy. Gerstner swore as she leapt away from the flashpoint and dodged into the middle of the fight. "Weapons Two, see if you can cover her," he ordered.

"We've enough to do covering ourselves—" Reese began.

Gerstner chopped his hand down, cutting off that protest. "Insane courage could turn out to be a useful trait in an ally; if the Enemy hits 'em, they'll be no use to anyone."

Reese made a conceding gesture, but Gerstner feared the little ship couldn't be saved. Regret bit sharp, though he hadn't even known how much he'd hoped to see an alliance forged between mainline humanity and this particular complicated lost-and-regained population—a chance to turn the tide, set the Enemy back good and hard—probably he'd been a God-damned fool to even let that hope cross his mind, and it was too late now anyway—

Three saucers disappeared from the surrounding cloud of Enemy ships, one-two-pause-and-three, and it dawned on Gerstner that the little ship had targeted just those three saucers and no others, a peculiarly specific kamikaze run. Then the Enemy unexpectedly scattered in disarray, their formations stuttering and dissolving into confusion. Gerstner leaned forward, riveted. Somehow, he had no notion how, those people had known *exactly* which saucers carried the brain of the swarm.

No time to think about that right this second—opportunity was knocking good and loud. *Implacable* seized the chance and dove toward the main body of the task force, deploying her defenses to tie into that common lattice. That was all very well, in fact that was *excellent*, but following didn't look like an option, the geometry was all against *Vengeful* getting over there herself. And even if they managed it, they'd be stuck, just as Reese had pointed out.

Gerstner snapped instead, "Nav, flashpoint, best speed! Weapons One, cover our little friend."

"ETA three minutes fifty-two," Lieutenant Vaughn sang out.

"Can't cover 'em unless they get themselves tucked in—" began Lieutenant Grigson at the same moment, then went on with hardly a break, "They're tight, they're right in our shadow, sir, we've got them covered! Our little buddy's a smart mover."

Reese glanced Gerstner's way: *Maybe a little* too *smart, you think?*

"Smart enough to figure just which saucers to take out, did you see that?" Gerstner answered that look. *"And* smart enough to pay a debt." His tone made it clear that there was no such thing as *too smart* for the commander of a ship that had just pulled *Vengeful's* bacon out of the fire. *Implacable's* too*:* two dreadnoughts pulled out of the fire and dropped back in the frying pan. That was a hell of a coup for a little ship like that one.

Reese frowned, his gaze going back to that little ship. After a second he nodded, an acknowledgment that he'd missed the vital importance of that ship's targeting, that he ought to have understood it.

"Happened damn fast," Gerstner said. His Exec shrugged, meaning he knew he should have seen it anyway, which was true enough. Also meaning he wouldn't miss something like that again, which was probably also true. Reese had been underestimating that little ship, those people with their nice civilian outfits and their damn feathers and those aliens right beside them, that was the problem. So had Gerstner. He didn't expect either of them would make that mistake again.

"Flashpoint in thirty seconds," said Vaughn. "Twenty-five seconds!"

And then they were through, and clear, or clear until the Enemy came after them. Gerstner snapped, "Our friend still with us?"

Keith Maxson at Signals reported at once. "Flashed through right behind us, sir, and tucked up in our shadow again, very smooth little ship when it comes to close maneuvers."

Sun Grigson added, "Just our buddy so far, sir—no sign of pursuit." *Yet*, trembled in the air, but no one said it.

Gerstner fed a course to Annette Vaughn, a fast arc that would sweep *Vengeful* away from the slide and into the radiation envelope of the distant gas giant, a course that'd force them to stutter hard as they picked up and then shed vee fast, but would get them tucked up invisible and safe against that giant planet as fast as possible. "Signals, feed that course to our little friend, and if they can't figure it out fast enough, we'll find out just how smartly they can move." He added to Reese, "We won't show the Enemy the other flashpoint if we can help it. That'd be very damn unfriendly to our new buddies, plus we may want that line of retreat ourselves. We'll tuck ourselves down into that planet's radiation signature, turn invisible and see what follows us."

"Something will, I expect," Reese murmured.

Gerstner expected that too, unfortunately. Considering that, he also tapped Doug Bateman on Weapons Two. "Countermeasures, Lieutenant, drop fifty right now and spread 'em out wide. If the Enemy comes through right on our tail, let's slow them down, right?"

"Sir," Vaughn and Bateman acknowledged in slightly ragged chorus.

Gerstner had already turned to Lieutenant Maxson. "Signals, how's our buddy doing? Let me know if they seem to be having any trouble keeping up. Shaking the Enemy off our tail before they even get on it, that would be a very good thing, but let's not allow our countermeasures to lose us our friend, got that?"

"Got it, sir," Maxson agreed with clear sincerity. "Wouldn't dream of it, sir. I'll pulse them every thirty seconds once the countermeasures are—starting the pulse now." He paused, then added, "She's still with us, right and tight."

"So, have we got a plan?" murmured Reese, his low voice meant just for Gerstner's ear.

"We do indeed, Exec, in the short term," Gerstner returned. "We'll catch our breath and give firecontrol a chance to do its job, and while we do that, we'll have a little chat with our friend and see if we can't come to some common agreement. We get enough help from those people fast enough, maybe we can break the task force clear."

Reese raised his eyebrows. "You certainly are optimistic today, sir."

"Of course, if you have a clever plan for shooting *Vengeful* back to the task force, single-handedly destroying a thousand Enemy fighters and however many motherships, pulling the commodore's chestnuts out of the fire, and saving the day, I'd be happy to hear the details."

Reese cleared his throat, but only shrugged. Restrained from acerbic comment by the dire situation, no doubt, because Reese Kennon's tongue certainly wasn't ordinarily likely to be quelled by mere captainly sarcasm.

Gerstner said, as firmly as though he really believed this, "They'll hold, Reese. With that formation, they'll hold." They would. For a good while. A day wouldn't be a problem, two days. The task force could certainly keep up that defense for two days. Three, maybe. Then they'd start running low on munitions and materials to make more, plus people would start making mistakes from sheer exhaustion, and the task force would start losing ships out of that lattice until their defense broke entirely. That would probably happen sometime during the fourth day.

In practice, probably the Enemy would throw a rock at them before that happened. But ... maybe not for two days, or three, or maybe even four.

They had that long to find a much better option. Gerstner knew just the option he wanted to find. He said out loud, "We've got time to consider the possibilities inherent in this situation. Maybe make more possibilities if we don't like the first set."

Reese nodded, but he said, "The Enemy will find a rock eventually. All they have to do is stop Aleph from getting away through a flashpoint—and they won't have any trouble stopping Aleph getting through a flashpoint because the minute Aleph breaks that formation, they'll destroy them in detail. But if our people can't break their formation—"

Gerstner moved a hand to stop him.

The Enemy, if they were patient and determined enough, could pin the task force in place, find a decent-sized asteroid, kick it into more or less the right trajectory, fit it out with a slowdrive, and send it slamming right through any formation human ships could build. And that would be that.

The term *slowdrive* had been coined as someone's idea of a joke, but once the Enemy found a rock they liked and fitted it out, a slowdriven asteroid would leap through this system like a bat out of hell. Nukes were handy for handling asteroids coming in at a natural vee. Detonate them just a bit beside a big rock and you could knock the asteroid off its disastrous course.

But there was nothing anybody could do to deflect the kinetic energy of a miles-wide asteroid stuttering through normal space at a good proportion of the speed of light. The only choice when someone threw that kind of rock at you was to get out of the way, which was not good news for the task force because a slowdriven rock could change course a hell of a lot faster than a bunch of ships locked into a tight formation could maneuver. If Aleph broke their formation, every ship could outfly a rock, no problem. But outnumbered as the human ships were, they'd be torn up the second they broke their formation.

Disaster either way. The choice was immediate or delayed disaster. That was it. That was the choice. That was why Gerstner wanted—optimistically, yes, even though he wasn't, generally speaking, an optimist by nature—but he really, seriously wanted to get a real alliance hammered out in doublequick time, with the descendants of lost colonists or troll-centaurs or the devil himself, if he appeared in a flash of sulfur and with a big enough infernal host to get the job done.

Get an alliance fast enough and maybe, possibly, there might be a chance to get Aleph that help.

Vengeful was coming up now on that gas giant, big enough it'd obviously just missed becoming a star. Lots of radiation, exactly what they wanted, that should definitely provide the energy necessary to feed into the masking confounders and keep *Vengeful* off Enemy scans. Once Lieutenant Vaughn got her settled in close orbit, it would hardly matter if a hundred saucers and five hundred arrowpoints and a whole damned mothership came looking. Any number of ships bigger and flashier than *Vengeful* could hide in this planet's skirts just as long as they had the right kind of confounder suite, the energy to feed into the confounder shields, and the patience to sit still.

"Settle us in," Gerstner ordered quietly. "And then we'll hail our friend. Ops, do they seem to have shielding tech?" He nodded at the affirmative. Good. Anyone with both slowdrive and gravitics tech ought to have figured out the shielding utility, but who knew. But yeah, when he checked the boards, he could see for himself that the little ship's signature was thinning out, every kind of radiation bending around her, blurring her out until you'd just about have to trip over her to spot her.

That little ship had proved itself a fine ally and those people, strange as they were, ought to feel the same way about *Vengeful.* Damn sure they had something to build on. They just had to build on that foundation fast. Right now, today, they had to build something they could *use.*

Working out an alliance over screens, sure, maybe. Or maybe it'd be too damn slow, plus you couldn't get a good feel for people if you held them at a distance. They couldn't afford slow, damn sure they couldn't afford mistakes. A face-to-face meeting ... Gerstner wanted that. After what had just happened, he wanted that a lot, and he was going to get it. He could tell the other commander so even with the limited vocabulary they had between them, because everyone already agreed on the meaning of *you* and *come.*

***

The other commander made no effort to pretend he didn't understand, once Gerstner got him on screen. He said *Yes*, recognizably *Yes*, and bowed his head in response to Gerstner's order; surely that was acknowledgement or agreement, even among these foreigners on that flamboyant bridge, surrounded by those massive centauroid aliens, speaking that tongue-twisting alien language. Gerstner was just about certain he'd made it clear exactly what he wanted: for the man himself to come here, right here, to *Vengeful's* deck.

But he wanted one more thing. Because Reese had been perfectly right when he'd pointed out the problem of a shared but way too limited vocabulary.

Gerstner pointed at the commander of the other ship and said, slowly and deliberately, "You. *And* the one who talks." Because judging from the earlier exchange, the alien's accent and intonation were truly dire, but if it could manage an actual conversation, they were going to need it. He didn't trust the idea of an alien translator—but better that than no translator at all. Maybe. Probably. They had all better hope so.

The other man bowed his head a second time, his expression guarded but not fearful. Or so it seemed to Gerstner, and caution seemed understandable under the circumstances. Then the signal flicked off, as, presumably, that foreign commander and his weird half-alien crew debated whether to obey Gerstner's orders. Hard to imagine there wouldn't be a debate. But Gerstner thought he knew which way the decision would come down.

Gerstner had met a woman from Terabithia once, during a diplomatic function. Come to think of it, Commodore Marchetta had been responsible for getting Gerstner into that uncomfortable situation too. The woman, not much older than Gerstner, had been extraordinarily handsome but also extraordinarily hard to read: expressions had come and gone across her lively face, but he'd found them impenetrable. He had known she was amused by his confusion, but whether she'd been scornfully amused or delightedly amused or something less identifiable had been impossible to guess.

This man, now. This man, Gerstner almost thought he understood. He certainly hoped so. He glanced at the bridge entrance, wondering how long it would take for that little ship to send over a shuttle, assuming they really had understood him and really were going to follow his orders, not do something crazy and unpredictable and alien instead. Probably best to wait long enough to be sure a shuttle was actually on the way—

"Sir," said Reese, breaking in on Gerstner's thoughts. His tone was level, but a kind of level that made his objection clear.

Fine; better to have every objection—Gerstner assumed there would be more than one—and every answer on the record. He said, his own tone neutral, "Yes, Commander? Lay it out."

Reese Kennon raised an eyebrow, but he got the idea about putting everything on the record and therefore said readily, "Sir, you're putting yourself into a first-contact situation."

Yes, and that was not exactly according to regs, not that anybody had ever run up hard against that particular regulation in the entire history of the Imperial Republic. But that reg was there with the Enemy in mind, not this kind of crazy sort-of first, sort-of second contact scenario. Gerstner answered in a quiet tone that would nevertheless carry. "Commander Kennon, I am making a command decision, on the basis that we need help *right now* to pull Aleph out of the fire. I know that ship is small. But these people have got guts, they've got friends, and they've got something else. You saw what they did back there: they knew *exactly* which saucers to hit. I want that, I want it fast, and I'm not putting the job of getting it on anybody else. This is my decision and I'm making it. If it goes wrong, you can say *I told you so,* if you've got time."

Reese snorted. "Oh, that's fine. You leave me holding *this* bag and I swear I'll file for a transfer."

Which was his way of saying, *Be careful.*

Then Lieutenant Lockwood swiveled his chair around, half lifting a hand, requesting permission to speak—drawing on his status as Falconer's appointee. Gerstner hadn't exactly expected that and didn't welcome it. He paused for half a second, a hair from shutting Lockwood down hard. Under the circumstances, he wasn't real worried that would come back to bite him in the ass.

But ... he'd let one of his own people speak up. *Any* of his own people. Lockwood was a decent officer, dedicated as far as Gerstner could tell, smart, not likely to throw his connection to Falconer around for no damn reason. Not actually fair to shut down a political officer just because Gerstner didn't altogether like the concept of political appointees.

He said curtly, "Keep it brief, Lieutenant."

"Yes, sir," Lockwood said. "Just a query, sir: meaning no offense, but you're allowing *an alien* onto *Vengeful's* decks?"

All right, fine. That was another reasonable objection; Lockwood was hardly going to be the only member of the crew who objected to that idea. Gerstner ought to have answered that objection up front, not waited for a query. He answered it now, for the record as well as for the moment, speaking in a quiet tone that would nevertheless carry. "Lieutenant, *allowing* is not the term. I am *ordering* more than one foreigner onto *Vengeful's* decks, including, indeed, an alien. It appears that the alien speaks some English, which, as we have observed, the human personnel aboard that ship do not. I would not be surprised to learn that we have already heard nearly their commander's full repertoire of English. I don't believe we have quite the leisure to send kindergarten language modules over to that ship and wait for her crew to get past See Spot Run. I have complete confidence that our personnel will be able to accommodate the presence of..." he chose a judicious phrase and finished, "Potential allies attached to our lost colony. Especially if they may be of use in getting Task Force Aleph clear of the Enemy. If they'll ally with us, I don't care how monstrous they may appear."

A slight stir of reaction from all quarters of the bridge: as intended, everyone had heard that. Lockwood didn't frown; he had too much sense. He said, "Yes, Captain," and swiveled back around to his station.

Reese Kennon said briskly, "Yes, sir, well put. I think we're all on board with getting help to break Aleph clear if we can." That was a show of solidarity. But he added, "On the other hand, allying with aliens, that's something else."

"Quite so, Exec," Gerstner agreed. "If we can break Aleph out of the trap they're in, we'll hand the whole situation with the aliens over to Commodore Marchetta, and I expect Viceroy Modhwadiya will take over from there." Nobody could reasonably object to that, plus it was absolutely what Gerstner wanted to do. He added more gently, for the record as well as for the moment, "You know, Exec, the only way to meet someone is to meet him."

Reese glanced at the screen, at that alien bridge with its wide-curving walls in shimmering blues and its arching rainbow-colored banks of stations and most of all its frightening, massive centauroid crew, one alien stationed with every person, an arrangement that couldn't help but fuel wild speculation. "Yes, sir," he said, but he also lifted one shoulder in a minimal shrug. *You're the captain. If you let an alien aboard* Vengeful *and it turns out to eat people or mess on the floor, you'll be the one to clean up after it.*

Gerstner smiled in return, deliberately. *You're my Exec. Cleaning up messes would actually be* your *job.*

Reese, by the way he cast his gaze up to Heaven and sighed, understood the exact shade of his captain's smile.

"Sir," Keith Maxson interrupted, waited for Gerstner's nod, and went on quickly. "We've got a pulse, a double pulse, and now we have a singlepod exiting that ship. Or, it's not exactly a pod," he added conscientiously. "The energy signature's too low, and it's too big, and if it's armed at all, I think its weapons must be powered down. But some kind of little boat, anyway, a pod or a shuttle or something like that."

"That was fast," murmured Reese.

"And just as well, as I think we'd do well to get acquainted before the Enemy flashes into this system. It's also good to know our allies—potential allies—can make decisions expeditiously when that's advisable. That's excellent. Open the bay, if you please, Lieutenant Vaughn. Light it up, and rotate to show them where it is. Lieutenant Maxson, if you would alert Commander Keay and Dr. Chandratre and ask them to step down to the bay. Exec, you have the bridge."

"Sir," Reese acknowledged, with no humor at all. This time he didn't even lift an eyebrow. Gerstner expected Reese to have a good deal to say, later, after they stood down. Presuming all went well. If Gerstner actually had made the wrong call and it all hit the fan, then Reese Kennon would never say a word about it, even if he got the chance.

But if Gerstner called this one wrong, then Reese would make a fine commander for *Vengeful*. It didn't work the other way around: Gerstner didn't trust anyone but himself to make this first contact.

If one could call it a *first* contact, given the peculiar circumstances.

Gerstner strode off the bridge, nodded to the marines on duty at the hatch, ran down the ladder from the bridge level, swung immediately onto a dropdisk, shifted it onto a priority track, stepped out moments later on Deck One, and caught the fastest ripwalk toward the bay. The arches flashed by, flick-flick-flick, rings of bright light and relative dimness, punctuation to a journey that seemed much longer than merely from one end of the ship to the other.

He could hardly imagine what this was going to be like. Troll-centaurs, God above. Or, hell, call them just plain centaurs. He'd make it official, because that didn't sound so bad. Though the aliens really didn't look much like mythological centaurs. Pig-ugly, four arms ... used to working with humans. He could hardly imagine that either.

Esaias Keay was already near the main terminal of the bay when Gerstner got there, at the head of a short company of front-assault troops. Keay transparented his faceplate, courtesy to the captain, and offered the merest suggestion of a salute. Gerstner returned a nod. He thought of saying, *Remind your troops these are not the Enemy.* But Commander Keay knew his business and would be justifiably offended if the captain said anything of the sort. He said instead, with a brief glance along the double line of troopers, "Good to know your people have my back, Esaias."

"Be a change from clearing Enemy drones and robots in close combat, sir," the marine commander answered. "And a substantial change from setting my boys and girls up in kami runs. We can talk to this lot, I gather. The screencopy was certainly memorable. We've all seen it, and we're all dead keen to see what the continuation of war by other means looks like in practice." He was completely deadpan, but one of his eyelids shivered in the merest suggestion of a wink.

Marines never had much to do aboard a dreadnought, until they had a lot to do. If the Enemy tried to peel open a ship or a station instead of standing back to destroy it, well, marines were what you needed at moments like that. Or if you found yourself with the chance to raid an Enemy station for tech, once again, marines. Though that had become less important over the past fifty or hundred years, as decent human tech had caught up with Enemy capabilities ... more or less caught up, as far as people knew, and after that damned disaster unfolding right this minute around Aleph, Gerstner wasn't so sure that was an accurate supposition.

Gerstner said merely, "Indeed," with a grave nod. He gave no sign he recognized this was deliberate reassurance, that Keay was really telling him he had his people well in hand and no one was going to panic at their first sight of an alien centaur. Gerstner hoped this was true. On the screen, those damned aliens had looked ... just really big.

He turned to Dr. Chandratre, just arriving. Chandratre had come in from Science and thus had been required to make his way across the whole width of the bay. Even on a fast ripwalk, that took time, because the bay was enormous, easily the largest single space in *Vengeful*.

Singlepods lined one side of the bay, tiers of them ranked all the way from deck to ceiling because they doubled as lifeboats. They were little things, but flash-capable, moderately decent fighting ships that could defend themselves if they had to and hold a good, brisk acceleration for quite a long way. They were also cramped, claustrophobic, and ugly; uncomfortable if you had to stay in them for any length of time; and possessed just enough power that it never seemed to be quite enough for whatever you wanted to use them for. Everyone hated them. But they were by far the most usefully flexible small craft a big ship could carry into the dangerous waters outside the Shallows.

Far more popular were the shrikes that occupied berths on the other side of the bay. Those crewed six—the singlepods, despite their name, generally crewed two though they could manage with anything from one to four. But though the shrikes were sleek and fast and had a sharp attack that was worth something, they had no flash capacity at all. Trade-offs there as in everything. For example, there were definitely tradeoffs in deciding to bring aliens inboard rather than keeping them at a distance: Fleet authority might rightly question the wisdom of that move. But Gerstner wanted very much to see what that other commander would do: if he'd come, and who—what—he'd bring with him.

Doctor Chandratre made no attempt to mask his own deep curiosity. Chandratre was Gujarati, from Abhilasha, a world that since its founding had produced a good many of the best physicians and naturalists and field biologists in human space. A sound man. Solid to the bone. Gerstner would have taken another dozen just like him on *Vengeful* if he could.

Chandratre was an older man, built tall and narrow, with angular eyes and a high-bridged nose. He was quite dark skinned, as was nearly everyone from Abhilasha—a fine world, but subjected to more intense solar radiation than some; gene-tweaking ensured children born there were suited to the intensity of their sun. Sharp-witted and sharp-tongued, Dr. Chandratre was quite famous in Fleet circles for his intense desire to capture living Enemy, keep them alive and figure out what made them tick. He wanted to know what they were, what drove them, why they acted as they did, why they were seemingly so committed to burning the entire universe clear of all people other than themselves.

Gerstner was more practical. He simply wanted to burn the entire universe clear of the Enemy. If these weird foreigners with their alien centaurs could help with that, he was interested.

What would it *do* to people, to live among giant four-armed centaurs? Gerstner could not imagine. Maybe Dr. Chandratre could imagine it. Gerstner was curious, but did not ask after the other man's thoughts. Better to form his own independent judgment. He only nodded to him, a brief formal nod. "Doctor."

Dr. Chandratre nodded back, strict and restrained, but anticipation lit him from within despite his formality.

"Sir," said Commander Keay. "Doctor. The ... alien craft is making its final approach. ETA five minutes. We're not clear about their docking protocols, of course. It might be advisable to step to the side, in case we should need to deploy blast shields or ... whatever."

The blast shields were meant to protect personnel in case of a hull breach or other disaster. Gerstner could not imagine what form disaster might take, under these peculiar circumstances. No doubt Esaias Keay had spent several intense moments imagining various possibilities. He didn't argue, only jerked his head at Dr. Chandratre and moved to the side, exactly as Keay indicated.

Keay stepped back, blanking his faceplate again, all business—no doubt focused on the approaching alien boat and on his own people.

The alien's craft came in awkwardly. It was brightly colored, which Gerstner ought to have expected after the colorful bridge. Green and gold in a pattern that might mean something or might be purely decorative. He couldn't help feeling like it had to be a civilian craft and that ship out there a civilian ship, despite the clear evidence that those people knew damn well how to handle themselves in battle. Maybe the very categories of *military* and *civilian* made no sense for these people.

It was a sizable craft. Fat, clumsy, unaerodynamic—Gerstner could not quite imagine anyone trying to fly that thing in atmosphere; it would be like putting wings on an armored tank. Perhaps it was meant only for use above gravity wells.

But its pilot was not unskilled. The clumsy-looking boat cleared the entrance to the bay and came into the internal gravity of *Vengeful* with a lurch that stabilized with commendable speed. Then it pivoted ponderously on its vertical axis and settled with a surprising lack of fuss to the deck, about thirty feet from Gerstner's party.

There was a pause. A ripple of almost perceptible tension had gone through Keay's troopers, but no one lifted a weapon. Gerstner made a mental note to commend the commander, and waited. Everyone seemed to wait.

"Maybe they want a personal invitation?" muttered Dr. Chandratre. "Or they're testing the atmosphere, or debating who should venture out first—"

"No," said Gerstner. "That won't occasion debate. Their commander will be first out."

Dr. Chandratre gave him a quick look and, after a moment, a nod.

With a sighing sound, a wide section of the alien boat's hull, about ten feet high and fifteen feet wide, depressed inward and drew aside. The foreign commander stepped into view. He stood for a moment, looking out or letting them all look at him or both. But he didn't stare around at the bay. His attention was on Gerstner.

Gerstner gave him a small nod. Then he beckoned, deliberately.

The man returned his nod and stepped down to the deck. It was an awkward step for him; that cane was clearly not just decorative. The brown robe he wore over loose-fitting tan clothing was certainly exotic, like a dancer's costume, or a Terabithian priest, or a bit like formal dress on Pallas Athene, actually. The sleeves of the robe were embroidered with patterns in gold and light blue and ivory; the shapes might have been flowers or stars, or might just as well be some kind of alien writing, Gerstner supposed.

From this distance, in the flesh, despite his exotic robes, the man himself looked ... ordinary. He certainly would not have looked out of place on one of the Gujarati worlds, Kanan or Hemadri. Tall, but not unusually tall. Dark-skinned, but not as dark as Chandratre; not even as dark as Esaias Keay. Brown hair, medium short and medium wavy. An ordinary face, with strong cheekbones and a small mouth, tight now with nervous tension. Anything could be hidden beneath that loose robe. But his hands were in plain sight, and he met Gerstner's eyes with straightforward courage.

Undoubtedly there would be many points of difference. It would be a mistake to take anything for granted for a good long while. Even so, Gerstner felt he understood quite a few important things about this man.

The brown-robed man turned and looked back at the alien boat, and so Gerstner was not surprised when a woman appeared and stepped cautiously down to *Vengeful's* deck. Or he was not surprised by the fact of a crewmember's existence on that boat. By the woman herself, yes. He had not expected the other commander to bring so *young* a woman. Seventeen, eighteen, if she were older than that, he'd be surprised. If anything, he'd actually guess she might be younger. Gerstner couldn't help but find her presence reassuring ... possibly a mistake, but nevertheless. It was hard to imagine including a young woman like this in a party that expected or meant violence. Surely it was a good sign the man had brought her rather than a bunch of armed soldiers.

The girl was small, pretty, with an oval face. She had the same light brown skin, wide cheekbones, and small mouth as the man—they might be kin. She wore a diaphanous pale gold blouse that left her arms bare to the shoulder, tucked into sleek tan leggings that covered her legs to the ankle. Her feet were bare, which was mildly shocking—*very* different idea about suitable dress for first contact situations. The girl took the man's hand and jumped to the deck, though with an understandably nervous look at Keay and his men.

Then a great dark shape moved within the alien boat, and Gerstner stopped thinking about the girl, or about the other commander.

The aliens had looked huge on the screen. But they had not looked like this.

This one was, like the others, a four-armed pig-tusked centauroid creature. But this one absolutely dwarfed the ones they had seen on screen. Gerstner had guessed the aliens must mass nearly a ton; this one looked like it would mass three times that. It was bulkier, heavier in every dimension. When it stepped down out of the boat, it had to duck to clear what had seemed a very generous hatchway. Muscles rippled in its shoulders and ... other shoulders, and back, and ... everywhere. One could see its anatomy plainly, as it wore nothing but a harness of webbing, dark blue against its hairless mahogany-colored hide. It looked like it could pick up a singlepod all by itself, twist it in half and throw the pieces the length of the bay. All the aliens had tusks thrusting up from their lower jaws, but this one's tusks were longer than a man's hand, making its broad, craggy face into something straight out of a fairy tale—the kind where trolls ate careless children.

Then it turned its head and gazed right at Gerstner, and he took a step back before he could stop himself, his heart hammering in his chest. Its eyes were nothing human. They were bright lambent yellow, slit-pupiled like the eyes of a cat. The eyes of a predator. The eyes of a monster.

Gerstner was aware, barely, that Dr. Chandratre was also backing up; he was aware of the rattle and muted crash of weapons being brought to bear; of Esaias Keay muttering fervently, *"Jesus Christ son of God who is our savior."*

He was more aware of the girl shrinking back against the alien with a muted gasp, of the alien wrapping its two left arms around her, tucking her against its side, stiffening and leaning forward, seeming suddenly even larger and far more aggressive. Gerstner caught his breath, and the other commander, his eyes wide, stepped in between the alien and the leveled weapons and spread his arms wide.

Coming to his senses, Gerstner flung out a hand, palm down. "Keay!" he snapped. "You have my permission to dismiss any marine who can't keep fire discipline."

There was a very slight pause. Then Commander Keay answered stiffly, "Naturally all my people can be trusted to keep fire discipline, sir." Followed, after a second, by the faint, embarrassed rattle of weapons being lowered.

Gerstner did not turn to look. He assumed that situation was under control. He wanted to stare at the alien, make sure *it* was under control. He fixed his gaze on the man instead, with an effort.

He said to Dr. Chandratre, deliberately, with careful attention to his tone, "What did *you* see just now, Dr. Chandratre? Because what *I* saw was that—" *monster* "—centaur ready to face live weapons in order to defend a frightened human girl." It still looked ready to do that, in fact, and just how much firepower would it take to stop a creature that size?

It took a long time for Dr. Chandratre to answer. Probably he, too, needed a few seconds to make sure his voice would come out even. But he said eventually, "Yes. I believe I saw that, too."

"And you saw that this human man was clearly ready to do the same, to defend the alien as well as the girl."

"Yes." This time Dr. Chandratre sounded more certain of himself. "Yes, definitely. I think that was quite plain. Indeed."

"Well," Gerstner said, making certain his tone was thoughtful. "Well. That's a start. Let's just be sure no one feels it's necessary to defend anybody."

"Yes, sir," Keay said behind him, firmly.

Gerstner nodded. He didn't say that they had all better hope that the giant troll-centaur agreed. That didn't seem like a very useful observation to make out loud, just now. What would be useful to actually *do* right now ... that wasn't clear.

Without looking back at his people, he took one step forward.

5

Daamon had assumed the cousins would find Kaamharaa alarming. He had *not* guessed he might open the hatch to find not only the foreign commander, but also fourteen uman in polished gray armor, all exactly alike, their faces hidden behind smooth, featureless armor. Each of those people was carrying a personal weapon as long as an uman's arm. That was terrifying enough, but then five of those faceless people brought their weapons up on the mere sight of Kaamharaa, who was the most tolerant turun in the world and who had never in the whole of his long life raised even his voice to any uman.

Daamon stepped in front of those weapons at once, sharply waving Kaamharaa back when the uturun, rumbling a protest, stiffened defensively, ready to defend them all—to defend Taya, who cowered back against him. Thankfully, the commander also flung out a hand, speaking in a sharp tone, and those weapons went down. For that first instant, Daamon had been absolutely sure of disaster; he had nearly *seen* all his hopes crashing down in blood and fire. But now, thank all the beloved gods, everyone was standing still.

Then the other commander took one step forward, and stopped, looking at Daamon rather than staring at Kaamharaa, which seemed ... better, maybe. Possibly. The man spoke again, still nothing Daamon could understand. Daamon wanted to ask Kaamharaa for a translation, but did not dare—he didn't even want to look over his shoulder at Kaamharaa because he didn't want to take his eyes off these people. One of whom spoke, perhaps answering the commander. This was the only other unarmored person: a tall man with much darker skin, set off by his clothing because he wore warm tan with red flashes rather than black. Other than the color, the clothing was identical.

Probably black signified something specific and tan something else. Now, too late, Daamon remembered Taya's suggestion that they make clothing more like that. Maybe someone had even done it; he hadn't thought to ask, he'd been too anxious about bringing Kaamharaa here—Taya—worried for himself as well, to be honest. But he'd thought a face-to-face meeting might be just exactly the right next step, until he'd stepped out on this deck and found these faceless armored people with their weapons and their terrifying response to Kaamharaa.

The commander spoke again. This time he spoke clearly, deliberately, to Daamon.

Daamon took a deep breath, because he might be wrong, he might be wrong at any moment and bring disaster crashing down on them all. But he took one step forward to match the other man. Then, without turning, he beckoned his little sister with one finger, as close as he could recall to the gesture the other battlecommander had used. "Come," he said, carefully, in cant. "Talk."

Taya had obviously not expected those faceless men with their long weapons; who could have? She was brave, but she was not battlecrew, and Daamon knew she hadn't wanted to come on this mission at all. But she had wanted even less for Kaamharaa to come here alone. Since she'd been barely old enough to toddle, Taya had made it clear she didn't believe anyone took care of Kaamharaa properly except herself. Kaamharaa had been just as reluctant to risk her, but everything was a risk—that was very clear by now—and Daamon had felt it best to bring the best uman linguist they had, in case it took the cousins time to get used to Kaamharaa.

Now, expecting the cousins to *ever* accustom themselves to Kaamharaa seemed wildly optimistic. Fortunately Kaamharaa was exercising the most extraordinary restraint, considering all those weapons these people had pointed at Taya.

Taya obviously thought Kaamharaa's restraint was amazing too, and knew they had better do something to stop any other violent gestures like that if they could. And she *was* brave. So now she gulped and nodded and moved gingerly away from Kaamharaa, edging up beside Daamon. "This was a *terrible* idea," she whispered to him. "If we all get shot, I'm blaming you."

She meant to make him smile, but there was too much truth to it. If they all got shot, he would definitely blame himself. Daamon could hardly say so. He bumped her shoulder with his. "Go on. Say something. Be polite."

"Polite!" she whispered back. "I'm not the one pointing *guns* at people!" But then she straightened, tossed her head in an uman echo of the turun gesture, and stepped forward, pretending to a confidence Daamon knew was mostly an act. She brought her hands together before her chest and said to the other commander, "Taya sepu Kaamharaa. Name is." She spoke slowly and carefully, watching the man, clearly nervous. But he only nodded, a surprisingly normal gesture, and repeated, "Taya sepu Kaamharaa."

His accent was strange, cutting the long vowels short and the short vowels nearly to nothing, exaggerating the *y* in *Taya*. But the effort was understandable. And he had answered, like a civilized person. Possibly—probably—*surely*—like someone wanting an alliance. In his place, Daamon would absolutely want the fastest possible alliance, and this foreign commander couldn't think he could get that by shooting people he had invited onto his ship.

Taya too was smiling in clear relief that the commander was behaving like a rational person. "Name is," she repeated, and touched Daamon on the shoulder. "Name is Daamon sepu Kaamharaa. Nda Daamon, battlecommander of *Nkaastu.*"

"Keep it simple," Daamon muttered to her. "Keep to cant."

Taya shrugged impatiently. "They should know you're important! And cant doesn't have those words." But she stepped back and laid a hand on Kaamharaa's lower shoulder, which was as high as she could comfortably reach. Kaamharaa looked down at her, covered her fingers with his own far larger hand, and tenderly tucked an errant wisp of hair back behind her ear.

Taya was looking up at Kaamharaa at that moment, and Kaamharaa was looking down at her, so only Daamon saw how the uman man in tan and some of the faceless armored people flinched. He looked quickly at the other commander, but that man, at least, showed no response. So Daamon took a breath and let it out and nodded to Taya, meaning she should go on.

She nodded back, smiled, patted Kaamharaa's lower shoulder, and said proudly to the cousins, "Kaamharaa. Name is Kaamharaa."

Daamon could see how badly his sister wanted to say *Tsuumat Kaamharaa* and list all his earned honors and granted titles, make the cousins understand Kaamharaa's fine record and high reputation. But she left it all unsaid. She only stepped forward, carefully and slowly, and put her hands together again, tipping her palms toward the other commander. "Name is?" she asked him. "Name is?"

These cousins had long, difficult names. Also, it was difficult to get further than names because every time Kaamharaa said something about interior consonants or complex fricatives—every time he said anything at all—at least half the faceless people flinched, which made Daamon very nervous. It was also, slowly, making him angry.

Then Kaamharaa, who had been trying to speak quietly, suddenly declared, in booming tones of pleased discovery, "Taya, I believe *Kabtaan* is a title, very like *Tsaa*," and every single foreign uman in the ships' berthing hall flinched at the sound, two of the ones in armor half-raising a weapon. Kaamharaa, embarrassed at having forgotten himself, rumbled soothingly, which didn't seem to help: more weapons twitched and rose, not quite pointing at the turun, but close, way too close. Daamon stiffened as Kaamharaa drew into himself, trying to look smaller, a hopeless effort.

Taya snapped, *"Kaamharaa* didn't do anything wrong!"

"He certainly did not," Daamon agreed, hearing the heat in his own tone. After a heartbeat's consideration, he added, even more emphatically, "This is not acceptable." He walked straight forward, to face the nearest of the armored persons, trying not to limp too obviously. He reached out, rested the tips of two fingers on the barrel of the man's weapon, and pressed it slowly down so that the muzzle pointed straight toward the decking. "No." He spoke firmly, as though addressing a young child, except in cant instead of Uom. He said again, "No."

The commander or captain or whatever he was, Kabtaan Lehm Gehersner—Taya thought that wasn't quite right, but it seemed close to Daamon—said something curt. The armored person slung his weapon over his shoulder by its strap and said something in rapid uman language, by its tone an order. All his fellows did the same.

Daamon tipped his chin up in approval. "Yes." Then he turned and walked back to lean against Kaamharaa's reassuring bulk, hoping the weakness in his knees didn't show.

"That was utaaru," Kaamharaa told him, putting a lower arm around Daamon's shoulders, a welcome support. The word meant half-audacious and half-stupid, a word almost always applied to young males, uman or turun, the kind of male who was much more reckless than Daamon was supposed to be. It was a reprimand, but Kaamharaa's tone was also pleased and proud because uturun admired audacity.

Taya punched Daamon lightly on the arm and said, "Stupid!" Her choice was a far less ambiguous word, but she only punched Daamon lightly because she, too, had not been happy at all with the way the cousins treated Kaamharaa.

"I think it was necessary to insist on better manners. I hope it wasn't stupid. Do they look angry to you?" It was hard to tell.

"They've no call to be angry! They ought to be ashamed of themselves." Taya frowned at the cousins, laid a hand on Kaamharaa's nearest lower arm and urged him, "Speak now, and let's see what they do."

"Ask something useful," Daamon said. "He wanted us to come here; we're here; point that out to him and ask him what now. Those were his people under such violent attack in the other system; what does he mean to do about it, what does he expect *us* to do about it? One would certainly think uman cant must be suited to express ideas about *enemies* and *overwhelming odds*. He needs to understand, *Nkaastu's* not even a half-fighter. We're only a half-fighter tradeship; we can't expect to survive major action of that kind. But we can return to Aam and ask Siiv u Kaoluun for help. Can you express all that?"

Taya rolled her eyes. "I don't see how, big brother! Ask for a romantic epic, why don't you?"

But Kaamharaa tilted his head, considering. Then he said in his deep, deep voice, "Kabtaan Lehm Gehestner." For the first time in his life, Daamon realized just how different a turun's voice was from an uman voice, and found himself doubting that the other commander could possibly understand. Kaamharaa went on, "Come, we. Here, is. Now is?" But though no one flinched and the weapons stayed at rest, even those simple cant words sounded sonorous and flowing in a way that the cousins' language just did not.

"Everything they say *sounds* so different even if the words are sort of the same," Taya said, frustrated. "And it's hard because Kaamharaa can't really do the fricatives." Then she went on, sounding much more fluent than Daamon would ever have imagined. "Kabtaan Lehm Gerrstter, come we here, now here is we, now is you where?"

The other commander said slowly, correcting Taya's pronunciation, "Captain Lem Gerstner. Captain Gerstner. Captain."

The difference in how he said the words was not obvious to Daamon's ear, but Taya nodded, her lips moving as she repeated the words to herself, settling the sound of them in her mind. She did the same when the commander indicated his companion and said, "Doctor Chandratre."

The commander then added carefully, "Taya sepu Kaamharaa." His pronunciation seemed creditable, though he still shortened the vowels in Kaamharaa's name so that the word sounded almost like kamhara—the word meant *arrogance*, so it wasn't entirely inapposite. But then Captain Lem Gerstner went on, sharp-sounding phrases too complicated for Daamon, who found that despite the other man's careful enunciation, he himself could hardly even pick out where one word ended and another began.

Taya was frowning in concentration, nodding occasionally, listening to the sound of the language even if she couldn't understand the meaning. When the man stopped, she opened one hand and then the other, meaning *maybe yes and maybe no*. She said slowly, "Now is? Want is? Oh, I don't know how to ask about—wait, Kaamharaa, what's *family* in cant?"

Kaamharaa could not even approximate the word, which included several sounds impossible for a turun. He tried to draw it out in the air in linguists' symbols for Taya, but Taya waved this effort away impatiently and said instead, remembering to shorten all her vowels, "You, you, you, all you, all enemy, now is?"

Then she went on for several more phrases, hopefully less confusing. Daamon, studying the other commander, caught a word or two. The cousins all listened attentively ... one presumed the faceless ones in armor were listening; they stood like statues. Armed, frightening statues, but at least not actively threatening anymore.

Captain Lem Gerstner. Some difficult syllables in that. Daamon rehearsed the sounds of the name in his mind, wanting to get it right if—when—he needed to pronounce it himself. Kaamharaa said the first word was a title. That was good to know. Less cumbersome, certainly.

They seemed to use the same word for *uman,* once Taya got that far. Or nearly the same: their pronunciation was a little breathier, but close enough. *Turun* was easy to get across, as long as no one cared about fine distinctions. *Uut* was difficult. Taya gestured around them to the cousins' ship. "Uman, good." Then she pointed to the transport, bright in Aanuku green and gold. "Turun, good." Then she swept her hand up and around, a vague *out-there* kind of gesture, and said, "Uut, bad. Many, many, lots uut, bad. Many uman—human—turun, good. Many lots uut, bad. What do?"

Daamon was impressed. That was really very clear. Or it seemed very clear to him.

"Captain," said the one called Doctor Chandratre, turning. He said a lot more after that, rapidly, while Captain Lem Gerstner listened, frowning.

"Uut," Taya told Daamon, listening intently. "Us, them. It's hard to follow. I can't catch anything important."

Daamon certainly couldn't. He studied the others instead, keeping an eye on the armored people.

At last Captain Gerstner turned decisively, interrupting Daamon's thoughts. He took one step toward Daamon, then gestured away across the berth. "Come," he said, and all the armored people shifted to one side, clearing the way.

"Daamon ..." Taya touched his arm, glancing wide-eyed at the armored people and then over her shoulder toward the transport. "I don't know ..."

Daamon put an arm around his sister's slight shoulders. "We came this far." He stopped himself, just in time, from adding, *It makes no difference where they take us; they could kill us all whenever and wherever they wanted.* That would not be a helpful thing to say, even though it was true. Still, he considered walking back toward the transport instead. He would like to know whether those weapons would stay slung. Were they prisoners or guests? Or some strange combination of both? In historical finance-dramas, nturun of one matriline would sometimes accept high-ranking hostage-allies from an unrelated matriline as part of an effort to build an alliance. In the dramas, the fate of such persons was not normally enviable. Even if everyone began with the best of intentions, blended loyalties almost inevitably led to tragedy. Only in contemporary uman-authored romance-adventures were kinder outcomes likely.

This situation was actually a good deal more like an uman romance-adventure than seemed quite comfortable. Daamon wished he'd grown up watching the cousins' historical and contemporary dramas so that he could have had a better idea what hidden expectations and beliefs informed their actions.

"Tsuumat Kaamharaa?" Daamon asked. "I know my own inclination in this. But I would value your opinion."

Kaamharaa tilted his head, pleased to be asked. He opened one hand in tentative assent. "My belief is that we have come far, but not yet overfar; and that these your cousins have half-offended, but not yet fully offended. They were frightened, as such small and delicate people may reasonably be frightened by so large a person as myself. But they overcome their fears, as civilized persons will do. Would you defy this uman captain so that you may observe his response? I believe *he* commands *you* for just this reason."

Daamon hadn't considered this. But he could see it must be true. Every order the other commander issued to Daamon or his people *was* a kind of test—a kind of *question*. Captain Gerstner issued an order to come; that *was* a question. Obedience or defiance were each potential answers. Command or refrain from commanding, obey or refuse to obey, trust the other or choose mistrust, accept risk or shy away from risk ... well, it was too late for that last. From the moment *Nkaastu* had encountered this foreign ship, there had been no way forward but straight into the teeth of the north wind.

"All right," Daamon said out loud. "Let's try this. Tell them I suggest we go back to Aam right now, this minute, their ship and ours, and ask for alliance with Kaoluun. Can you get that across yet? It shouldn't be that complicated, surely? Us, them, go Aam ... I admit, I have no idea how to say *alliance.* Much less explain matrilines and the Ka' Taand and ..." He shrugged. "Everything."

"*Us* and *you* and a lot of waving our hands around," Taya said. "Anybody should understand—especially since they *have* to want alliance. Of course they do! Only I don't know if *Kaoluun* will. They have lots of other alliances already, and they'd *definitely* lose ships taking on all those uut, and they—we—don't *know* these people. And if Kaoluun is against the idea, the Suund isn't likely to decide in favor."

"Let's not leap quite that far off the cliff." Daamon was fairly sure he could get Siiv u Kaoluun to give him a hearing, at least. Getting Tnakaa u Kaoluun to listen would be Kuotaan's problem. But just getting these cousins back to Aam where they could negotiate with real authorities was all Daamon really had to worry about. With luck, they'd each be able to offer the other such advantages against the uut that Kaoluun would swing their considerable influence behind alliance. Taya was right: as Kaoluun went, so many other matrilines would go, and probably the whole Suund in the end. And if the beloved gods were beneficent, the cousins would turn out to be trustworthy as well as powerful.

He said, "Just get them moving, Taya. Kaamharaa, I would very much appreciate your assistance in this."

"To be sure—" Kaamharaa began.

"Come," the other commander ordered, his tone insistent. "You, come, all."

"You come *us,"* Taya countered, pointing to the transport. "We go Aam, all go talk Aam."

For a long moment, everyone looked at each other, no one moving.

Doctor Chandratre said something rapid, not quite under his breath, Captain Lem Gerstner answered, his tone curt. Some of the armored men moved suddenly, so suddenly Daamon couldn't suppress a flinch and Taya squeaked and tucked herself back against Kaamharaa, who straightened and brought one foot down against the deck in warning, a heavy booming stomp.

No one pointed weapons at anyone, so that was good. That was excellent. But those armored people wound up between them and the transport, in a line, facing Kaamharaa, and that was a clear enough statement that nobody could possibly mistake their meaning.

"I think we're going to have to work on the concept of *alliance,"* Daamon murmured, keeping his voice level.

"I think they've got the concept of *hostage* straight right now," Taya countered. "I don't like this! What should we do?"

The other commander, Captain Gerstner, actually did not look hostile. Or even aggressive. Not as far as Daamon could tell. Intent. Focused. Tense. He certainly should be tense, pushing an uturun of Kaamharaa's reputation ... he was probably *afraid* of Kaamharaa. That was difficult to keep in mind, but it was probably true.

"We can't get the transport out of this berthing area unless they let us," Daamon said, trying to keep tension out of his own voice, his own manner. "They've got us if they want us. But did you notice, they haven't starting pointing weapons again? Even though they're afraid of Kaamharaa." They hadn't. All those weapons were still slung. He added, "I think Kaamharaa's right. I think this is a question, and a test. They might be just posturing, true." He used an edged term, not very polite, for the behavior of young males, but then went on. "But it's also possible they've got a perfectly acceptable reason to want us to come with them. They could want to take us somewhere more comfortable to talk. Maybe even to a contemplation garden or something."

"Sure," muttered Taya.

"No, this seems possible, even likely," argued Kaamharaa, obviously pleased at this idea. "That would be a perfectly appropriate gesture of hospitality, and if they also make a gesture of dominance, who can blame them?"

"We'll go a small distance, for a short time," Daamon decided. "And, if necessary, we'll see what happens when we decide to leave." He beckoned to the others, and began to walk the way Captain Gerstner had directed. And stopped, becoming aware that the other commander was holding up a blocking hand, beckoning Daamon to come with him while waving away Taya and Kaamharaa. Directing them back toward the other man, Daamon couldn't remember his name and at the moment couldn't bring himself to care.

He meant to separate them.

Daamon stared at Captain Gerstner. Then he said flatly, "No." And in Uom, "Absolutely not. Under no circumstances. We stay together." And in cant again, forcefully: "No!"

"Really, no," Taya muttered, not quite under her breath. She edged forward to take Daamon's hand in one of hers; on her other side, she gripped Kaamharaa's nearest hand. Her glare at Captain Lem Gerstner should have dissolved him on the spot, though the man met her anger with impassivity. Daamon drew his sister close and braced himself solidly to show he would not be moved, like an uturun with a reputation to defend—a symbolic gesture from an uman, but he meant it. He could feel Kaamharaa's reassuring bulk at his back, and was glad of it: *no one* would move *Kaamharaa*. That certainty gave Daamon the strength to set himself, cane and all, as though he were rooted right to the center of the world.

For a long moment, they stood facing one another. Daamon couldn't read anything from Captain Gerstner's carefully inexpressive face.

"Yes," said Captain Gerstner. Stepping back. Yielding the point, just like that. He said, with a sweeping wave that clearly took in all three of them, "All come. Daamon, Taya, Kamhara, come."

"You see? He wished to see what you would do," rumbled Kaamharaa.

"Is that what you think?" Taya demanded. "*I* think he was *rude!* That was *awful!*"

Daamon gave his sister's hand a little squeeze, warning her to remember her manners. He used Kaamharaa's formal title for the same reason: "Tsuumat Kaamharaa, I believe you are correct." He stared narrowly at Captain Gerstner, who remained impassive, as if it were all one to him whether his prisoners-guests-hostages-allies obeyed his commands or not.

Daamon didn't believe that. No. He *believed* that Captain Gerstner had posed a question, exactly as Kaamharaa suggested. It was exactly the sort of risk a battlecommander would take, in order to better understand his ... potential allies. He studied the man's face, wishing he could tell what Captain Gerstner was thinking.

Did he approve of Daamon's own answer, or was he coming to the conclusion that their two peoples might be potential enemies?

But he knew he could have given no other answer; that he would never give another answer to that particular question. And he certainly had no intention of letting Captain Gerstner conclude that *Nkaastu's* people would meekly follow any order given by these hardly-known uman cousins.

He said, "We'll obey their commands where it seems expedient or wise. But we won't be separated. Taya, don't make faces. Be polite."

"Oh, polite!" Taya tossed her head, scornful of the very concept. "These people aren't polite to *us,* so I don't see why we should be polite to *them!* A contemplation garden, sure!"

"You represent the dignity of sepu Kaamharaa, and of Tsuumat Kaamharaa himself. Our dignity is not contingent on anyone else's manners," Daamon told her, with a little snap to his voice because he shouldn't have had to remind her of that.

"Huh!" said Taya, but she did smooth out her expression.

"We'll *all* come," Daamon said firmly, using the cant word for *come.* He led the others toward the patiently waiting Captain Gerstner. Whose patience was actually an answer in itself, Daamon realized, to a question he hadn't even been aware of asking. He offered the cousins' commander a little dip of the head, acknowledging the exchange between them, command and response, defiance and patience. Captain Gerstner inclined his head in return. It might be an answering acknowledgement that they had begun to understand one another. Or maybe not, hard to say.

The ship's berthing area was truly vast. Walking any distance pointed out how vast. Daamon was frankly not certain he would be able to walk far enough to get wherever Captain Gerstner wanted them to go, and not pleased at the idea of demonstrating his weakness, though he supposed the cane made that clear enough.

The bay was interesting, however. The little ships lined all one side of the berth, like rows of ornaments arranged on shelves, only these ornaments were spaceworthy craft. Almost certainly little fighting craft. Even now, Captain Gerstner must be worried for his fellows, must long to return to succor them—almost certainly hoped for an alliance with the Ka' Taand. Daamon was almost certain that was the man's aim in all this. Perhaps, if the beloved gods were kind, the uman ships had tucked up in a defensive geometry that would let them hold and hold despite all the uut could do. Paaol had said he thought they could hold for a long time.

Not forever. Frightening as they were, these foreign cousins needed allies. That was probably why, tense as they were about Kaamharaa, they had allowed Daamon to correct their excessively bad manners.

They came to a different part of the berthing area and paused, Captain Gerstner and his people halting, and so by necessity Daamon and his. Captain Gerstner moved aside to provide a clear view of a strip of decking perhaps four or five strides across, which glided along at a considerable velocity. The outer stride or so of the sliding conveyer strip moved fast, but not as fast as the next strip in, and the center section glided along faster still. Then on the other side the velocity stepped down again, then picked up with the movement in the reverse direction.

"Now *that* is clever design," Daamon commented. It was an application of engineering that he had never thought of and for which he immediately saw innumerable uses.

Taya obviously had exactly the same thought, because she exclaimed, "Oh, Guuan *needs* that! Big brother, you have to make them give us the designs for that! Think how much faster it would be to get from the central clanhouse to any of the peripheral holdings! *So* tiring and tedious," she added in heartfelt memory of her year at the Guuan matriline holdings on Gaatuu.

"Mmmm," Kaamharaa rumbled, tucking his chin in disapproval. "While brokering trade in some new and broadly useful technology would surely please Aanuku, I am alarmed to hear that matriline territories no longer utilize public service transports for the benefit of their uman people. I am certain I have seen references to such."

"Public service transports *never* go where you need to get to, especially not when you're in a flying rush—"

"Better to ask an nturun sister to carry you if you have no uman transport available. You uman folk are fragile. What if you were to lose your balance and fall? Observe the velocity of the swiftest strip. A fall—"

Taya whacked the uturun on the nearest arm, not gently. "Kaamharaa, we are not either fragile! Honestly, anyone would think our bones were made of spun glass!"

"They nearly are," Kaamharaa began. "Chitin is a more sensible material—" but all the foreign uman people had startled when Taya hit Kaamharaa and Taya, catching this reaction and already nervous, now crowded back against Kaamharaa's side for protection. Obviously weary of tolerating risks to his favorite, Kaamharaa wrapped his lower hands around her waist, picked her up, twisted, and deposited her on his back, where she stood with easy balance, gripping his upper shoulders, sheltered by his upper torso.

"You see?" Kaamharaa told her, his tone severe. "You are always safer on the back of a friend."

Daamon had tensed when the uturun picked up his sister, guessing what the cousins might think or fear or do at that move. But perhaps the uman foreigners were becoming accustomed to the uturun. Many of them had their hands on their weapons, but no one was pointing a weapon actually *at* anyone.

And that was as well, because at that moment, a savage rising wail sounded, a terrible sound, and everything suddenly seemed to happen at once.

Captain Gerstner called out urgently, as did others, but the deck beneath their feet jolted and tilted and sent all the bipedal uman people staggering. A great grinding scream of tearing metal drowned out every uman cry.

Kaamharaa boomed in alarm, audible even over the tumult. Taya wrapped her arms around his thick neck and clung tight, and Kaamharaa grabbed Daamon before he could fall, snatching him up protectively in his left arms, bracing himself on his four powerful legs, tossing his head to display his tusks in a thoroughly uncivilized warning to any enemy that might appear. But Kaamharaa also caught the staggering foreign commander; nor in this crisis did Captain Gerstner shy from him. He clung to the uturun's arm, salvaged his balance, and snapped rapid, steady phrases to the air—a personal link, Daamon realized after the first startled instant, and wished savagely for the information feed the other commander had no doubt accessed.

"Nkaastu!" Daamon cried, but he knew as he shouted that the foreigners wouldn't understand, and knew as well that Aanuku's little half-fighter tradeship wouldn't, couldn't be a priority for the cousins whose own ship had come under such unexpected and surely disastrous attack. He had no way even to demand to know what was happening. The armored people had mostly fallen to their knees or prone, deliberately, he saw now, because once down they could brace themselves and their weapons far more effectively—but against what attack he had no idea; ship's weapons were nothing a man could face with a weapon hardly longer than his arm!

How, how, *how* had any uut formation found them here, practically buried in the gravity well of this gas giant; how had the enemy approached closely enough to attack without being painted by scans; *how* could they have defeated all the confounders and darkmasking, *how could any of this be happening?*

The metal of the ship was tearing apart, the whole far end of the berth peeling open as a turun would open a tough-hulled ndao nut. Daamon, horrified, saw metal twisting awry and the starfield beyond growing and growing. Disaster shields were slamming down, sectioning the vast area of the berth, but the shields, too, twisted and folded out of true. The ship's gravitics held, establishing an airshield and preventing depressurization despite the terrible breach of hull integrity, a remarkable feat of disaster-engineering. If the gravitics had failed, everyone in the vast berth would probably have had just enough time to know they were going to die before the atmosphere blew out into space and carried them all with it. Or maybe not the armored persons; suddenly that armor and those face shields suggested a purpose other than sheer intimidation. But he still didn't understand the weapons, or their obvious expectation of some kind of attack they might actually be able to repulse—

An uut Disk flashed right into the berth through the torn hull, jerking down and then recovering as it compensated for the gravitics within the bay, spinning rapidly, but the spin slowing as Daamon watched in horror. It looked different in its actual physical bulk than any icon in the tank display; that was his first mad impression. It wasn't glowing red like the icon of a Disk; it was polished, glassy black and translucent gray, transparent around the sharp-edged rim, looking like nothing so much as an ornament made of fine obsidian.

And it was big. Vastly bigger than any of the little uman transports docked in this berth; far bigger than the turun transport. Daamon had had no idea a Disk would look so immense when seen in person, but it took up a huge amount of volume, instantly making even this enormous shipbay seem cramped and crowded.

Then the Disc stopped spinning. Transparent glassy tentacles writhed out of the Disk, all along the anterior rim, slender bifurcating tentacles like the limbs of some horrifying sea creature, and immediately Daamon found out what the weapons were for, because the armored uman persons were shooting steadily as the tentacles lashed forward, their beam weapons withering the tentacles—obviously they had expected exactly this kind of attack, even though Daamon had never heard of uut deploying any such mode. Uut fighters tried to get past orbital defenses and burn worlds; if they couldn't get close enough to use nuclear fire, then they tried to slip into a system unseen and hurl high-vee asteroids from a distance. They tried to hull stations, behind them they left airless hulks and scattered debris and savaged worlds, but they did not try to tear a way *into* a turun ship and take *prisoners*, only that seemed exactly what *this* uut Disk was trying to do.

And there was nothing he could do to protect any of them, nothing he could do to protect himself but hold tight to Kaamharaa.

The uturun gathered himself and surged into a heavy canter, carrying Taya and Daamon and Captain Gerstner with him with no trace of effort. The uturun leaped right over a prone armored uman, landed with an echoing crash that seemed almost to shake the whole ship. Someone was screaming, an uman voice, but Daamon couldn't see what was happening. A glassy tentacle flashed in front of them, as big around as Daamon's wrist, not flailing blindly but lashing toward Kaamharaa's legs. Kaamharaa boomed in threat, rearing back; Taya screamed, sharp and piercing. The tentacle snapped forward, writhing. Kaamharaa boomed again and trampled it savagely, tearing at it with the short, thick claws of his forefeet. That tentacle jerked back, but another struck, twisting about his lower limbs. It jerked the uturun off his feet, and not even Kaamharaa was heavy enough or strong enough to fight that attack. Though he tried. The uturun let go of Daamon with his lower arm, grappling with the tentacle, trying to tear it loose, but it lashed tight around his powerful wrist.

Then Kaamharaa thrust Taya into Daamon's arms and hurled them both away, hard.

Daamon tucked himself around his sister and took the impact of their fall mostly on his thigh and hip—his good leg, fortunately—skidding rather than tumbling, until they both slammed into some solid obstruction with a force that knocked his breath from his lungs and felt like it might have broken all the ribs on that side. He couldn't get breath enough even to gasp, though Taya uttered a fervent curse he'd had no idea she even knew. But she leaped up with no regard for Daamon and would have run back toward Kaamharaa if he hadn't grabbed her ankle and jerked her down into his arms. She hit his chest hard enough to blind him with an explosion of bright agony. Since he didn't have the breath to shout at her, he shook her, but she cried out wordlessly, pointing, and Daamon finally saw how Kaamharaa—and the foreign commander—were being pulled rapidly back toward the uut Disk, glassy tentacles wrapped around them both. They were both alive, both struggling, but obviously unable to get free. He tried to stagger back to his feet, and Taya grabbed his hand and heaved, and he found a handhold on the casing of the machine that had so brutally stopped their fall. He made it up, mostly, but it was obviously much too late for either of them to *do* anything, even if he'd been in perfect health and had some idea what might actually help.

The armored persons were *trying* to help, at least. The tentacles reached after them, but flinched away from any direct contact, one more use for that armor; Daamon wished fervently the turun had something like that—that Kaamharaa had been wearing something like that. But none of them had guessed the uut might attack like this.

Kaamharaa had torn himself partly free of the tentacles' grip, but the tentacles kept bifurcating and wrapping his limbs, and he couldn't reach back far enough to grip the tentacles twined around his hind legs. Even his enormous strength was plainly not going to be enough to get himself free—he knew it, he had stopped trying to free himself, he was tearing with his two free hands at the tentacles gripping the foreign commander, but even as Daamon watched, one of his remaining arms was tangled and restrained.

"No! No!" Taya was shouting, as ineffectual as Daamon—all Daamon could do was hold her back, keep her from pointlessly rushing into danger—worse danger.

The armored persons were advancing in rapid order, half of them firing to cover the other half, then reversing roles as they gained ground, obviously a practiced tactic, obviously not something unarmored, untrained uman people could help with. *They* might have gotten Kaamharaa and their commander free, the tentacles were unable to touch them and their weapons made the tentacles wither and twist and darken and fall away. But they couldn't fire directly at the tentacles gripping their commander or Kaamharaa, and then the Disk leaped forward, its remaining tentacles shortening and retracting, a mouth spinning open to swallow its captives. Someone shouted and someone cursed, but there was nothing any of them could do.

Then there was, or might be, because a couple of the little uman transports suddenly twitched out of their positions, raced forward, and began to fire far more powerful weapons at the underside of the Disk. Daamon hadn't guessed such tiny craft might be armed, but thank the beloved gods, the Disk staggered and wobbled in the air.

But blowback ripped through the berth, sheeting across equipment and armored men, and Daamon twisted to get Taya behind him as the fire and pressure surged toward them. Heat and pressure slammed him back to his knees, carrying Taya down with him; even as he caught his breath with pain, he was grateful it wasn't worse. If the fire brought down the Disk, the risk of blowback would have been worth it—he squinted, trying to see what was happening, and through the confusion of smoke and steam saw that, instead of falling or tearing apart, the Disk, opaque and dull where it had taken the force of the attack, nevertheless began to spin again, faster and faster. Then it jerked away, back toward the torn hull, and vanished from sight into the yawning emptiness beyond.

The sudden quiet was staggering. Daamon felt stunned. Blank. Helpless.

Furious.

The Disk had taken Kaamharaa. The uut had taken *Kaamharaa*.

"They took the foreign captain, too!" Taya cried, her voice shaking with the same terror and outrage Daamon felt. "Our cousins *have* to go after their captain—we'll *make* them help us rescue Kaamharaa!"

Daamon couldn't quite manage an even tone. "Our cousins were armed and armored for just that kind of attack. They knew the uut might try to take prisoners, so surely they must know what they do with prisoners. They must have gone after their captured people before. They have to know what to do now. Except we don't even know how to *ask* them."

"I'll find a way!" Taya promised fiercely. "I'll learn their forsaken language and I'll *make* them help us!"

"Don't curse," Daamon told her quite automatically. He rubbed his face and looked around, trying to think. He found he had sorted out, by some cue of bulk or posture, the armored commander, and from that realized he had also sorted out a possible course of action. He had been gripping the apparatus against which he'd fallen. Now he transferred his grip to Taya's shoulder, straightening cautiously as she helped him back to his feet. His breath snagged with the pain of the movement, so that his sister finally swept him with a summing glance, looked around to find his cane, and went to get it for him without a word.

Daamon took it gratefully and braced himself upright. "That, I think, is actually their battlecommander," he told his sister, nodding toward the armored man. "Help me over to him, and we'll *both* make him help us."

Which was a brave, forceful thing to say. But he knew, as Taya had to know, that neither of them had the least chance of making the cousins do anything they didn't want to do.

But they would do it anyway, because they couldn't rescue Kaamharaa alone and so they had no choice.

6

Obviously Daamon had to return to *Nkaastu* as soon as he possibly could. Taya understood that. Of course she did. Daamon *had* to go back to *Nkaastu*. Taya tried just to fix her mind on the certainty that Tsaa Kuotaan needed her battlecommander, which she *did*. Saraa u Aanuku might be smart and brave and determined and audacious, but she wasn't *Daamon*.

Even so, Taya had never been more frightened in her life than when she let go of her brother's hand and stepped back and smiled and pretended to be brave while he boarded the transport without her. The transport lifted up and slid away, and she was alone on this huge echoing foreign ship where she didn't know *anyone*, where the very *air* smelled flat and wrong. Nothing she'd ever done had ever been so hard. Not ever.

Not even when she'd left Kaamharaa's household for the first time, going to live with her u Guuan cousins for a year. She'd been upset then, not wanting to leave the household and live among a great crowd of kin she didn't know. Now all those worries seemed so childish. She'd had nothing at all to be afraid of, and she'd known that all along. Her near-sister Daana had come to meet her as soon as Taya stepped off the public transport onto u Guuan soil. Daana had explained who everyone was and shown Taya everything, and later Taya had made friends with Daana's nturun half-sister, Ndeh. Ndeh's mother was only a servant and so Ndeh would never have the chance to be anything but a servant herself unless she took the huge, risky step of trying to break off the main Guuan line and establish a new matriline. Daana had promised to help if Ndeh tried that, but that had been years ago and Taya didn't know whether they had ever done it.

It was so much easier to be uman. An uman was welcome anywhere and free to build her reputation within a matriline or independently or in association with an uturun, whatever she wanted.

This was different. It was *so much worse*. Everything was *so awful*. She wanted to go home so badly now, *right now*. She wanted never to have left. She wanted for all of them to be back there, in the graceful, sprawling house of sepu Kaamharaa. She wanted to run her hand down the smooth trunk of the graceful ndao in the courtyard, a tree older than she was, older than Daamon, older even than their parents. She wanted to trail her fingers though the pool where the orange-finned kasukasu darted through the dappled shade and sun. She wanted to be there with her near-kin and half-kin, her parents and her brother and her second-parents and their toddler twins. Most of all, she wanted to be there with *Kaamharaa*.

If Kaamharaa were really lost, that home wouldn't even *exist*, and no one there would even know it yet. Everything was so awful, but she couldn't upset these armored cousins, faceless and frightening as they were, or who knew what they might do? Daamon trusted her to get them to help, *Kaamharaa* needed them to help, so she pretended she wasn't frightened at all.

Chin up and head high, Taya turned to the armored uman commander, the one Daamon had said might be the battlecommander for this ship. *"Nharutsuukaa uul, taam kuannaas uul,"* she whispered to herself. *When far from home, it's best to believe in the goodwill of strangers.* Her mother had reminded her of that when Taya had gone to live with the Guuan matriline. It was a good saying. It was true. At least, it had been true at Guuan.

These people were *cousins*. How scary could they be?

But with those shiny, featureless helmets over their faces, they *were* frightening, no matter what she told herself. She was sure this man already understood why she'd stayed behind. She was sure she'd explained that clearly enough, even with the *extremely limited* vocabulary that was all she had to work with.

"Nda cousin," she began, and got stuck, fumbling for some way to express urgent phrases such as *I have to learn to talk to you* and *How are we going to rescue Kaamharaa and your captain?*

The battlecommander might not be able to talk to her, either, but *he* didn't fumble around. He said something brusque to one of his people, then took Taya's arm in a firm grip—she squeaked embarrassingly before she realized this was guidance rather than aggression—and led her toward the moving conveyer strips set into the decking. His manner was definite but not, Taya decided, actually *meant* to be intimidating.

Taya had looked forward to riding on those strips. But that had been when she'd had Daamon with her, and Kaamharaa. Now her earlier delight in the idea had all been lost. Nevertheless, when the foreign battlecommander showed her how to step from the ordinary deck to the first moving conveyer, and then from that one to a faster one, she followed quickly. None of the other armored persons came with them.

Riding the moving conveyer wasn't actually difficult at all, even at the center where it was fastest. It was certainly much easier than riding on a turun's back at a full canter across the savannah, standing up so you could see over his upper shoulder, your bare feet giving you good purchase on his second back, your hands gripping his lower shoulders ... she might never have that again, *Kaamharaa* might never have that again.

They were still traveling. Taya had thought *Nkaastu* was big. And it was, for a half-fighter tradeship. *Nkaastu* couldn't transport thousands of tons of ore or grain like some of the big full-tradeships, but it could carry several hundred cannisters of high-value tradegoods from one world to another, and fight off any pirates that might try to steal its cargo, and even—maybe—face a formation of uut fighters if it absolutely had to, supporting full-fighters to protect the worlds of the Ka' Taand. But Taya could *walk* from front to back of *Nkaastu* in only a little more than two chimes if she strode along at a proper pace, and that was even counting the sideways jog in the middle where the cargo areas intersected with the duty stations of the crew. She'd done that several times right after she'd come aboard, just to see *Nkaastu* and learn her way around the ship.

This ship was just ... so much *more*. She could probably explore this ship for a *year* and still not see everything.

The conveyer had carried them out of the huge boats' berth and along a great corridor, still very broad but not nearly so vast as the berth. The corridor was ribbed like a giant marine animal, except the ribs glowed bright as the savannah sun, while in between the ribs, the ceiling was dark, so they slid through bars of light and dusk, light and dusk. It was a little disorienting, a little dizzying, but Taya refused to close her eyes because there was so much to see. For the first time there were a lot of people, thronging everywhere, coming and going about their mysterious business. She was relieved ... mostly relieved ... that hardly any of the people she glimpsed were in faceless armor. Except they nearly all wore that gloomy black clothing, with flashes of color only at wrist and throat. A few were in tan, one in white. No one seemed to wear any proper *colors*. Not a single person was barefoot, which seemed really strange in the controlled environment of a ship. Taya curled her toes uneasily against the smooth surface of the conveyer.

Some people had red flashes on their clothing, sometimes yellow, sometimes white. No one had two different colors at once. It could have been some kind of very weird artistic taste, but Taya was sure the colors *meant* something. She realized with dismay that all these unspoken signals must be like a whole separate language to learn. There was *so much* to learn.

The battlecommander raised a hand to his face ... and suddenly he *had* a face, not merely a blank faceplate.

It was such a relief to be able to see her intimidating companion properly that at first Taya couldn't help but stare. He was not tall, but he was solid. His square-featured face suited him. He had broad cheekbones and deep-set dark eyes, very short black hair going gray at the temples, and skin almost exactly the same shade as a turun's hide.

The battlecommander looked grim, maybe angry, but Taya was almost sure he wasn't angry at her, and if he was angry at the uut, that was fine. Only she wished she knew where he was taking her.

"Esaias," the battlecommander told her. "Esaias Keay." He tapped himself on the chest with one black-gloved finger. She understood this was his name. Or title, or anyway something she was supposed to call him. The words were difficult. The first had something like a hiss at both beginning and end, and a light, thin-sounding vowel sound in the middle. The second seemed to consist mostly of a different short, light vowel.

"Esaias," she tried, but it came out more like *Ehsaa'as*. The battlecommander gave her a small nod, but Taya wasn't satisfied; if she couldn't do better than that, she would never make the cousins understand her. "Ehsaaeh," she tried, experimenting. "Ehsa'ehs." That seemed pretty close, and she looked at the man hopefully.

"Esaias," he said again, smiling a little—the smile lightened his grim expression more than she would have expected, and she was relieved at his apparent willingness to be friendly, but the word was both sharper and more sibilant than Taya had yet managed.

She wondered if this man really was a battlecommander the way the Ka' Taand meant the term. Probably not exactly. But it helped to think of this man as kind of like her brother. She wondered if he had fought a lot of times. She couldn't see any scars. But sometimes scars didn't show on the outside. She had realized that after Daamon had come back from the far edge after that last battle, when everything had been so awful and terrifying. All the news had been so frightening: Nguaa burned, the worldlet Ta' Nguaa hit with a high-vee rock, stations destroyed, ships lost, *Daamon's* ship lost.

Then her brother had came back after all, following close behind the horrifying message about his ship, and everyone had been so glad. Their full-mother had cried, and Kaamharaa had been so relieved and then so silent, because Daamon had been badly hurt, much more badly than Taya had understood at first. Daamon had come back with that cane, but that was nothing. He'd also come back thin and silent, with shadows at the backs of his eyes, and she hadn't been able to help at all.

Finally, a year or so later, their full-parents and Kaamharaa had made the alliance with Aanuku, choosing Aanuku partly because it was a good alliance for Guaan and partly because Aanuku mostly ran tradeships with just a few half-fighter tradeships to guard against piracy, and partly because Aanuku was most interested in building its presence along the near edge and not the dangerous far edge. Daamon had gone to *Nkaastu*, and their near-brother Paaol had followed, and some others. And Kaamharaa. That was why Taya had come. Because Kaamharaa had decided to firm up this alliance with Aanuku as strongly as he could, for a lot of reasons, but partly for Daamon.

Maybe this foreign battlecommander had a family behind him too. Of course he must. A family and alliances and a complicated life, and more than likely shadows at the backs of his eyes.

Before she could make another attempt to pronounce his name, the battlecommander took Taya's elbow in a firm grip and led her from the fast center of the conveyer toward the slower section to their right. She let him help her, stepping and then stepping again and then hopping neatly from the conveyer to the unmoving decking.

Beyond the doorway, a wide cylindrical channel speared vertically upward, filled with round platforms that rose and sank, each at a different velocity. People rode on the platforms, up or down. Most of the people in the corridor had been too far away or too busy or too polite to stare at Taya, but a lot of these people stared as they went by, eyes wide, craning their necks. Pointing at one of the rising platforms, Taya asked in cant, "What?" Then she frowned and amended that to, "Ehsaeh'as, what?" She still couldn't get his name right, and tossed her head irritably, trying again. "Esaae'as. Esaaeas. Esaaeas Kaay."

The battlecommander gave her a small, approving nod as she got closer to the proper pronunciation, but corrected her, demonstrating once again the sharp vowel in the middle of the word: "Esaias." Then he pointed to the same platform she'd indicated and told her, "Updisk." then, nodding toward one of the descending platforms: "Dropdisk." A sweeping gesture took in the whole vertical channel. "Elevator shaft."

Taya repeated these words, fixing them in her mind with the little mental *thump* that would keep them there. More sibilants, sibilants in every word, plainly this language was filled with them. Cant might have more sibilants than Uom—or the other less common turun languages she half-knew, Tku or Maarou—but even cant didn't have as many sibilants as the cousins' language. It was hard to believe cant had degenerated from this very language. Maybe both had changed a lot since Taya's ancestors had been abandoned or lost on Ymaa so long ago. Or maybe cant and the memory of cant had changed to better match turun languages. Taya could imagine that, too: that very first lucky uman family teaching Tsuumat Nkaarusapaa their poor degenerate language, learning to adjust their words to what he could pronounce.

Nkaarusapaa had been so lucky too, to suffer his famous accident where uman people could find him and help him—where they could help each other and learn about each other. What an astounding time that had been, and how very, very lucky for everyone.

Imagine if those ancestors had been discovered first by these cousins instead. Everything would have been so much easier.

But then her ancestors wouldn't ever have established a presence in the Suund or helped create the Ka' Taand. Taya herself would have been born on some uman world where no turun had ever set foot, grown up in an uman family with no Kaamharaa to tease and cherish ... she couldn't imagine it, shied away from trying just as she shied away from imagining where Kaamharaa might be right now.

Much, much better to think of how much he would have liked these platforms, these *updisks* and *dropdisks*. They did look like great fun, only she wished *so much* Kaamharaa were here to enjoy all these strange new experiences. She had to learn as much as she could as quickly as she could, so she could explain to these cousins how important it was to rescue Kaamharaa.

She shook herself free of the battlecommander's grip in order to jump onto the rising updisk he'd indicated. It didn't exactly look safe—oh, there was an *airshield*. Of course there was. Taya should have expected that feeling of pressure, of pushing through a half-solid wall. She made it through the shield, it was only about as thick as a finger, and bounced on her toes as the battlecommander stepped up to join her. She felt much happier now that she knew nobody could just fall off because of a second of carelessness.

No doubt getting off would be just as easy. The platform wasn't moving all that fast, really. Obviously a person would have plenty of time to jump off the disk as it rose past the level of the decking, even though it didn't pause.

Surely the platform wouldn't squish a person against the ceiling if she failed to jump off at the right time. Taya was sure it wouldn't. No one would design a danger like that into a transport system like this. She resolved not to worry about it.

The updisk rose higher and higher above the corridor, while Taya poked her head through the airshield to look over the edge and watch the decking dwindle away below. After a few moments, the battlecommander gave her a nod, beckoned—a perfectly familiar gesture—and pointed to the edge of the vertical channel, where Taya could see they were coming to a doorway edged with light. He pronounced a few words slowly, but she couldn't guess whether he was naming their destination or just saying *There it is* or something completely different.

Their destination turned out to be the bridge. Taya had seen this place on the display capture, but it looked bigger and more impressive in person. She'd been on the bridge of *Nkaastu* once or twice, just to see it. This space was very different, but it had the same kind of important look. Or maybe it was the people who looked important.

Everyone in this place had his or her own separate station, the consoles set into individual pedestals. The pedestals were square and abrupt, made of plain undecorated metal; and the consoles were all black glass with lights glittering under the glass; and everyone was uman, and they were all *staring* at her.

Well, that wasn't quite true: there was a big, oddly flat tank display in the front of the bridge, showing a rapidly shifting view of the giant planet and space, overlain with icons Taya didn't recognize—she hoped one of those icons represented *Nkaastu*, and she hoped Daamon was back on *Nkaastu* right now, and she hoped very much that he was finding out that things weren't so dire as they seemed. Here on this giant foreign ship, everyone was dividing their attention between that display and their own consoles and her. But it *felt* like they were all staring at her.

Taya had watched the recording of Daamon's very first exchange with these people; she'd watched that recording over and over, studied the people and listened carefully to the sound of their language. She didn't *know* these people, but she *recognized* them. It made her feel a little less lost and scared, especially because she'd learned to see their expressions, a little, even though they mostly seemed to keep their faces deliberately quiet. Maybe she should try to do that too. On the second hand, there was no hope of *her* blending in, but on the third hand she didn't want to cause offense. On the fourth hand, though, she honestly couldn't tell what might give offense, so there was probably no point in worrying about it.

She knew the man at the central station was important and guessed he was a secondary captain, maybe a battlecommander, but most likely in charge now that the primary captain was ... missing. She didn't want to think, *gone*.

The secondary captain spoke. Nda Esaias answered him, and they went back and forth while Taya listened as hard as she could, trying to sort out what they were saying to each other. She caught a few words: *talk* and *captain* and *no*, but such small words were meaningless in the rapidity of this argument or discussion or whatever it was. The secondary captain's tone was quiet, but not very friendly-sounding.

Taya patted Nda Esaias on the arm, and when he looked at her, she gently pulled free of his supportive hand and stepped forward. She pretended that the secondary captain was someone important from Aanuku or Guuan, maybe some government official from the Suund. She knew how to talk to someone like that—at least, she knew how *Kaamharaa* talked to people like that, how her parents talked to them. She might not have that kind of reputation or authority, but she knew the right kind of manners.

She straightened her shoulders, looked the secondary captain in the face, and said with authority, "Captain Lem Gerstner, go. Tsuumat Kaamharaa, go." She didn't know how to say *taken*, but that *go* ought to be clear. She made a broad, slow gesture, taking in the bridge and by implication the whole great ship. "We go, all go, you, us, I talk, you talk, Daamon talk, we all talk, we all go, bring Captain Lem Gerstner, bring Tsuumat Kaamharaa." She wasn't sure of the word she'd used, *bring*. Maybe it should have been *come?* Or *get?* On second thought, she was pretty sure she should have said *get*.

The secondary captain was studying her. He had seemed angry before. Taya thought hopefully that he didn't seem angry now. Not *so* angry.

"Taya sepu Kamhara," Esaias said helpfully—she was almost sure he was trying to be helpful. Then he added, this time to Taya, with a little indicative wave of his hand, "Commander Kennon."

Taya offered a small bow and repeated this name or title or whatever it was, trying her best to pronounce the words correctly. She studied the secondary captain's face and the way he stood so that she could be sure to recognize him again. Commander Kennon. Those words weren't so hard. She had to do this *right* or she'd be no help to anybody.

The secondary captain frowned at her, but gave her a sharp little nod and said something that didn't sound angry. Battlecommander Esaias said a bunch of stuff back, of which Taya mostly caught the word *talk*. Commander Kennon nodded again and looked around the bridge, his expression searching.

Another man swiveled around in his chair, received a nod, and spoke. His manner implied that he expected the secondary captain to listen to him. He was light-colored: pale skin and pale hair, with long bones and long hands and a long face. He spoke rapidly and emphatically, too quickly for Taya to understand, and he gestured sharply toward her with an abruptness she felt expressed anger, or maybe disdain. She moved a little closer to Esaias while the other two men spoke to each other, a fast exchange she didn't understand. Then the unfriendly man nodded sharply and looked Taya up and down, and yes, she was pretty sure that *was* disdain. Or at least some kind of dislike. "Talk," he said to her. He touched himself on the chest and added, "Lieutenant Samuel Lockwood. Lieutenant. You say that. Understand?"

From his tone, he didn't expect her to be very smart. The sounds weren't too difficult, except for that strange lippy *muu* sound in the middle of one word and the *wuh* sound in the middle of another. She tried it out determinedly, "Luu tehn nahnt aam muueh lohk uud." She knew she had to learn how to say it better, especially if the man didn't like her.

The secondary captain said something in a crisp tone, and Lieutenant Samuel Lockwood answered, his tone more respectful this time. One of the women swung her chair around and said something, and the secondary captain nodded to her. She stood up too, touched herself on the chest, and said to Taya, "Lieutenant Sun Grigson."

That was easier. All the sounds were normal, though some of the combinations were strange and every syllable was about half as long as Uom would have made it. Also, the woman smiled and looked friendly. She was older than Taya, maybe about Saraa's age. She had light brown skin and dark brown hair, a round face and a stocky build. Going part by part, she wouldn't have looked out of place anywhere in the Ka' Taand, but somehow taken all at once as a whole person, she still looked foreign.

Taya smiled back and repeated the woman's name. Name and title. She was pretty sure now that *lieutenant* must be a title, and that both of these people must be the same rank.

Then the woman—Lieutenant Sun Grigson—tried to lead her to one side, but Taya resisted. She didn't want to make trouble, but she couldn't leave the bridge without at least *asking*. So even when Lieutenant Samuel Lockwood rolled his eyes and spoke sharply to her, Taya stayed where she was. When the secondary captain turned his stern attention toward her, she bowed and tried hopefully, "Daamon? Daamon? Talk Daamon *Nkaastu*?"

There was a slight pause. Then Commander Kennon pointed to the flat display, and when Taya looked where he was pointing, she saw one of the icons blinking on and off. Then a tone sounded, three tones that all ran together, and the secondary captain said something fast and hard. She waited uncertainly, and the display cleared, and filled up again, this time with a view of *Nkaastu's* bridge and Daamon, just where he should be, beside Tsaa Kuotaan.

Taya was so relieved she could have cried.

7

Daamon had never done anything worse in his life than leave his little sister behind, alone on the cousin's huge ship. Unless *Nkaastu* was destroyed and they all died and that huge ship survived. In that case, Taya might be the only one of them to live through this wild cascade of disasters, and leaving her on that foreign ship might be one of the best things he'd ever done. One couldn't know; one could never know; one did the best one could and the rest was in the hands of the gods.

The moment he arrived on *Nkaastu's* bridge, he ordered, "Reports, please, all reports to my console. Where, by all the forsaken gods, did that cursed Disk get off to? Tell me we tracked it."

"Sure, we tracked it!" Paaol said. He tossed his head aggressively, all those clips of feathers swaying. "We need to go after that Disk, Daamon! We can't let the uut take Kaamharaa!"

Daamon very much wanted to agree. Almost all his hesitation, almost every wish someone, Siiv u Kaoluun, could take over this whole problem had disappeared into the dark right along with Kaamharaa. But he didn't say *Yes*. That wouldn't be politic—in fact, it would be entirely impolite. He therefore only signed half-agreement with one hand, careful not to glance at Kuotaan, and said, "Gen, what've you got? Put it in the tank."

Lots of icons bloomed in the tank, including an enormous red sphere to represent that giant uut ship. "I threw a lot of drones after them, Daamon," Genru assured him. "Powered way down so the uut won't spot them. We're not going to lose track of a ship that big for a good long time."

"Their accel is nothing special," Saraa added, coolly certain. "Provided they don't run it up too much higher, we can keep up with them just fine. I've run calculations, and I'd stake quite a bit of reputation that if we start after them within the chime, we can catch them. If somebody decides that's not the stupidest and most deeply forsaken idea in the entire lexicon of stupid and forsaken ideas." She added acerbically, "You know, Daamon, they have a perfectly good tank display in Medical."

"Just a lot of bruises." Daamon wasn't actually certain this was true. He limped across the bridge to the station he shared with Kuotaan and, though he didn't look up to meet her gaze, leaned against her side, accepting her steadying hand on his back. His ribs didn't hurt worse than his leg, but he was *used* to his leg, to the weakness and constant ache that came from losing a big chunk of muscle and part of the natural bone. It had been too much damage to entirely repair even with the best medical techniques available; not enough to make use of a full prosthesis. None of these new injuries could possibly prove so inconvenient. However they felt at the moment.

Kuotaan studied the recording over Daamon's head. It was grim enough; hardly less terrifying to view from this angle even after the fact. A giant uut ship, nearly the size of a worldlet, peeled open the side of the cousins' ship, leaving behind torn strips of metal. Disks and Blades swarmed out of the huge ship like nilgiim out of a disturbed hive, tiny in this view. Though the cousins' ship tried to fight back, the giant uut ship shrugged off every blow like a turun pricked by pahao thorns.

Then all the Disks and Blades fled the cousins' ship and withdrew, the little fighters and the giant ship together, presumably taking its prisoners away, racing inward toward the system primary.

"Did we know they'd do that? Take prisoners?" Genru asked. He meant, *Did our cousins know?*

"They must have known it," Daamon answered grimly. "They had arms and armor against just that kind of attack. Too bad they didn't mention the possibility to *us.* Not that cant has the vocabulary for it. We *need* to be able to talk to these people. Especially if we have something useful to say." He could hardly imagine what that might be. They could go after that ship, sure. For all the good *Nkaastu* could do, following along after an uut ship large enough to host perhaps hundreds of ordinary uut fighters.

This was a disaster. And yet it could so easily get worse, in so many ways.

Daamon wished fervently that *Nkaastu* was simply, calmly, orbiting Aam, finalizing details of their delivery. The weightless cargo plus the various high value trade goods that could be carried by the little half-fighter tradeship: current installments of popular dramas and a broad selection of new finance-adventures and romance-adventures; medicines and medical patches; enamels and dyes. But also, much more relevant at the moment, electronics and components for weapons systems. The matriarchs who had invested in Aam and its associated worldlets and stations were not so sanguine as those whose matrilines kept to the heart-stars. Living out at the edge meant constantly remembering turun space was small and the universe wide. Those who settled Aam had constructed orbital defenses right along with comfortable residential stations. Now that caution seemed not merely wise, but prescient.

If only *Nkaastu* had been safely tucked up in close orbit near Ta' Aam, if Siiv sep' Upuonnu and *Sepuuk* had been the ones to meet a lot of unexpected uut and even more unexpected cousins ... nothing would have happened to Kaamharaa. Taya would still be on board and safe. True, probably *Sepuuk* didn't count among its crew anyone as gifted with languages and linguistics as Taya, far less Kaamharaa. But if *Sepuuk's* whole battlegroup had been with the cousins' ship when they found their people besieged, everything might have been resolved already. A full-fighter like *Sepuuk* would have been in a much better position to do something, to do *anything*. A man like Siiv would probably be so much more confident about his *options*.

Daamon blew out a sharp breath, dismissing all those wishes for what might have been. Everything had happened as it had happened. Wishes were pointless. Options. Fine. The first step was definitely to sort out the options that actually existed. *Then* decisions. Thinking of it that way clarified at least the next immediate steps. "I am aware we must discuss all these matters," he said to Kuotaan. "If you will permit me to speak first with this other commander, if he will speak to me, Tsaa Kuotaan."

"Of course, Nda Daamon," Kuotaan rumbled, as he'd known she would. He thanked all the beloved gods for an unshakeable nturun captain.

"Get the foreign battlecommander in the display," Daamon told Genru. "If he'll talk to me, I want to talk to him."

Gen raised his eyebrows, but moved to ping the cousins' ship.

Daamon waited, taking shallow breaths and trying to put his thoughts in order. On the first hand, he was practically certain the cousins knew more about the uut than he did. On the second hand, if they had known about those giant uut ships, he was seriously annoyed that they hadn't found a way to mention the danger. On the third hand, if they'd known this kind of attack was likely, surely they wouldn't have hidden somewhere they could be found, settled down, and invited new-met relatives over for cakes and tsuaeh. On the fourth hand ... on the fourth hand, Daamon probably shouldn't reason too far out in front of what he knew.

"Display," Genru said. "Incoming feed."

Daamon straightened, painfully. The bridge on that other ship looked almost familiar by this time. Taya was there, utterly out of place. He was intensely relieved to see her. He hadn't dared hope the cousins would have brought her up to their bridge, but there she was. To Daamon's experienced eye, his sister looked nervous and uncertain, but not actually afraid. That was almost as great a relief as her presence.

She gave him a tiny little wave, plainly just as relieved to see him. Daamon smiled at her, though he was also measuring the new commander. This man, presumably a secondary captain, was taller and not so solid as Captain Lem Gerstner. But his stance hinted at a different kind of strength, and possibly at the kind of aggression that always wanted to move forward.

Daamon hoped this impression was accurate. And that both of them—all of them—were facing the same direction, toward the same enemies. He was bitterly aware that they had lost their best hope of communication, and desperately glad Taya was on that other bridge even though at the same time he hated to see her there.

He said, sticking to urgent business, "Taya, we can follow that uut ship. It's heading insystem, either toward a planet or a station or a near-in slide, but wherever it's going, we've got a trail of drones after it. We've got them powered down low and they're using fingerwidth signals, so if the gods love us, we can follow that ship and not be seen ourselves. But is there any *point* to following it? What are the uut going to do with our people, and what can we do to stop them?" He paused, and then asked, looking not at his sister but at the other commander, "If *Nkaastu* goes after that ship, are our cousins willing to come with us? Can you ask them that?" He added, even though he knew exactly how Kuotaan would hear it, "Can you tell them we'd take their help in this as evidence they'd make good allies?"

Beside him, Kuotaan rumbled, almost too deep for uman ears to hear. He felt the vibration of it in his bones and teeth. Ouch, yes, he was becoming fairly certain he had a couple of cracked ribs. He didn't let his expression change, but he couldn't help but tighten his grip on his cane and her lower arm. Her rumble cut off as she realized she had hurt him.

Taya was wide eyed and nervous, but she turned to the new commander on that ship and spoke carefully in cant. Daamon understood a word here and there, not enough to guess whether she might manage to make the other commander understand him. The man listened to her, but he spoke not to Taya, but to the man beside her. There was a rapid back-and-forth involving several men and two women. Daamon couldn't follow this at all. Taya seemed to catch some of it; she broke in, her voice rising passionately.

Daamon said to Saraa, "Let's set a course after the uut greatship."

"Sure," agreed Saraa. "Hold it ready or actually move? If we move, that'll get a response from our relatives over there, I expect." Her sideways look was pointed: *Do we really* want *to force our cousins into a response?*

"Yes, let's just see what they do. Move gently until we're clear of the cousins' ship, then pick up a little more accel. We'll see if they follow or sit right here or just what they do. If they don't follow, we can reassess."

"Unless they fire on us to stop us provoking that huge uut ship," Saraa suggested pessimistically, but she laid in the course.

Daamon felt reasonably confident the other commander wouldn't do that. He might range them, which would be a warning. Which Daamon would then have to decide whether to obey or disregard. Or he might fire a warning shot, which Daamon would ... almost certainly have to obey. That would tell them all a lot about these cousins and the sort of *alliance* they might want. He set his jaw and studied the other commander. Saraa was right: they were almost certain to see *some* kind of response.

"All right, we're moving," Saraa said laconically. She glanced at Genru, who was working with Suumat to lay in the sorts of alternate courses they might want in a hurry—a course for either the nearer or farther wayout slide, though they would surely not want the near one, forsaken gods knew how many uut ships might be directly on the other side of that slide by this time. But Saraa stayed on the course they actually wanted, straight in toward the system primary, right after the giant uut ship. She had actually handed that course over to Tsumon, resting her own hands lightly on the enamels, ready for the fast, violent, instinctive moves of battle navigation. Just as Paaol hovered over the console he shared with Aanhk, all his attention on the cousins' ship. Just in case.

Daamon didn't watch any of them. He kept his eyes on the other commander.

He knew exactly when the man realized *Nkaastu* was moving. One of the others spoke, a man with light coloring and long bones. His words were short and sharp, his tone accusing. The commander glanced at this man and then turned back to stare straight across all the space between them straight into Daamon's face. He rapped out a short phrase.

"What is?" Taya asked, apparently translating this demand. Then she smiled suddenly and added, sounding a lot more like herself, "Oh, good idea, big brother! They'll *have* to help if you go first, or die of very shame for letting *Nkaastu* go alone to face their enemies."

"I don't think you should put it quite that way," Daamon warned her. "And it may not work. They might even shoot at us."

"They won't shoot at you! This will work!" Taya promised him, meaning she would *make* it work, and Daamon really thought she might, because his sister turned immediately to the other commander, stepped close to him, laid a hand on his arm, and looked appealingly up into his face. "Commander Kennon, we all go," she said to him. "We all go, us, you. Captain Lem Gerstner. We go get."

Daamon actually understood all those small words. Taya's pronunciation had improved amazingly even in this short time; to Daamon she sounded almost exactly like one of the cousins.

The commander frowned down at her. He touched a finger to the back of her hand and made a short gesture, clearly forbidding. Taya took her hand quickly off his arm. She tucked her hands behind her back, ducking her head but not retreating. "We go get," she told him again. "*Daamon* go get Captain Lem Gerstner. *You* go get?"

There was a stark silence. Everyone had heard that. Everyone had to have understood Taya's question. Daamon leaned forward, helpless to snatch his sister out of the way if that foreign commander turned out to have a temper.

But though his frown deepened, the commander only transferred his forbidding look to Daamon. "You," he said, and something unrecognizable and filled with sibilants.

Daamon tipped his chin down, though he doubted the other man would know he meant he did not understand. But if they knew their captain was dead, Daamon thought, surely this man would have found a way to say so. But it couldn't be true. If the uut had wanted to kill everyone right away, why take prisoners at all?

He said carefully, "Commander Kennon." Probably he had the pronunciation all wrong, but he tried. He wished he knew how to say *please*. As far as he knew, cant included no such word. He did not know what to say, but met the other man's hard gaze and said very quietly, "Saraa ... double our accel."

Alone, *Nkaastu* had no chance against that giant uut ship. Daamon could try to be devious and clever, but he knew, realistically, they had no chance. The idea of someone from *Nkaastu* somehow sneaking aboard that ship and finding Kaamharaa was even more ludicrous, if possible, than the idea of throwing *Nkaastu* into battle against it.

If they didn't catch up to that ship soon, if they couldn't stop it or get Kaamharaa off it somehow, it was probably going to go through some near-star slide. He wouldn't be able to go after it. Kuotaan would never permit it. She would decide instead to retreat back toward turun space so that she could make a full report to Siiv u Kaoluun, to the Aanuku matriarchs and to the Suund, in that order. And she would be right to make that decision. Daamon would not be able to argue against it. Even if Commander Kennon agreed to help, Daamon was going to have to hand this big a decision over to Kuotaan. He could not possibly argue that *Nkaastu* was caught up at this moment in the heat of battle.

But if Commander Kennon agreed to set his own ship alongside *Nkaastu*, Daamon would at least be able to argue that they should risk going ahead for the present—at least until the uut actually did go through another slide.

He said quietly, "Saraa, double our accel again."

Saraa obeyed this order without a word; without, this time, even the flicker of a glance. Bold by nature, Saraa u Aanuku. Mothered by the north wind. Daamon did not look at her. He kept his gaze steady on the other commander's face.

On the other ship, someone murmured. Commander Kennon glanced that way. Then he met Daamon's eyes again and smiled. It was a tight, grim smile, but not without humor. "Daamon sepu Kaamharaa," he said, with quite creditable pronunciation. "We go get." He tapped his console and the cousins' sleek razor-edged ship began to move, matching Nkaastu's acceleration, on a parallel course.

Daamon let his breath out. He bowed his head to the other man, a careful, deliberate gesture. Then he said, "Let the feed go. Double our accel again. Let me know if the other ship doesn't match us." Then, at last, he turned to Kuotaan.

"Tsaa Kuotaan, Captain," he said formally. "We are very far out in this system. Most likely we'll take a long time to arrive at the uut ship's destination, whatever that may be. We might choose to approach that ship before they arrive at that destination, but even this possibility surely need not concern us immediately. Our cousins do not seem inclined to fire upon us, nor yet to abandon us. Although the universe is unpredictable, I foresee a period during which the chance of battle is low. Will you resume command?"

Kuotaan inclined her head. "Nda Daamon, we will. Tuutka, we will consult." She raised her voice. "Battlecrew, rotate off. Main crew, please resume your stations. Tsumon, take command. Nda Daamon, we see you are injured. Do you require immediate care?"

"Bruises," Daamon promised her. "I'm fine, Tsaa Kuotaan. I know we have to talk."

"Indeed. We are aware you must be weary, yet we would be pleased to consult, if you are able to accommodate us." She tipped a hand toward the rear of the bridge and the entrance to the Aanuku contemplation garden.

Daamon followed her, trying not to wince in anticipation of the coming argument.

***

Kuotaan, like any competent, experienced nturun, never started an argument by arguing. She made tsuaeh instead, for herself and Daamon and for Tuutka, who as secondary captain would always participate in every important decision.

Nturun never liked to make fast decisions and never liked to make decisions alone; hence the nturun plural and the slow ritual of making tsuaeh. The breeze riffled the soft foliage of the timhk that concealed the bulkheads, filling the space with a comforting susurrus. The humid air was fragrant with the blooms of the nsann set around the low table, until a tired uman could almost believe he was actually in a real garden back on Gaatuu.

Kuotaan concentrated on the tsuaeh. She ground the dried leaves and the bark and the spices, each separately; heated the water; made and filtered the first infusion and the second, and then combined both with a little heated wine before adding the sweetening. All her movements were smooth and unhurried.

Daamon lowered himself, with some difficulty, onto a broad, flat, uman-sized cushion, trying to find a position that didn't hurt before he set aside his cane. He leaned an elbow on the table, feeling the muscles in his shoulders and back slowly begin to unknot. When Kuotaan set the pot and the cups down on the low table of carved and polished wood, Daamon was able to lift the pot and pour for them all with something like equanimity, even though he felt the weight of the pot all through his back and side. It hurt, but not too much. Maybe those ribs were not actually cracked. He managed to set down the pot with no more than a quiet tap of porcelain against wood, and after that picking up even a big turun-sized cup presented only a minor challenge.

Daamon held his cup in one hand, finding his ribs hurt a little less if he kept his other arm pressed against his side. He breathed in the comforting steam for a moment before sipping. Then he tipped his head back to meet Kuotaan's one golden eye.

She set her cup aside. "Nda Daamon. Your audacity is an asset to *Nkaastu* and to Aanuku, and a credit to Kaamharaa. These are most unusual and unsettled circumstances. We have sent a drone back through the slide to Aam. We will send another, and whenever some moment brings an event of note, another." She paused and then added wryly, "If we continue on your suggested course, Nda Daamon, we fear our supply may run short."

This, despite her tone, was a joke. *Nkaastu* crewpersons were perfectly capable of making more drones. Daamon tipped his chin up.

"Definitely audacious to pursue that ship," mused Tuutka. The variant of the word she used was not precisely complimentary. Ordinarily Daamon got along with her very well, but it was her job to slow Kuotaan down and help her think through important decisions, especially decisions with broad implications for the Aanuku matriline. Every decision right now had broad implications for everyone; Daamon certainly couldn't argue otherwise.

"If we follow that ship and we are discovered, *Nkaastu* will probably be destroyed," Daamon admitted. "If we follow and come up on that ship's position and we are not discovered, I don't know what we'll do. In either case, I don't know what our cousins may be inclined to do, or what they might be able to achieve. But if we follow, perhaps we may learn things that will be useful to Aanuku and to the whole of the Ka' Taand."

Kuotaan sipped tsuaeh. After a time, she observed, "We have already learned a great deal."

Daamon gestured agreement. But he said, "We have no idea what the uut look like and less idea what can possibly motivate them to behave with such violent hostility. Acquisitiveness, fear, anger ... philosophy, religion ... who knows? Perhaps, even if we fail to recover Kaamharaa, we may find some relevant information. And," he added deliberately, "we will certainly learn something useful about our cousins, as we observe their response to any attempt we put forward. We might learn many useful things about them, about their people, even if the attempt is unsuccessful. Further, gaining a firm alliance with our cousins will give us access to any knowledge *they* may have regarding the uut. Surely they would freely share such knowledge regarding a common enemy."

Kuotaan lifted her cup again, sipping tsuaeh by way of declining the argument. Not a good sign. That was a tactic nturun used when they did not agree or meant to refuse one's request, but wished to avoid confrontation. Kuotaan would never have abandoned a female of her own matriline. Pointless to blame her for considering abandoning a male. Kaamharaa was important to Aanuku ... but only since uman people had woven together the broad Ka' Taand had nturun begun to frame their relationships with uturun differently.

Daamon said, keeping his voice steady, "It's true that losing Kaamharaa will break my sepu family. It's true that would distress me. But that's not why I think we should go after him. We've seen uut as uncountable as stars in the sky, very little removed from familiar space. This will alarm everyone. Debate is probably taking place within the Suund already. Who knows what will be decided? Perhaps the Suund, always cautious, will choose to abandon Aam." The Suund, the primary deliberative body of the whole Ka' Taand, was infamously slow to come to any decision about anything, but even more infamously unwilling to take risks.

Daamon went on. "That would be difficult for the Aanuku matriline, with settlements nearing completion on Aam and multiple matriarchs established at Ta' Aam. Worse, perhaps the decision will be made to abandon Hanaa. Should that happen, no degree of diligence will enable Aanuku nor her sister matrilines nor her allies, acting independently, to prepare such defenses as would seem advisable against such uut numbers and ships as we have seen. Someone less cautious might wish to gain instead an alliance with powerful uman cousins who can defend this side of familiar space. Matriarchs are always more likely to agree to a broader alliance if individuals of those families first demonstrate the efficacy of that alliance."

Tuutka poured more tsuaeh. This time, that was not a bad sign. She was politically astute, and if she disagreed, she would say so.

Daamon opened one hand. "If we assist in recovering our cousin's captain, or even cooperate in an effort to do so, they may well be inclined to favor alliance with Aanuku. Furthermore, should we manage, through the beneficence of the beloved gods, to recover Kaamharaa, one can hardly help but observe that, should the Suund hesitate, an uturun of unassailable reputation might persuade cautious officials to favor alliance of at least one clan with these cousins. Should highly ranked uturun reputationists be persuaded of Aanuku's solid commitment to alliance with sepu Kaamharaa, their assurance on that point might set an avalanche of alliances in motion—whatever the legislators of the Suund may prefer. Should broad alliance with our cousins prove favorable, that would see Aanuku rise throughout the Ka' Taand."

"Tsuumat Kaamharaa would certainly acquire considerable accent to his reputation, should he prove able to elucidate the nature of the uut through his unique experience," Kuotaan mused. "It's certainly true that alliances spreading out through uturun and uman families would stabilize a broader base of support for Aanuku. We should certainly find it possible, even inevitable, to establish beneficial and profitable trade for our matriline and our allied matrilines. This is, we acknowledge, greatly to be desired. Yet this is not an uman romance-adventure. The risk you propose is not inconsiderable. If we were *Sepuuk* ... but we are not Tnakaa u Kaoluun and her secondary captains, and though we have every confidence in the ability of our battlecommander and battlecrew, you are not Siiv u Kaoluun sep' Upuonnu."

Tuutka made a slight gesture of satisfaction, meaning that she had intended to say much the same.

"Indeed," Daamon agreed. "All this is true." It certainly was. He didn't permit himself to pause, but continued at once. "It's true we haven't the experience of *Sepuuk's* people. But we do have experience of our own. We don't—we can't—expect to engage in pitched battle. Subtlety rather than direct aggression seems much the wiser course. But many potential advantages accrue to moving forward rather than retreating." He hesitated, putting his thoughts in order.

Then he went on. "I do want very much to regain Kaamharaa on behalf of my sepu family. Nevertheless, I hope no one believes I would hazard *Nkaastu* merely on that consideration, nor that I would mistake myself for the protagonist of a romance-adventure. Nor do I mistake the estimable captains and main crew of *Nkaastu* for the protagonists of a finance-adventure. Nevertheless, I am contemplating the loss that will accrue to the forward-thinking and astute matriline of Aanuku should the political asset represented by Tsuumat Kaamharaa be lost—as I'm sure you must be as well, Tsaa Kuotaan, Tsaaku Tuutka." He paused.

Then he added, "Let me remark as well that we need not commit now to great risk. We only need to follow that uut ship at the farthest reasonable distance." That was actually truly reassuring to consider. He added, which was also reassuring, in a way, "If we lose track of that ship, our further decisions will certainly be simplified. If we don't, our eventual decisions may become more complex, but we don't need to make those decisions now. Kha Taya will learn to talk to our cousins and we'll be able to consult more easily. If we are able to work together, we would all find that useful to know, surely."

Kuotaan tipped her chin up. "We must commend your conscientiousness toward *Nkaastu* in assigning your close-sister to such hazardous duty."

Daamon bowed slightly—his ribs felt that gesture, especially when he straightened. He ignored the pain. "It's not all that hazardous." He hoped this was true. "Whether they meant to try to recover their captain or otherwise, I think it's clear they badly need our help. At the moment, they undoubtedly want an alliance even more than we do, if not to recover their captain, then to rescue their many companions in the other system. They surely hope to ask someone for help against the uut. As we are here, they will ask us. Should a broader alliance eventually be contemplated and established, a matriline that acted decisively in such a moment would surely be preferred to all others. An entire *epic* of finance-adventures would probably be composed in honor of a matriline whose decisive action in the face of unknown but considerable risk resulted in a close, unique, and potentially exceedingly beneficial alliance with a previously unknown but powerful polity. One can hardly imagine the rising prosperity such an alliance might offer Aanuku and the allies of Aanuku."

A long pause. That was a potent argument, to nturun. Alliances were the social network upon which matrilines rose and fell. Prosperity, and the proven judgment that brought prosperity, was the essential coinage of alliance. Aanuku had always been bold, for a matriline. If they hadn't been, they would hardly have established settlements at an edge-world such as Aam.

Tuutka set her cup down and said, "Strangers are not as trustworthy as kin," which was so basic it wasn't even an aphorism. But she added, "Therefore, when considering alliance with strangers, it's better to learn quickly whether they have the courage and decisiveness and loyalty desirable in allies."

Kuotaan considered this. She considered for what seemed a long time, but probably was no more than a tenth-chime. Finally she set her cup down and turned it through four deliberate quarter turns, signaling that she had reached a decision. "Very well. We shall follow that uut ship and pray the beloved gods grant us adequate time for scrupulous consideration of the quality of these presumptive allies and of our options."

Daamon bowed to show he had heard all this and accepted it. His ribs had stiffened even more. He couldn't bow as deeply as he ought, but managed at least something of the proper form.

"In the time available, *you* should surely go and rest," Kuotaan told him in a far less formal tone. "Do not insist to us that these are merely bruises. Plainly you are hurt. Must we *order* you to have your injuries properly seen to?"

"That won't be necessary," Daamon promised her.

"Then, go." Kuotaan reached across the table to assist Daamon to his feet. "We shall pursue the uut ship with all possible caution and summon you when the need appears more immediate. All battlecrew must take this chance to rest. The primary crew may rotate according to our ordinary schedule." She kindly did not say anything about human fragility compared to turun sturdiness, though she was undoubtedly thinking it. She merely added, "Though all the battlecrew should rest, we will wish a sensible uman eye on the bridge. Send one of your uman sep' kin to us. Mattu, perhaps. Someone who will not be too frightened to speak to these cousins of yours if they wish to speak to us."

Daamon bowed slightly, acknowledging this. That was a good notion. And was he surprised Kuotaan would know exactly which uman among those of Kaamharaa's household would be steadiest under pressure and which spoke a little cant? He was not. He bowed a final time, shallowly, indicating his respect without stressing his ribs too badly.

Kuotaan did not rise, of course; the captain had no such obligation and getting up and down was a considerable business for even the smallest nturun. But Tuutka worked her way up and declared, "We shall assist you to Medical, Nda Daamon."

"No, no, I'm perfectly capable, I promise you," Daamon assured her. He could manage. He was determined to. Even in Medical he expected to keep one ear tuned to *Nkaastu's* whistles, listening for any alarm Mattu might sound from the bridge. He was glad Kuotaan had thought of bringing more uman people onto the bridge. Mattu was a good choice. He would have watched all the recordings, and he had the quick, keen judgment that made uman crew better for unpredictable battle situations. ... Tuutka was not moving out of his way. She stood four square, solidly in his way, regarding Daamon with the exasperated affection of a turun faced with unreasonable, wrongheaded uman demands for independence. She would step back if he claimed autonomy. But she would be offended. And she would be right.

Daamon sighed. "Very well. Thank you, Tsaaku Tuutka, I would appreciate your assistance."

Rumbling in approval, Tuutka stepped forward and picked him up, carefully, mindful of his bruises. She had plainly been watching closely enough that she had a very good idea where the worst of those bruises were.

Daamon allowed himself to relax against her muscled chest. Tuutka wasn't Kaamharaa. But she was kind, and careful, and he was glad after all to let go of immediate responsibility and rest. At least he'd had a chance to see Taya, to be relatively confident his sister was all right among the cousins.

He tried not to think of Kaamharaa at all.

8

Gerstner came to himself in darkness and pain and confusion. His eyelids were gummy and stuck together; when he got his eyes open at last, he squeezed them shut again immediately, swallowing, because glaring ribbons of light plunged down through the dark and spun upward again, some actinic blue-white and some flaring yellow and all of them painfully bright, moving according to no pattern he could understand. Then the lights flicked out, and the hot, close darkness pressed in on him again. A darkness that *breathed*. Slow, heavy, rhythmic ... his own breaths came shorter than that, faster.

His head pounded, his eyes stung and watered. The streamers of light returned, swooped sickeningly through the darkness, one and another and a third. His stomach heaved, and he swallowed convulsively. His mouth tasted metallic, bitter, like bile and chalk and copper. His throat hurt. The air tasted terrifyingly wrong, tainted in a way that made him fear fire or chemical leaks. He was lying on his back. He tried to sit up, but something was wrong with his left arm and shoulder, stabbing pain that made him gasp. Worse, something held him in place, a bar across his chest, rounded, as thick as his thigh, made of something like soft leather rather than metal or composite. He tried to push against that with his good arm and the bar shifted, but when he tried to sit up, his left arm failed and he fell back, clenching his teeth. Something important was definitely torn or broken in that shoulder.

Near at hand, *right next to him*, a deep, deep voice spoke. "Kabtaan Lehhm Geherrtner."

Memory crashed back. *Vengeful's* ship's bay, the huge alien centaur, the newfound human people, the Enemy mothership tearing *Vengeful* open. Tentacles *dragging* at him, pulling him into the saucer. Convulsing, Gerstner jerked up. The bar—good Christ, it was the alien's *arm*—shifted to let him up, but a different kind of restraint caught at his legs. He fell sideways, tried to catch himself, and abruptly lost his balance completely. For a moment he seemed to swing dizzily over a vast and endless dark. And was caught before he could fall, a massive hand and arm holding him in place with limitless strength. He clung to the alien, which suddenly seemed the only solid support in the darkness, breathing hard, waiting for the dizziness to pass. He was breathing too fast, his vision going, streamers and specks and dots scattering in front of his eyes. He squeezed them shut, managed to slow his breathing.

"Calm," rumbled a deep, deep voice. It said it again and then once more, drawing out the word, slurring the vowels, lengthening the consonants: "Calm. Calm."

By the third repetition, Gerstner could make out the word. He certainly recognized that deep slow voice, the way it lingered over every element of the word. The massive troll-centaur had been seized along with him ... of course it had. The alien had tried to get clear, tried to get its own human companions clear, it had actually managed that, or he thought it had succeeded at that part. It had tried to get *him* clear, too. It had torn at the tentacles that clung to him. Its effort had failed. But he was almost sure it had tried. Its arm across his chest seemed possibly meant as support or protection rather than restraint.

Trapped in the dark, on an Enemy ship, with a huge troll-centaur alien that sort of spoke English and might or might not be friendly. Gerstner almost wanted to laugh, it was so far beyond ludicrous. He didn't allow himself to make a sound. He held still, not fighting the centaur's powerful hold. *Calm* could mean a couple of different things, and God knew what it meant to the centaur, or why it thought *calm* was so important. Opening his eyes once more, he turned his head cautiously, looking around. He could make out almost nothing with any certainty; the illumination here was too strange, too random, briefly far too bright and then far too dim.

They had to be on the mothership. Or maybe still aboard the Enemy saucer. Not much hope to grab onto, either way. *Vengeful* ... probably *Vengeful* was all right, at least. A mothership that did a snatch-and-grab usually took whoever and whatever it could seize and took them ... somewhere. For some purpose.

He was going to personally find out all about that. A terrible sinking fear threatened to swamp everything resembling rational thought. Gerstner fought it back, clenched his jaw, and opened his eyes again. He tried, carefully, to sit up.

The centaur gentled its hold, but it didn't let him go. It patted his shoulder with another hand, astonishingly like a human hand, same basic five-finger design—four and a thumb. But huge, with thick, broad digits; thick even in proportion to the size of that hand, with heavy black nails. Gerstner couldn't quite keep from flinching when it touched him, though there was nothing at all threatening in that gesture.

He was starting to better make out his surroundings, almost starting to get used to the swooping ribbons of light and the sickening waves of darkness that made him lose his balance ... the centaur's hold tightened, and he winced, trying to keep from struggling.

Then he realized he'd had it wrong. The gravitics here, God, something was going on with the gravitics. *Down* was sometimes *sideways* and he was so out of it, he hadn't even realized that. If the centaur had let him go just now, he'd have fallen ... somewhere. Away. He couldn't see well enough in this strange intermittent illumination to figure out how far, or what he might have landed on, or in, or ... among.

Better not to think about the possibilities. Bracing himself against Kaamharaa's massive arm, he waited for the pounding dizziness to pass. The arm he held was bigger around than his own thigh.

"Good," rumbled the centaur. "Good."

Gerstner stared back at it. Its face was no more than a couple of feet from his own. He could make it out better now, when the light was momentarily in the right place. It was better when he could see it, ugly as it was. Tusks as long as his hand jutted up from a powerful jaw. It could probably bite a man's face right off.

It had given him no reason at all to think it might do anything of the kind. He couldn't read its expression, but it was trying to help. He was almost sure of that much. He was embarrassed to have even thought about its tusks. "Friends?" he asked it, keeping his voice low. "Friends? Do you know that word?"

The centaur stared at him, utterly unhuman. "Kabtaan Lehm Gerrstter," it said. "Rennd." Its voice was so deep and slurred all the words; it had trouble with some of the consonants and all of the vowels. But if he concentrated, he could understand it. As long as he already had a pretty good idea of what it was trying to say. He guessed maybe *f* sounds were impossible for it, but otherwise that wasn't bad.

He thought for a second, and then tried, "Kamhara."

The alien hummed, a soft sound deep in its chest. "Kaamharaa," it said. "Yes."

"Kaamharaa," Gerstner agreed, stretching out the vowels. He laid his good hand on his chest and said seriously, "Under the circumstances, I think you can call me Gerstner. Gerstner," he repeated more slowly, careful on the *s* and the *t*. "Or whatever you can manage is fine." He pushed again against its restraining arm, though wary of gravitic fluctuations. This time the alien eased its hold. Gripping its forearm, he managed to sit up, not quite suppressing a grunt at the various pains that all got suddenly worse.

Bracing himself against that massive arm, he waited for the pounding dizziness to pass.

Kaamharaa had turned his whole upper body, shifting what seemed like a lot of arms to help Gerstner brace himself upright. The arm he gripped *was* bigger around than his own thigh. Attached to a torso twice as broad as a big man's torso, and that was the smaller part of the centauroid body. Damn, he just could not get used to the alien's sheer *massiveness.*

The alien wasn't actually using the lower arm on the far side, Gerstner realized. That arm was cradled close to the centaur's body. So it was hurt, too. Its front legs looked all right. Powerful, thick, ending in feet that seemed tipped with thick claws rather than hooves ... probably the lab people would have some long involved explanation for why neither term was accurate. Gerstner didn't care. He cared a lot more about what was going on with Kaamharaa's rear legs. Brilliant streamers spun past, not quite as disorienting as he got used to this insane lighting system. He found it worked best to look quickly after his eyes had adjusted to a flare of light, then consciously wait for the next whirling band of light to pass over and around them so he could look again.

He was almost sure the alien's rear legs were held by shining metal bands. He was definitely certain that his own legs were wound about with metal. He could see those bands now, wrapped around his legs, a pair of thin metallic strips just above his ankles and another pair midway up his shins. He explored the higher bands with his fingertips. Metal or some composite, not too sharp-edged, not too thick, a little flex in it.

The gravity spun around them, shifting abruptly one way and then another, the changes coming fast and hard, crushingly hard, a whole lot harder than one gee. Gerstner held tightly to Kaamharaa's arms. The alien bowed its body forward and braced both of them against the violence of the shifting gravity. Not that either of them could *actually* fall, not bound as they were, but the gravity was sometimes strong enough, the changes abrupt enough, that Gerstner feared without Kaamharaa's support, his bones might very well snap against the metal bands.

That would be just delightful: trapped in the disorienting light-and-dark of an Enemy saucer with *two broken legs*. Torn ligaments in a shoulder were nothing. Amazing what you could be grateful for. Certainly you could be grateful that if you had to be trapped aboard an Enemy ship, a friendly giant alien centaur was trapped with you.

Gerstner was distantly amused at how fast he'd gone from his first instinctive recoil from the monster in the dark to trusting that the alien was on his side. He was less amused to realize how much stress Kaamharaa's body must be taking, every time the gravity cut in and out and around like that. It couldn't be easy, bracing such massive weight against the angled walls here. Now that he was sitting up, he could see—hell, he could practically *feel*—the centaur's muscles ripple and clench all through its back and shoulders and legs and ... its other back, and other shoulders. Centauroid anatomy needed more terms.

Somewhere not too far away, something trilled like a bird, a liquid up-and-down warble that for one disorienting second took Gerstner right back to Pallas Athene, the concourses and parks where canaries and parakeets and Terabithian tikitiki nested. Here, that sound was utterly out of place—and it sounded different anyway. There was an oddly metallic sound to it ... not exactly metallic. A bit like glass chimes, or ... not exactly like that either. It sounded like a cross between a lot of birds and a harpsichord with some windchimes thrown in, and it sounded ... Gerstner was almost sure it sounded like it was coming closer. "Calm," the alien rumbled. It wrapped its powerful arm around his chest. This time, Gerstner knew better than to object. He tightened his own grip on the powerful wrist, and the gravity shifted again, abruptly and violently. It felt very much as though they spun, dizzily, in a complete circle, though they weren't moving at all. Then the gravity settled, possibly not quite at the same angle it had held previously. Gerstner swallowed against nausea and listened. Nothing, now. But whatever had made that eerie birdsong-and-glass-chimes sound was still out there. Somewhere. In the dark.

If they both lived through this, they would probably share a set of unique nightmares. If giant alien centaurs had nightmares.

This was definitely not a tenable situation. Gerstner pushed lightly against the alien's arm. It loosened its grip—*he* loosened *his* grip, time to stop thinking *alien, it,* and start thinking *person, friend*. Gerstner didn't know whether Kaamharaa was male, but his eye wanted to read those ugly features that way. Or more that way than as female. He didn't actually care, but it was definitely time to pick a pronoun that wasn't *it*. What the hell was the name of the species? He'd heard it. Turun, right, something like that. Time to start thinking *turun* instead of *weird alien centaur*.

Kaamharaa had eased off enough for Gerstner to sit up again. He rubbed his face, his mouth. His lips stung a little, and his eyes. Something in the air? Not good, but nothing he could do about it.

Perceived gravity shifted, and shifted back. Not as violently this time. Gerstner waited out the disorienting changes, setting his teeth against nausea. Then, bending carefully at the waist, ignoring protesting muscles and abused ligaments, Gerstner ran his good hand over the metal bands that held his legs. Tight. He could barely get a finger between the band and his uniform trousers. There was a little more room where the loops entered the floor, or wall or whatever it would turn out to be when the gravity finally settled down. If it settled down. Surely the Enemy would choose one basic *down* eventually.

Or maybe not. No way to guess.

He pushed at the band around his right shin with the tips of his fingers, pulled lightly—yes, the band gave just a little. The band was maybe an inch wide, but not very thick. He couldn't tell about the loops around his ankles. He thought those might be narrower. That little bit of flex ... not enough to suggest human strength could break or bend the metal. On the other hand, a giant alien centaur was right here. Turun, whatever, but whatever he called it—him—Gerstner couldn't begin to estimate how much stronger Kaamharaa was than a person, but *enormously stronger* seemed like a safe bet. But there was no way the alien could get one of his thick fingers through that gap.

While he thought about how to *use* that strength, he asked, speaking clearly and slowly, "Is this the saucer? Or are we on the mothership? Mothership?"

He had not really expected to be understood, but Kaamharaa rumbled for a moment and then answered, "Mother. Mother. Not. Mother not." He went on for several incomprehensible rolling words or phrases, hell, maybe he was reciting poetry. Probably an epic about heroes who died tragic deaths far from home.

Gerstner stared at the huge, ugly face so close to his own. He wished he thought that if he asked the turun, *How do you know? What does the Enemy want with prisoners? What's going to happen to us?* Kaamharaa would actually answer, in detail, pointing out bulleted items on a damn screen presentation.

Probably it had never lost consciousness. It was so damn big, it would probably take a full company of marines half an hour to knock it out.

Him. Not 'it.' *Him*. Kaamharaa.

Giving up for the moment on freeing his own legs, Gerstner twisted around and tried to get a look at Kaamharaa's bonds. He couldn't quite touch even the closest, but the arrangement looked similar: loops of metal around the centauroid legs below what ought to be the knee but probably did not quite correspond to the human joint; more loops around the leg just above the feet. Hooves. Claws. Whatever. The metal looked a lot more fragile around such massive limbs.

Who the hell bound prisoners with thin loops of metal around their legs before subjecting them to mad changes in gravity? If it was deliberate cruelty, it was a strange way to be cruel. If it wasn't meant to be cruel, it was an even stranger way to handle prisoners. Gerstner didn't want to imagine what would happen when Kaamharaa got too tired to brace himself against violent changes in gravity. If an enormous centauroid type of creature took a lot of damage to his hind legs, he would probably be in very serious trouble. Possibly more than a human.

Gravity slammed one way and then the other. Kaamharaa tightened his grip, and Gerstner grunted with pain, but unpleasant as they were, the shifts weren't *that* disorienting, not as long as you knew what was happening and trusted your turun buddy to keep you safe. A man could get used to anything. Except these damned ribbons and streamers of light that would not stay *still.*

He ran a speculative fingertip across the metal band around his right leg. He wasn't even carrying a pocketknife. Not that a pocketknife would have helped, probably.

The gravity jolted, and jolted again, harder than before. Gerstner grabbed for Kaamharaa's arm, but it wasn't necessary; the turun had already caught him. The lights whipped through the air faster and more unpredictably than ever, orangish now instead of blue or green.

Then the gravitics grated around in a long disorienting half-circle, flipped at an angle nearly perpendicular to the half-circle curve, and snapped into place with a solidity that was completely different from anything that had happened before, leaving the floor down—or actually at a slant. But mostly down.

Gerstner let out his breath, only then aware he had been holding it. When he took another, the air smelled of ozone and, bewilderingly, of burning sugar. "Well," he said, and coughed, and cleared his throat, and tried to sit up. After a long moment, Kaamharaa's protective grip eased, cautiously. Gerstner was grateful for that caution, but he thought ... he was almost sure that a sense of vibrating motion he hadn't even noticed before had ceased.

"We're there," he said out loud. "Wherever 'there' is." The mothership, maybe. Their saucer had taken its own sweet time about docking, if that were the case. Or else they'd gone through a flashpoint and the saucer was now coasting. Or they'd been in a battle and the Enemy had won, their saucer luckily surviving. If that could be considered lucky.

Whatever was going to happen next, it was probably going to happen soon.

Without another word, he took off his uniform shirt—an unpleasant operation considering his injured shoulder, but he was highly motivated. He threaded the thin edge of a sleeve beneath the metal band around his right shin, pulled the shirt through until he had a good thickness of cloth under the band, twisted the cloth as tight as he could, and handed the ends of his makeshift sling to Kaamharaa. "Pull," he said, gesturing. "Pull."

Kaamharaa braced himself and pulled, slowly and with increasing force.

Gerstner was not at all sure this would work. Worst case, and maybe not all that unlikely, the metal band would deform and crush his leg before the turun realized something had gone wrong. Gerstner was prepared to slap Kaamharaa on the arm fast if he had to, and hope he realized that meant *stop*. Less bad, the shirt would rip, which would leave them no worse off.

But the microfibers in modern uniforms would not burn, would not melt, would not stain, could not be cut, and were very,

very resistant to tearing, so he was not actually surprised when it was the metal that gave, sending Kaamharaa lurching back with an expression that might have indicated surprise. The metal *did* deform before breaking. It would leave bruises. That was fine. Gerstner held out his hands for the shirt and smiled, grimly. "Good," he said. "Let's do that again."

It took less than five minutes to free himself. Getting Kaamharaa free was harder. The bonds were tighter, especially those up near the knee, cutting into the flesh in a way that would be seriously not good for a human; Gerstner hoped the turun's circulatory system was different enough that even bonds as tight as that hadn't caused dire damage. The leg below the tight band seemed as warm as above. Hopefully that was a good sign.

The bonds just above the feet were not as tight, but though Gerstner could get the shirt under those metal bands, Kaamharaa could not reach down far enough to take hold of the cloth. Gerstner considered this for about one second, grimaced, pulled his shirt back on and took off his trousers. How amusing it would be to face the Enemy without trousers. Well, if this worked fast enough, he'd get them back on in just a few minutes. A little baggier, judging by the shirt. If he got a chance, unlikely as that might be, he'd have to let the manufacturer know that enough pressure on the fibers would deform the cloth. He bet they'd never tested the uniforms they produced quite the way he was testing his.

Damn tight fit, getting one trouser leg stuffed through the band around Kaamharaa's left rear foot. He was never going to get anything this size through the higher bands ... worry about that later.

The legs of the trousers were just long enough for Kaamharaa to take hold of the cloth, if he bent his upper body enough. The way the alien bared his teeth probably meant this hurt. He certainly had a damn heavy, powerful jaw. Gerstner could not, at this point, manage to be afraid of him, even with those tusks.

Kaamharaa straightened his body with a grunting effort, and the band broke even faster than Gerstner's bonds. After that the second band, and after *that*, Gerstner found that yes, indeed, the upper bands were too tight to get anything under them. If he'd had a pocketknife, he'd have jammed cloth under the metal with that and never mind if it hurt the alien, but he couldn't manage it just with his fingers, even when he tried hard enough to risk jamming his knuckles.

Somewhere not far away, birds trilled. Birds and harpsicords and windchimes, the sounds delicate and lovely and infinitely creepy. Gerstner jerked upright, and Kaamharaa flexed the lowest joints of his hind legs, set his broad feet—hooves, whatever—against the floor, heaved his whole body around, and slammed upward with a powerful surge of muscle and rage that sent Gerstner stumbling back.

The remaining bands broke, with God knew what kind of damage to Kaamharaa's legs. But the giant turun was up, all the way up, and seemed likely to stay that way. *God*, he was big. His head was at least five feet above Gerstner's. He swiveled his head, his whole upper body—his teeth were bared, those tusks flashed in the dizzying light—he was holding his injured arm tucked close to his body, but despite that he looked just about as unstoppable as an armored crew carrier. Gerstner almost pitied any Enemy who now appeared. Or not really.

He grabbed for his trousers, but before he could wrestle them on, Kaamharaa snatched him up off the floor, amazingly fast for such an immense creature, whirled around, and thudded into a powerful run, leaving the warbling bird calls and harpsichords behind.

Gerstner could hardly see through the swooping lights and whirling shadows, definitely not well enough to dash recklessly through this unknown place, not even if *down* were going to stay down, and they really had no guarantee about that, either. He clung to Kaamharaa's upper torso, tucked his head against the massive chest, and tried to trust that the alien was not going to smash headlong into anything unyielding.

Kaamharaa's gait slowed, and slowed again. Then he stopped completely, gathering himself up, settling his weight into his hindquarters as though he might rear up. He turned about in a circle instead, rumbling in his chest, metal clanging and booming under the blunt hoof-like claws of his feet. Then he swung Gerstner down to the deck.

At first Gerstner could make sense of nothing he saw. He had to hold onto Kaamharaa's lower arm to keep his balance in the confusion of light and shadow; he wasn't even certain that the gravity wasn't shifting again. But no, he could feel the stillness underfoot; the ship was still quiet. He blinked and blinked again, trying to force his vision to adjust—then gritted his teeth, shut his eyes entirely, and pulled on his trousers to get that taken care of while he let his vision adjust, or tried to get his brain to adjust, or whatever.

Then he steadied himself against Kaamharaa's shoulder and looked again.

Now that he had taken a moment to settle his nerves and remember how to cope with the flaring, intermittent light, he saw they had come to a dead end, a place where the deck rose and the ceiling came down and the walls closed in. A huge object bulked to their left: a flattish platform or dais with regular cylindrical shapes lined up along it. A loaded cargo trolley? Empty munitions containers, to be replaced with full? Equipment of some mysterious kind? He saw nothing that looked like connections for power or any kind of input or output, nothing that looked like controls, but who knew. The whole thing, counting the cylinders, was maybe twelve or fifteen feet long and about eight feet tall. Whatever it was, another one just like it stood some distance behind them—light swooped, orangish and then greenish, and Gerstner saw there was a whole line of the things.

A ledge above Gerstner's head, no more than two feet wide, its edge shining and reflective, ran forward the way they had been going, followed the curve of the nearest wall up and around and then went straight through a door or hole or tunnel that pierced the wall they'd run into.

The ledge and doorway presented no problem at all for a reasonably agile man. But there was no conceivable way a creature the size of Kaamharaa could fit through that doorway, even if he could balance on so narrow a ledge, which anybody could see must be impossible.

Behind them, trilling birdsong was clearly audible.

9

Eleven chimes after collapsing onto the far too empty sleeping platform in Kaamharaa's quarters, Daamon drifted back to awareness. He levered himself carefully to a sitting position, sorting out recent memory. His back ached, his ribs, but no longer badly. His leg ached as well, but that was always true and something he was used to ignoring.

Paaol was sprawled across another part of the platform, tangled in the coverlets uman people needed against the chill of the sleeping chamber. No one else was in the chamber, but Daamon could hear quiet voices from elsewhere in the apartment.

Someone, probably Karuu, had taken away his discarded clothing and set out new: dusty green and dusty taupe, an outer robe of muted blues and grayed golds ... colors that evoked the last glimmer of a summer sunset on the savannah. Daamon thought of the stark black the cousins preferred, and of his sister among people of such foreign tastes ... pushed the thought aside. He just had to assume Taya would manage.

Before he went out into the living areas of the household, he paused before the niche to study the mosaic where the beloved gods were invited to rest. His eye automatically searched out patterns in the ever-shifting stones, which at a first glance suggested the eye and long curving jaw of a predator. Hopefully that was just chance or mood; Daamon wasn't particularly gifted with holy perception.

Mattu and Karuu were in the solar, and Nkan, Paaol's mate. The children were not present. Sent away to stay with friends, probably, because it was too upsetting here with Kaamharaa missing. Karuu rose quietly to offer Daamon her seat. She ladled a bowl full of rich nsaa stew, filled with chunks of tender meat and thickened with pounded ndao nuts. Slices of ndao fruit drizzled with perfumed laotk syrup were arranged on a rectangular green plate, squares and crimson triangles of richly savory puaand jelly on a round black one.

Despite everything, Daamon was starving. Gesturing appreciation, he took the offered place, leaned his cane against the table, lowered himself to sit, let his breath out in a long sigh, and tasted the stew. Spicy, the way Taya liked it.

"Taya is well," Karuu told him, always sensitive to the words someone did not quite say. "She has spoken with the bridge crew again since you very sensibly went to bed. She says that she is learning English as fast as possible. She has good teachers, she says."

Daamon nodded. "I thought I saw a predator in the mosaic."

Karuu smiled at him. "*I* saw a ndao."

"Did you? That's much better." The ndao tree suggested the close attention of the beloved gods and good luck to come. Daamon felt himself relaxing a little. Karuu was more sensitive to the gods than anyone else in the household. "Very good. Thank you. Who's on the bridge?"

"Vaeh," Mattu told him. "She'll stay until you're back up there. She says nothing important has happened and you're not to rush."

Daamon nodded. Vaeh, Mattu's daughter and therefore Daamon's near-cousin, was cool-natured, observant, calm in a crisis—a good choice. She'd be as upset about Kaamharaa as the rest of the sepu family, but she'd hold it together. He asked, "What else should I know?"

"The course of the uut ship appears constant," Mattu said. "The cousins' ship parallels our course. The cousins are all very quiet as well."

That sounded much less bad than he might have feared. Daamon nodded again.

"Your side? Your back?" Nkan asked. Paaol's mate, she'd only joined Kaamharaa's sepu family two years ago. She suited Paaol perfectly: calm, impossible to rattle, she loved his enthusiasm and fire. She went on. "I talked to Ngakuu. She said she expects you to have some pain today and more tomorrow, then likely less after that. She sent more painkillers."

Daamon shrugged his shoulders illustratively. "I think I've slept through the worst. Did you have to make Paaol take a sedative?"

Nkan smiled, a swift flash of white teeth in her brown face—u Guuan before she'd joined sepu Kaamharaa, Nkan had the dark coloring and small, delicate features common in uman belonging to the Guuan matriline. "What do you think?"

"I think you're the only one who could have made him drink it without throwing a fit that would've woken the whole ship. Good job. I don't think I need another painkiller, though, so no need to talk me into taking one."

Nkan raised an eyebrow in uman skepticism. "Will you still think so when you've been on your feet a couple of chimes? Ngakuu swears this kind won't dim your thoughts or make you sleepy, and, you know, if you take one now, you won't have to think of it later. You're supposed to take it with food." She held out a tube.

Daamon started to demur, but Nkan raised her eyebrows and he sighed, shrugged, accepted the tube, and shook out an uman-sized tablet. He should have known better; no one could ever talk Nkan out of anything. That was another reason she suited his sep' brother. Daamon chased the tablet with a bite of stew. Then he paused. "Saraa."

"Mm?" Mattu raised an eyebrow.

"I want to shoot ideas at her and see how many she deflects." His brain finally seemed to have started working, and he added, "All the battlecrew. Karuu, will you give them a whistle? I suppose we might wake Paaol, if you think that's all right, Nkan. And all of you; you're certainly welcome to stay. Mattu, may I take over the tank display?"

"Not until you finish your stew," Karuu said firmly.

Daamon stared at her for a moment. Then he said, "Fine. *Mattu*, please give me a summary with *your* tank display." He took another bite.

Three tenth-chimes later, Saraa arrived with, to everyone's surprise, her half-sister main-crew partner Tsumon. The nturun stared around the solar and ducked her head shyly, never having been past the screens of the reception chamber. "Very tasteful," she observed. "Very beautiful and tasteful. We could nearly believe ourselves planetside. These rooms are certainly entirely suitable to a trade negotiator of unimpeachable reputation."

"You sound like you want to have his baby next time you're ready," Karuu observed, not unkindly. She used the nturun singular *you* that was only appropriate when speaking of exactly such matters.

"Perhaps I will. Tsuumat Kaamharaa would be a perfectly reputable choice," Tsumon said without the least embarrassment. "It would only be courteous after I have ventured so far into his territory."

If Tsumon was also using the nturun singular, that meant she really must be willing to consider bearing a child to Kaamharaa, so her presence within Kaamharaa's apartment could not possibly be considered insulting. It was certainly kind of her to speak as though the possibility continued to exist. Daamon said, "I'm sure Kaamharaa would consider your presence here an honor, Kha Tsumon, and I hope he'll eventually tell you so himself. Saraa, look at this display, if you will—both of you, please observe the display." Then he paused. "Where's Paaol? Let's not start twice when once will do."

Paaol came out of the sleeping chamber just at that moment, sleep-tousled and yawning, seeming much younger than his nearly thirty. "Sorry. Nkan's fault! She's the one who fed me that forsaken drink." Nkan punched him lightly on the arm and he pretended to stagger, but also put his arm around her waist and pulled her against him. "Violent woman," he said affectionally. "You all right, Daamon? You were looking kind of rocky after all that mess yesterday."

"I'm fine—" Daamon began.

"Well, better, I guess," Paaol allowed, studying him critically. "I don't expect you'd be much good as a nkaanru partner the next couple days."

That made Daamon smile. Nkaanru had begun as a sport for young uturun, a game that wasn't quite a game. It honed their physical competence before they left their matrilines and set out to build their early reputations. Not every young uturun had to actually fight for a place, of course; not in the modern era. But for an uturun who was not outstandingly intelligent, nkaanru was one of the more common paths to build reputation.

For uman men and a few women, nkaanru was purely a sport; one that for some involved a great deal of dedication and passion. Daamon didn't mind watching tournaments, but he'd never participated in nkaanru and would be a terrible partner for someone like Paaol, who was always more than competent at anything physical.

"I'll do adequately for gentler pursuits, I'm sure," he said. "You awake enough to track the drone data?"

"Absolutely. That uut stop yet? What's it led us into, a nest of ten thousand kin and allies?" Dropping to sit cross-legged on a flat cushion, Paaol pulled Nkan down beside him and looked expectant. Already eager for something to do, preferably something tricky and dangerous: that was Paaol.

"Not quite yet," Daamon told him. "Let me call up the most recent drone data. Karuu tells me nothing important has changed. Yes, here we can see the giant uut ship's course, thus, continuing inward toward the system primary. At their current acceleration ... Saraa, work the math out for me ..." He brightened the display to show the appropriate course, overlaid on what little they knew of this system. Kuotaan or someone had chosen pink to delineate the giant ship. That seemed reasonable, since Disks were red and Blades white.

"Another thirty chimes at least before that ship starts dancing with the star's corona," Saraa said promptly. "Of course it's quite likely to reach a station or a near-star slide long before that. We haven't spotted any rocky planets big enough to help stabilize a slide, nor anything that looks like an inhabited world, but for all we know there's a whole handful of planets our scans haven't painted yet. We entered this system so far out we were practically interstellar. Even now, we're nowhere near the primary's habitable zone."

Leaning back on his cushion, Mattu remarked, "Gods know what that gas giant was doing out that far, but no doubt its presence out there explains the stability, maybe the formation, of slides so far out from the primary. I've written it up—this is actually a very interesting system, architecturally speaking. It has implications for explorers; we might want to start routinely dropping drones much farther out in systems with extremely distant gas giants, find out if they spot slides near those giants."

Daamon nodded. "More to the point, we probably have less than thirty chimes to do something before that ship arrives wherever its going. Possibly much less. I can think of four basic scenarios, and I want you all to spend some time thinking about options for all four, plus if someone comes up with a crazier scenario than I've thought of—"

A low whistle sounded, low to high, and he stopped. On the display, the system diagram vanished, replaced by Kuotaan's somber features. "Nda Daamon," the captain said, and considered the rest of them. Tsumon hunched down a little, but the captain made absolutely no comment about her presence among the uman people in Kaamharaa's personal quarters. She said generally, "Khand. How useful to find you all together. Allow us to efficiently inform you all at once that our latest recaptured drone shows us the uut ship has begun to decelerate. We suspect that it is approaching its destination."

"Much too far from the primary to be a near-star slide—" Saraa began.

Mattu lifted a cautioning hand. "The architecture of this system is highly peculiar—"

In the display, Kuotaan lifted her much larger hand. "At this moment, we do indeed theorize an out-of-position slide, possibly a slide dramatically less stable than those found in more typical arrangements. We should be able to discern such details in one to five chimes, depending on the decisions we make regarding our own acceleration and course. Then we will need to rapidly make further decisions. Nda Daamon, we would appreciate your participation regarding all these decisions."

Daamon made an acknowledging gesture. "Battlecrew is on the way, Tsaa Kuotaan."

"Main crew anticipates your arrival," the captain assured him gravely, and disappeared from the display.

"No slide has any business anywhere near there," Saraa muttered. She was already on her feet, absently lending Daamon a hand to rise, but she added aggressively, "I'm with the captain: I'll take a bet against any of you that if a slide's there, it's unstable as a plate boundary on Ymaa and that's why we've never had uut come at the Ka' Taand through Aam before."

Mattu shrugged. "I'll take that bet. It's a nice theory, so probably it's wrong. Listen, send the feed from the bridge display down here, will you, Daamon?"

Daamon murmured wordlessly, already involved in trying to sort out *Nkaastu's* options if that giant uut mothership was indeed nearing its destination ... way out here, well before they'd anticipated it might ... he shouldn't have slept so long, he should have left really firm instructions to get him up in half the time. Now all the possibilities that had lain in front of them were going to narrow down, and he didn't feel at all ready.

But he knew it didn't matter. Eventually—soon—the possibilities would shrink down to just one. The uut would do something and then, however prepared or unprepared he and *Nkaastu* turned out to be, they would respond. *Vengeful* would help, they would all work together, and they would win. Anything else was unthinkable.

10

Taya was learning English. Lieutenant Samuel Lockwood was teaching her. She didn't like him. Maybe he didn't mean to seem dismissive and contemptuous ... no. Taya was sure he *did* mean to seem dismissive and contemptuous. He didn't like her and she didn't like him, but she had to learn English and he was a good teacher. Sun Grigson came sometimes and she was nice; Doctor Chandratre came sometimes and he was nice; but neither of them understood how languages worked the way Lieutenant Lockwood did. She had to learn from him because how else could their two ships act together to rescue Kaamharaa?

She tried not to think about Kaamharaa. It had been many hours since the uut had taken him away in their Disk.

An hour was measured in sixty minutes. A tenth chime was about four minutes and a full chime about forty minutes, so that was easy enough. There were twenty-four hours in a day, which made a day here a little shorter than a Gaatuu day, which was forty chimes. There were three hundred sixty-five days in a human year, so a Gaatuu year was not as long, but not that much shorter. Humans also said that seven days made a week and some greater number of days made a month, but the number of days in a month changed over and over during a year. Months definitely seemed more complicated than necessary.

However you measured time, it had been almost a full day since the uut had taken Kaamharaa. And all Taya could do to maybe help him was learn English as fast as she could, whether Lieutenant Lockwood liked her or not.

'Lieutenant' was a word like *kha*. It meant he was a crewmember of good reputation. She was supposed to say 'Lieutenant' every time she spoke to him. One didn't use someone's personal name unless invited. One addressed a person by his title and his family name. Every one of the cousins seemed to have a different family name, which seemed very strange since they were all on this one ship.

Putting the title with the family name was different from Uom, but it was easy to remember. English was filled with things that were harder to remember. It was much more complicated than cant. The uman—human—people on Ymaa had lost so much, each generation less than the one before. Knowing less, remembering less, breeding less, until they had nearly died out, except then Tsuumat Nkaarusapaa had found his uman family—found wasn't really the right word. Nkaarusapaa had practically fallen on top of those uman people. From that lucky accident everything else had followed, right up to the establishment of the Ka' Taand.

For turun, Ymaa was a fine world. For uman people, it had been very bad. Too many predators, too many earthquakes, too hot, too heavy, plus the red-spot illness that had slowly been killing everyone. Taya couldn't imagine why any uman had ever wanted to settle on Ymaa in the first place.

There were still a few uman on Ymaa even now. Every year, two or four or ten uman were discovered and rescued. Taya had never thought about how difficult it must be for those people to learn how to speak Uom and how to be civilized people. Next to that, Taya did not have to be brave at all. Lieutenant Lockwood might not like her, and she didn't like him, but she wasn't *afraid* of him.

Human was the correct word. *Humans* was the correct plural. Plurals were another complicated thing in English. The verbs changed as well as the nouns, and in the opposite direction—taking a sibilant ending for the singular instead of the plural, except there were lots of exceptions for both verbs and nouns. That was so much more complicated than the cant uman people spoke on Ymaa.

Taya's own grandmother had been born on Ymaa, though she said she did not remember the world very well, except for the fear and loneliness. Taya's grandmother had been truly alone, all the way alone. Her family on Ymaa had all died when she was a child, leaving her as alone and lonely as an uturun with no uman family. But she had been lucky enough to stumble across one of the turun reclamation teams, so she had grown up on Mhkaehn, the station above Ymaa where a lot of uman lived. She had wanted to go farther away from Ymaa, and so eventually she had joined Guuan. Then she had met Taya's grandfather. Taya knew all that, but she had never met her grandmother. Now she wondered about her a lot more than she had before. Her grandmother had had one life and then stepped into another. Her life had changed completely.

If Kaamharaa died, Taya's life would change completely. If he died, everyone who had been sep' Kaamharaa would have to go to a matriline, probably Guuan or Aanuku, unless they accepted another uturun into Kaamharaa's territory and home. Taya knew she would never go back to Kaamharaa's house if he were not there. Maybe she would go to Ymaa and join one of the teams that searched for wild uman people living lost in the jungles.

Her mind was drifting. She was so tired. She had tried to sleep earlier, but the sleeping chamber here was so empty and lonely. She had just gotten up again and gone out into the main room and resumed working with the language modules. Lieutenant Lockwood had looked at her sharply and said something that sounded unfriendly, but then he had gotten her a hot beverage and a sweet pastry. The beverage had been bitter; she might have thought it another way to be unfriendly, except the pastry had been good. So she didn't know what to think.

She should not worry about Lieutenant Lockwood. She needed to think about this.

"Lieutenant," she said, turning the *computer screen* around to face her companion. "I finish this." It wasn't entirely true, but she had mostly finished, only leaving a few blanks. She had finished it *enough*.

The man said shortly, "I *have finished* this. Pay attention to the verb tenses." But he knew she only said she was finished when she was. He checked her work quickly. He made a few corrections, sharp and scornful, but he must have agreed that the module truly was finished enough because he loaded the new module he had been working on. "Important words," he told her. "Useful words. Learn them fast and maybe we can get somewhere." He copied her completed module to his screen so he could look for mistakes. He would probably like to find mistakes so he could correct them. But corrections were good. She had to learn to say things right. He was helping her, even if he wanted to make her feel stupid.

She could tell he didn't like Uom. Taya was helping him build a lexicon. She used both the English writing symbols and the decorative Taehm script, which was honestly a little too formal for just compiling a lexicon, but it was the script she knew best because it was Kaamharaa's favorite. Lieutenant Lockwood practiced the Uom words, but the way he held his mouth made it clear he thought the language tasted ugly. Taya pretended not to notice. He was learning, she was learning, that was what mattered.

I and *you, we* and *they, man* and *woman, go* and *come, close* and *far, approach* and *retreat.* Many words came in pairs, never in fours. Doctor Chandratre had pointed out that difference. He had seemed happy about it. Taya didn't understand why it mattered, but she had seen at once that it was true that many turun concepts came in fours. Far-kin and half-kin and near-kin and close-kin; those were Uom. English said merely *unrelated* and *related.* Or again in Uom, illegal, half-legal, near-legal, and legal. The concept came in fours. English offered *illegal* and *legal,* just two possibilities, as though everything really fell into just those two categories.

She had already learned a lot of easy words: *head* and *eye, mouth* and *teeth, eat* and *drink, bread* and *sandwich* and *lemonade*—that was a kind of sweet-tart fruit juice that Taya liked far better than the hot, bitter drink Lieutenant Lockwood had brought her. But she was feeling more awake and the headache that had been pressing behind her eyes had eased. Maybe the drink was medicinal. That would explain why people drank it.

Lieutenant Lockwood had also taught her the connecting words, which were sometimes difficult. *Into, out of, beside, before, behind. Do* and *doing, act* and *action.* Lieutenant Lockwood was impatient and unfriendly, but he knew what was important.

What will you do? I will walk across this room. I will throw this bread. I will catch this bread. *What are you doing?* I am walking, I am throwing, I am catching. *What have you done?* I have walked, I have thrown, I have caught. *Do* was for questions about actions in the future, except that sometimes it was for questions about the past. *Doing* was for questions about actions now. *Done* was always for questions about actions in the past. Verbs were like that; they changed for future and present and past, except they didn't change all the time or all in the same way. Taya had developed a real dislike for English verbs.

Because—that was a hard word, like *why*. She knew other questions now, mostly easier: *What* and *who* and *how*.

This new module was teaching her words that were bigger, more difficult, more important. *Together. Separate. Attack. Defend. Protect.* Those were all clear. She could see how useful those words would be.

Sun Grigson came in just then. That was good. Taya liked Sun, who had said Taya could call her by her personal name.

Lieutenant Lockwood looked up and said in a sharp, dismissive tone, "She's doing her best, I suppose, but we'll never get anything important out of her at this rate!"

"Rate is what?" Taya asked in her nicest voice, as though she hadn't noticed his tone.

The man sighed impatiently, but he always answered questions about language. He said curtly, "Speed, velocity."

Taya nodded, tucking this away. She'd already learned *velocity*. Words for basic physics were easy to explain.

Lieutenant Lockwood was going on, speaking quickly, his words meant for Sun and not for Taya, "How many worlds do *something something*, how much *something* do they *something*, what kinds of *something* do they have? We haven't got *something* answers to any of that. I think she's *something something something.*"

Taya caught enough of that to guess the man was accusing her of being deliberately secretive. This wasn't fair—in fact, it made her wonder if *he* were being deliberately secretive. But before she could answer, Sun said, in careful small words so Taya could understand, "We will come to those questions soon. I see she is learning the fifth module."

Lieutenant Lockwood raked a look across Taya that felt searingly scornful. "Yeah, well, when she gets to the sixth, maybe we'll be able to learn *something something something*. Maybe we can also ask her how her people gave up their own language—and what else they gave up."

This time Taya understood almost every word, and guessed he had deliberately chosen small, easy words because he wanted her to understand he was being insulting. She felt hot and embarrassed, and she wished very much that Kaamharaa was here—let this unlikeable person try to insult her then.

Kaamharaa was not here. That was the whole point. She said nothing.

But Sun said in a calm tone, "Sam ... I think you need to take a break."

For a second, Lieutenant Lockwood only stared at her. Then, to Taya's surprise, he glanced at Taya, blew out a breath, got to his feet, and walked out. He didn't apologize. But walking out without a word almost seemed like an apology, under the circumstances.

"He not like me," Taya said. "But he good teach. Is good teach. How should I say?"

Sun sighed, shrugged, pulled a chair around, and settled into it. "It's not you, Taya." She didn't correct Taya's sentences even though Taya had asked her to always correct and explain mistakes. She was nice, but she really was not as good a teacher as Lieutenant Lockwood. She only said, "Those turun, your Kaamharaa. Very big, very scary. Sam—Lieutenant Lockwood—thinks of your Kaamharaa when he sees you."

Taya said scornfully, "Him should know, Kaamharaa is important person."

"Him is the object form. *He* should know. Yes, he should, but we're not used to turun. Only Enemy. Only us and Enemy, many years. No turun. Aliens bad, *something something*. Humans yes, aliens no. You see?"

Taya had not quite framed the situation like that. She thought about it now. Only uman people, lots of uman people, and besides them only uut. And the uman language cast everything into pairs: one contrasted with another without room for things in between. It was a little hard to imagine. But she thought she could see it might make people scared of turun. Except it should be *perfectly obvious* to anybody that the turun were *not at all* like the uut.

Before she could say that, Sun went on, "It does worry me a little, because Lockwood's on Falconer's staff—*staff* is like a work group—the same as I'm on the viceroy's staff. Never mind, that is too much to explain."

Taya suspected it might be like the complicated alliances between and among nturun matrilines. She asked, "Your viceroy same thing Falconer?"

"Not the *same,* but just as important, maybe more important."

That seemed good. Taya wanted Sun to be at least as important as Lieutenant Lockwood. She looked back down at the words on the computer screen, but she found herself hesitating. *Attack. Defend. Protect.* Those words were all clear. But obviously if you could decide to protect something or someone, you could also choose *not* to protect that thing or that person. She saw no word here for that, for deciding not to protect. She wanted that word.

So she said, "Sun?" When the other woman looked at her, she set a bit of bread on the table between them and walked one hand toward the bread, making her fingers stalk like a knifefang predator toward a little animal. Then she set her other hand between and shoved the predator away. "Protect bread," she explained.

Then she did it again, but this time she moved her protective hand out of the way and let the knifefang hand leap on the bread and smash it. "What?" she asked Sun. "Not protect, walk away, let enemy go attack, what word?"

Sun did not frown at her, but Taya could tell she was unhappy. She hesitated. But finally she said, *"Abandon*. That is *abandon*." She set another piece of bread on the table. "*Vengeful,*" she told Taya, which was the name of this ship. Sun took the smashed bread, tore it into crumbs, and scattered the crumbs across the table. *"Task Force Aleph,"* she said, words Taya didn't know. Sun went on with words she did know: "Many ships. Many Enemy." She put the bread that was *Vengeful* near the group of crumbs, then moved it quickly away. "Abandon."

Taya was pretty sure she understood that. She patted Sun's hand, wishing she could make the other woman feel better. She didn't know how to say, *If we had stayed in that other system, we would all be dead.* Even if she had known those words, she was pretty sure it wouldn't have made Sun feel better. She patted her hand again. "Friend," she said. "You, me. *Vengeful*, *Nkaastu*. Not abandon."

Sun smiled a little then, though Taya could tell she was still unhappy. *Friend. Ally. Enemy.* She could only hope she had those important words right.

"Task Force Aleph?" she asked Sun.

So Sun pulled up a display and showed Taya pictures: *Star, world, station, ship. Superdreadnought, dreadnought, cruiser, freighter.* She showed her one picture: *flagship*, and said Ronsard Falconer and Viceroy Modhwadiya were both there, which made Taya wonder. If those people were like matriarchs of rival matrilines, it seemed strange they would share territory on one ship. Maybe they were more like matriarchs of the same matriline. But uman people, a purely uman society, who knew what they might do?

Taya couldn't show Sun images, but she gave her the best approximations she could for the ships of her people: *Full-fighter, half-fighter, half-fighter tradeship, tradeship, explorer.* She taught Sun *slide* and learned *flashpoint*, but did not know any of the more specialized words the navigators and explorers used for other kinds of wormholes.

Sun showed Taya other pictures: *Saucer. Arrowpoint.* Taya taught her *Disk* and *Blade* in return. Taya thought soon they would both be able to ask the kinds of questions that *mattered*. She hoped they would both like each other's answers. She hoped either of them *had* answers.

Then Sun showed Taya a different kind of picture. A map. Obviously a map of stars and slides, that was easy to recognize, almost exactly like the kind of star map the Ka' Taand used: bright points with little notations beneath them, the lacework of the slides stretching between and among the stars. Sometimes a slide made the distance between stars very small even if the stars were a long way from each other in ordinary space. Other times, the slides wove in and out so that stars much closer to each other required many days' travel. The slides on the map were different colors, probably showing their stability because anyone would definitely want to know that, but maybe something else.

On Sun's map, seven stars were very bright and linked by slides that were colored green. Some of those stars were far from the others, but the slides made them close, never more than two slides to connect any of those stars. Those might be the heart-stars for the human people. If Taya had drawn this map, those would certainly be the heart-stars. She thought that had to be what this map indicated. All the other suns were dimmer and linked to the bright ones by many more slides colored white or red.

"Home world human people one these stars?" Taya asked.

Sun glanced up, surprised. Then she smiled, not a happy expression, and drew a rapid series of slides away from the bright stars. She put one star there at the end of that long path. "Human home," she said. "Earth. Do you know that name?" Then, without waiting for an answer, she made the slides go dim, one after another and looked up again, shrugging. "All flashpoints go. The word is *destabilize,* have you learned that word yet? Flashpoint gone. *Gone* means *go and not come back*. No way home."

That was very sad. Taya didn't know the word for *sad.* She hadn't realized before that this was an important word, but of course it was. She asked softly, "Why all flashpoints gone?"

"I don't know how to explain it." But Sun sighed. "The Enemy came, Taya. Earth only had one flashpoint. They had to close it. We don't know if they did it soon enough. We don't know if Earth is still there. Everyone on the wrong side of the flashpoint had to forget Earth, run fast, look for a safe place, anywhere no Enemy would find them." She patted Taya's hand. "Never mind. It was a long time ago." Turning back to the map, Sun tapped the bright stars. "Here. Shallows."

Then she traced a lacework of slides away from the bright stars—the Shallows. "The Deep," she said, and made a lot of tiny pinpricks of light appear a long way from the heart-stars. She traced threads of light looping one way and another, slide, slide, slide, slide, more slides than that, eight slides altogether before those little lights connected to one of the bright stars. "Aleph," Sun said, looking intently at Taya.

"Yes," Taya said. "I understand. Long way home, many slides. Flashpoints."

"Yes," Sun agreed. She drew two more slides leading away from the trapped battlegroup, showing the way toward Aam. "Your people?" she asked. "Deep or Shallow, where we meet? You show?"

Nodding, Taya touched the controls of the display. She drew a line from Aam to the juncture system, then another to Hanaa. Then the short, direct pathways that wove through familiar space, star, star, star, star. She put in the eleven heart-stars with Gaatuu much brighter than the others, then the tangle of slides of the far edge. That was tricky to draw, though she knew more or less how it looked, the complicated lacework that wove in and out of familiar space but actually led away to the far edge, many days' journey from the heart-stars no matter how close anything seemed in ordinary space.

"Eleven stars in your Shallows," Sun said, tracing the slides from Hanaa to Gaatuu and some of the others.

Taya started to tip her chin up, caught herself and nodded instead. "Seven stars your heart-stars," she began, but a soft tone sounded—actually a series of tones that all ran together, not the more familiar whistle or resonant hum of signals aboard *Nkaastu*.

After almost a day, Taya knew what that was: it meant someone wanted to talk to Sun using the wrist link the woman wore. Sun touched the link. A voice, clipped and sharp, said, "Lieutenant Grigson, report to the bridge, please. Bring the girl with you."

Taya sat up straight. "Is something happen? I come, yes! I talk much better now."

"I hope so," snapped the voice, and cut off.

11

Gerstner stared up at the walkway above his head and the doorway that led into or through the wall. If it was a doorway. The ledge that led to it *looked* like a walkway. What could that lit edge be *for,* if not a guide for someone in a hurry, to keep them from falling off the ledge? On the other hand, a guiding strip would make so much sense, when nothing in this place had made a particle of sense before. Maybe that glittering strip was decorative. Or meant *keep out.*

Even so, with that strange birdlike trill getting closer, that ledge and the opening looked a lot like a way out. For a person, though. Not for an enormous centauroid alien. Maybe the Enemy were small enough to get through that opening. Gerstner had no idea.

From time to time, somebody had managed to recover Enemy remains, if you counted various smears of weirdly acellular goo as *remains*, but no one had ever managed to recover a more-or-less undamaged dead Enemy, far less take one alive. No record suggested anyone had managed anything of the kind during that first shocking series of attacks that had forced the decision to destabilize Earth's only known flashpoint, isolating Earth and stranding every ship that had been on the wrong side of that flashpoint. Definitely no one had done it during the years refugees had struggled to survive, nor after the Imperial Republic had been established, nor during these recent years of the tentative new human expansion.

This was not the way Gerstner would have chosen to get his own personal up-close look at an Enemy.

"Right," he said out loud. "Options. There's got to be a way to get cargo or equipment or whatever into and out of this damn saucer. Say these things here, these cylinders on these platforms, *are* cargo or something." They could be. They looked a lot like cargo canisters. Even crazy aliens who did insane things with light and gravitics only had so many ways to package up materials, right? "Cargo, munitions, whatever those things are, no damn way is anything like this going through that opening up there. If they move at all, some big door's got to be here somewhere."

Kaamharaa rumbled. It might have been an answer, but if there were words in that sound, Gerstner couldn't make them out. He took a step back and studied the wall in front of them. Or tried to, with light that swooped overhead and would not just sit still and let a man *see* what he was looking at. As far as he could tell, the wall was utterly smooth and featureless. A big red button labeled PUSH TO OPEN would have been nice. Likely the door, if there was a door, was controlled by some kind of automated system somewhere else. There ought to be manual controls. On a human ship, there would've been manual controls. Maybe there were controls on the other side. Maybe he could get through that opening and figure out some way to open bigger doors before the Enemy got here.

How dangerous could something that sounded like a flock of canaries and windchimes actually be?

He didn't want to find out, actually. By the sound, it or they were getting close. Too damn close to fool around trying to find controls that more than likely wouldn't be findable.

Turning, Gerstner said, "Kaamharaa," and pointed emphatically back the way they'd come. "You can't get out this way, so we need to go back that way, fast before whatever's making that damn noise gets any closer. Understand?"

If Kaamharaa understood, he did not agree, because he picked Gerstner up and set him on the ledge, shoving him toward the opening. The birdsong sounded like it was practically on top of them, though Gerstner couldn't see a damn thing even when light flashed and swirled through the darkness. *Something* chimed and rang, like ceramic or glass ringing against metal. Like they were being pursued by a whole host of bells as well as birds.

"Listen, I'll find a way to get the damn door open," Gerstner snapped. "You hear me? Don't get your damn centaur ass killed, you got that?" Then he turned and strode up the walkway, ducked low as he got to the opening, and went straight in. He held his good hand out in front, hoping he didn't run into any kind of ... God knew what. In an adventure story, this would be a trash chute, and he'd be hurrying right toward the trash compactor or shredding blades or disintegration ray or whatever.

It was definitely a chute or tunnel, not a simple doorway. It sloped up at first, then down, not in a smooth arc, but weirdly asymmetric. About four feet wide, about five feet high; surely that meant the Enemy were indeed rather small. He had to duck, but at least he didn't have to crawl. The walls weren't metal. Some kind of ceramic, maybe. Curved edges, no right angles in sight; that's what made it look so much like a tunnel rather than a hallway.

The glimmer of light by his feet meant he wasn't quite blind in this place, once his vision adjusted. The disorienting swooshes of brighter light didn't seem to reach into this tunnel, which actually made it easier to see despite the dimness. But there was nothing *to* see but a blank tunnel. He hadn't thought to count his steps. He hadn't come more than ten meters or so. If anything terrible were happening behind him, he would hear it. He already knew that Kaamharaa boomed and roared when he fought ... Gerstner couldn't even hear birds and bells now. Could there be some kind of sound baffle in this tunnel?

If anyone, any*thing* came into the tunnel after him, would he hear it?

Light raked across his field of view and vanished. Gerstner gritted his teeth, squinted, set his good hand cautiously on the tunnel wall to steady himself as he reached the end of the passageway, tucked himself low, crept to the edge, and looked out. And out, and farther out, and down.

His first impression was that he was looking out into the concourse area of a station, something at least the size of Pallas Athene's concourse. Yellowish light flared, rippled, streamed sideways, swept across an immense open area, and died. Gerstner leaned against the wall, shut his eyes, and tried to make sense of what the light had so briefly revealed. Mostly flat, some movement as a line of gliding ... things ... moved. Not living things: a whole lot like platforms with big cylinders on them, in fact. He was more sure than ever that those were cargo trolleys of some kind. Whatever, they'd been moving toward something way out in the middle of the open area, a cluster of long writhing nightmare tentacles.

Every instinct he owned insisted tentacles had to belong to some kind of monster. But the Enemy used tentacles a lot, so some kind of mechanism seemed more likely than any sort of giant tentacled monster. Opening his eyes again, Gerstner waited for the rippling bands of light to return. Refused, this time, to blink. This time, knowing where to look, he got a better idea of what was down there. Tentacles, yes; but he was fairly certain they did indeed belong to some kind of cargo-handling machine. Lines of those trolleys with their cylinders trundled toward those tentacles, got swept up and pulled down, and disappeared. All right. Unloading cargo, loading emptied munitions containers, something normal like that, no matter how weird it looked. Definitely not a monster. He told himself that, firmly.

The floor of the bay was maybe twelve feet below the tunnel's mouth. It almost seemed like it was covered with grass or moss, something organic and growing. A peculiar luxury in a shipbay. Or it might have additional uses. Maybe on alternate Tuesdays, Enemy soldiers came to this place and had picnic lunches, ham salad sandwiches and cake.

A ham salad sandwich would be excellent right now. And water. He was aware of tearing thirst as soon as he thought of water. Not helpful.

Something else had moved down there, way off to one side, pale and indistinct and rapid, vanishing even as he'd spotted it. Whatever that was, it had been far enough away that he hoped he didn't have to care about it.

Possibly more important, those trolleys were moving from wide, arched openings all along the periphery of this ... had to be a shipbay, what else could it be? They'd been on an Enemy saucer; the saucer seemed to have docked. So this had to be the mothership, or maybe a station. This tunnel might be some kind of docking tube by which Enemy personnel went back and forth, and yes, there damn well *was* a cargo door right here, only this one was closed, not open. Probably because a giant centaur had gotten loose aboard this saucer and the Enemy didn't want giant centaurs getting out into the station. That'd make sense. Go with that.

In that case, a lot more saucers and maybe arrowpoints must have docked along this bay, and each doorway probably led to one of those. So if he had that right, where were all the Enemy personnel?

Maybe the Enemy had disembarked right away and were already gone. On the other hand, maybe if he waited five minutes this whole space would be teeming with Enemy and he'd find out exactly what kind of aliens burned human worlds and had voices like birdcalls and harpsichords and windchimes.

Maybe all the Enemy personnel were behind him, trying to recapture an enormous centauroid turun who'd proven to be more of a handful than expected. How many of the Enemy would that take? Wouldn't they just use those tentacle things? Maybe recapturing escaped prisoners was a spectator sport and everyone who wasn't involved was watching, cheering on the sports stars who tackled Kaamharaa one at a time for the sheer glory of it. Maybe *anything;* he couldn't guess.

Get Kaamharaa out into the big space down there and if nothing else, he'd have room to run. Not necessarily any place to run *to*, but all those openings from which emerged those cargo containers or empty munitions or whatever offered possibilities. Not good possibilities, probably, but still.

Actually, maybe those doorways, probably entrances to other ships, might offer *some* kind of possibility. No good getting out of one saucer and into another, Gerstner couldn't see any use to that, but getting out of the saucer and into an *arrowpoint* might offer better chances, different chances. Way, way smaller, arrowpoints. Fewer crew, probably. Maybe. Easier to defend, maybe. Possibly.

Easier to steal, easier to *fly?* That chance was too damn remote even to bother thinking of it. Embarrassing even to hope for that. But ... could be Kaamharaa might know something about Enemy tech, Enemy controls. Tiny chance, stupid even to call it a chance. *But.*

Except he'd left Kaamharaa behind. If he was still alive back there, big if; if he was still free, what then? Getting the giant alien out into this shipbay was a problem Gerstner was no closer to solving. From where he crouched, he couldn't see a damn thing that looked like any kind of controls. The wall on this side seemed exactly as smooth and featureless as on the other. Damn sure no big red buttons.

Everything about this place was so appallingly *alien*. Maybe that door would open on its own.

Sure, probably after the Enemy re-captured the giant centauroid turun, or killed him, real helpful possibility there.

At least ten minutes since he'd fled into this tunnel and left Kaamharaa behind. If the alien centaur *were* still alive, probably there was nothing a human could do to help him.

But it was definitely time to find out, because there was no way he could go on without at least checking. He didn't like the silence, not that he would have been any happier if he'd been hearing birdsong mixed with screams and roars and explosions.

The tunnel seemed even longer and dimmer going the other way. This time he counted his strides. Eighteen, nineteen, and he realized the tunnel definitely curved just a bit, imperceptibly, as light rippled across the tunnel and he saw the entrance in front of him. Nine more strides, shorter ones, quiet steps, and he was finally able to tuck himself close to the wall and peer cautiously around the edge, back into the cul-de-sac they'd run into those few minutes ago.

No one was there. Kaamharaa was gone.

Gerstner had had worse moments. Hell, he'd had worse moments *today*. But not by a whole lot.

***

All right. This was bad, but it could be worse. There was no blood or other mess. Cannisters lined up on trolleys, waiting for the cargo door to open, and that was it. Whatever had happened, it must have happened fast and apparently without the kind of struggle that left body parts scattered around. It was hard to imagine how the Enemy had taken Kaamharaa down that fast, but it seemed possible they'd taken him alive. They'd gone to a lot of trouble to take live prisoners in the first place, so it'd make no sense to kill the alien centaur now.

Strange the Enemy had not come through that tunnel after *him*. Maybe they knew exactly where Gerstner was and thought that was a fine place to leave him. Or maybe they hadn't realized he was with Kaamharaa at all. They must have seen that both their prisoners had escaped. But maybe they hadn't realized they'd fled *together*. That might explain why they didn't seem to be searching for their human prisoner in the obvious place. Who knew what crazy alien reason they had for anything.

Whatever the reason, Gerstner was still free, and it seemed reasonable to assume Kaamharaa was still alive. Just ... not here.

Option one: search this whole damn saucer until he found him, then battle his way past whatever had captured a three-ton centauroid alien and rescue him. Option two: write him off, go back through the tunnel and try to steal an Enemy arrowpoint all by himself.

The first option was almost certainly hopeless. But the second would be contemptible.

He would probably fail to find the giant centaur anyway. Setting his hands on his hips, Gerstner stared around into the darkness, then blinked and flinched as swooping lines of harsh, actinic light swept past, its glare briefly revealing strangely angled walls and the line of cargo trolleys.

A horrifying image leaped into his mind, vivid and terrible: the turun lashed to a cargo trolley, aware but helpless, sliding out into the shipbay, gliding into that monstrous tentacled mechanism in the middle of the bay, heading for God alone knew what fate.

Gerstner had wanted to find a way to open the cargo doors. Suddenly he wanted, almost more than anything, for that door to stay closed—at least until he had time to examine each of the waiting trolleys. He was not at all keen on the idea of searching an empty saucer until he was recaptured or died of thirst, whichever came first, while Kaamharaa had already been taken away to suffer imprisonment or vivisection or whatever the Enemy had in mind. Trolleys first, and then he could think about where to search next.

Sudden movement, rippling and liquid. Gerstner flinched back, jumping up to the ledge, ready to retreat—then realized that the cargo doors were opening at last, not sliding or folding so much as flowing aside. In front of him, the line of trolleys began to move.

Dark echoing space; chemical stink; moving trolleys; brilliant streamers of light that first dazzled a man and then left him blind ... Gerstner threw caution aside and scrambled up onto the nearest trolley, grabbed the edge of a cylinder and dragged himself up on top of that, then crouched down and waited for the light to return.

When it did, he stood up and looked, really *looked,* at all the surrounding trolleys and at their cargo. He had just seconds to figure out what he was looking at, and then he had to leap down because his trolly was just about to pass through the cargo doors and there wasn't enough room at the top for a man to ride a cylinder out. He jumped off the trolley, sprawling as he lost his balance. He hit the decking hard and badly; his shoulder felt like he had a knife jammed up under the shoulder blade. Scrubbing his good hand across his stinging eyes, he forced himself up. The violent lights swooped past and he couldn't see a damn thing, but the moving trolleys were so big he felt them moving past him, so he could count them off.

One ... two ... three ... he scrambled up on the next trolley as it came even with his position. *This* one hadn't held canisters. This one, if he'd counted right, had held a single bulky, uneven shape that *might* be ... if God happened to be looking out for him and Kaamharaa both ... actually it *would* be interesting to see how the Synod responded to the turun. Not that, absent divine intervention, Gerstner seemed likely to get a chance to follow the debate.

He couldn't *see*, and was reduced to patting with his good hand across the shape he'd glimpsed. Soft textures, slick and plastic-y under his fingers, nothing familiar. That was disturbing. But the shape could be right. The bulk seemed right.

When even touch failed, it was his sense of smell that made him sure. Beneath the chemical reek he could smell something organic and oddly herbal, a little like bay leaves and a little like sesame, with a musky note underneath. He hadn't had any idea he'd even noticed the alien's smell earlier, yet here when he found it again amid all the chemical and metallic odors, it was both distinctive and familiar.

He wondered what he smelled like to it. Nothing too unpleasant, he hoped.

The trolleys were moving slower than a man could walk, he was pretty sure. But not *much* slower. The distance from right here to the tentacled transport thing wasn't *that* great. Kaamharaa wasn't moving. Gerstner was fairly certain the alien was lying flat on his side, all his legs out one way, his upper torso the other. Unconscious? Dead? No easy way to tell.

The slick surface covering the alien gave under his prodding fingers. A lot like plastic. The bay-and-sesame scent, though. Would he have been able to smell the alien through layers of airtight plastic? That didn't seem likely. Then this plastic stuff must be permeable, not airtight—he could hope so, at least.

Gerstner felt his way forward toward the alien's head. Arm, yes, and another arm, peculiarly set shoulders, here was the thick, relatively short neck, here the heavy jaw with its tusks, unmistakable even through the layers of plastic. Those tusks were nearly as broad at the base as Gerstner's thumb, about as long as his hand. He traced the outline of the nearer tusk, pressed the plastic material against the pointed end. It was actually a fairly blunt point. He pressed harder. Forced his bad arm into service despite the ripping pain from his shoulder. Maybe he was trying to save a dead alien. No way to tell. He pressed harder still.

The layer of plastic gave, gave farther, stretched, and *finally* tore. The alien's tusk was not as convenient as a knife. Gerstner swore if by some miracle he got back to *Vengeful*, he would never again leave his quarters without a service knife in his pocket or clipped to his belt. He made it a formal vow to God, all the while working to widen the gash in the plastic and peel the material away from Kaamharaa's face. Paused to hold his palm in front of the broad, slack mouth, try to feel if the damn alien was breathing. He couldn't tell … but honestly, he thought not. The thought of the turun's death made him angry, and it made him sad, and frankly the thought of being stranded here alone terrified the hell out of him. Surely it was still *possible* Kaamharaa was alive.

The cargo trolley seemed to be moving faster.

So. Work fast. Clear a couple inches more plastic away from Kaamharaa's slack face. If he were human, Gerstner could perform CPR. Breathing for the alien … the idea of that macabre echo of a kiss turned Gerstner's stomach, but it didn't matter; the alien's mouth was so massively outsized and strangely shaped, he couldn't imagine anything of the kind could work. Chest compressions on a creature this size … and this peculiar shape … except some kind of respiratory organs had to be in there *somewhere.*

Feeling his way down the upper torso, Gerstner found a spot that seemed relatively similar to the sternum on a person's chest. He hit the alien there, hard, and then harder, as hard as he could, with one hand and then both, ignoring the lancing pain from his bad shoulder. Nothing … nothing … more nothing; he couldn't tell whether he was having any effect at all.

So. Down again, past the massive foreleg to the lower chest, where he guessed the equivalent of lungs might be. Or the main lungs, possibly. He hardly knew what to do even if his guess was right. Kaamharaa was so big that Gerstner could probably jump up and down on that massive body without the slightest risk of injuring the alien.

That was a thought. There seemed no reason not to try it. Except the risk of losing his balance and falling off the damn trolley and breaking his neck. That would be a ludicrous way to die. And anyway, the alien was probably already dead.

Ribbons of light rushed past. The trolley was more than halfway to the tentacled thing.

Gerstner got to his feet, backed up, took two fast steps—set one foot on the alien's flank, jumped, and landed with both feet on the side of the huge barrel chest. Staggered and fell, taking the impact straight on his bad shoulder. He couldn't restrain a short scream, bit it off into a sharp, panting series of breaths.

Kaamharaa stirred, trembled, jerked, and lifted his upper body. The plastic coating ripped and tore with a lot of loud popping noises, but seemed to offer no restraint. The centaur rolled to lie more or less upright. He wrapped an arm around Gerstner's waist and lifted him effortlessly to his feet. "Gerrstner," he rumbled. "Gerrstner."

Standing, with the centauroid alien lying down, Gerstner found their heads more nearly at a level. He still had to tip his head back to meet Kaamharaa's eyes. Which caught the light and flared gold. Alien, strange, unhuman ... familiar, welcome. He had been *so certain* the alien was dead. He gripped Kaamharaa's nearest forearm and found himself smiling. Grimly. But it was a smile. Then he pulled, pointing urgently. "Let's go, let's go, move!" he ordered.

Getting to his feet was more of a production for the alien than Gerstner had realized. Kaamharaa started with his front, heaved himself up in the rear, surged up in the front again, and finally pitched upright. The thumping clatter all this produced was loud enough anyone with ears probably heard it on the other side of the bay. The Enemy had already shown their ability to handle Kaamharaa. They would undoubtedly find a single human male, somewhat the worse for wear, a much easier target.

More immediately a concern, if they fell into that cluster of tentacles, which was *way too close*, he was sure they wouldn't get out. "Let's *go*," Gerstner snapped, and pointed again, even more urgently. "*Off* this damn trolley, understand?"

"Go," agreed the alien. He picked Gerstner up and jumped off the trolley. It was only about three feet to the floor, but Kaamharaa landed heavily enough that Gerstner imagined he could feel the entire station tremble. It made him wonder what kinds of sensors the Enemy might have in this bay. It was hard to believe that any kind of sensor could miss Kaamharaa, who was now striding forward, heading back toward the outer wall of the bay. Long, seemingly slow strides, but they were moving faster than a person could walk.

Someplace not too far away ... was that possibly a birdlike trill?

Kaamharaa's nearest ear twitched and swiveled. He surged forward powerfully, not running full out, but fast enough to cut between two of the trolleys. Sharper, closer birdsong broke out. Gerstner twisted, trying to get a glimpse of the creature that made that sound, see if it matched the tentacled monster of his imagining. But light flared and died, too bright and then too dim, and he couldn't tell whether he saw anything but shadows. Maybe a pale blur darting from a passageway, not large, moving fast. Gerstner wasn't sure what he'd seen, or even that he'd truly seen anything.

Kaamharaa had veered now to run along the wall. Huge cargo doors opened up in that wall, one after another, but the centaur didn't seem inclined to head into any of them. Gerstner wasn't exactly keen on that either, but ... he peered ahead as the light flared and swept past ... up ahead, maybe those doorways were smaller. Yes, definitely smaller and a lot closer together: likely enough they'd reached the arrowpoint docking area. If that assumption was correct, if any of his assumptions were correct, staying out in the shipbay hardly seemed sensible. The darkness of those open cargo doors yawned to their right, and he hit Kaamharaa on the shoulder and pointed urgently.

A creature this big should have moved laboriously, changed direction ponderously. Kaamharaa reared, pivoted, came down with a thud Gerstner felt all along his spine and *way* too clearly in his bad shoulder, and headed for the open doors at a pace no human could have matched on his best day.

These narrower cargo doors didn't offer much scope for a creature Kaamharaa's size, but the turun slowed down and picked his way through. His feet thudded on the hard surface of decking as they left the grassy area of the shipbay. The shadowy doorway led into an open space that reeked of bitter chemicals.

No Enemies Gerstner could make out, but God knew there could be a whole crowd of tentacled monsters in the dark and he probably wouldn't be able to tell. Or fast-moving little pale things; he still wasn't certain he'd really seen that. No arrows painted on the deck with glowing letters declaring *This Way To The Bridge*, unfortunately. A human would put the controls in the nose and the loading area in the rear. After a slight hesitation, Kaamharaa seemed inclined to head forward, too, though maybe he was just thinking *away*.

Gerstner hit him on the shoulder and pushed away from the alien's hold. "Put me down! Down. Listen, put me down."

Gestures or words must have gotten the message across because Kaamharaa stopped and set Gerstner on his feet.

"Got to be a way to get those doors closed," Gerstner told him, out loud because why not. "God knows what's coming up behind us! We've got to at least slow them down. Where would you put manual controls? I'd put them here somewhere by the doors ... at about chest height for me, but I guess we could be talking anywhere from floor to ceiling, if there *is* a manual control." He added, in case Kaamharaa might understand him, "Close door, lock door, find door control."

Kaamharaa tilted his head one way and then the other, listening, rumbling. It was impossible to guess how much of that he'd understood. But he had taken a sturdy, four-square stance that suggested he was prepared to stand right here and wait while Gerstner figured out what he was doing.

Gerstner couldn't hear anything warbling, not at the moment, but he figured it probably wouldn't be long. And it was all too easy to visualize a hundred predatory tentacled monsters slithering toward them ... though if so much was automated, maybe it would be a hundred unstoppable tentacled mechanisms. Wielding plastic wrap.

What a hideously ridiculous situation this was. Equally ridiculous to hope they could get out of it. On the other hand, neither of them was dead yet. Nor toppling into a tentacled mechanism, nor strapped to a dissection table. *Alive* and *free* and *together* were a start, but not likely to last unless he could get this door *closed*. And, while he was asking for miracles, the arrowpoint launched, out in hard vacuum and moving fast, so he knew nothing could get that door open again.

Normal design would suggest a wheel or lever set into the wall, probably painted some contrasting color and very possibly with arrows indicating which way to turn the wheel or shove the lever on the off chance someone unfamiliar with the ship might suddenly be pressed into emergency service.

Ribbons of light that flared and swooped around randomly and went out again suggested that contrasting color might not be a big thing for the Enemy. If not visually obvious ... something raised, or inset. A change of texture, a pressure-sensitive plate that all the Enemy knew about and anyone else would have to step on by pure chance ... God, it could be *anything* ... or simply absent, maybe the Enemy thought all their mechanisms were best operated from some central control area. In that case, Gerstner and Kaamharaa should be making a dash forward, looking for that control area. Not that it'd make any difference if they found it; they probably wouldn't have the right-shaped tentacles to fit the controls, never mind their complete ignorance about Enemy engineering.

Even so, Gerstner rapidly and carefully felt his way along the wall on one side of the cargo entrance and then the other, knelt to run his good hand across the floor, stared upward in case controls might be up above his eye level despite his best guess otherwise.

Light flared off to the high left, streamed through the air, and Gerstner pivoted, eyes wide, tearing copiously as he tried not to blink. He was certain he'd glimpsed motion, *some* kind of motion, but it might have been simply the swooping motion of the lights. It was a hard, white light, glaring painfully off walls and decking. Except for a crescent-shaped matte-dark region of the deck, directly in front of the cargo door. Gerstner stepped hastily sideways and set his foot firmly on that crescent—then both feet—then jumped up and down on it, gritting his teeth and gripping his bad arm with his other hand. So far as he could tell, none of this had the least effect.

A smallish pale shape skittered through the cargo doors, something pearly white that darted into view, then jerked abruptly to a halt. Not the sort of monster Gerstner had had in mind; he didn't get a good look, but his first impression was that it kind of resembled a Terabithian silverpede, except it was a lot more delicately built, no more than eighteen inches high, but long—maybe four feet—honestly, a *lot* like a silverpede except it had even more limbs. It had come in fast, but now it jigged in place as though surprised or alarmed, the front part of its body rearing up, three-four-five segments, each with little clawed limbs. At the top, still only about as high as Gerstner's waist, a delicate head almost like that of a bee, but instead of eyes or other ordinary features, a comma-shaped patch of slender, glassine tentacles on either side of the head. Behind the head, a rippling mane of longer tentacles that reached and recoiled.

Gerstner got all that in one fast impression. Then birdsong warbled. Tiny claws, or something like claws, chimed and rang against the decking as the creature dropped low and skittered away as fast as it had come, zipping off the floor and up onto the wall as it left the arrowpoint. With no change in speed, either, just *zip,* up and around, heading for the ceiling out there as far as Gerstner could tell. A silverpede certainly couldn't do *that*. That trick made Gerstner think of the tiny orange centipedes that had come along with some of the botanicals from Earth.

That was an Enemy? Maybe it was a pet. Or a prey animal. Whatever it had been, it was gone.

Then the doorway was filled suddenly by something slithery and dark and much bigger, something that glided with a smooth rippling wiggle thoroughly at odds with its size. *That* was an Enemy, Gerstner had no doubt of it. There was a sudden ringing as of dozens of little bells, a liquid trill of birdsong, a rising hiss.

Gerstner recoiled, but Kaamharaa reared up and crashed back down, his voice booming out, resonant echoes crashing through these metal-lined spaces. Kaamharaa in a rage was *terrifying*. But the black slithery thing kept coming, slithering like a serpent, trilling like a flock of canaries. Kaamharaa leaped over a sudden effusion of slender glasslike tentacles that sprouted from the thing and *roared*, the most incredible sound. He came down on the back of the Enemy, slamming down with such force that the deck underfoot really *did* shake. For a long, stretched second, Kaamharaa pounded the Enemy with fists and front feet. Then he leaped away from reaching tentacles. A ripple went through the huge slithery thing, which was now moving rather awkwardly. So Kaamharaa had hurt it—no surprise there, hard to imagine anything *not* being hurt by that kind of assault—but the Enemy had overcome and captured Kaamharaa before. Twice.

Gerstner fell to his knees and started to press the palm of his good hand against the surface of the crescent—changed his mind at the last second and made himself use his left hand instead, steadying his left with his right, just in case something reacted the wrong way to his touch. He could just imagine disabling his *other* arm. But no; nothing. He drew a fingertip from one tip of the crescent to the other. Nothing. In desperation, he leaned down and breathed on the crescent, and at just that moment there was a sharp trill of birdsong and Kaamharaa *bellowed*, a sound that might almost knock a man right off his feet, and Gerstner, flinching in anticipation of disaster, looked up.

The centaur had reared up, hardly a pace in front of the cargo doors, which ... were closed.

"You *breathe* on it? Seriously?" Gerstner asked the wide universe, incredulous. Maybe the doors had closed coincidentally—or the little white creature had closed them from its side—or the controls had responded to one of the trills the big dark Enemy had made.

No matter what had shut that door, the Enemy would probably open it again as soon as they'd gotten together enough reinforcements to overcome Kaamharaa. Who was battering the slithery black thing—not to a pulp, exactly, but literally to pieces. It wasn't moving very much anymore. Well, most of it wasn't moving. Gerstner wanted very badly to examine the thing, see just what Kaamharaa had destroyed. Animal or mechanism? There was no organic smell, so now he suspected the latter. But figuring out what they had here couldn't be a priority. The priority *had* to be figuring out how to launch this damned arrowpoint. It had damn well better *be* an arrowpoint, and not some random little cul de sac in the middle of some station or mothership, all Gerstner's guesses and suppositions shown to be utterly wrongheaded.

The little passageway-tunnel for, presumably, the use of actual crew, might still be open; hard to tell from here. He couldn't see any glowing edge along the ledge. Maybe that entrance had closed too. Or maybe not. If this was an arrowpoint and he got it into space and away and that tunnel was still open, the gravitics had better be set to create an airshield at the slightest hint of depressurization.

On the other hand, there were plenty of worse ways to die than sudden depressurization. Gerstner had been trying not to think of quite a few of them since he'd woken up in the dark. Definitely time to see if breathing on the main controls would automatically initiate a launch.

Yeah, well, they could hope.

Gerstner was torn between asking Kaamharaa to come forward with him and leaving the massive centaur to guard the entrance. There might perfectly well be Enemy in the control part of the arrowpoint, either the little white centipede-like kind or the big slithery black kind, but that wasn't primarily why he called, "Kaamharaa!" and waved for the centaur to come with him. The real reason, stupid and irrational as it might be, was that he just couldn't stand the idea of exploring this little ship alone—or the risk that he might by some miracle get the arrowpoint launched, then come back to find Kaamharaa and discover that the Enemy had killed—or, worse, recaptured—him. That they had dragged the centaur off the arrowpoint and Gerstner had left him behind *again*.

That thought was truly unendurable.

***

Gerstner started to lead the way forward, only to discover that Kaamharaa had a decided opinion about that, and his opinion was that centaurs went first. Gerstner found his objections comprehensively ignored. Obviously there was no possible way he could *make* Kaamharaa do any damn thing. Ludicrous even to try. So he gave in and followed the turun, who advanced along the wide corridor-like space with commendable caution. His golden eyes flared with reflected light whenever the swooping illuminated ribbons passed overhead, his ears twitched and swiveled. He put his huge feet down so delicately his blunt claws made almost no sound, though he was moving fast enough that Gerstner had to jog to keep up. Every step jolted his shoulder. He finally stuffed his left hand into his waistband to help stabilize his arm. It didn't really help, but it made the problem a little easier to ignore.

The centaur strode along so smoothly it was easy to forget he'd been injured as well. His hind legs had to hurt where he'd broken his bonds; and a creature that size had to need plenty of food. Probably water, too. But he showed no sign of suffering. He seemed completely focused on the mission. Though it was iffy to describe a nebulous hope of getting the arrowpoint launched as a *mission*.

But Gerstner found himself reevaluating the turun. For some reason he'd been thinking of Kaamharaa as a peaceable sort, probably a herbivore. The alien's kindness ... or maybe it was the alien's sheer size ... had made Gerstner assume his people were peaceful herbivores.

Now he thought again. Kaamharaa's tusks certainly looked like they were meant for business, when you came right down to it. Hadn't he thought immediately of pig tusks when he'd seen the aliens? He dimly recalled once hearing someone from Haven comment that wild pigs could be nasty customers. Come to think of it, any Terran-native animal that managed to go wild on Haven had to be pretty tough.

Any way you sliced it, the way Kaamharaa was behaving, Gerstner had to think that this wasn't his first sortie into enemy-held territory. That was reassuring in one way, though it raised definite questions about his kind when you thought of them as possible allies.

Where the interior of the saucer had been wide open, everything about this place was narrow. The damn lights were the same, coming and going in painfully bright streamers, too fast for Gerstner's eyes to adjust properly. Kaamharaa didn't seem to have nearly as much trouble with the lights. The turun might be inwardly cursing the illumination as fervently as Gerstner himself, but he moved with purpose. If he could actually handle this insane lighting system, that was another reason to be just as glad he was in front.

Gerstner knew exactly how big arrowpoints were: ninety-one point three one meters from nose to stern, twenty-eight point three one meters across at the widest point, seven point three one meters high. They were all exactly the same. The flattened, sharp-edged shape naturally gave them their name; a narrow concavity running fore to aft even suggested the exact shape of flint arrowheads. Gerstner had actually seen a couple of real arrowheads once. Somebody, no one knew who, had tucked the contents of a decent museum onto one of the ships that had gotten out through the flashpoint. That must have been just before that flashpoint had been slammed shut, when a lot of people thought Earth itself might be burned to a cinder. Hopefully that hadn't happened, hopefully they'd closed that flashpoint fast enough, brutal though that had been for all the people left stranded.

Thank God both Haven and Kanan had been such welcoming worlds. Those early refugees hadn't even known how lucky they were. Not a single world since had been quite so suitable for human settlement. Not even Terabithia or Abhilasha. Certainly not

Hemadri or Hades. To this day, every habitat and terraforming effort depended mainly on biotas from Haven or Kanan, plus canaries and lemon trees, cats and pigs, honeybees and earthworms, and just a very few other salvaged animals and plants.

And to this day, the greatest threat to every human habitat and world was posed by Enemy arrowpoints. Arrowpoints carried world-breakers—startlingly small hydrogen-confinement bombs that had to be a terror to store. If they could find a world-breaker on this particular arrowpoint and figure out how to set it off, maybe they could pull off some truly worthwhile sabotage.

Figuring out how to launch or set off a world-breaker would probably be as impossible as figuring out how to launch and fly the arrowpoint itself. But a man could hope. Gerstner didn't know whether to hope this particular arrowpoint was currently deserted or hope that its crew—probably forewarned—was waiting in front of them. He had no ideas about how to force an Enemy crewmember to launch the arrowpoint, but surely there was more hope of managing that than of figuring out how to fly the little ship himself.

Biological remains had several times been recovered from arrowpoint debris. But those had all been in the form of frozen, charred, or pulped smears, the kind of remains you got when gravitics failed, nothing that would let the lab people figure out what the Enemy actually *looked* like, how one *functioned*, what kinds of senses or appendages they had. Tentacles were assumed because of the snatching apparatus used when a saucer tried to take prisoners, and certainly everything Gerstner had seen supported that idea. The weird lights and those tricks with the gravitics suggested senses and appendages that weren't a lot like a regular person's. Little claws that could let a creature run up a wall, say, and who knew what weird senses those tentacles permitted. It would be astounding if anything about Enemy control systems made sense to a human. But if they couldn't make an Enemy launch this arrowpoint for them, Gerstner couldn't see a lot of options better than trying to do it himself.

Maybe Kaamharaa would surprise him again and turn out to be brilliant at figuring out unfamiliar alien technology. Maybe his people already knew the Enemy language and Kaamharaa could talk to them—though that was probably too much to hope for. Still, hope was free. Maybe Kaamharaa's people had had better luck at capturing Enemy ships intact, and he already knew just how arrowpoints worked and exactly how to fly one. While he was at it, Gerstner could hope the centaur also knew how to backtrack the saucer's course and locate *Vengeful*.

Right.

Ninety meters seemed a lot farther when you were hurrying through an arrowpoint with Enemies possibly before and almost certainly behind you. The corridor narrowed, and then narrowed again, strongly suggesting the external shape of an arrowpoint. Gerstner suspected they had to be getting close to the pointy front end ... ribbons of light curled and uncurled overhead; not very far overhead in this place. From this distance, he could feel the heat as those ribbons swept past, but not as much heat as seemed likely with that brilliance. They seemed to bring that acrid chemical odor with them as well.

In a moment when light faded to darkness, Kaamharaa stopped. He came to a halt smoothly, but so abruptly that Gerstner had to take a quick step to the side to avoid running into him. "Bulkhead?" Gerstner asked him out loud, and edged around the centaur.

It was not a bulkhead. It was the sharp-pointed nose of the ship. Or so it seemed. The floor, which seemed to be made of black glass, ran out into a sharp tip, but on either side of that tip spread out a starfield so vivid and clear there might have been nothing at all between them and the infinite depths of space. A screen seemed likely; a perfectly transparent bulkhead most unlikely; Gerstner supposed either was *possible.*

For the first time, illumination was clear and steady. This part of the arrowpoint was illuminated by the light of a distant star and by the dim radiance of a nearby flashpoint. Seen with the naked eye, the flashpoint looked like a thin cloud of gas, a grayish-gold cloud of uneven shape and thickness and variable luminescence. It would be big enough to encompass a ship, even a very big ship, even a station; but in astronomical terms, it was tiny. The radiation it produced was peculiar and hard to detect. Even specialized explorer craft had difficulty finding flashpoints. But they did produce some energy in the visible light spectrum, and that, along with the system primary, produced a light that was far easier on human eyes than Enemy lighting systems.

The system primary itself was blue-white, bright enough that Gerstner was careful not to look straight at it. He couldn't tell whether the star out there was the primary of the system where *Vengeful* had been attacked or the primary of a different system entirely; they might have gone through any number of flashpoints on their way to this place and there'd be no way to tell. But if he'd been unconscious much longer than a day, he wouldn't just be tormented by thirst, he'd be weakened by it. That star was the right color. It seemed at least plausible this was the same primary and they were still in the same system.

If that was so, *Vengeful* might be out there. Gerstner had no idea whether Reese Kennon would have followed the mothership or fled, possibly in company with Kaamharaa's ship. That would have depended on what else had happened after the raid. He couldn't help but waste a few seconds searching the starfield for *Vengeful's* raking lines, though he knew the naked eye was useless given any practical distance. He made himself stop looking out at space and start looking for some way to control the arrowpoint.

Ship's controls ... nothing obvious. No boards showing readouts and command functions. No wheels or levers or yokes or anything of the kind. This whole area of the ship seemed entirely empty. "Where the hell would you put controls in an arrowpoint, if not in the nose?" Gerstner asked Kaamharaa in exasperation. Maybe in the stern, and they'd wasted all this time rushing forward to find nothing but some kind of visual display area.

The centaur rumbled unintelligibly back at him. Gerstner patted Kaamharaa's lower shoulder and squatted down to squint along the floor. Shiny, shiny, shiny ... matte and dull. Not a crescent this time. A circle, right up close to where the floor narrowed to a sharp point and then looked like it just stopped, a sharp ledge jutting out into empty space. He crawled awkwardly forward to examine the area more closely. Behind him, Kaamharaa rumbled some sort of comment, but Gerstner ignored him.

Here, at the very tip of the arrowpoint, he found matte shapes on the walls as well as the floor. The nearest was not quite an even circle; more of an uneven sort of ellipse, narrower at one end than the other, a bit like the shape of a falling drop of water. A little farther on, an elongated isosceles triangle. Beyond that, a more symmetrical ellipse.

The transparent wall or screen wasn't entirely featureless, either. Not when you got up close to it and looked carefully. Faint, relatively opaque areas spread out across what looked like emptiness. Crescents and ellipses on the left side of the point, and then the point itself, and then on the right, another of those long arrowpoint-shaped triangles and one true circle, the only curved shape that seemed precisely circular. Gerstner touched the unseen wall right beside one of the shapes, carefully, with just a fingertip. He still couldn't *see* even the faintest suggestion that anything physical was there, but it felt like touching glass: cold and ungiving and solid. He touched the nearest ellipse, cautiously, not knowing what he expected.

Nothing. So far as he could tell, nothing. Except the surface didn't seem quite so cold. Just as hard and unyielding, but ... no, he was almost certain it wasn't as cold.

The only shapes that suggested anything at all were the triangles. The one on the floor was pointed forward. The one on the transparent bulkhead was pointed down. Otherwise they seemed exactly alike: About a foot from tip to base, a couple of inches across at the base. Familiar proportions, to a man who was thoroughly acquainted with arrowpoint dimensions.

Gerstner set the tip of one finger on the triangle on the black floor, ran his finger forward to the tip. Nothing happened, naturally. Leaning close, he breathed on the shape. Still nothing, not entirely to his surprise.

Behind them, barely audible, something hissed, long and low, a sound that changed tone and volume even as Gerstner jerked around. But he said grimly, "Kaamharaa, you handle that," and made himself turn back to his examination of the shapes.

The turun had already gone, with a muted thudding of massive blunt-clawed feet.

Gerstner tried not to pay attention to anything behind him. He had enough to occupy himself right here. Crescents and ellipses and triangles—his first guess was definitely that the triangles in some way represented the actual arrowpoint. The others could be anything: controls for loading or unloading munitions, fire control, navigation; hell, they could turn on entertainment channels; he had no way of knowing.

"If I were making one of these damn things a *start* button, which would it be?" he asked out loud, though Kaamharaa was not here to listen. He could work his way from left to right, first across the floor and then the transparent bulkheads. Or he could guess. If anything at all happened when he touched one of these shapes, at least it would be a clue about how to handle these controls.

If these shapes *were* controls, then if he were picking the start button, it'd be … the exact circle, he decided. It was the only shape that had no counterpart elsewhere among the shapes. Of course it could be anything, up to and including a self-destruct button. But if there was an on-off switch, *he* would have wanted it to be unique. Of course, you might say the same about a self-destruct button. And he knew perfectly well that human design principles meant nothing here. Less than nothing.

But he had to do something and start somewhere.

Leaning forward, Gerstner set a fingertip in the exact center of the circle.

12

Taya stood near Commander Kennon's place at the center of *Vengeful's* bridge, nervously pleating the hem of the short jacket Sun had given her and then smoothing the cloth straight again. The black clothing was a little too warm as well as gloomy, and the footwear was uncomfortable and seemed totally unnecessary on shipboard. She was glad to wear this clothing, though, if it made the commander approve of her.

Half of the flat display at the front of the bridge showed little white icons for *Nkaastu* and *Vengeful*—white was certainly an odd color for friends, since it ought to mean arrowpoints—plus a blue dot for the system primary, a glittering smear that represented the slide, and a big round red icon for the uut mothership. Apparently everyone agreed red was the right color for danger. The display also showed a stream of little tiny red sparks moving away from the mothership. Those were apparently Blades and Disks, though they were all the same color and shape, which made it hard to tell the Disks from the Blades.

The other half of *Vengeful's* display was much better. That half showed an image of *Nkaastu's* bridge, with Daamon and Saraa and Kuotaan and Tsumon and everyone. Taya was so glad to see them all she could hardly make herself stand still and quiet. Her brother stood at the station he shared with Kuotaan, looking relaxed and calm, which he had said once was half his job as battlecommander. The captain rested her lower left hand against Daamon's back, projecting support for her battlecommander. That, Taya guessed, was part of *her* job as captain. Their console was not quite turun high, not quite uman low; it was at a compromise level that suggested whichever of them was in command was willing to take advice from the other. She supposed that made sense, though she would have felt better if Daamon had already been in command.

That would have meant *Nkaastu* was definitely planning to *do* something about that mothership.

So far no one had said anything, except Daamon had said *Commander Kennon*—he had pronounced that pretty well—and the commander had answered *Nda Daamon*—he had not pronounced *Nda* at all correctly, but he had tried. Now, with both of them making that gesture toward courtesy, Daamon looked straight across all the space between them. "Taya, I know you haven't had much time. Can you talk to these people at all?"

"Much better," Taya promised her brother. She was too nervous to look at Commander Kennon, but she added in English, "I learn lot. I talk better now." And in Uom again, "What's going on? Things are happening, right? All those uut fighters moving over there by the *mothership*." She used the English term for the giant ship. "Do you know what that's about?"

"We have a guess," Daamon told her.

There was a tense excitement underlying his calm, not visible in his face, but Taya heard it in his voice. She leaned forward.

"It's kind of a mad hypothesis, but we think—please ask Commander Kennon to observe this one Blade." Daamon glanced at Genru. "Can you split the display again? Show them our tank display?"

Gen muttered to Suumat, then made several adjustments at their station. Suumat rumbled, a pleased sound. She stamped one dappled rear leg in satisfaction as she made a final adjustment. Daamon's side of the display divided top to bottom, the top showing the unchanged view of *Nkaastu's* bridge, but the bottom focusing on *Nkaastu's* tank display. The icons there were a lot easier to distinguish: *Nkaastu's* display, fed from a drone far in advance of their own position, showed a much more restricted area with a far larger representation of the mothership and the uut fighters, colored appropriately red and white for Disks and Blades.

In that display, a single narrow white icon brightened sharply. Daamon went on. "The loose structure of this formation is strange, and its composition is odd—it's mostly Disks—and you know Blades never center formations, but this time, Paaol and I agree, every fighter out there is definitely arranged around this one particular Blade."

Once her brother had pointed this out, Taya could see it herself. The stream of uut fighters was heading in a peculiarly straight line, at a peculiarly variable velocity, for nowhere in particular. The formation was too big, too amorphous, dozens of Disks and some Blades, all of them swirling around in the strangest way. Just as Daamon had said, they all seemed to be oriented on the one bright Blade near the front of the swarm.

"Tell Commander Kennon, the behavior of these uut fighters is unlike anything we've seen before," Daamon told her. "He can surely see this Blade is the source of the peculiarity. We see no obvious reason for its behavior. It may be crippled, but then why not move back toward the giant ship instead of away? The other uut fighters may be attempting to assist; several times a Disk has moved to intercept. But the Blade responds to this by increasing its velocity, which to us looks like a threat to ram. Every time so far, the Disk has moved out of the way rather than risk a collision. Is *any* of this behavior familiar to him?"

Trying not to show her mounting excitement, Taya turned to Commander Kennon. "Daamon say look that bright arrowpoint in front. He say all other Enemy saucers and arrowpoints follow that one. He say some time saucer go in front that arrowpoint, then arrowpoint try hit saucer, saucer move away. He asks, is *Vengeful* confuse—confused—by how arrowpoint move, what it do? I mean, what it does. Is—*has Vengeful* watch—watched—many arrowpoint moved same that arrowpoint?"

Commander Kennon listened carefully to Taya's clumsy English. Then he spoke, too fast and with too many unfamiliar words for Taya to understand.

At her station, despite Lieutenant Lockwood's scowl, Sun Grigson lifted a hand, received a nod, and clarified quickly, "We don't understand either. We have never seen the Enemy behave like that. The commander asks if Captain Daamon has a supposition—that means a guess, Taya."

"She says it's weird and they don't understand it either," Taya translated quickly for her brother. "Commander Kennon asks if you have a guess." She was so tense she could hardly stand it. "You do, don't you? You think you know." She almost thought she could guess herself, but didn't quite dare in case she was wrong. Gripping her hands together, she asked, "Do you think—could it be—do you think this *could* be—?"

"Let's not leap ahead farther than our knowledge can take us," her brother cautioned her. But he was smiling; a grim, tight smile. He went on, "We wonder if maybe it's not uut flying that Blade. Paaol and I agree it doesn't *feel* like uut. Saraa thinks the Blade could be severely crippled, but though that might explain its limited maneuverability, we don't see how that could explain how it's acting or how the rest of the uut are reacting to it. Among the others—" in the display, a handful of Disks brightened. "We think all these are heart-Disks. That's a *lot* of heart-Disks for one formation, even a big formation. But even the heart-Disks are orienting themselves according to that one Blade. It all seems very strange, and it's strange in ways that make us think it *could* be their captain flying that Blade. Maybe there's some other reason they're all acting like that. But it *could* be their captain."

"And Kaamharaa?" Taya demanded, coming up on her toes. "Do you think Kaamharaa's on that Blade, too?"

"Don't leap ahead," her brother reminded her again. "We can't know, can't even guess, but I'm afraid if *one* person were to figure out how to fly an unfamiliar ship, it would be their captain, not our Kaamharaa."

Taya let her breath out. "I guess," she said, not very happily, and turned back to Commander Kennon. "Daamon say—says—Nda Daamon says, that arrowpoint, not uut. Not Enemy. Not move right, not feel right. He says that arrowpoint, maybe your Captain Gerstner."

Everyone on *Vengeful's* bridge reacted to that, some studying the displays and some turning to their secondary captain to check his response. Lieutenant Lockwood glared at Taya. She kept her own gaze on Commander Kennon.

The commander studied the divided display, particularly the part echoing *Nkaastu's* own display. "Commander Keay to the bridge," he said at last. And, with a comprehensive gesture that took in the entire bridge, "Thoughts, people?"

Lieutenant Sun Grigson said immediately, "That *something* isn't acting like any Enemy I ever saw, sir."

Lieutenant Lockwood snapped, "*Something something* because the alien *something* girl's put that in your head! Way too *something* and *way* too convenient. Have some sense!"

Someone else argued, "Yes, but *forward* would be a good start on figuring out alien controls in an alien ship, wouldn't it? So would *go faster.* If the captain *is* flying that ship, those would be functions he'd want to get first. I guess *something something* might be *something.*"

Sun said, in simpler language that Taya could understand better, "Commander, if the captain could run, he would try; and if he were going to try to take a craft, an arrowpoint is the obvious choice. Also, that turun was with Captain Gerstner; maybe the turun understand more about Enemy *something.*"

Across the bridge, another person added, "Besides, it's true that it's damn hard to understand what that arrowpoint is up to if it's being flown by the Enemy."

Esaias Keay, stepping onto the bridge, added in his deep, brusque voice, "Threatening to *something* an Enemy saucer would be a *something something* thing to do, if it were Captain Gerstner in that arrowpoint. If the Enemy doesn't want to take the person or people aboard, why not shoot it out of space?"

Commander Kennon frowned, clasped his hands behind his back, and considered the strange swirling movements of the uut fighters around that one Blade, which continued on its unvarying course.

"I wonder what the range of that *something* arrowpoint is," Esaias commented. "If they want it back bad enough, they can just sit on it and wait for it to *something* out, I suppose. I wonder how long it will take for that to happen?"

Commander Kennon shot him a look.

Taya thought she understood a lot of this despite the far too liberal scattering of important words she didn't know. She thought Esaias was saying that if the Blade was threatening to ram any Disk that got in its way, that only made sense if it wasn't an uut flying the Blade. And the other uut ships weren't firing on the strange one because they could just wait for it to run out of fuel and then collect it and whomever was aboard. That made horrible, horrible sense.

Turning to Commander Kennon, she pointed to the display and said determinedly, "Take once is bad, take again is very *very* bad! Get away is hard; get away again is very very *very* hard. Maybe your Captain Gerstner do this hard thing get away. Let Enemy take again, no! Go get!"

Commander Kennon considered her.

Lieutenant Lockwood said vehemently, "They want to *use* us to get back their *something* alien."

"Well, yes, that seems fair," Sun Grigson put in, her tone much more neutral. "Considering we would love to use them to recover our captain. We're all using each other, aren't we? That's what an alliance is, really. In the best alliances, everyone benefits."

"Come on!" snapped Lockwood, confusingly, but from his tone this was a vehement objection. He glared at Sun, then said urgently to Commander Kennon, "Listen, it's impossible to *ally* with aliens; we don't know them and can't *something* them and who knows what they'll do when push comes to *something?*"

"These particular aliens are already allied with humans—" began Sun.

"Allied with, or keeping as *something something something*? Way too trusting, Lieutenant!"

"That's not what they say and not how they act. *Way* too damn *something*, Lieutenant!"

Commander Kennon did not interrupt, and the exchange rapidly became too fast and emphatic for Taya to catch more than a word here and there. She could tell that Lieutenant Lockwood did not want to cooperate with *Nkaastu* to do anything. She couldn't tell what the commander thought. She could only wait tensely, clutching her hands together and hoping.

And she didn't even know whether Kaamharaa was on that Blade. None of them could even be sure Captain Gerstner was on that Blade. She felt desperately certain that if they didn't find out, she would never be able to live with not knowing.

Eventually, Commander Kennon held up a hand, stopping the argument. He said in a mild tone, "Our knowledge is necessarily *something*. We can only do our best, and then work hard to ensure we have an opportunity to explain all of this to our various *something*."

"Sir—" Lieutenant Lockwood began.

"Yes, Samuel, I'm aware of your *something*, and of the possible *something*. I don't actually disagree. Nevertheless, Lieutenant, aboard this ship, the decision is mine. I'll hope for the chance to discuss all my decisions with the commodore and possibly Witness Falconer at some later date." Turning to Taya and pointing at the display, he said slowly and carefully, "You must make your captain understand, *Vengeful* cannot fight a mothership. Without a—never mind." He paused to consider his words, then went on with the same care, "If those fighters go far away from the mothership, we can attack them. The mothership will *something* and we will *something*, and your ship must *something something*—"

"Sir," Sun said quietly, obviously seeing that Taya was completely lost. At the commander's impatient gesture, she took over: "Taya, if those fighters go away from the mothership, *Vengeful* can attack them, but they must go far far, understand? The mothership will try to attack us, but we will be too far away and we will go very *very* far away fast, *run* away, you understand? The mothership will *something* and *Kaastu* must get that one arrowpoint because *Vengeful* won't be *something something*—"

Lieutenant Lockwood snorted. "Listen up, Taya. Sun's trying to say, *Vengeful* will not get the arrowpoint. We will fight the Enemy, get the Enemy to pay attention to us. The ship that will catch the arrowpoint has to be your *Nkaastu*. But if that is *not* our captain, or your lost crewmember, then taking the arrowpoint aboard may be very dangerous for your people. Do you understand?"

He had used only words she knew, and he had spoken every word so distinctly she knew she had understood everything. Taya felt so relieved, she could hardly speak. She managed after an instant, "I understand very good, yes!" To make sure, she turned to Commander Kennon. "*Vengeful* attack Enemy fighters. *Vengeful* run, mothership follow. *Nkaastu* get arrowpoint, find out if Captain Gerstner is aboard arrowpoint." She didn't mention Kaamharaa. Better to focus on their captain. She finished, "*Vengeful* run away, safe. *Nkaastu* get arrowpoint and run away, also safe. If Captain Gerstner on arrowpoint, him also safe. This all correct? I understand, yes?"

"Yes," Commander Kennon agreed. "After this *something* we will both make our way through the *other* flashpoint, obviously not this one—" he pointed toward the display with its glittering icon of the slide—"but the one far out in this system, the one that goes back toward *your* space. We will come back together there. Where we met for the first time. Yes? You understand?"

Taya understood perfectly. She hadn't thought that far ahead, but obviously that was a very important part of the plan—there was no way their two ships would keep track of each other if they did what Commander Kennon was suggesting. And if the commander was planning for a rendezvous, he must truly be intending to go ahead with this plan. She clapped her hands. "Meet again same first meet, yes!" she agreed, and spun back toward the display. "Daamon! We have this great plan!" She outlined it quickly for her brother.

Daamon listened to her explanation. Then he nodded, frowning, and turned to Tsaa Kuotaan. "I think this is a good plan," he told her. "It's simple, it's direct, it assigns each ship a suitable role, and in my estimation it offers a good chance of success. Though there is some risk, capturing an intact Blade would be extremely useful—so useful that I believe the risk is not too great given the potential benefit."

Tsaa Kuotaan tilted her head, considering. "You assert we have the capacity to carry out the proposed maneuver."

Daamon nodded. "I think we do. This isn't exactly a battle maneuver. The battle will be carried by our cousins, not by us. We'll need to manage some tricky flying, but we can handle it. Paaol? Aanhk? Saraa?"

"Whatever part of that formation our cousins' ship doesn't clear out of the way, we can manage," Paaol said confidently. "We've had plenty of time to get our tusks sharpened and we're ready to challenge."

"Yeah, and we can definitely catch that Blade," Saraa added, finishing some quick calculations. "Definitely. We'd have to dump the largest cargo bay, but if we're willing to do that, we can catch that Blade almost exactly the way we'd pick up a low-gravity load at a station."

Aanhk rumbled. "This situation would not be precisely parallel, Kha Saraa." But she tossed her head to show her tusks and make her feather accents swing. She wanted to do it.

"Oh, it'd take some fancy work with the gravitics, but Tsumon and I can handle it," Saraa assured her.

"We can," Tsumon agreed, patting her partner's shoulder with immense approval. "Saraa is clever—and I am also clever. The Blade will occupy roughly one-eighteenth the volume of the bay. This is by no means a prohibitive volume."

"Yet to do this, we would have to dump the bay entirely." Kuotaan sounded pained.

Taya looked at Daamon, expecting him to answer this. She knew *Nkaastu* was carrying electronics, components for weapons, things like that—all more valuable than ever now that they knew the uut had come this close to the near edge of Ka' Taand space. But surely under the circumstances ... but Daamon didn't say a word. He leaned his hip against the smooth rising curve of the crash railing and crossed his arms over his chest, letting everyone else argue.

At least everyone else seemed *willing* to argue. Saraa's main-crew partner Tsumon swiveled her upper torso, ran a lower hand across the enamels of her console to tighten the display to just the one Blade and the nearest other uut fighters, and observed, "Bringing an intact Blade to the reputationists and the craftspersons of the Ka' Taand would be an enormous coup for Aanuku, more than offsetting the proposed losses as well as the losses already sustained during all these unexpected complications. We need to understand better what we have found. That would surely gain Aanuku much support in the Suund. Such a feat would also be a most suitable topic for a romance-adventure; we may be certain someone would write one."

"Our own efforts in that direction would surely win acclaim," Kuotaan observed, a little drily. "Especially as no other author of these tales will be able to speak from personal experience."

Tsumon rumbled, amused. Kuotaan might say *our efforts,* but everyone knew that aboard *Nkaastu*, Tsumon was the only turun who more than dabbled with adventure stories, both the finance-adventure beloved of nturun and uman-style romance-adventure. Of course Tsumon herself couldn't say this. She said, "We dabble merely. Still, we might hope our skills might be sufficient to enhance Aanuku's reputation and increase the line's profit."

"Kha Tsumon is too modest," Suumat protested. "She should indeed write such an epic. We can't be too forward if we suggest an adventure tale composed by Tsumon u Aanuku might lead to the Kaoluun matriline supporting Aanuku in the Suund. We've seen all these uut, so many! These giant ships, so big! And so few slides removed from turun space! We need to understand better what we have found. Kaoluun is certain to agree."

"Yes, and anyway, we need to make our uman cousins be our allies," Taya put in quickly, since this was obvious. "That's important, too, Tsaa Kuotaan! We made them come with us after the mothership, so we can hardly say now we won't help with this plan–"

"Enough," Kuotaan told them all. "Nda Daamon, you believe this can be done?"

Daamon stepped away from the crash railing, bowing slightly in a way that made him look *perfectly* confident. He said, "With your permission, Tsaa Kuotaan, and with our cousins to help us, and with the beloved gods providing a very reasonable number of favorable dice, I think it's very likely we can do this. I think we should attempt it. Which of us can say with assurance what other system may prove suddenly at risk? What we learn here may prove invaluable."

Taya watched anxiously. *Surely* the captain would agree?

After a long pause, Kuotaan shrugged, a complicated gesture that involved all her arms, acknowledging the complexity of the situation. "Aanuku policy here is ambiguous. However, we agree. We shall carry out this plan. Nda Daamon, you may assume battlecommand for this purpose."

Daamon tipped his chin up in agreement.

"Yes!" cried Taya, and while her brother reached to bring the console down to uman height, she whirled back to Commander Kennon. "Tsaa Kuotaan say yes! Daamon say yes. We do what you say. *Vengeful* attack Enemy, make safe way for *Nkaastu*, and *Nkaastu* get arrowpoint. Yes!"

The secondary captain sighed, glanced around his bridge, and said to Esaias in a dry tone, "I guess that's a go, Commander." And to Sun, "Please summon Ensign Genee to the bridge. When she arrives, she will *something*. You, however, may set aside your *something* duties for the *something*; please serve as our *something* to Taya and her people."

"Sir, I—" began Lieutenant Lockwood.

"Certainly, Samuel. Both of you, then," Commander Kennon said mildly. "They also serve who stand aside and translate."

"Sir," Sun acknowledged, her tone quiet, and Lieutenant Lockwood nodded, looking annoyed but satisfied.

Taya bounced on her toes. She didn't care if Lieutenant Lockwood hated her. She was confident that her brother would catch that Blade, and she was sure Captain Gerstner and Kaamharaa would both be aboard, and then everything would be *so much better*.

13

Daamon strongly suspected that neither Commander Kennon nor his battlecrew nor anyone else aboard the cousins' ship was capable of distinguishing a heart-Disk from any other uut fighter. Spotting the heart-disks required an odd trick of unfocusing the gaze, a talent that was at least partly heritable. Paaol had it, Daamon had it, Taya had it—the talent was common in uman people from Guuan matriline, as he assumed it was among the uman people belonging to the Kaoluun matriline. That was surely one important reason Kaoluun had put together so many full- and half-fighter battlecrews so quickly. But he'd always thought it was just common throughout the uman population.

Now he wondered whether that trick of perception had evolved, or at least been strongly favored, on Ymaa. Certainly Ymaa had presented every kind of challenge for the uman colony stranded there, especially after they lost their technology. Whatever had led to the difference, as far as Daamon could tell, the cousins just did not seem to have that ability. Given that weakness, finding a way to share that perception seemed of the utmost urgency. Daamon had therefore asked Paaol to keep track of the heart-Disks. Paaol understood the issue and was now tightly focused on continuously updating the position of each heart-fighter in the tank display.

Daamon had also asked Paaol's partner Aanhk to coordinate *Nkaastu's* display with *Vengeful's* people to ensure the cousins could not possibly lose track of that one particular Blade they needed to separate from the rest, though he hardly saw how anyone could have the slightest trouble distinguishing that one from the rest; it was so plain to him now that he could have spotted it at a glance even if Paaol hadn't painted it a vivid, brilliant pink in the display.

It was nturun who said too much hope was as dangerous to clear thought as too much fear; that was not at all an uturun attitude. But in this case Daamon thought the nturun were right.

Asking Aanhk to do anything involved with battle was a little closer to truly illegal than half-legal. But handling communications with an ally was not quite battle. Daamon pretended it had not occurred to him that there could be any question, and Kuotaan made no comment. Aanhk herself probably truly did not realize there could be a problem; among all the nturun aboard *Nkaastu*, she was probably the least concerned with legality and propriety. He happened to know that when it came to Aanhk u Aanuku, Kuotaan's official register was heavily sprinkled with the words *diligent* and *industrious* and *ntuo*, but never once used the term *meticulous*.

Saraa was rapidly sorting through possible courses, first to intercept that vivid pink Blade and then to get away again. Daamon saw no need to involve himself with that; Saraa was thoroughly meticulous, in her independent and aggressive way. Tsumon was leaning thoughtfully over Saraa's shoulder, making an occasional low-voiced suggestion. Kuotaan didn't seem to have noticed, which Daamon didn't believe for a moment.

Genru had taken on the job of setting up for battle maneuvers using the nearby slide; slip-courses that would take them into the slide and out again along wildly divergent vectors; snap-courses that would take them in and immediately snap them right back along the exact approach vector but at a much higher vee. Nothing that would take them into and *through* the slide; that seemed sensible; they hadn't the faintest idea what might be on the other side. If it came to using those maneuvers, Saraa would choose which to use, but she didn't need to personally oversee this initial preparation; Genru wasn't as aggressive, but he could direct the priorities almost as fast as she could.

Suumat u Kaoluun had taken up the task of trying out different theoretical maneuvers for capturing a free object the size of a Blade in their largest cargo bay. She modeled the maneuver with different vees and relative orientations for both *Nkaastu* and the Blade. In about half her attempts at these simulated maneuvers, the bay gravitics failed to contain the Blade, resulting in various kinds of disaster and mayhem for *Nkaastu*. Also the total destruction of the Blade in question.

Beside Daamon, Kuotaan thoughtfully ran a fingertip across one pattern in the enamels and then another. Suumat glanced over her shoulder at the captain in evident surprise, made an adjustment, and ran another scenario. This simulation resulted in the captured Blade hanging suspended in the middle of the cargo bay, at the cost of significant wear on the gravitics.

"Our repair crews, skilled and diligent as they are, wouldn't be able to bring the primary gravitics back up to spec after something like that," Daamon commented.

Kuotaan inclined her head. "Secondary and tertiary gravitics would remain optimal in this scenario. Though scrupulous attention to detail is always desirable, occasionally it is boldness in pursuit of success that separates rising matrilines from falling. Observe, Nda Daamon: your-and-our cousins are beginning their run."

Daamon leaned forward. The sharp lavender icon that was *Vengeful* slid forward, increasing acceleration once and then again. As far as Daamon could tell, Commander Kennon intended to make a completely straightforward attack with nothing of subtlety about it. At that acceleration, the uut fighters at the forefront of that swarm ought to pick up *Vengeful* in ... he worked out his best guess absently ... zero point one four. If the sensitivity of their sensors was normal. Considering the giant uut ship had found

Vengeful even when the cousins' ship was fully masked, possibly this was not a reliable estimate.

They knew far too little and depended on guesses and hypotheses far too much. But what choice did they have?

Daamon glanced at Saraa, who tipped her chin up in acknowledgment and told him, "I'm feeding *Nkaastu's* course to your console now. If that Blade continues along that course, and I don't know why it should change considering it hasn't varied its direction one bit so far, we'll be in position to intercept it in ... zero point five three. If they add or drop vee, we'll adjust, but obviously that would change the time to intercept."

Daamon nodded.

Paaol lifted a hand for attention. "I'm going to complicate that, cause I figure we all like a challenge. I'm guessing our cousins'll clean up the leading uut and fix the attention of the swarm, draw the whole lot off, and if that's the way it goes, we'll be fine, but listen."

"Right," Saraa said, just as Daamon saw where Paaol was going and sighed in disgust.

"Right, you see!" Paaol answered them both. "Once we're set up for intercept, we'll *have* to sit still or risk tapping the capture way off center, which I'm guessing would not be helpful, so if we've got any uut shooting at us at that point, that would be bad. I'm figuring on maybe battle maneuvers right up until the actual intercept, then an absolutely steady course till we've got the Blade secure. Sorry, Saraa, I know that makes it impossible for you to run decent projections."

Saraa shrugged. "If the beloved gods throw favorable dice our way, the uut will be so busy with *Vengeful* they won't notice us till we've already caught that Blade and started our run out into the far reaches of this benighted system at our very best accel. We'll have to go dark, I expect, if any of those uut do leave *Vengeful* to pursue us."

Daamon nodded. "Assume some will. Hit our best accel, but prepare to drop confounders, kick us onto an orthogonal course, and run inertial and darkmasked off this way." He sketched the course he had in mind, one that should—might—get *Nkaastu* well away from the area the uut would probably search most strenuously, and take them out toward a semi-handy asteroid belt where they could tuck themselves behind a rock and let the energy-expensive darkmask go.

They'd be almost safe at that point. Probably. Unless something else went wrong.

Vengeful was well out toward the cloud of uut fighters now, moving fast and still picking up vee. As yet there was no perceptible response from the uut; he guessed that couldn't last much longer. The cousins' ship was already closer than he'd expected it to get … ah. "See here," he murmured, highlighting a double handful of Blades that whirled away from the swarm of uut fighters surrounding the one pink Blade.

Vengeful shed ten little lavender sparks in return; Daamon thought of the small vessels he'd glimpsed at rest in their berths in the great ship's docking bay and wondered what kinds of weaponry those little ships might possess, what kind of crew they carried. The display flickered as they shifted to a direct feed from *Nkaastu's* own sensors rather than a drone relay.

"Real time, no delay," Saraa announced. "That pink Blade is adding vee, but as you see, its escort hasn't abandoned it yet."

"At least they're still not firing on it, either," muttered Paaol.

This possibility hadn't occurred to Daamon. Now he realized that the uut might possibly destroy the peculiar Blade rather than let *Nkaastu* capture it. He couldn't guess whether that was the sort of thing uut would do or not, so better—far better—if they didn't guess *Nkaastu's* intention. He took a breath, let it out, and told Paaol, "Listen, if any uut are still in range on our last approach, *we* will fire on that Blade—carefully, but try to make it look real. Let's not let the uut figure out what we're really after till the last moment. Can we do that?"

"Oh, we can definitely do that! Especially if the Blade doesn't vary its exact course. Good idea, Daamon."

"Clever," Saraa conceded. "Probably scare whoever's in there practically paralyzed, though."

Daamon cupped a hand, meaning he didn't see any good alternatives.

"Right, right, I know," Saraa agreed. "That'll make us the very first ship to fire on that Blade. Or look like we're firing on it. Let's hope they truly do not have weapons capacity."

"They won't fire on *us!*" Genru protested.

"If that's our people on there, we don't know what kind of sensors they've got working, or if they can read them at all. Even if they know it's us, the uut use so many mechanisms, the weapons might be fully automated."

Paaol opened both hands, wide-eyed. "Well, gods be forsaken. Good point. Let's throw some confounders out when we start firing. And plan to do some clever dodging."

"And fire a little wider than necessary," added Daamon. Though none of that might help if that Blade tagged *Nkaastu* as actively hostile. He started running damage control estimates based on *Nkaastu* taking damage during final intercept maneuvering. "We'll want to limit the time we spend in our actual intercept position to ... point one three or less, if we possibly can, Gen, if you would add that to your calculations."

"Yeah, this wasn't looking interesting enough before. All right, fine, point one three. Or less."

Far out ahead of them, *Vengeful* engaged with the first of the uut Blades, deploying insystem-driven missiles, faster than light weapons, which forced the uut onto the defensive. The little lavender sparks were definitely fighters, cleverly used to attack any Blade that seemed likely to get itself into position to return attack against *Vengeful*. This allowed the cousins' ship to hold its course without much need for evasive maneuvers or defensive interceptions. The skirmish, over almost before it had begun, did not even slow *Vengeful*, which slashed on at an angle that would carry it past the leading edge of the swarm of uut fighters and directly toward the giant ship.

"If you think it wise, we should pass this tactic on to every tactician allied to Aanuku," Daamon said to Kuotaan.

Kuotaan tipped her chin up in agreement. "Half-fighter tradeships would probably have to give up too much cargo space to carry tiny independent attack craft such as those, but perhaps half-fighters and full-fighters might find their options expanded by such means."

"Yes, and if crews were made up only of uman khand, the little craft could be made even smaller without compromising weapons capability."

"All laws regarding uman autonomy aside, the Suund probably would not approve subjecting uman battlecrew to such disproportionate risks," Kuotaan observed, her tone not quite neutral because she definitely did not approve either.

It was always difficult to get turun to accept risks to uman people. That was the whole point of the autonomy laws. Daamon considered arguing, but it didn't seem an urgent question just at the moment. Instead, he studied the display, where a significant number of Disks and far too many Blades were concentrating along *Vengeful's* course. But *Vengeful* would have made the best and newest Kaoluun full-fighter look like a lumbering tradeship.

"Giant pink ship's figured out there's a problem. It's releasing more fighters," Saraa announced. "I make it another twenty Disks so far, and fifteen Blades. Lag means we're behind at least zero point six, so I put the new formation about here." She painted her best guess of the new formation's location into the display, red and white icons flickering with uncertainty. "Assuming they're moving to intercept at any kind of decent vee, we should paint them for real in about zero point one. How many uut would it take to pull down our cousins, do you suppose?"

"Fewer than they're facing," Daamon answered grimly. "They'll have to pull off. How long till we intercept? Gen, listen, we'll want to cut right out of here the instant we've got our captured Blade tight in the bay." Once they had the Blade, *Nkaastu* and *Vengeful* would both have more options. But of course they had to capture the Blade first. At least its course was still invariable. Beloved gods forfend it change now.

"Zero point two two to intercept," Saraa said. She was leaning forward tensely, Tsumon right beside her. Tsumon didn't say a word, but she moved a finger, tapped the console, and Saraa said immediately, "Point two zero, and they're still adding vee, Gen, that's a lot of mass for our gravitics to handle—"

"We've got it, we can handle it, Suumat's double-checked my numbers, but it'd be great if they went dead in space just about now."

Daamon nodded. "Let me know if it looks like we can't catch them, Gen." He began to figure a secondary option for getting *Nkaastu* out of the way if the intercept became impossible. Odds for a second try ... hard to calculate, but probably poor.

"Daamon—" Paaol said warningly.

"Yes, I see them." Most of the uut fighters had gone after *Vengeful*, which had battered its opponents in passing, specifically clearing out the fighters closest to that one Blade. Now *Vengeful* was heading threateningly straight toward the giant ship. That was fine; many of the remaining Disks and most of the Blades had swept off in pursuit, and Daamon assumed Commander Kennon had a plan besides taking his ship directly into the fangs of all the uut in the universe and letting *Vengeful* get surrounded and battered to pieces.

Of more immediate relevance, half a handful of Disks and two Blades had maintained their pursuit of that one pink Blade. Not too many for *Nkaastu*, or it shouldn't be too many, but on the other hand *Nkaastu* was not actually free to maneuver, either. Any moment now the uut had to paint *Nkaastu* no matter how their attention might have been pulled away by the drama *Vengeful* was providing. Daamon didn't have to actually run the numbers to see that *Nkaastu* could not possibly intercept the pink Blade without entering attack range of the rest of the uut.

"Drop a handful of confounders," Daamon ordered. "Also, let's drop a drone—two drones—and set them up to ram this Disk here; Paaol, do you agree?" He brightened the Disk he meant. It was hanging back in the way that heart-Disks generally held back and would be far out of attack range as the nearer Disks and Blades engaged.

"Absolutely," Paaol agreed. "Good idea. The Disk'll take out our drones, of course, but they should distract it for a moment or two. And, you know, I think I'll run one in noisy and one in quiet and we'll just see if the beloved gods feel generous."

Before Daamon could answer, Saraa announced, "Our target's increasing accel again. Time to intercept: zero point zero seven. Gen?"

A slight pause as Genru and Suumat exchanged a long glance. "We can do it," Suumat stated in her firm, deep voice.

"Suu—"

Suumat tossed her head. "*Nkaastu* can do this. Tsaa Kuotaan, it won't push our gravitics much beyond specs, and we know there's always give in the specs. We can do it." Her big hands moved as she shunted calculations to the captain's console.

Daamon left Kuotaan to make that decision, rapidly updating the abort-and-try-again course and feeding it to every station on the bridge. "It's an alternative," he told them all.

"Yeah, a terrible one," Saraa said grimly.

"I know that—"

"Perform the intercept," ordered Kuotaan. "*Nkaastu* will endure the shock. But if that Blade adds more vee, we will abort."

"I concur," said Daamon, making that order officially unassailable.

"Yes, great, but listen!" Paaol said urgently. "Do we want to pretend to fire on that Blade? Time to do it if we're going to."

"Any uut fighter in position to fire on it?"

"Just one Blade, but another will get in position *way* before we can grab our little friend."

"Set us up so we look like we're planning an attack run that starts with the pink Blade, range it, and see if you can't fire past it at the two closest Blades instead. Got it?"

"Right, Daamon."

"Point zero six chime-down," Saraa chanted. "Point zero five ... point zero four five chime-down ..."

The first drone slashed in toward the suspected heart-Disk, vanishing from the display as the heart-Disk destroyed it. The second drone, which had slipped stealthily into an intercept course with that Disk and gone dead, was not visible in the tank, but Paaol had painted its presumed location with blue glitter. If the heart-Disk didn't spot it ... and didn't change course ... it occurred to Daamon that fitting drones to drop a load of tiny explosives might make this kind of tactic more useful, but he didn't have time to make a note of the idea ...

"Point zero four," Saraa said coolly. "Point zero three five chime-down."

"Start firing past our Blade," Daamon told Paaol. "Genru, set us up for the intercept." He bit down on an urge to add, *Be careful.* Instead, he sent a warning tone to the repair crews he knew were standing by and a collision alert to the whole ship, then threw Kuotaan a tense smile as she set a second steadying hand on his back.

"Intercept position," Genru said crisply. "Holding intercept position."

"Whoops, I guess they've figured it out," Paaol announced. "We've lost confounders—we need to *move,* Daamon—"

Daamon, every console on the bridge mirrored to his, said, "Hold, hold. Zero point zero zero two to intercept."

Way out behind the rushing pink Blade, the heart-Disk suddenly stuttered in the display as it detected the silent drone. With no time to fire, the Disk jinked sharply to evade, and then the Disk was past the drone and closing fast. But its instant of distraction had indeed cost the uut; in that last instant, not a single uut fighter fired on *Nkaastu.*

"Intercept!" Saraa declared, her voice sharpening in pitch.

"Intercept!" Genru agreed just as the pink icon disappeared from the tank display.

"We have seized it tightly!" declared Suumat, tossing her head in aggressive satisfaction.

Daamon had for some reason expected to *feel Nkaastu* capture that Blade, even though he knew perfectly well that if the gravitics worked properly, there would be nothing to feel. He said crisply, "Evasive maneuvers, confounders; Saraa, give us a random walk and prepare to darkmask; Paaol, that heart-Disk?"

Paaol waved an irritated acknowledgment. "Forsaken thing's too smart to get in near-range and too aggressive to just pull off.

I've got solutions for the nearest Disk and those Blades ... holding ... holding ... firing now!"

Daamon counted to four and then nodded sharply as one of the Blades disappeared from the display and, an instant later, the closest Disk stuttered and dumped vee, dropping almost instantly out of range. Saraa had initiated a random walk, which was generating a lot of noise around *Nkaastu's* ultimate course, which was basically just *away*.

"We need to get off their scans," he said out loud. Safe to assume the big uut ship had extremely good sensors; pouring energy into the darkmask until they could get themselves tucked behind a nice big rock seemed to be the best option. They'd want to drop a drone or three so they could see what else might happen in this system, but first they would have to get rid of the other three Disks and the remaining Blade. They should be able to do that, though he wished very much they'd managed to destroy the heart-Disk with that drone maneuver.

All this went rapidly through his mind, and he added, "Tsumon, program a drone to emit the brightest signature possible and get ready to drop it. Paaol, I'm going to want more confounders. Tsaa Kuotaan, we don't actually *know* who, or what, might be aboard that Blade we're holding in our cargo bay."

"Nda Daamon, our khand are taking appropriate precautions," Kuotaan told him calmly. "We have detailed a handful of nturun to occupy the access corridor between the bay and the other areas of the ship."

Daamon shrugged in chagrined agreement. He should have thought of that himself. "Paaol, those Disks?"

"*Working* on it!" snapped Paaol. "They're stringing themselves way out, which at first I figured was fine because we're not in range of any but the one Disk and that last Blade, but on second and third thoughts, I don't think it's good at all, Daamon, and on fourth thought I think it's a gods-be-forsaken disaster. Look back at the giant ship, that's the real problem."

It only took one glance to see that at least a hundred uut fighters were streaming away from the giant ship. Red and white, brilliant in the display; a lot were moving to engage *Vengeful*, but far too many were coming straight after *Nkaastu*. Which ought to be out of sensor range unless they knew exactly where to look.

"They're using those other two Disks as signal relays," Daamon said, realizing this at last. He should have caught on much faster. He kept his expression calm, but inwardly cursed his own lack of experience.

"They figured out what we were doing with our drones, I guess," Paaol agreed. "We taught them a new trick! Aren't they clever?"

Saraa raised one hand. "Think *we've* got problems? Take a look at our cousins."

Daamon followed her advice and took a deep breath.

When Commander Kennon decided to support an ally, he evidently went *all* the way. Because *Vengeful* had surged straight into the cloud of uut fighters, and through that cloud, and was now attacking the giant ship directly. Pink glitter spread outward as *Nkaastu's* computers found evidence of damage.

"Well, it *is* working," Genru said in a tentative tone. "If any fighters were coming after *Nkaastu*, I think they've changed their minds. That means we only need to deal with—"

"Firing," Paaol said, and the blade behind them disappeared from the display.

"These last three Disks," Genru finished. "We can handle three Disks."

Indeed, *Nkaastu* almost certainly could handle three Disks, unless they were unlucky or careless. But it was impossible to find this very cheering now that they could see how all the red and white icons in the tank display were folding back toward the giant pink ship, plainly intending to engulf and destroy *Vengeful* ... or surround it, tear it apart, and take a lot of prisoners.

Saraa said, "We have to remember, we're lagged by point eight seven. Whatever's happened back there, it's probably already finished."

Daamon nodded. "We have to get off their scans. Paaol, I want that nearest Disk destroyed. Get a firing solution and put us wherever you have to in order to let *Nkaastu* take it. Saraa, when Paaol takes navigation, let him have it. Tsumon, you've got a drone set up? Give it to Genru. Gen, on my order, drop that drone and the confounders. Saraa, the instant that drone is away, put *Nkaastu* on this course—" he shunted it to her console. "Then drop power to everything nonessential and bring up our darkmask. Let us drift, but deploy sensor drones to keep our eyes open. Everyone understand?"

Murmurs of subdued agreement.

In the tank, the lavender icon, looking uncharacteristically small against the giant pink uut icon, skated along the side of the giant ship, then dropped away from it into the swarm of tiny red and white icons. Lavender glitter puffed away from *Vengeful*, then more lavender glitter ... and the cousins' ship changed course almost upon a single footprint, clawed for vee, and ... disappeared into the slide. Into gods knew what.

Paaol, not watching the larger drama unrolling in the distance, snatched control of *Nkaastu* and violently switched out of Saraa's random walk onto an attack course. *Nkaastu's* targeting computers instantly executed his priority attack on the nearest Disk, which dissolved into a flare of red light.

"Move, move," snapped Daamon, not shouting, and there was a flurry of activity—the confounders away, followed immediately by the drone. Saraa coolly took back navigation, slipped *Nkaastu* onto a quiet dead-ship course orthogonal to its original course and killed every possible ship system, feeding power to the darkmask instead.

Then they merely stayed quiet, watching through trailing drones too small and cold to attract attention, as the other two Disks passed them by, going after the confounder drone.

That much was good. But *Vengeful* had not returned. The giant uut ship had gone after *Vengeful*, pursuing the cousins' ship through the slide. Even now—or, correcting for the increasing lag, more nearly a full chime ago—a whole lot of little red and white icons followed it. Hundreds of them. Literally hundreds. And Daamon knew *Vengeful* was already damaged. Maybe badly damaged.

"Daamon?" Genru said, a little hesitantly. "What do you think we ought to do now?"

Daamon drew a deep breath and let it out. "Stay as we are. Take a broadly circular course and wait to see if *Vengeful* returns."

"How long will we wait?" Kuotaan said, which was only half a question.

Daamon turned his head, meeting her one eye.

She dipped her head in regret, but not with any suggestion she might change her mind. "We must consider how long to linger before bearing our report to Aam."

Daamon couldn't deny this. He hated it, but he knew Kuotaan was right. He let his breath out and said steadily, "Tsaa Kuotaan, you are, of course, correct. We will follow the plan to rendezvous at Aam. But of course we must remain passive until we are certain no uut remain near enough to perceive our signature in their scans." Another breath, and a glance at Kuotaan, who acknowledged with a tip of her head. "In the meantime," Daamon added, "We must certainly open up that Blade." He tapped his cane gently on the decking. "Though I would wish to handle that personally, Tsaa Kuotaan, I can't say I feel this would be the most practical choice."

Kuotaan eyed him. “Indeed. You will retain battlecommand; all battlecrew will continue in their places. Tsumon u Aanuku will personally inspect this captured Blade, if she is willing. Kha Tsumon?”

Both Daamon and Tsumon bowed acceptance. Tsumon was too polite to show open satisfaction with an assignment Daamon wanted and could not take, but it was obvious from the swift brevity of her bow that she was pleased to be asked.

Kuotaan was already continuing. “Kha Tsumon, if you will select a handful of khand to accompany you and assist your efforts. As physical danger seems more than a remote possibility, let us not unnecessarily risk uman khand. Select only nturun for this task.”

Daamon cleared his throat.

“Indeed, Daamon, we are fully aware of the impropriety of restricting uman people from assuming necessary or appropriate risks, but we consider this task suitable for turun and do not perceive any great benefit from uman participation.”

Daamon couldn’t argue that uman skills or talents were uniquely useful in breaking into that Blade. If they cracked it open and discovered enemies waiting inside, he had to acknowledge, turun were probably a much better choice. He opened both hands in a gesture of concession.

“Yes,” rumbled Kuotaan. “Also, Kha Tsumon, we consider that you might wish to ask Ngakuu or another physician to accompany you.”

“Indeed,” agreed Tsumon with another brief little bow. She patted Daamon on the shoulder in passing and promised him, “We will be careful, Nda Daamon, and polite if your uman cousin is on that Blade; and more polite if we are so fortunate as to encounter Tsuumat Kaamharaa.”

"And more *careful,* if it's uut aboard after all!" Saraa warned Tsumon, her tone tart. "If you're so overconfident you get yourself killed, I'll add *careless* to your reputation flag, Tsu!"

Tsumon rumbled amused reassurance, added an nturun's three-handed salute for good measure, and disappeared off the bridge.

14

Lem Gerstner could not remember ever in his life being so tired and afraid.

One or the other, yes. The instructors at the academy deliberately ran plebes ragged in those first months, then did it again to anyone who came back for officer's training. Find out who had nerve and grit and the ability to stay focused through exhaustion and effort, that was the point. He ought to be able to get a grip on himself, focus on the problem at hand.

Granted, it was a hell of a problem.

They'd done a pretty fair job staying out of the Enemy's hands—tentacles—for a good while, given the only controls he'd ever figured out were *forward* and *faster*. And yes, fine, he'd been lucky to get even those two controls sorted out, but it hadn't been nearly enough. He'd known almost from the beginning that they weren't going to get clear. But he'd thought at least they might be able to ram a saucer, take a handful of Enemies with them.

No. They'd been recaptured. He'd failed to get them clear, failed even to manage a heroic kamikaze death, and now ... here they were. Back in a damned saucer. Or they would be, as soon as the Enemy opened up this arrowpoint and hauled them out.

Gerstner had stared failure in the face once or twice. Everybody did. His very first battle as a baby lieutenant under Captain Lawes had been bad, though—perhaps fortunately—he'd lacked the experience to realize just how bad.

Or later, when Fleet had faced terrible odds at Kanan, the Enemy suddenly breaking into the flashpoint web of the Shallows from an altogether unexpected direction. An unknown flashpoint, a new flashpoint, some abrupt rearrangement of web geometry—whatever had led to that incursion, they could have lost everything, right there, for every single person on Kanan. He'd been afraid then: of failure. Of losing. Of letting the Enemy get past him. The desperate terror of those long, frantic days, holding back the Enemy, knowing that some other task force searched, with equal desperation, for the knot in the web that had let in the Enemy, not knowing whether they'd find it in time.

They had, of course, or Gerstner wouldn't have found himself in *this* dire situation. James Dawson had found the right flashpoint, and sacrificed his ship to destabilize it, and finally Fleet had been able to make decisive progress against the Enemy swarm ... all that came back to Gerstner now, the terror and relief, the grim satisfaction as the tide of battle finally turned, the sorrow of the memorial afterward, held in honor of all those lost.

All those moments, all those disasters, but through all of that, Gerstner had not been *personally* afraid, afraid for himself, like a child or a coward. Not until now.

He'd been staring through the transparent hull of the arrowpoint into the starfield, waiting for another saucer to get in front of them so he could signal for *faster* and force it to back off. He hadn't guessed, hadn't had any way to figure out, couldn't read whatever sensors might be screaming warnings, that a saucer might be cutting in close at an angle from which he couldn't see it, that it might get in front of them so fast he'd see nothing but the empty starfield and then *boom*, black. Maybe the saucer had flicked its slowdrive, literally just appeared in front of their arrowpoint.

Didn't much matter exactly *how* the Enemy had caught them. The fact was, they were caught. Ramming would almost certainly have been preferable. Using their time to find out if this arrowpoint had a world-breaker on board and how to set it off would *definitely* have been more worthwhile; with luck they could have taken out far more than the one saucer that had caught them. The whole mothership, even, with *enough* luck. Maybe they could still manage that, but probably they'd run out of time.

Gerstner rubbed his eyes with his good hand. They burned—chemicals in the air or plain exhaustion, he had no idea. "I don't think I'll be much good in a fight," he told Kaamharaa.

"I fight," the centaur declared, with a rumbling boom, and stamped one huge foot; the solid percussive *thud* of the blow boded ill for any monstrous Enemy snakey thing that got in Kaamharaa's way.

"Yes," Gerstner agreed. "Yes, I know you will."

The turun's attitude was definitely aggressive, even eager. Gerstner would never have imagined he could stand this close to a supersized aggressive alien and just not worry about it. Of course, threats from every other possible direction would give anybody a different point of view about a giant four-armed centaur, as long as he was on your side. Gerstner devoutly wished he thought Kaamharaa's bravery and willingness to fight would be enough. He knew it couldn't be. But in the end, what else was there to do besides fight for as long as breath and muscle would answer?

He drew another breath and promised the centaur, "Well, I'll help. I'll do what I can." Then, in smaller words he hoped Kaamharaa would understand, "Yes, I fight too."

"No," Kaamharaa rumbled, his voice pitched so deep that Gerstner felt the sound in his bones. *"I* fight. You, no."

Dictatorial bastard. Or protective. Or maybe realistically assessing both of them as potential fighters. Conceivably thinking ahead to keeping Gerstner free to mount yet another rescue attempt, if it came to that. Possibly all of that at once. Gerstner didn't argue, partly because arguing didn't seem like a sensible use of anyone's energy, and partly because tactical realities did suggest he should probably let Kaamharaa take point while he himself stayed back to observe.

Which was still an idea that felt like utter cowardice.

Regardless, Gerstner would have chosen to wait at the narrow prow of the arrowpoint; keep the closely angled walls at their backs so that nothing could come in behind them. Maybe some of those whirling streamers of light would whoosh through whatever space was outside the arrowpoint now; probably wouldn't help, but he'd have liked to get a glimpse. Not that having a chance to *see* lots of writhing tentacles engulfing the arrowpoint would actually make anything better.

But it didn't matter. Wherever they were, it stayed pitch black out there, and Kaamharaa made it clear that staying put didn't suit him at all. The centaur strode back toward the wider stern with great determination. Gerstner could see a creature Kaamharaa's size would do better with lots of room to fight and move. And if horrible tentacled monster things tried to wrap him up in plastic somehow, again, maybe this time Gerstner could figure out a way to stop them.

Well, he could hope.

Unless the saucer started doing crazy things with its gravitics. Gerstner had to hope the Enemy wouldn't realize how easily even Kaamharaa could be defeated by violent shifts in gravity. The arrowpoint hadn't seemed inclined toward such madness with its gravitics. No doubt it was lucky Gerstner hadn't accidentally triggered whatever controls might have subjected them to that kind of thing.

He took a couple hurried steps to catch up to Kaamharaa and tapped the centaur on one haunch to get his attention.

Kaamharaa whirled around so fast Gerstner took an involuntary step back, but at once the turun visibly collected himself. "Gerrstter," he rumbled. "Go fight."

"I know, yes, but remember the gravity on the saucer? Maybe it would be better to stay here, on this arrowpoint, wait here for the Enemy. The gravity here's been constant—so far—but if we're going to fight, better have *down* stay *down*, right?"

"No," Kaamharaa said definitively. Whether he understood what Gerstner was trying to say wasn't clear, but his opinion certainly was. "No. Out. Go. Fight." He pivoted again, surprisingly graceful for so massive a creature.

"Jesus Christ who is our savior," Gerstner muttered. He wasn't extraordinarily devout, but this was definitely that kind of day.

The cargo entrance at the stern of the arrowpoint was still closed when they approached it, which was both a frustration and a relief. Debris from the slithery black thing Kaamharaa had fought was scattered across the floor, half visible in the poor light, some pieces shining dimly. There was no organic smell or obvious blood or whatever. Gerstner more and more believed it must have been a mechanism, not a creature. Or maybe a monster cyborg thing, God knew. He couldn't quite decide whether that would be more or less horrible than a living Enemy alien.

Kaamharaa's yellow eyes glowed as the light flared and passed overhead and died. "Open!" he boomed, stabbing two hands toward the cargo doors.

"Right," Gerstner muttered. He was not at all sure he *could* get those doors open, but he hunkered down to inspect the crescent on the floor and look for other shapes that might be controls. He still had no idea whether he'd somehow closed those doors in the first place or whether the Enemy had coincidentally closed them right as he experimented.

"Crazy damn controls," he muttered, laying a hand on the crescent.

The arrowpoint was shuddering. He could feel the vibrations under his hand: subtle but distinct. He couldn't remember having felt that before. It didn't feel quite like anything he'd expect from a live ship underway. More like … a *lot* like somebody trying to cut their way through the hull.

Jumping up, Gerstner slapped Kaamharaa's nearest arm. "Back, back. Back up." He set a hand firmly on Kaamharaa's chest—well, about at the place the upper torso joined the lower; call it the chest—and shoved.

After a startled pause, the turun took half a dozen steps straight back. As the vibration got stronger, he halted, lowering his tusked head, opening and closing his great fists. A grinding whine started up. A line of painfully bright light drew a line straight across the cargo doors, then down. Then down the other side.

Gerstner looked around for a weapon—for anything that could be used as a weapon; a simple club would be enough—well, not *enough*, but he'd feel better with something in his hand. Kaamharaa collected himself, making a deep, deep rumbling sound that Gerstner thought he could feel in his bones. He tossed his head; Gerstner had seen him do that before, but only now, as the dim light picked out one hand-length tusk, did he recognize the gesture for the threat it was. The centaur took one long stride forward, moving protectively in front of Gerstner, and as a large section of the bulkhead lifted and slid away, letting in streaming yellow light, Kaamharaa reared up and came smashing down again with tremendous force and a deafening *boom*.

God knew, Kaamharaa was going to be the center of attention. Gerstner ducked sideways, trying to get a clear line of sight as the Enemy came through the hole they'd made. Maybe he could do something while they were focused on the turun—he could certainly *try*. He could see great bulky shapes moving against the light; he had no idea what he was looking at, except they were big—not as big as Kaamharaa, thankfully, but big, with a lot of limbs … sort of centauroid shaped, in fact …

He stared from the newcomers to Kaamharaa, realizing at last that if you put the centaur in some kind of pressure suit ... yes, Kaamharaa would look just about like the newcomers. Except bigger.

Kaamharaa had recognized his own people first, of course. He had already settled, rumbling in a completely different tone and register, and began to speak in his own language, with broad gestures of three arms and far more expression than Gerstner had seen from him before. All of the newcomers were answering, and two had reached up to their helmets—not really helmets; more form-fitting and less rigid, Gerstner thought.

He would never have expected to feel infinite relief because he was surrounded by giant four-armed pig-tusked centauroid aliens. But he did. He most definitely did. Kaamharaa rumbled and growled in his own language at the newcomers. Gerstner could make out nothing but his own name, which was enough and more than enough; all the desperate focused strength that had kept him going was now running out of him like water, and he had to grip the centaur's arm to keep on his feet.

"Vengeful?" he asked them. *"Vengeful?"* But of course they couldn't understand him, so he said instead, "Daamon?"

"Nda Daamon!" the foremost of the smaller centaurs said with enthusiasm, waving two great hands.

"Daamon sepu Kaamharaa," Kaamharaa declared. He gripped Gerstner's good shoulder, pulling him forward to stand beside him. Tilting his head, he stared down into Gerstner's face and rumbled firmly, "Good. Good. Come."

Gerstner was perfectly willing to believe this reassurance and go wherever Kaamharaa wanted him to go, but he did delay to look ostentatiously around at the dim arrowpoint. "Not safe," he warned them. "Be careful!" He added, "There could be a world-breaker somewhere here," though he knew they wouldn't be able to understand him. But maybe they'd understand his tone.

Kaamharaa boomed, though quietly, and two of the smaller centaurs rumbled and growled back and waved various tools or weapons they held. Gerstner would have preferred Esaias Keay and a full company of marines, but maybe the turun could handle whatever they found, whether Enemy or some kind of mechanism or a neatly packaged bomb in a little box saying *Do not fold, spindle, or mutilate.*

Kaamharaa seemed to have no doubts. Fine. Let the other centaurs deal with the arrowpoint however they saw fit. He just hoped they were competent engineers. Surely they were. He hoped they'd find something useful. He followed Kaamharaa toward ... he had no idea where they were going, and hardly cared. He did not look back.

***

Where turned out to be some kind of sickbay. First lots of corridors, wide and warmly lit, weirdly decorated with fancy mosaics and things which Gerstner might have appreciated more if he hadn't been working so hard to stay on his feet. Mostly he appreciated the lighting, which was just normal lighting, like normal people would want on a ship. He'd probably appreciate ordinary, regular lighting for the rest of his life.

Corridors, and then a big open space, though Gerstner didn't realize this room was a sickbay until one of the smaller turun—they all seemed small compared to Kaamharaa, and way too big compared to a person—began to poke at Kaamharaa's injured arm. Kaamharaa folded his legs up in a movement that seemed clumsy and yet smooth at the same time, lying down on the floor to make it easier for the other centaur to examine his injured limb. He was so much bigger than the others that his head was nearly at the level of theirs even when he was lying down and they were standing up. Gerstner had known his centaur was oversized compared to the others, but he had to stop himself from staring as he compared them now. It wasn't just the size and the bigger tusks. Kaamharaa's features were harsher, sort of a cross between human and gargoyle, so far from human he didn't exactly strike Gerstner as ugly. The smaller ones somehow looked both much more human and much uglier.

The smaller centaur examining Kaamharaa, surely a physician of some sort, rumbled and purred and eventually took out a kind of hand-held scanning tool to image Kaamharaa's damaged limb. The scanner extruded stiff sheets of black and white images, like radiographs, which the smaller centaur held up to the light for careful consideration.

Meanwhile, another of the smaller turun approached Gerstner, who steeled himself to stand still and look it—him—in the face. Her? Some of the turun struck his eye as more masculine and some more feminine, but for all he knew they were sexless until they got as big as Kaamharaa and then sorted themselves out. A discreet peek underneath didn't tell him anything; whatever genitals these aliens might have were not immediately evident.

The size difference might be sex based, but it might just as easily be based on age, or race, or God knew what. This one had small tusks, hardly as long as a man's thumb. To him, this one's features were ambiguous, but wasn't it usually the males of whatever kind that had bigger horns or antlers or tusks or whatever?

Whatever it was, the turun spoke to him, which of course Gerstner could not understand, and Kaamharaa growled and rumbled. The smaller centaur turned and trotted away across the room. The sickbay.

The sickbay itself did not immediately present a professional appearance, yet at the same time, it tended to inspire confidence. Unidentifiable equipment was placed all around the large central area. Nothing looked purely utilitarian; most of the equipment was colorful, and the floor was covered with soft rugs, green and blue. It seemed it should be difficult to keep rugs clean, but the colors were bright and the rugs showed no sign of wear or dirt. The walls were painted in more greens and blues, and potted plants were set here and there amid the equipment.

The door they'd come through, if you could call it that, was actually a kind of curtain made of hundreds of strings of tiny beads. Mostly the beads were a tawny amber color, but some were a brighter yellow material and some glossy gray. They might be glass or natural minerals or even ceramic; Gerstner couldn't tell. It was a nice effect, but he couldn't help but wonder what precautions, if any, these people had taken in case of a depressurization accident. He hoped airshields would automatically deploy, or at least that there were real doors concealed in the bulkheads.

The overhead lighting was diffuse, steady, and cast a quiet warmth—so much like sunlight through clouds that, with the soft colors and the plants, he might almost have believed himself in an outdoor setting. The air smelled like outdoor air, planetary air. It smelled like growing things and faintly of some floral fragrance. He hadn't realized how awful the chemical stink of the Enemy ships had been until now, in this clean and pleasant place.

The turun that had moved away now returned and approached Gerstner again, offering him a narrow, deep bowl of clear water and a smaller bowl of some hot milky-brown liquid. The water was enormously welcome. It was hard to manage the bowl with only one good hand, like a really big cup with no handle. He almost spilled it, which would have been unendurable. The turun saw the problem and steadied the bowl for him. Gerstner didn't object. He was even grateful, and that was a hell of a thing, but he was long past worrying about an alien holding a cup for him. He drank half the water at once, hardly pausing for breath. It was cool and faintly sweet and very possibly the best water he'd ever tasted.

He didn't touch the other bowl, which eventually the centaur set aside on a counter or table. Then it—he, she, whatever—began, gently, to try to remove Gerstner's shirt. Gerstner stepped back quickly. "No, thank you," he said forcefully.

"Calm," rumbled Kaamharaa, suddenly looming up right beside him. He patted Gerstner's good shoulder. "Good. Good. Calm."

"Good," Gerstner echoed, mostly to show he was paying attention and willing to cooperate. He was, more or less, but he was not at all interested in letting an alien doctor poke at his shoulder. "Listen, do we know where *Vengeful* is? Can you ask them about *Vengeful*?"

Kaamharaa rumbled, a sound which might have contained words, or maybe not. Leaning forward, he lifted the narrow bowl of steaming liquid from the table—the bowl looked much smaller in his huge hand—and offered it to Gerstner himself, adding a firm little flourish. "Take," he ordered. "Take."

Gerstner hesitated. But after all, these turun lived with people. They could not possibly poison him accidentally. Yielding to Kaamharaa's certainty, he first sniffed and then cautiously tasted the hot liquid. It smelled peculiar, but not unpleasant. It tasted bland, a little sweet. Its thick, creamy warmth soothed a throat Gerstner had not even realized was raw. He waited a moment, but felt no ill signs from the single sip. Kaamharaa, watching, made an impatient gesture, miming drinking, and Gerstner sipped again.

When his physician turun tapped the floor with a front foot, a largish section of the floor where Gerstner was standing rose up about two feet—a much more convenient height for a big creature to examine or treat a human-sized patient.

"Thank you," Gerstner told the alien, easing back from its touch as it again tried—still very gently—to take off his shirt. "Thank you, but no. *No,*" he emphasized, certain that was a word Kaamharaa understood. "Listen. Listen, where's *Vengeful?* I'd prefer a human doctor, no offense. Is *Vengeful* here? Where are we? Your ship, I know, but beyond that, where? Where? *Vengeful?*" He gestured around with his good hand, hoping it was clear he meant a broader question than just about the sickbay. The half-dozen words he shared with Kaamharaa didn't really stretch to fit questions like *Are we still in the same system, did we go through a flashpoint, is my ship all right, what the hell has been happening*—it was hopeless.

On the other hand, this was a whole different kind and quality of *hopeless* than aboard that arrowpoint. Or before that, on the mothership or the saucer. He was deeply grateful to be here, aboard Kaamharaa's ship, but *where* was *Vengeful?*

The turun looked at Gerstner blankly, purred at him, and patted the surface of the platform, plainly wanting him to sit down and cooperate. When he didn't move, it—*he,* dammit, or maybe *she*—turned and talked to Kaamharaa in the centaurs' rumbling, purring, coughing, unintelligible language. Gerstner rubbed his face with his one good hand. He supposed that these aliens probably did know how to treat human injuries. Maybe he should let one of them look at his shoulder; maybe they knew what they were doing. He was so tired he almost didn't care.

He stayed on his feet. *"Vengeful?"* he asked quietly, stubbornly. "Look, isn't there someone human I could talk to?" He looked at Kaamharaa. "Humans? I *know* there are humans here on this ship ..." For a wild, disorienting moment he wondered if this could actually be a *different* turun ship, one with no humans aboard after all, so that he was completely alone. The idea sent a sharp chill down his spine. Crouching, he jumped awkwardly off the raised table-platform, which produced a jarring explosion of pain all through his shoulder and arm, plus his back and neck as well. It took a breath to recover. Then, ignoring the pain, he headed stubbornly toward the curtained doorway, evading the smaller turun who exclaimed and reached out to him.

Before he reached it, the bead curtain clattered gently and a woman stepped through it.

This was no one Gerstner recognized, but she was a woman, she was undeniably human, and he immediately felt himself begin to relax.

She wasn't a young woman, but not old—maybe a little younger than Gerstner himself, somewhere in her early forties. She was not beautiful, but attractive: full figured and broad hipped. Her face was round, her mouth generous and smiling, her coloring dark but not unusually so. She might have been from Kanan or Hemadri or any Gujarati habitat; she had that kind of look. She wore a narrow dress, patterned with circles and triangles of brown and soft ivory; and over that a loose robe of some soft, sheer fabric in different shades of green, all sorts of shades that blurred into one another. Her shoulder-length hair was thick, black, and decorated with strands of little wooden beads that clattered gently when she moved. Her feet were bare; her toenails tinted chocolate brown.

The woman smiled at him, perfectly friendly, but the smile she directed at Kaamharaa was entirely different: a wide grin of pure, uninhibited relief and joy. "Kaamharaa!" she said, and something else, quite a lot else. Striding forward, she took one of his hands in both of hers and brought that huge hand to her cheek, and Kaamharaa cupped another of his hands around the back of her head and stroked her hair. Gerstner saw the woman was blinking back tears and looked away, feeling strongly that he was intruding.

But a moment later, the woman had pulled away from Kaamharaa and turned to Gerstner. She met his gaze, smiling, and brought her hands together before her chest. “Karuu,” she told him. “Karuu sepu Kaamharaa. Captain Lem Gerstner.”

Her pronunciation of Gerstner’s name was all wrong, but it was wrong in a completely human way. The woman’s voice was warm, her tone friendly, her manner confident; and when she spoke to the smaller turun and then gave Gerstner a stern look and pointed back toward the platform, he understood her perfectly and couldn’t help but smile.

The turun doctor had backed away a couple of steps and crouched down a little. That didn’t make it look any less alien. Him. Her. Whatever. Fine, *her,* and if he was wrong, no doubt he’d find that out eventually. For now, say the little ones were female no matter what they looked like to his eye; that way at least he’d be using pronouns fit for people and not monsters. *She* was a doctor, probably perfectly competent. She probably worked with human patients all the time. The woman, Karuu, was speaking in a soothing tone and making little patting gestures, and she could not have been communicating more clearly if she’d spoken decent English. *Stop making a fuss, you idiot, and let the doctor do her job.* Hell of a situation, but he *was* being an idiot. If he couldn’t be on *Vengeful*, with a real doctor fixing him up ... fine. Gerstner blew out a breath and finally let the centaur help him back up on the platform.

The doctor tried to cut his shirt off, discovered it wouldn’t cut, and eased it off over his head as gently as possible. Getting it off made spots close in around the edges of Gerstner’s vision. His shoulder actually hurt worse now because he was less distracted by thirst and horrible lighting and weird shifts in gravity and sheer terror. There was something seriously wrong with that shoulder, but he tried to pretend he trusted the turun doctor. He set his jaw, and the doctor purred and hummed and said things to Kaamharaa, and Kaamharaa purred and hummed back and told Gerstner, "Good, good, calm," in a tone as reassuring as a giant centaur could manage. Which was actually pretty reassuring, under the circumstances. The woman, Karuu, perched on the edge of the platform and patted Gerstner's good shoulder, and he was embarrassed to admit that was also fairly reassuring.

The doctor did something that hurt like hell. Gerstner gritted his teeth and stayed put and thought about other things. He needed to find a way to ask about *Vengeful.* He *had* to find out what had happened, language problem or no language problem. They had to understand he was asking about his ship. They couldn't have failed to understand that. He didn't want to think they were deliberately refusing to contact *Vengeful* for him. He couldn't believe, didn't want to believe, that she'd been lost. Maybe his ship was nowhere nearby. Would Reese have let the little alien ship go after the Enemy ship all on its own? Well, he might, obviously, depending on what else had happened after Gerstner been snatched out of the bay. He didn't *know* what had happened; that was the whole problem, and he didn't have a way to ask, and he couldn't stand it but couldn't do anything about it.

Another of the smaller centaurs came over and handed the doctor a thing like a flat, broad syringe, complete with a long needle. Gerstner immediately pushed himself up. "No!" he snapped, and slid off the platform again. Just a couple feet down to the floor, but the movement jarred his shoulder. Gerstner grabbed the edge of the platform, swaying, and the doctor caught him with her two lower hands, and maybe she just meant to steady him, but he tried to jerk away and *that* hurt badly enough he staggered and sagged in her hold instead, dizzy and sick. The woman, Karuu, was speaking urgently, and Kaamharaa boomed something, and the doctor picked him up, put him back on the platform, and then unexpectedly let him go and took a step back and boomed something that made everybody else shut up.

Gerstner braced himself with his good hand, sweating and sick, and glared at the turun doctor. She met his eyes. Hers were bright gold, completely unhuman. He couldn't read her expression at all, but she said something, very slowly and quietly, in a voice that would have seemed resonant and deep if he hadn't gotten used to Kaamharaa first. She held up the syringe in one of her hands, reached out with another hand, and very gently touched one fingertip to the back of his hand. She was obviously big enough to make him do anything she wanted, but she didn't grip his hand or wrist. Just that light touch. She was saying. *I won't force you to let me treat you, but you are being a complete idiot and you should stop that.*

"All right," Gerstner said. "Fine. Dammit. All right." He was so tired his eyes burned and felt gritty at the same time, and his shoulder felt like someone had shoved a knife into the joint, and he couldn't speak the damn language. But he let her give him the shot. The needle barely stung, going in, and when he fell slowly into gauzy darkness, the alien centaur had plenty of arms left to catch him.

15

Taya mostly kept her eyes squeezed tight shut. It was just too terrifying to watch the displays. So many red sparks that were uut, and the mothership so close, and everything was happening so fast; every time she opened her eyes she immediately got so scared she had to shut them again.

Even when she dared to look, she couldn't make sense of anything. She could hardly understand the tank displays, but she felt how the ship trembled, and trembled again. She had no way of guessing how much injury the cousins' ship could absorb, but she was sure *Nkaastu* would have been destroyed within a tenth-chime if it had gotten itself into such a terrible position. Not that Daamon would have let that happen. She hoped he wouldn't. Hadn't.

She peeked once more, and now they were skating so close to the mothership that the icons in the display merged in the most horrifying way, as though the mothership were in the act of engulfing *Vengeful*. The display was filled with the white sparks that meant the little human fighters, sweeping in among the dense clusters of red ones nearest *Vengeful* and then turning into diffuse puffs of light. As soon as Taya realized that, she understood what might be happening. Maybe those were drones, but ... she was pretty sure they weren't drones. They didn't fly like unmanned drones. She couldn't have explained how she could tell. It was like saaom, or like picking out heart-Disks from an uut swarm. She just didn't think those were drones.

She was pretty sure those little uman fighters were deliberately sacrificing themselves to clear a way through the attacking uut swarms.

The strategy was terrible, it was unspeakably terrible, but it was *working*. Taya suspected none of those little ships would make it back to *Vengeful*; she was pretty sure none of them meant to try. She hoped their bravery saved *Vengeful*. It was so ugly to hope someone else would die to save you; Taya had never imagined hoping for anything like that and it was awful, but she couldn't help it.

Because the little uman fighters were drawing away so many of the uut, *Vengeful* was not at the moment in very great danger. Except once the white sparks were gone, the red ones would come back and attack *Vengeful*. No one had to explain that to Taya. It was obvious. And there were still so very many little red sparks.

But then, startlingly close, a vast glittering cloud came into the display. Taya knew this had to be the slide even though the last time she'd had the nerve to look at the display it had been much smaller. It had never occurred to her that they might go through it—surely the other side must be uut territory—but now she could see that maybe going through an unmapped slide into unknown space might be the best thing they could do, if everything else was worse.

Commander Kennon did not actually look frightened at all. He was on his feet, leaning one hip against the arm of the chair he wasn't sitting in, and he had his arms folded over his chest, and he looked not merely relaxed but mildly amused. This impression would have been more comforting if Daamon hadn't explained to Taya how the battlecommander always had to look like he wasn't upset, even when terrible things were happening.

If you think you're going to lose, you can make it happen. He'd explained that to her. As soon as her brother pointed that out, Taya actually understood perfectly. It was the same for a young uturun who'd just left his mother's matriline and headed for a reservation; he had to look confident, because if he looked like he doubted his strength, he would draw challenge after challenge. And then eventually he would lose.

She wondered if Commander Kennon thought he was going to lose. If he did, she couldn't tell. The bridge crew spoke to one another in those short, clipped phrases Taya couldn't understand, and did things that were no doubt useful and appropriate, but she couldn't bear to watch anymore and squeezed her eyes shut again.

Near at hand, Commander Kennon said something in a drawling tone, and a ripple of laughter passed across the bridge. That made Taya peek in sheer astonishment, and so she saw the displays all go to silver glitter. And then *Vengeful* turned inside out.

Almost at once the ship twisted itself back rightway round again. Even though she'd expected Commander Kennon to take *Vengeful* through the slide, Taya could hardly believe he'd truly done it. But she guessed it must have been a good idea after all, since *Vengeful* didn't seem to be under actual attack anymore. The displays were clearing again, everything overlaid with red but nothing yet resolved into clear images. *Vengeful's* crew and computers must be trying to figure out where they were; the ship's sensors must be hunting for signals, urgently striving to paint in the icons of any enemy ships or structures.

The bridge crew were all busy, probably trying to help their computers figure out what all was out there—Lieutenant Maxson was doing something fast and complicated, and so was the woman beside him, whose name Taya had forgotten—no, she remembered: Genee. A squeaky sort of name, one that sounded wrong to an ear trained to turun voices and Uom.

Commander Kennon hadn't moved; he leaned on the arm of his chair, swinging one leg idly, his attention divided between the big display and whatever his own boards were telling him. The big central display was slowly resolving, which was a great relief. They'd come through a slide that seemed oddly placed in the system, neither near the primary nor way out in the distant reaches of the system. Now she figured out that the computers seemed to think *Vengeful* had entered a double-star system. That was unusual. Mostly double-star systems had few planets, and so stable slides rarely formed in such systems. Maybe the slide they'd come through was actually not at all stable. As long as it didn't close down while they were actually stuck on this side of it, that would probably be a really good thing.

Both stars looked purplish in the display—Taya assumed they were really blue, but everything in the display was overlain with a wash of red. At first she thought this was because they were just assuming this was uut space and always colored their display like that when they ventured into Enemy territory.

Then the red overlay began to resolve into icons, and she realized that it wasn't an overlay, exactly. It was just that the system was *filled* with uut ships. Besides the ships, there were other things that didn't make sense at all, and those were colored red, too. *Everything* was colored red.

Fine. At least that made sense, horrifying as it was. But nothing else did. Taya had learned to recognize ships and slides in the cousins' displays, but what *was* that bar extending right across the screen? Not exactly solid, fuzzy around the edges ... she couldn't even guess.

"What in the name of God is *that?*" Sun Grigson asked. Taya was so grateful the other woman had put the question into clear, understandable words that she could have hugged her.

After a slight pause, Commander Kennon answered, "Well, now, Sun, I do believe that's a Niven ring, or something close to it. Those *something* might be fairly well spaced out, but offhand I'd say that's probably more than we want to take on all by ourselves."

Taya had no idea what a *Niven ring* might be and didn't dare ask. Apparently everyone else knew, because no one asked. There was another pause.

Lieutenant Maxson broke it, asking in a plaintive tone, "Damn, sir, why don't *we* have one of those?" All across the bridge, people glanced him and smiled. A few of them laughed.

Commander Kennon said drily, "Get these images on file, Keith, and I'll be sure to put your proposal before the *something something*. I imagine the *something* will be most enthusiastic," and everyone laughed again.

Since no one seemed exactly worried about the crowds of uut, and for some reason none of the uut were firing on *Vengeful* any longer, Taya hesitantly raised her hand. "Enemy not attack?" she asked, hoping that there might be time for someone to explain.

Apparently there was, because Sun glanced at the commander for permission, then did something that made one little red icon light up in the display and take on a white halo. "Us," she explained to Taya. "The second we hit the flashpoint, we *something*. We can't go all the way, um, all the way black, we don't have enough power for the *something*, but we can ... we can change light, change how light goes around us, so to Enemy who look at us, we look round, flat, like Enemy saucer."

"We hope we do," said Commander Kennon. He was leaning against the arm of his chair again, perfectly relaxed. "We won't be able to keep that up *something*, but long enough, let us *something*. That damned mothership shouldn't have been able to spot us masked all the way down in the *something* of that gas giant, yet here we are, so let's not get *something* about Enemy *something*, right, people? Any close scan is certain to pick us out of the *something*, so let's have a nice saucer-appropriate course toward that Niven ring."

"*Toward* it?" asked a woman, though she began to do things that that sent the white-haloed icon skimming along with some of the Enemy ships, matching their general course and velocity.

The commander shrugged. "Well, now, Annette, when a single *something* flies the wrong way, anyone can see it's not part of the *something*. I do think it's *something* to join the flow right along with everyone else and not make ourselves obvious, yes?"

Taya didn't have to understand all the words to get the general idea, but this new plan seemed horrifyingly dangerous to her. She wished Daamon were here, and Paaol. She trusted her brother's battle sense and Paaol's eye. She wasn't at all sure she trusted these people. That they were brave and determined, yes. But even though she'd tried hard not to look while they fought the uut, she thought, she was *almost* certain, that no one here could see the heart-Disks. Not even the people handling the targeting computers. No one.

But the woman, Annette, seemed reassured. She only answered, "*Something* is definitely the aim, yes, sir."

Commander Kennon considered his board and then studied the main display. "Also, if we can keep a great many ordinary fighters between ourselves and the mothership for the next hour or so, that might be *something*."

"Yes, and between us and all those other motherships," added Lieutenant Maxson, gesturing at his board and doing something that made a scattering of points on the ring brighten.

Commander Kennon glanced at him. "Why, yes, Keith, I imagine that would probably be *something* as well. And what is your estimate just at this moment?"

"I can't tell whether I'm picking up a hundred thirteen motherships or a hundred thirteen habitats or what, sir, but I can definitely say there are a hundred thirteen power signatures near enough and strong enough that I'm prepared to worry about them."

"One hundred and thirteen. What a *something* we are having, to be sure," murmured Commander Kennon. "Annette, if you would kindly see about working *Vengeful* toward the perimeter of this swarm. We'll just see if we can't *something something*. Then perhaps we'll be able to eventually make our way back toward the flashpoint before we run out of *something*. Keith, where is our own personal mothership, do we have its signal in *something?*"

Lieutenant Maxson tapped his board, and the round icon representing the mothership brightened in the display. "They haven't *something* us yet, sir, or if they have, they're being *something* about it. If I were guessing, I'd say they think we're somewhere back here." He did something else that started a cone of space flashing on the other side of the slide, broadening as it reached away into the far reaches of the system.

"Not a *something something* idea, in fact," murmured Commander Kennon. "But if we'd actually tried that, we'd have needed quite a pair of legs to get out of sensor range fast enough."

"They might think we *have* legs. But they might figure it out when they don't find us back there. I'm guessing we might not want to get too comfortable with our idea of their *something* sensitivity and range."

"Quite right, of course." Commander Kennon considered the display. "Picking us out of this crowd does possibly seem to be beyond them, however."

"Maybe," Lieutenant Lockwood muttered, but not very loudly. "For now."

"Indeed, Samuel," Commander Kennon said, his tone bland. "We shall by all means avoid overconfidence."

"Sir." This time, for once, Lieutenant Lockwood sounded apologetic.

The images in the display were beginning to take on greater definition as *Vengeful's* crew or computers or both began to get a better handle on what sensors were telling them. The many red sparks of uut fighters were obvious, but Taya found herself treating all those sparks as just a kind of background. So many other things were scarier now. The nearby mothership was scarier, but falling farther behind *Vengeful* as it continued to search for the uman ship in the region of space "behind" the slide, instead of among the swarms of red uut fighters.

Taya could see now that the ring was not solid. It actually consisted of a lot of red icons, widely scattered through a ribbon-shaped noncircular loop of space. Many, most, of the icons seemed much bigger than even the mothership, but some smaller.

"So many!" she said softly. They must be stations, like Ehnuuk or Aramaa, two of the larger stations that orbited Gaatuu. Or hollowed-out asteroids, like people used to make really big tradeships and sometimes worldlets. But these mostly looked even bigger than famous worldlets like Nnumpauk. Though Taya had never actually seen Nnumpauk herself, only read about it in stories, she knew it was supposed to be almost a twentieth as big as Gaatuu.

"A few too many for *Vengeful* to challenge," Commander Kennon agreed, which Taya hoped was a joke. "It does seem odd to see so many habitats when there aren't any obvious worlds in any similar orbit. Keith? Genee?"

"Not that we can see, sir," Lieutenant Maxson answered. "Extrapolating from what we *can* see, even spread out as they are, I'd guess the Enemy has more living area in those habitats out there than any hundred—thousand—Haven-sized worlds could provide."

"How very alarming." Commander Kennon didn't sound alarmed at all; merely thoughtful. He continued in the same musing tone, "Well ... let's see if we can avoid investigating the ring too intimately, however fascinating it may be. Annette?"

The woman nodded and threw a possible course into the display; then a second; then a third. Each drew itself out, flickering white lines that stretched out in front of *Vengeful*, showing different alternatives for curving gently away from the greater masses of red sparks heading toward the ring.

The woman made the longest, smoothest course flicker more brightly. "Option A *something* more *something* course changes and keeps us at the outer edge of the swarm, which might help us stay *something*. But it also takes us most of the way to the ring, *something* us *something* close to one of those bright unknowns that concerns Lieutenant Maxson, and keeps us in this system a little over eighteen hours, which would take us right to the edge of losing our false image. Here's the quickest option." Another of the white lines brightened. "As you see, this one gets us heading out in less than six hours, but you'll observe it crosses against the *something something* of Enemy *something* and eventually takes us back close to our own mothership, unless that mothership moves out of our way."

"And the other alternative *something* the difference," murmured Commander Kennon. "Let me see, nearly twelve hours. Hmm. Yes, I believe we shall attempt the middle option, Annette. I believe that will give firecontrol sufficient time to make repairs without risk to our shield confounders ... Samuel, if you would be so kind as to confirm that ... and allow us to take a fair look at that ring and this system without, I hope, quite patting the *something* on the nose. As an added benefit, it offers a reasonable amount of time for the mothership to go somewhere else. We shall devoutly hope it becomes bored with sitting by the flashpoint. Esaias ... let's rotate the shrike and singlepod crews. I want every single one we have left to maintain launch readiness." The commander paused and touched his console, his tone becoming formal. "Lieutenant Lockwood, log this. If *Vengeful* does not survive, it is of the *something* importance that word of what we've found here get back to *something something something* and to the *something*, or failing that, to *something*. Every singlepod will take this as its *something* priority. Back up the main log to every singlepod now, and we'll be streaming all our observations of this system as well; singlepod crews will confirm receipt. Commander Keay, if *Vengeful* must launch all her small craft, the priority of the shrikes will be to ensure that as many singlepods as possible get out of this system. Log that, please."

Esaias Keay signaled acceptance of this order with one of the sharp little gestures the cousins used for such things.

Commander Kennon nodded and went on, "Run the numbers for four shrikes; those four will carry a heavy payload and a *something* crew. Singlepod and shrike crews, acknowledge as you bring your craft online, please."

As a murmur came back through the sound feed of Commander Kennon's board, Taya raised her hand. "Sir," she said quickly, not waiting for permission in case he might not give it, "Aam very close, maybe easy go to Aam, one slide—I mean flashpoint—maybe not Enemy there."

"Oh, God, no," said Lieutenant Lockwood, not very quietly.

Taya glared at him. She said to Commander Kennon, as firmly and calmly as she could, "Maybe go to your people hard, maybe Aam better! Go to Aam, quick to go, maybe more safe, singlepod talk everyone at Aam, talk say Enemy and big ring, very important Suund—turun—know all this!"

Commander Kennon studied Taya wordlessly for what seemed like a long time, though it was probably not more than a twentieth chime. He asked at last, "Those aliens will listen to my people? My people will be safe among your, uh, turun?"

Lieutenant Lockwood snorted, but softly. Taya avoided looking at him. "Safe, yes," she promised the commander, because she was sure of that part. "Very obvious your little ships not uut—not Enemy. Very different, you. I tell your people what say, words make sure they safe."

Siiv sep' Upuonnu himself had been at Aam. Taya was *positive* he would listen very carefully indeed to anything the cousins told them. If officials had come from the Suund, it was harder to predict what they would think. Their response would probably depend on their matrilineal connections and on their complicated political alliances, but also on what the fighter captains thought. But no Suund officials would ever destroy a lot of little uman ships. There was no way they would do that.

If *Nkaastu* was already waiting at Aam, that would make everything easier. Taya wanted so much to be sure *Nkaastu* would be there. But either way, the battlecommanders would listen. And their captains. She said firmly, "Listen, yes. Everyone scare of Enemy. Singlepods ping turun ship—ships—" she wasn't sure what the English was for *ping*, but surely Commander Kennon would understand. "*Vengeful* people tell turun ships, *uman*." She exaggerated the word, drawing out the vowels. "Say *Nkaastu tsuung*, Aanuku *tsuung*, Ka' Taand *tsuung*. Ally of *Nkaastu*, ally of Aanuku, ally of all Ka' Taand. Can say this? Any part good to say." She cupped one hand and then the other and added, "Or just say *tsuung*, good, anyone would listen."

"Commander—" began Lieutenant Lockwood.

Taya raised her voice enough to speak over him. "*Want* is all true. I want, you want. Good to say. Say it make it true."

"A most *something* observation, I believe," Esaias Keay murmured. "Commander, I agree this is a good suggestion and, if *Vengeful* doesn't get clear, I fully support sending some number of singlepods, maybe a third of the total number, toward alien space."

"Log that," ordered Commander Kennon. "I grant there are risks; there are always risks. Lieutenant Lockwood, I understand your reservations. You may log a protest if you wish."

Lieutenant Lockwood scowled, but he shook his head in the way that meant refusal or disagreement.

Commander Kennon nodded and looked around the bridge. "Anyone who has objections, log them, but I concur with Commander Keay. Log that as well, and—" his tone became ironic—"we shall indeed hope that declaring an alliance makes it true. Signals, did you get all that?"

Lieutenant Maxson nodded. "Logged, sir, and I'm passing it to every singlepod now. Shrikes too, just in case, though it seems unlikely shrike crews'd get a chance to use it."

Commander Kennon nodded absently and tapped his board. "Singlepods A through Q will plan to retreat through flashpoint designated four oh six. Singlepods R through Z will attempt to *something something something something*. All singlepods, log that order. Commander Keay, we will try to recover any shrikes that must be *something*, but if any shrikes must launch, we'll wish them Godspeed and good luck now."

Low murmurs of disembodied acknowledgement from unseen speakers. They must be brave, all those people. Though the commander had said *Vengeful* would try to recover shrikes, she was pretty sure that most or all that launched would be lost—expected to sacrifice themselves for *Vengeful* and for the singlepods. She understood that uman pilots could probably outfly drones, that probably they could do better than unassisted drones even if they couldn't see some things about uut fighters. She understood the strategy of making deliberate sacrifices. Things like that happened all the time in uman romance-adventures. But it was different when she was sitting right here watching Commander Kennon give orders to all the little fighters *Vengeful* carried.

Maybe it wouldn't happen. Maybe they'd just swim along with all the red sparks like one more fish in a very big school of orange-finned kasukasu, glide unnoticed past the Niven ring and back out away from the ring toward the slide, and get out of this system without any uut ever figuring out *Vengeful* wasn't one of them.

Maybe it would be just like that. Maybe it would.

16

Gerstner woke slowly, as though he were rising gradually upward through dark water toward light and air. It was a peaceful feeling. He knew where he was before he was fully awake. Scents of bay leaves and flowers and, faintly, sesame. A low susurrus, not exactly familiar but not disturbing; and beneath that the utterly familiar hum of engines, more felt than heard. Close at hand, people talking quietly in a language that wasn't English or Gujarati ... human people, human voices. Farther away, Kaamharaa's rumbling voice.

Memory came back, equally slowly, without any particular sense of urgency. The turun doctor; the open, airy sickbay; turun everywhere, huge four-armed alien centaurs ... the memory was not, now, charged with much alarm. Kaamharaa, so much larger than the rest. The human woman, Karuu.

His memory drifted further back, but still without much alarm. The Enemy ... yes, but that was over. He remembered the frantic desperation, but with a sense of unreality, as though it had been a dream. A nightmare. It had been strange enough to be a nightmare. Birdsong and harpsichords and windchimes and tentacles; violent shifts in gravity and confusing, swooping ribbons of light. Kaamharaa, roaring in challenge ... it had really happened. All of it. But they had gotten out of that. Kaamharaa's ship had found them, somehow. An honest to God miracle in that. A whole series of miracles.

Vengeful. He had no idea what had happened to his ship. *That* was urgent. He opened his eyes and pushed himself up. With his right arm; his left was supported and confined by some kind of bandage that held his arm against his chest. His shoulder ached, but not badly. Not nearly enough to distract him now that he'd thought of his ship.

The nearby voices had stopped.

He was lying—half sitting now—near one edge of a truly enormous bed, maybe a foot off the floor. He was surrounded and half buried by pillows and fluffy, thick blankets. The light was soft, indirect, but bright enough he could see the room clearly. The bed itself was round, and significantly bigger than his whole bedroom aboard *Vengeful*. It was almost entirely surrounded by low planters containing waist-high narrow-leaved plants; it was the soft, continual movement of those leaves, stirred by a gentle breeze from some unseen ventilation system, that he'd half-heard. That and a faint rattle from the hundreds of strands of beads in the doorway—two doorways, one on either side of this enormous bedroom.

About ten feet from Gerstner, four people, ordinary human people, sat together on the other side of the bed. The woman, Karuu, he recognized after half a puzzled second. The human commander of this ship, Daamon, would have been easy enough to recognize even without the cane. There was another woman, younger than Karuu, whom he thought he recognized from the bridge. Also an older man Gerstner was fairly certain he didn't recognize at all.

They had been waiting for him to wake up, probably. He might have felt uncomfortable, knowing they'd been in this room, watching him sleep. He did feel a little uncomfortable about that, especially as he realized he was naked beneath the blankets. But none of them looked uncomfortable at all, and somehow that helped. Not intruding. Or they didn't mean to intrude. They were just ... here. As though it were the most ordinary thing in the world to settle in this room for a chat, even with somebody, a stranger, a foreigner, asleep in the bed. Their bed, maybe; it was more than big enough for all four of them plus a dozen more people. It was big enough for *Kaamharaa*, if centauroid aliens liked pillows and fluffy blankets. Maybe this was Kaamharaa's bed.

But Gerstner was not very interested in the customary sleeping arrangements of these people. He focused on the commander. Daamon. *"Vengeful?"* he asked. He knew this man would understand him. He'd know there would be only one possible question Gerstner would ask.

He did know. Gerstner could see that. He frowned, not angry as far as Gerstner could tell, but unhappy. That wasn't good. Gerstner braced himself. "Is she gone? Was she destroyed?" He knew the other man didn't speak English, but he couldn't help asking. "Look," he said. "You know what I'm asking. I bet you do. Just tell me. Yes or no, we've got those words sorted out, right?" He waited. Nothing. Just that steady, grave expression. He said, exasperated, "You've got to have a log. Do you keep a log? You can just show me what happened, right?" He added, deliberately, *"Vengeful?"*

"Captain Lem Gerstner," Daamon said. His pronunciation was not bad. He touched himself on the chest. "Daamon sepu Kaamharaa."

"I think we got that far before everything went to hell."

The man ignored this. He gestured toward the other people, one after another. "Karuu sepu Kaamharaa. Mattu sepu Kaamharaa. Saraa u Aanuku."

"Call me Gerstner. Or Captain Gerstner. Or whatever the hell you want. Look, nice to meet you all, I'm very grateful for the rescue, thank you, good job, I want to hear all about it, but what I want *right now* is to hear about *Vengeful*."

"Vengeful. Yes," Daamon said. So that was a start. But then the man said something else, completely incomprehensible. One of the women, Saraa, also said something and that started a whole conversation, nothing Gerstner could understand.

Karuu picked up a bundle that had been lying on the bed and brought it to him, smiling with warm sympathy. Clothing.

All these people were wearing those loose, floating, civilian outfits, greens and browns and blues and different shades of yellow from lemon to golden-tan, but the bundle the woman handed him was black. It was, in fact, his own uniform, cleaned and folded. The cloth smelled faintly of flowers. For the first time, Gerstner realized there wasn't a trace of the chemical reek left on himself, either. He didn't much like knowing somebody, maybe these people, maybe turun, had stripped him and bathed him and put him in this bed, all while he'd been unconscious.

Which was stupid. He'd sure as hell needed a bath; he'd probably needed full decontamination of some kind; God alone knew what kinds of chemicals had caused that stink on the Enemy ships. He touched his eyelids lightly, remembering the way his eyes had stung and watered. They felt okay now. Mostly okay. There was a faint, residual itch, now that he thought about it. The skin on his face felt a little tight, a bit like a mild sunburn. He was thirsty and, now that he took a second to notice, starving. But he felt a hundred times better than when he'd staggered off that Enemy arrowpoint. Not just physically. Trapped on an alien ship, by himself, among people he couldn't talk to, completely helpless, and yet the only thing that worried him was *Vengeful*. He couldn't dredge up a single shred of worry on his own account. It was amazing how a man's attitude could be adjusted by just one horrifying day aboard an Enemy ship.

He could see now how close to the edge he'd been by the time he and Kaamharaa had been rescued. Making a godawful fuss about letting that turun doctor look at his shoulder. He remembered that. He was embarrassed, in retrospect.

The alien centaurs had taken care of the shoulder and cleaned him up, and then these people right here had put him to bed, if he wasn't mistaken, in their own quarters. He was pretty sure he had that right. Damned ungrateful to make another fuss now. If it were anything but his ship, he wouldn't. He had to find out what had happened to *Vengeful*. This ship had to keep a log of some kind, a record. Surely they did. If not that, then surely Kaamharaa could find a way to explain what had happened to his ship, even if he had to use one-syllable words and charades to get it across.

He could hear Kaamharaa's deep voice. He was sure he recognized that incomprehensible rumble.

There were two women here. But he had no way to ask for privacy, and no one else seemed concerned about it. He tossed the blankets back, swung his legs over the edge of the bed—the bruises on his shins were impressive, and hurt as soon as he saw them. His whole left side ached, not just his shoulder. He ignored that, got his feet under him, and stood up. A little light-headed, right at first. He ignored that too. Everyone was looking at him. One more discomfort to ignore. He got himself half dressed, which was a hundred percent better, but paused because the webbing over his shoulder was a problem.

It unsealed. Karuu showed him that, how to make the webbing release along tabs he could feel with his fingertips. Here and there the texture of the bandage material was stiffer and could be pulled apart. He got the webbing off and his shirt on—careful as the woman was, helping him, that was not fun—and the webbing on again over the shirt. He needed Karuu's help for all that. She was thoroughly matter-of-fact about it, a bit like a doctor herself. Maybe she *was* a doctor and that was why she'd come to the sickbay in the first place; he had no idea.

Kaamharaa's voice told him which way to go. Gerstner headed for the door, brushing the strands of beads out of his way and once again wondering, distractedly, about emergency airshields or doors. He didn't stop to look for anything like that, only went into the adjoining room.

And yes, *here* was Kaamharaa. This was another big room—probably all turun rooms would strike a regular person as oversized. At the far end, a thick, translucent column that looked like smoky glass and might be a screen or display surface; down the middle, a long, wide table, also made of smokey glass. This was lower than a normal table, maybe two feet or so off the floor. Small round cushions were arranged down both sides of the table. Settled comfortably on the floor, his huge lower body recumbent, rested Kaamharaa. His lower left arm was slung up in webbing just like the kind supporting Gerstner's shoulder. He was doing something, drawing or writing directly on the table, with his lower right hand, but his upper two arms waved as he described or explained something to two people who sat, side by side, cross-legged, on cushions drawn up close to the table. One, a long-limbed woman in tan and yellow, had her elbows braced on the table and her chin resting on her knuckles. Her expression was cool. The other, a man, was laughing. He had feathers braided into his long hair. Gerstner definitely remembered that. One of the bridge crew. Amazing.

The man tossed all that long hair back over his shoulder and looked at Gerstner, his eyes dancing, as though he'd caught that thought. Despite the hair, he was a good-looking man. Devastating charm even without a language in common. A man like this would be trouble on shipboard ... on a naval ship. Here, maybe not.

Somehow, in this setting, in a place that almost looked ordinary, surrounded by all these humans, Kaamharaa looked even more alien. That rugged troll-face with the slight muzzle and the long, savage tusks, the deep-set yellow eyes, the four powerful arms ... amazing Gerstner could be glad to see this alien. But he certainly was. No other turun were present; only Kaamharaa and humans. He would have liked to ask about a thousand questions, about turun and humans and this ship and everything. But at this exact moment, he only had one question.

Kaamharaa had seen him now, and paused in whatever he had been saying. He held out his upper right hand and rumbled, "Gerrrrstner!" in a voice that might have made the table vibrate.

Gerstner couldn't help smiling. He didn't try to hide his relief at seeing the giant turun. He said, "Kaamharaa. Glad to see you. Seriously glad to see you. Good. Yes. Okay. *Vengeful?* Can you tell me what happened with my ship, do you know? My *ship*, understand?"

Maybe Kaamharaa understood and maybe he didn't, but everyone was getting plates and bowls out of a compartment across the room and bringing them to the table, and the giant turun patted the table next to him and said, "Gerrstter, good, sit, talk, eat, talk, sit," which was repetitive but clear. *Talk* had appeared in that list twice, which seemed possibly like a good sign. Gerstner was absolutely ravenous, but *talk* was the word that got him to walk over to that table and sit down on one of the little cushions next to Kaamharaa. The centaur waved a hand at the two humans and told Gerstner their names. The man's name was a lot like Paul, but different, the vowels—of course—drawn out. More like Paaul, or maybe Paaol. The woman's name was practically impossible: Ngan or Nkan or something like that. Gerstner nodded politely and repeated the names as well as he could. If he'd wanted to be a linguist, he wouldn't have gone into the command track. He assumed everyone would be tolerant.

Karuu brought a platter of golden-brown triangles of something to the table, and a wide, flat bowl of translucent red sauce that apparently went with them. The platter itself was nearly the same golden-tan as the triangles, which Gerstner noticed mainly because someone else set out green bowls filled with moist pink flakes of something sprinkled with a dusting of some yellow powder. Then there were black bowls filled with a pale, creamy custard, and a brick-red rectangular platter piled high with glistening round flat ... cakes, maybe. They looked like cakes. About eight inches in diameter and an inch thick. Delicate slices of some kind of yellow fruit, arranged in overlapping rows on a chilled translucent plate. Flat glass bowls of little spherical pinky-orangey things that might be fruits or confections or who knew what. Bowls of ice water at every place, and little cups—with handles—set out beside round ceramic pots at either end of the table. Nothing plain, everything presented with careful attention to detail. Dinner at a nice restaurant someplace might look something like this; nothing on shipboard. Certainly not on a naval ship.

He'd drunk whatever that was in the sickbay, and he'd let them inject him with some kind of medication, or maybe a sedative, and they'd taken care of his shoulder and solicitously tucked him into bed afterward. Worrying about the food after all that seemed pointless. And impolite. Especially since he *was* starving. There were flat spoons with arched handles for the custard and a kind of two-pronged fork thing for the pink flakes. Everything else was apparently finger food.

The triangles were crisp on the outside and creamy on the inside, with a flavor a little like very mild, fresh cheese. The translucent red sauce was tart enough that one taste was enough. The custard was sweet, and filled with beads of something that burst on the tongue. The pink flakes might be some sort of fish, or maybe not. Not bad. Rich, with a buttery texture. It was all certainly edible. Not a lot stranger than Terabithian food, really. The steaming beverage in the pots was a clear pinkish color and surprisingly astringent. Gerstner mostly stuck to the water, cautious of possible stimulants or who knew what. But after a few minutes, he said quietly, insistently, "Good. Thank you. Talk. *Vengeful?*" He used small words Kaamharaa might understand, but he looked, deliberately, at the commander. Daamon. Daamon sepu

Kaamharaa—friend or employee or who knew what, but attached to Kaamharaa somehow. Odd to find that attachment reassuring, but he did.

The man seemed young to be a commander, maybe in his thirties or so, but then Gerstner still didn't know how the command structure actually worked aboard this ship. The idea that an alien, a turun, might actually be captain ... he couldn't be comfortable with that, but the idea of human people under the command of aliens wasn't as horrifying as it had been.

With his coloring, Daamon looked a good deal like someone from Kanan or Hemadri, but not quite. Rounder face or something. People descended from specific colonies did take on a common cast of features, depending on how broad the initial gene pool had been. No way to guess which colony, of all those scattered and lost, might have given rise to this population. Not that it mattered. Here they were, and the important difference between himself and this man was that Gerstner was captain of a dreadnought for the Imperial Republic and Daamon was some kind of officer for this ship, from this strange, blended society of human and turun.

Gerstner could have said again, *Vengeful?* But he didn't have to repeat himself. No matter how huge the difference between them was, the other man knew exactly what he was asking, and that he wasn't going to stop asking.

Daamon met Gerstner's eyes. His mouth had tightened, and he laid down the little fork thing and folded his hands on the table with the kind of deliberation that made it clear he'd come to a decision ... perfectly plain body language. Not very reassuring. Gerstner waited, keeping his gaze steady, trying to communicate without words that *whatever* had happened, he wanted to know. Needed to know.

The man said something, quietly. He gestured, a little movement of one hand and a nod: *look over there*, perfectly clear. Gerstner followed that gesture, turning to look at the glass column, which yes, was indeed a display surface. A nice one: three-dimensional and with crisp, clear imagery. The little figures in the display were far more detailed than they would have been on a regular screen: the colors were brighter and clearer, and the three-dimensional depth of the images made it much easier to tell where everything was relative to everything else.

The man with the feathers, Paaol, jumped to his feet, stepped over to the column, and began tapping images. *"Vengeful,"* he told Gerstner. *"Nkaastu.* Uut. Uut, uut, uut."

"Not now," Kaamharaa rumbled. He waved one enormous hand. "Back. Back."

Gerstner nodded. He understood. The stylized lavender figure was *Vengeful*, the little blue-green one was this ship with its unpronounceable name, all the red and white figures were Enemy. That huge orangish sphere was obviously the gas giant whose radiation *Vengeful* had poured, unsuccessfully, into the shielding confounders, and that told him they'd backed up the display to start at the point he and Kaamharaa had been snatched away from *Vengeful*. That was fine. That was great. This was *exactly* what he wanted. "Good," he said. "Yes. Good. Go on." He gestured, trying to get across the idea that he understood what they were showing him and wanted them to go forward.

Images shifted and moved. He held his breath, but all the red and white figures swirled around and then streamed away, and the lavender representation of *Vengeful* was still there. Gerstner exhaled, a long breath of sheer relief. "Thank God," he said aloud, which was a mistake because they all looked at him and the display froze. He gestured again, urgently. "Go on. Please."

The blue-green ship followed the Enemy. A heartbeat later, *Vengeful* followed. Symbols scrolled past, a long line of symbols across the top of the display, probably time and date representations, unreadable. Probably this part had taken hours and they were compressing the time. He wanted to ask, wanted to try to figure out how much time had passed. Later. He'd try to figure that out later. For now he just watched.

The system primary, a blue star. All kinds of red and white, and the big mothership, pink. A smear of faint gold-grey, probably a flashpoint. The word for star was something like *taak,* with a very long *a*. That might mean *star* or *blue star* or *Enemy star* or God knew, but just for now assume everybody was trying to keep things simple, so just *star*. That was the word Gerstner gave in return. The word for flashpoint was *ehn*. Hard to complicate that one. Lots of other kinds of wormholes, but if you couldn't flash through them, they weren't any good to anybody.

The view tightened on a stream of white and red figures moving away from the big pink mothership. Mostly saucers, which were *guaan*, but some arrowpoints too—*suu*—all of them moving in a dead straight line toward nothing in particular. Gerstner was pretty sure he knew what that was. He was right, because Paaol pointed at the brightest white spark and then at him and then at the white spark again. "Gerrstter," he said. "Kaamharaa."

"Yes," Gerstner answered, leaning forward intently. "I understand." The lavender figure, *Vengeful*, approached the stream of Enemy saucers and arrowpoints, attacking—and moved past them, attacking the mothership. One dreadnought could not possibly take on a mothership. Gerstner's whole body tensed as though he could pull his ship out of that encounter by sheer force of will. Reese Kennon wasn't an idiot. He'd never throw *Vengeful* away on some pointless gesture. In and out, that was probably the idea; get the Enemy's attention and get away again. He'd definitely gotten their attention; nearly all the red and white symbols moved to pursue *Vengeful*. The blue-green image maneuvered to intercept the one bright arrowpoint. *Vengeful* continued her attack.

The white arrowpoint merged with the blue-green turun ship and vanished.

Vengeful sheered hard away from the mothership and disappeared through the flashpoint.

The display turned back into smoky, featureless glass. The end of the show, apparently.

Then it took on a new image. The flashpoint, not in quite the same relative position. Saucers and arrowpoints, lots of them, coming and going through the flashpoint and away into the reaches of the system—heading toward Task Force Aleph, Gerstner feared; or toward the centaurs' territory, or God knew. Maybe searching for *Nkaastu*. He had missed the dim figure until Paaol leaned over and tapped it. Yes. Way out in the dark reaches of the system, probably shielded all the way down, or as close as they could come without a serious energy source. No sign of the lavender figure that represented *Vengeful*.

So that was pretty clearly a representation of the present situation. Gerstner sat back, slowly. His ship had gone through the flashpoint and hadn't come back, and now *Nkaastu* was hiding. Waiting for *Vengeful* to come back, or—even more likely—waiting for a chance to run back for turun space without being blown to plasma by a thousand Enemy fighters. For a long moment, no one spoke or moved. The commander watched him with steady sympathy.

Sympathy might not be necessary. Reese was sharp. That hadn't been a suicide move; if Reese Kennon had wanted to play the kamikaze card, which he wouldn't, he'd have rammed the mothership, not hit the flashpoint. God alone knew what *Vengeful* had run into, flashing blind to God knew where, but more than likely Reese had had that option in mind from the beginning of the whole insane maneuver. Probably he'd decided it might be nice to get a peek through that flashpoint if he could, and why not, the option beat staying on this side while all those Enemy fighters pounded away at *Vengeful*.

More than likely getting a peek through that flashpoint wasn't the only thing on his mind. No, Reese, like Gerstner himself, had been thinking about Task Force Aleph. From the glimpse they'd gotten, two of the superdreadnoughts and seven of the nine dreadnoughts had definitely gotten themselves locked into a solid formation, tight around the smaller ships of the task force. If every ship just held on and took whatever punishment got through the common defensive envelope and guarded its neighbor's flanks, then Aleph was almost certain to hold for a good long time. They *should* still be holding now, unless Gerstner had been unconscious a lot longer than he'd thought at some point during the last couple of days.

But any stationary defensive position could be broken *eventually*. Ordinary weapons were one thing. Kinetic weapons were something else. One good-sized rock fitted with a slowdrive locked onto the task force, and that would be the end. Impossible for that many ships locked into a tight formation to outmaneuver a guided rock. Equally impossible to hold that kind of structured formation while also maneuvering to go through a flashpoint. But if the task force broke that formation, the Enemy would tear through it in a heartbeat.

Aleph needed help. Reese knew that, and he knew this weird society of humans plus turun was the only possible source of that help.

Gerstner had dumped quite a problem on his executive officer. Before the Enemy had got in the way, his own plan had included demanding help for Task Force Aleph from a position of relative strength. Then he'd gotten himself snatched, and Reese Kennon had been faced with a more complicated problem. So step one: rescue the snatched alien personnel, or at least show himself willing to try, plus maybe rescue Gerstner himself as a side benefit. Step two, point out that one daring rescue—even one good attempt at a daring rescue—deserved another. Step three, get a whole bunch more giant centauroid aliens and go pull Commodore Marchetta and the whole damn task force out of the Enemy's trap. Step four, dump the problem of what to do with a whole new civilization on Viceroy Modhwadiya and breathe a big, big sigh of relief.

The whole thing was insane, but it was exactly the kind of insane that Reese Kennon might try. *Vengeful* had good legs on her, and Keith Maxson was a good man to have on signals. If *Vengeful* hadn't been too badly damaged, she might have skated through that flashpoint and run, or cut off sharp, shielded tight and dark. If she'd pulled that off fast enough, she might've survived no matter how many Enemies were after her. It was possible. She might come flashing right back from wherever she'd got to, hopefully having shaken loose her pursuers. That could absolutely happen.

Or she could have been destroyed. Or worse, taken. His entire crew, whoever survived, might be prisoners right now, dealing with the lights and the gravitics and the God-damned birdsong and whatever all that had been leading up to. Except without a giant turun buddy to help break them free.

No. If it had come to it, Reese would have blown *Vengeful* himself. He would never have let that happen. That was actually a comforting thought, for certain values of comforting.

Whatever had happened, *Vengeful* has apparently not yet returned. But Aleph still desperately needed help. Instead of issuing demands from a position of strength, Gerstner was going to have to ask for that help very politely, from the weakest imaginable position. Beg, if necessary, on the strength of his own ship's sacrifice. He was willing to do that, if he could make himself understood. Because the basic situation hadn't changed a jot. Except the clock was ticking louder and louder with every second that passed.

All right. So he figured he had a decent idea of the basic situation now. He looked around the table, meeting nothing but sober looks. He asked, "So where are we now? We still sitting in the same system, or have you headed home, or what? Who's captain here? Daamon, you the captain? Is it Kaamharaa? Somebody else? Let's get that sorted out, right? Because if *Vengeful's* gone ..." he got that out almost without wincing. "If my ship is gone, or even if she's just stuck someplace, there's still Aleph. Aleph's the important thing here."

Gerstner knew perfectly well he wouldn't be understood. He was going to have to come up with a way to fix that. He looked around, picked up one of the round cakes, broke it into pieces, and began to lay them out on the surface of the table.

The older man held up a hand to stop him, pushed plates and fragments of cake out of the way, and tapped the table, which became translucent. He drew a little circle on the surface with a fingertip, cleared it away with a tap, and looked at Gerstner, opening a hand in obvious invitation.

Gerstner hadn't felt much like smiling, but he smiled at that. "Good. Thanks. You're Mattu, right? Good thinking, Mattu. Okay, let's see what we can do with this." He drew circles, rapidly, connecting them with lines. The geometry-defying Escher-like contortion of space connected by flashpoints, surely understandable to these people. He looked at Kaamharaa and said, trying to stick to small, easy words, "Here, we met. Here, this is your world, where we took out those arrowpoints. Back this way, one, two, three, and here we are, watching Aleph take a beating."

Big dots for the task force, little tiny dots for the Enemy fighters, one very big dot for the mothership. When he glanced up, everyone was watching. He was pretty sure he'd been clear enough, good. "All right," he said. "This is Task Force Aleph—let's keep it simple. This is Aleph. Aleph." He pointed at the drawing. "Aleph, understand? All these ships here. Okay. Then we, *Vengeful* and your *Kaastu*, came back this way, and here's where we hid—tried to hide, by this gas giant. Then Enemy—you say uut, don't you? All right, uut, here. Kaamharaa, me, this way, with uut. *Vengeful, Kaastu,* this way, follow. Here's the system primary, here's the flashpoint, here's the uut mothership, there goes *Vengeful*. Gone." He sat back, looked up. Met Daamon's eyes, because he was certain this man was at least an important officer, if not necessarily *Nkaastu's* captain. "Now. Aleph." He pointed, forcefully. "This is Aleph. I want your people to help me break Aleph out of this trap." He turned to Kaamharaa. "You, Daamon, *Kaastu*, turun, human, all of you, I want you to help Aleph. Is any of this getting through?"

"Gerrstter," rumbled Kaamharaa. "Aleph." He spoke to Daamon, to all the humans, and suddenly everyone was talking at once. Gerstner couldn't understand a word any of them said; if there was a single word in there he should have recognized, it was lost in the rapid flow of the alien language. If he had ever been in a more purely frustrating situation in his life, he couldn't remember it.

A series of tones, like breathy flute music, interrupted the chatter. Everyone stopped and looked up. Paaol said something. He was grinning. Daamon answered. He wasn't. He looked the way a captain might look if there was trouble. Something not too urgent, but potentially a problem. Daamon picked up his cane and set his other hand on one of Kaamharaa's arms, letting the turun lift him to his feet. The others were on their feet too, except Kaamharaa, who stayed where he was, but rumbled and purred in a tone that sounded possibly anxious or upset ... that idea could have been a projection; Gerstner definitely felt both anxious and upset. He stood up. "Enemy?" he asked. "Uut? Jesus Christ, I wish I could talk to you people."

Daamon looked at him. He said, apparently making a decision, "Gerstner. Come," and beckoned.

***

Nkaastu's colorful, crowded bridge was almost familiar: the smooth, symmetrical arches into which the controls were set, lots of them looking like enameled mosaics more than control stations; the ornate filigree of lights overhead, although glimmering right now in soft blues and pinks rather than the dark colors Gerstner remembered from his previous glimpse of this place, on *Vengeful's* screens. Turun. As many four-armed troll-centaurs as people: five of each, counting Gerstner himself. That was why it seemed crowded. All these were the smaller ones, maybe a third Kaamharaa's size, but they were still very damn big. He kept sort of interpreting some as male and some as female, but still didn't know whether those impressions meant anything. He'd forgotten to ask the right kinds of questions while he had the chance and now it was too late. Well, he'd pick whatever pronoun seemed right and worry later about how well his notions matched up with reality.

Regardless, the humans spoke to the aliens with the same light, easy manner with which they talked to each other. Lots of casual chatter; nothing like recognizable military discipline here. That bothered Gerstner a lot more than the uncertainty about pronouns, though he tried not to show it.

Every single person on this bridge touched the turun casually: patted a thick arm or a strangely jointed shoulder, leaned against a solid body. And the turun touched the people, too, on the shoulder or arm or back or head. That bothered him a lot more. Twice

Gerstner had seen a turun stroke someone's head, so much like someone stroking a pet that he'd had to look away.

They came in pairs, as far as he could judge: one turun per human, more or less. Saraa and Paaol were both bridge personnel and had their own stations down at those curves, but each shared that station with a turun partner. That seemed to be how it worked. Daamon stood up on a little dais with one of them, a scarred creature with only one eye. A second turun stood just below that dais, not at any specific station—Gerstner tentatively pegged that one as the equivalent of an executive officer. But she might be more like a marine or man-at-arms or something, because Gerstner had been told to stay near her. Closer than he liked, a lot closer, well within her arm's reach. This wasn't exactly his first choice, but Daamon had gripped his arm, a firm hold, guided him to this exact spot, and given him a downward gesture that couldn't have been clearer if he'd ordered *You stay right here* in English. Maybe every human had to have a turun partner or minder or something, and this one was supposed to be his.

The turun officer didn't touch him or even look at him. He couldn't tell whether this was because she was perceptive enough to realize he wouldn't welcome it, which would be fine, or because she was deliberately excluding him from the easy give-and-take between human and alien, which might be a problem. He couldn't begin to guess. He thought she might very well not like having a foreigner on her bridge. He would have been surprised if no one objected. If this had been *Vengeful*, he wouldn't have allowed a turun on his bridge—except Kaamharaa, and maybe not him. But he would have been delighted to have Kaamharaa beside him right now and not this other turun. Highly cognizant he was a guest on this bridge, he stood still, arms folded, uncomfortable and trying to pretend otherwise.

When Gerstner had first seen this bridge on *Vengeful's* screen, he'd have sworn the humans were in charge. Now it was obvious the aliens were. He had no idea how or why they switched back and forth. Maybe a clock would strike midnight and this ship would go back into human control. It could be just like that, he had no idea.

He did have some pretty good guesses about other things. He knew Kaamharaa wasn't the captain, nor any kind of officer, apparently. He was almost certain Daamon was some kind of co-captain with that one-eyed turun. And he knew the two of them didn't agree about their next step. He was fairly certain the turun captain wanted to go somewhere and do something, and almost as certain that Daamon wanted to stay put right where they were. That was as much as he could gather from the screen display and their gestures. Even if there was nothing he could do, he wished he knew which side he ought to be on.

He studied the big three-dimensional screen at the front of the bridge. The Enemy flashpoint glittered in the distance, Enemy fighters swarming around it like someone had thrown a handful of red and white glitter into the dark. More Enemy fighters scattered all through this system, more than likely searching for *Nkaastu*, or for whatever else they might find out here. Some of them had gotten too close; he thought that was what had happened. He couldn't be sure, but he thought that was the alarm that had gotten Daamon and the other humans up here. Certainly some of the narrow little white figures that represented arrowpoints seemed to have come pretty close to the dim blue-green figure of *Nkaastu*.

A breathy series of flute notes cut off both his speculation and the chatter. That could have been the same as the other signal; he couldn't tell. Though he studied the display, he couldn't see anything that looked like Enemy fighters approaching *Nkaastu*, but everyone had certainly stilled. Daamon had braced himself with his cane, but the centaur with him had positioned one of her—his—whatever, *her* arms, where Daamon could rest his hand on her forearm and brace himself that way as well. He accepted that support as though he hardly noticed it. There weren't any chairs, which seemed odd, but all the humans stood as though they were used to staying on their feet.

Saraa said something. A man named Genru answered, and one of the turun said something else. They were all doing things at their stations. The controls looked like patterns of enamel ornamentation, uninterpretable, but almost homey after the much weirder controls in the Enemy arrowpoint.

Maybe that unusual chime meant they were getting ready to move at last—it sounded again, and a third time. Gerstner folded his hands behind his back and tried to figure out what might be going on, even though the effort was completely hopeless.

A host of new figures appeared in the display, way off to one side.

Blue and lighter blue. Not, as Gerstner's first startled impression suggested, hundreds of them. But dozens. He didn't have to ask who they were. *Nkaastu* was turquoise, after all; not exactly the same shade as those new figures, but damn near. Those were turun ships—or turun-human ships, whatever. A rescue force, an exploratory force, the vanguard of a whole armada, he didn't care, he'd take any and all of the above. He didn't think, just stepped up on the dais and gripped Daamon's wrist. "Task Force Aleph." He gestured toward the newcomers in the display, not trying to disguise his urgency. "Them, us, Task Force Aleph, go, now, fast."

Daamon looked at him, really looked. His expression had that familiar studied neutrality ship commanders learned; the kind that said, *You are being a problem.* On a Republic ship, grabbing the captain would get you thrown off the bridge. Gerstner let go and dropped his hands to his sides, but he didn't back up and he didn't look away. The man *had* to have understood, even if the only word in that he'd caught was *Aleph*. Gerstner said urgently, "That many ships, that could do it, you drive *any* kind of wedge through to Aleph and they'll do the rest. Listen, you saw *Vengeful*, let me tell you, a superdreadnought'll really show you something. Listen, Daamon: you, us, them, Aleph, go!"

Daamon patted Gerstner on the shoulder, but he also gestured firmly: *Step back*. The turun officer to whom Gerstner had been assigned looked like she was going to come get him in about one second. Gerstner raised his hands, yielding the point. He stepped back, off the dais, but he also said, "Daamon! Aleph! Listen, we can do this, you, them, listen, I need to talk to Kaamharaa, can I talk to Kaamharaa? Kaamharaa?" Surely he could make *one* turun understand.

Daamon said something to the turun captain. Everyone else got involved. For several minutes there was a rapid give-and-take all across the bridge, a disorderly lot of voices, human and otherwise, that was utterly uninterpretable and completely foreign to anything Gerstner could accept as proper bridge protocol. He waited, grimly patient, in the near-certainty that speaking up again would not help his case.

Finally, as the turquoise figure that represented *Nkaastu* began to move toward the blue formation, Daamon turned to him. *"Sepuuk,"* he said, pointing, and several more words that were equally baffling. They might have been the names of those ships, or the names of their captains, or a description of the whole formation, or something completely different. Daamon apparently realized Gerstner could not understand him, because he made a frustrated gesture and stopped. He said something to the turun captain, they had a brief debate, and then Daamon adjusted the rainbow-colored controls and said something else, rapidly.

And Kaamharaa's voice rolled through the bridge, instantly identifiable. "Gerrstter. Rrend. They come. They, us, go Aam. Uut come, they, us, fight. We go *something something something* quiet not fight. Go Aam. Break *ehn*, break lot *ehn*, end all fight, go quiet, not fight."

Ehn was *flashpoint,* Gerstner remembered that after a second. Break flashpoint—he had a bad idea what Kaamharaa meant by that. Drop a big enough fissionable inside any flashpoint that was less than entirely stable and you'd break it all right: you'd turn it into the kind of violent wormhole nothing and no one would get through for the next twenty years, hundred years, maybe thousand, who knew.

"Task Force Aleph," he repeated, in his calmest, most determined tone. "Kaamharaa, us, them, go Aleph."

He knew Kaamharaa understood him. Kaamharaa spoke to Daamon, and for half a minute everyone got into it again. It sounded like a pretty good argument. But only for a minute. Then Kaamharaa's deep voice again "No Task Force Aleph. Go Aam. Break *ehn*."

Gerstner drew a slow breath and let it out again. He understood that. He was absolutely sure he understood it, and it was the worst possible decision—oh, not for the centaurs; for them it probably made all kinds of sense to duck back to their home stars and shut down every flashpoint on this side of space.

But it meant they had no intention of helping Task Force Aleph. No interest in working out an alliance, either. They were going to retreat and burn every bridge behind them, and they were going to take him with them. And he couldn't even argue, because he didn't speak the language.

Even if he did, even if he could explain everything to Kaamharaa and get the giant centaur to argue for him, how could he possibly persuade them? *Take a huge risk for strangers, come on, this is a fantastic idea, let's go risk all your lives rescuing a bunch of very, very distant relatives.* Even if he could make them understand, with no ability to speak to these people, he just had no way to make the case for alliance, much less for an *urgent* alliance starting *right* the hell now.

17

The uut ring became more and more impressive as *Vengeful* drew closer to it. It took a long time: chimes and chimes. Hours. Crew came and went, snatching a chime or two of rest while they could. There were chairs at the back, against the wall, for people who weren't really crew. Taya sat there and looked at the ring. The display was lovely: the ring twisted around the star like so many ruby taak berries loosely strung on black thread. It wasn't actually a simple ring, but a sort of wide, oddly folded river of gleaming red jewels. Lots of space between each gemstone and the next, but still, lots and lots. Hundreds. Maybe thousands, weaving through this system in that looping ring. Maybe a planet was somewhere over there, but too far away for *Vengeful's* sensors to pick it up. That might explain why the stream of ruby jewels folded around that way.

Either way, the ring was very impressive. So many ships, and so very many big structures—stations, worldlets, maybe small moons. She couldn't begin to guess how many uut might live in this system. Maybe uut lived like uturun, males—widely spread out, each one alone on a big territory.

The uut might even be *more* solitary than uturun, because even if uturun couldn't tolerate each other, nearly all of them wanted a sep' family, uman people who lived with them. These days, only very rare uturun really lived *alone*. Especially because uman absolutely *hated* it when younger males challenged *their* uturun. Sep' people headed off challenges when they could, blocked a challenger's way if they couldn't make him back up by just asking, and there wasn't an uturun in the whole Ka' Taand, no matter how aggressive, who would try to physically force his way through a lot of uman people, so males lived a lot longer now than they had and built up a lot more reputation. So not many young uturun challenged older ones, not anymore, especially because any young male who might live long enough to think about challenging would probably find some uman person, maybe a mated pair, asking him to join them. Almost any young male would say yes to that kind of offer. So, yes, Taya had heard of a real challenge now and then, but that was because *everybody* heard of that kind of challenge now, because it was really rare.

Maybe uut were even *more* solitary than uturun, except without uman to help bring them together in a way they could tolerate. Maybe that was what was out there: a whole lot of really big territories, but not nearly as many uut as it seemed.

Taya didn't like to think of that. That seemed ... just really sad.

The uturun had been so terribly *lonely* before the turun had discovered Ymaa and rescued the dwindling uman population there, as many people as they could find and persuade to leave the planet. They'd built sanctuaries for the uman people who didn't want to live with them, places without all the predators, and they'd found a vaccine for that horrible red-spot illness, and let the uman alone to live the way they wanted to. Horrible and primitive, but at least not so *desperately* awful, with extra food and civilized medicine for anyone who had enough courage to come to the turun who lived nearby, in their own settlements or on their own territories.

That had been a long time ago. The sanctuaries had all been empty long before Taya's grandmother's day, uman people going to live scattered among the nturun matrilines. That had been such an exciting time of discovery and change, as uman first proved how smart they were, just as smart as turun, and gained citizenship and then autonomy, and then gradually wove together the Ka' Taand and established the Suund. There were lots of uman-authored romance-adventures set during that time. And during the time after that, when changes kept happening, sep' uman who had lived scattered on male reservations finally getting the uturun recognized by matriline reputationists, slowly weaving the uturun into the Ka' Taand in a way that was different from the nturun, but that everyone could live with. Acceptance from the nturun matrilines, a lot less aggression among the uturun, and uman people stitching together the Ka' Taand from one end of familiar space to the other.

Maybe the uut were even more aggressive than uturun; maybe that was why they attacked everyone and tried to burn off living worlds: because they just couldn't stand to have anybody else near them.

That had been so terrible on the far edge, not just all the destruction, but the way the uut had closed off expansion of the Ka' Taand in that direction. If young uturun couldn't challenge older established males, they had to have a way to set up their own territories and build reputation a different way. Even when they had uman families, uturun had to spread out. They couldn't stand being crowded. That was why the uut forcing the closure on the far edge had been half-disastrous, and why finding uut on the *near* edge was going to be worse.

Eleven Gaatuu years ago, uut ships had appeared along the far edge of turun space and immediately attacked turun ships and worlds. There had been no hesitation, no perceptible attempt to communicate, just immediate attack. In that first year, one living world, Nguaa, had been completely ruined, its surface pounded by high-vee rocks and poisoned by nuclear fire, its two stations attacked and destroyed. Two million turun and close to twenty thousand uman had lived there, and only a few had been able to flee in time. Nearly everything that was beautiful and unique within Nguaa's ecosystem had been destroyed; only a tiny remnant of its native life had been preserved in a handful of worldlets. Aanuku had not been the only matriline to lose many investments and entire secondary lines; Kaoluun had also taken terrible losses. Finally Tnakaa u Kaoluun had handed battlecommand to Siiv u Kaoluun sepu Upuonnu—she had been the first turun captain to do that. They had led the ships that drove the uut back and closed the slides between Nguaa's system and the rest of familiar space. Even now about half the full-fighters of the Ka' Taand belonged to Kaoluun. Upuonnu himself and the uman of his sepu had designed many of the modern full-fighters. On full-fighters, the uman khand were mostly primary and the turun khand mostly supportive, the reverse of how it was on *Nkaastu*.

Both Aanuku and Kaoluun, having lost so much along the far edge, had supported the exploration and development of the near edge instead. And now this.

Even if the uut spread out even more than uturun, a lot more, a hundred times less dense than that, there must surely be a lot of uut here. As that wide red ribbon took on more and more detail, misgiving crept through Taya, a cold suspicion that there might be more uut in this one system than all the turun and uman people in all the eleven systems of the Ka' Taand.

She studied the ribbon of uut stations and worldlets twisting around this double-star and felt a sinking certainty that the Ka' Taand would have to interdict all the slides at the near edge of familiar space too. That the Suund would vote to close the slides completely. Aanuku and Kaoluun would take another serious financial loss if that happened, which was bad enough. Kaamharaa and Upuonnu, two of the males allied with those matrilines, would lose reputation, bad in a different way. And that would be the *best* that could happen, the very best. That would be something that would be a problem only if Kaamharaa were not a prisoner of the uut, or dead.

"Is very bad. Terrible," she said softly to Commander Esaias Keay. *Terrible* was a word that meant worse than *bad*. But she doubted it was a strong enough word to encompass what she meant.

He had said she could call him Esaias. It was a difficult word, but she had learned to say it right. He and Taya were mostly just waiting; others on the bridge were busy, but he seemed not to be, and of course Taya had nothing to do. So she had been asking about all the words she didn't know. Esaias wasn't as clever at explaining words as Lieutenant Lockwood, but he had *played back* the *log* of the recent exchanges on the bridge, so now she knew what the log was and what the command *log that* meant. He wasn't as good about correcting her mistakes, though, even when she asked him. He did not mind when she made mistakes, but Taya knew it was important to be able to speak correctly and pronounce words right. Otherwise no one would listen to her when it was important. She was going to have to persuade these human cousins to ally with the Ka' Taand and work with the Suund. She knew she had to do that, or there was no chance the Suund would vote to do anything but close all the slides on this side of familiar space.

Considering what she saw in this system, Taya wasn't even sure that would be enough. If the uut kept coming, they would find some unknown way into familiar space eventually. And as far as anyone knew, the uut always kept coming.

Vengeful's course was laid out in white, slowly sinking through the swarm of real uut ships as well as moving forward. Forward, forward, forward, but pretty soon *Vengeful* would bend its course into a smooth curve to pick up a different stream of uut ships moving the other way. Then back, back, back, all the time wondering just when the uut would realize *Vengeful* was not one of them at all, but foreign and alien and encroaching. The moment a real uut pinged or hailed the human ship, the illusion would surely fall apart.

Taya could hardly believe it hadn't happened yet. Surely the uut must talk to one another *sometime*. The terror of waiting for that felt like it must be almost worse than actually having it happen.

As though prompted by her anxiety, Lieutenant Maxson suddenly raised one hand and said, "Sir, I'm picking up more and more comm traffic out there. Of course we can't read it, but just let me put it over the bridge speakers."

Commander Kennon nodded, Lieutenant Maxson touched a sliding lever on his board, and birdsong spilled across the bridge. Rippling trills and buzzing whistles and vibrating warbles, and behind all the rest a sharp metallic chiming that rang all up and down a peculiar musical scale, like someone tapping a lot of different-sized metal and enamel bowls with a little hammer. There was no obvious rhythm or theme to any of it. It didn't sound like any kind of speech, nor like any kind of music, but it was pretty. How strange to be so frightened of something so pretty. Taya gripped her hands together.

"I can't interpret that, obviously," Lieutenant Maxson said. "But the small craft seem to start emitting aural signals as they approach the larger, uh, habitats, and I think I'm hearing a lot of repetition in some of the signals. Let me filter out everything but the signal I'm picking up from this group of saucers here. Listen to this."

"Aural?" Taya whispered to Esaias.

"Audible, auditory—something you can hear," he murmured back as a cluster of saucers near *Vengeful* started to flash in the display, and the birdsong and chiming suddenly thinned out, the sounds becoming no more comprehensible, but less ... jumbled.

Taya tilted her head, listening as carefully as she could to each individual note. Though as far as she could tell, there was still no pattern—no melody or harmony or progress or sequence.

But Lieutenant Maxson said, "It's going to start repeating in a minute. Wait for it ... wait ... here's where it starts over ... mark. All right, now, it runs a little more than three minutes long. Wait for it." And, after a pause, "Here it comes around again ... mark!"

The rippling birdsong did indeed start repeating. Taya could tell, now that Lieutenant Maxson had pointed it out. Commander Kennon frowned and shook his head. "Not that I don't trust your ear, Keith ..."

"You don't hear it?" Lieutenant Maxson seemed more resigned than surprised. "Wait, let me just ..." he made rapid adjustments to his board. "I'm going to echo the incoming signal with the recorded signal," he explained. "Wait for it ... here it comes ..."

Suddenly the birdsong seemed to double, as though two birds were singing the same song, not quite together. It was obvious that every note was exactly the same, except one half a beat behind the other. That gave Taya an idea what *echo* must mean.

"All right, Keith, you're obviously correct. And what does that suggest to you?" Commander Kennon asked.

"I don't know, sir. But that group of saucers is repeating that one particular ... song." Lieutenant Maxson hesitated over the term, as though not sure it applied. But he went on quickly, "This group over here—" he indicated a slightly larger cluster of saucers a little farther away—"is repeating a different song, and this group *here* a different one. That one's quite a bit longer. If I had time, I bet I could sort out more. And, listen, we're just starting to pick up some signals from the habitats or whatever those are. They're not matching the songs the saucers are producing, but I sort of think ... let me put this on speaker ..."

Another ripple of birdsong and chimes.

"Keith?" said Commander Kennon, patiently.

"Well, it's not an echo, but doesn't it sort of seem to harmonize with that first song? And look, isn't that group of saucers moving toward that habitat? Or," Lieutenant Maxson added, "I guess I could be fooling myself, sir."

"Possible. But let's assume you're correct." The commander was frowning thoughtfully. "You're thinking these are identification calls. Is that what you're thinking?"

"Sir. Yes, sir, I think they could be. And, as far as I can tell, we are, at the moment, part of this group *here*, going toward *this* habitat. Only of course, we're not putting out any kind of song."

"Indeed," the commander murmured, but not as though he expected anyone to answer. "Are they *all* giving out those signals?"

"I don't ... I'm not sure, sir. There are so many ... it's hard to tell." Lieutenant Maxson hesitated. "I think all the nearby groups are. Every individual ship ... I can't tell. But as you say, *we're* silent. I'm not sure that's going to work for us much longer."

"We could echo our group of saucers," suggested Esaias. "Of course, it might look peculiar if we've been silent all along and then start announcing ourselves. One might even call that suspicious. If we make a mistake with our signal, things could go very wrong very fast."

"And I hardly see how we could keep from making a mistake," agreed the commander. "We've been running silent for a good while so far and no one's shooting at us yet; let's hold our metaphorical tongue and see if we can just keep it up a little longer."

Taya raised her hand. Lieutenant Lockwood frowned at her in instant disapproval, but Commander Kennon nodded. She said quickly, "Sir, back—" she pointed at the display at the rear of the bridge, what they called the *aft* display. "Back to flashpoint, maybe that mothership still there, maybe it makes identification signals? Maybe *Vengeful* listen to saucers come toward that mothership, echo, make *Vengeful* look like the right kind of saucer later soon we go that way?"

"Keith?" the commander asked Lieutenant Maxson.

"I don't know, sir. I've never heard anything like this around a mothership, and I haven't read anything about it in Signals reports ... but I'm not sure anybody's ever been this close to a mothership when it wasn't engaged in battle. At least, I'm sure *I* haven't been. And for sure no one's ever listened to a mothership in this particular system. If Genee will take signals in near-space, I'll just see whether I can sort out anything coming from that mothership, or from saucers approaching it. If I can even tell whether it's still back there ... I can focus on the flashpoint, but there's a hell of a lag at this distance ..." his voice trailed off as he bent forward over one of his boards, one hand touching his ear where a little object fed him signals from *Vengeful's* sensors. The woman who partnered him took over the rest of his boards without comment.

"Lag?" Taya asked Esaias. "Like log?"

Lieutenant Lockwood threw another unfriendly glance at her. She pretended not to notice. Esaias said in an absent tone, "Lag—a short delay. A pause. The mothership's so far away some time passes before we hear any signal coming from it."

"Lag," Taya repeated, satisfied that she understood. "Yes."

Another of the bridge crew, Annette—Taya wasn't sure of her title or the rest of her name—said tersely, "Nineteen minutes till we're scheduled to make our first course change, sir."

Commander Kennon nodded. "Good, good. Plenty of time for Keith to sort out the twelfth overture from a harmonica duet, despite the lag. Samuel, status?"

Taya had no idea what a *twelfth overture* was, or a *harmonica duet*, but she could see that everyone else relaxed a little bit. Maybe Commander Kennon had made a joke. She wished she understood it. Nineteen minutes would be ... half a chime, more or less. That would take them very, very close to the ring. The nearest habitat already loomed across half the display, red and disquieting. The display traced black lines across that habitat, carved gaps into it, detailed breaks in its surface, spun silver filigree around it ... Taya had no idea what any of that meant, but it was strangely beautiful as well as frightening.

Taya made herself breathe normally. In, out. In, out. Just like she wasn't frightened at all. Looking at the giant red glowing shape growing larger and more complicated in the display wasn't helping. She shut her eyes. That didn't help either. She ought to have learned by now that closing her eyes didn't help. She opened them again.

"Five minutes," Annette said quietly.

A little more than a tenth chime.

Lieutenant Maxson raised a hand. "Sir, either our very own mothership or some other ship way back by the flashpoint is definitely, ah, singing."

"For want of a better word, singing will do. Well done. Please continue to listen in that direction. Genee?"

The woman nodded without looking up. "Lots of ... singing, sir, but nothing stands out to me. Just lots of ... song."

"Very good."

The giant red habitat loomed in the display. The little ships swirled around it like gnats. They were that small next to it. Maybe that habitat *was* like a hive; maybe the uut actually were like nilgiim, stinging when they were disturbed. Except nilgiim didn't rush out a long way from their hive looking for creatures to sting when they hadn't even been disturbed at all.

The habitat or hive or whatever it was swept up swarms of uut ships and spat them out again, in constant chaotic motion. If you were an uut, probably all that movement made sense. Taya could find no pattern in it.

"Two minutes," said Annette. Commander Kennon linked his hands behind his back and rocked gently onto his toes. Lieutenant Maxson bent low over his boards, his eyes closed, listening to his private channels. Lieutenant Lockwood rested his hands on his console, alert but calm. Sun leaned back in her seat, so relaxed she looked half asleep. Taya closed her hands hard on the arms of her chair and tried to slow her breathing.

"Initiating course change now," murmured Annette.

Commander Kennon nodded, and Taya held her breath until she had to let it out with a gasp. On the screens, the stylized view of the system and the ring and the huge habitat and all the uut ships began slowly to wheel past. There was no sensation of movement at all. It was exactly as though all the rest of the universe were turning around *Vengeful*, with the human ship the only still point in all the cosmos.

At last, after what seemed a very long time but was probably less than a chime, the view stabilized again. Now the forward screens showed a lot of empty space, though scattered with a lot of little red sparks that shifted and swirled in rippling, meaningless patterns. The slide—the flashpoint—was ahead of them again. And the mothership that had pursued them through it, and lots and lots of Disks and Blades. But maybe, if they could sneak past all those uut, maybe they would find *Nkaastu* on the other side of the flashpoint, with Kaamharaa safely back in his own apartment and even Captain Gerstner safe.

Taya glanced over her shoulder at the huge habitat just once more. It nearly filled the aft screen. If they'd been wrong about that one arrowpoint, then Kaamharaa and Captain Gerstner might soon be taken to a giant uut habitat like that one. Maybe that very one. It was even possible they already had been. How could she know, how could anyone know? If that were so, then when *Vengeful* had turned away, it meant they had left their people behind.

Thinking about this wasn't helping *at all*.

"How long to flashpoint?" she asked Esaias.

"Hours," he told her, gripping her shoulder briefly. "Go rest, eat something if you want. It'll be hours before we get anywhere."

Taya nodded, but she didn't move. No one else left the bridge either, though tenth chimes crept past and still nothing alarming happened. Nothing *more* alarming.

"Commander, our very own mothership's definitely singing," said Lieutenant Maxson, listening intently. "Or something big certainly is, at least; that's no little saucer I'm picking up. Sounds peculiar. I mean, more peculiar. Kind of like a clarinet's joined in with a bunch of birds. Permission to—"

"By all means, let's hear it."

Once again the bridge of *Vengeful* heard the rippling-birdsong-and-windchime sound of uut song. Or calls, or signals, or language, or whatever that was. For all they knew, it might as well be real and actual poetry, set to what uut thought of as music. Or it might be more like hunting calls. Parts of it actually sounded a little like the high, whistling call of hunting yuannkuu: a breathy sound that seemed to be scattered at very strange intervals through the rest of the ... song. Call it song; it seemed as good a term as any. That sound must be what Lieutenant Maxson meant by a *clarinet* joining in. She wondered what kind of animal a clarinet might be; whether it was fast and dangerous like a yuannkuu.

"Well," Commander Kennon said thoughtfully, "I suppose we could mimic a bit of that. It's an option, at least. Keith, select a portion and get it set up for playback. Annette, our ee tee ay to the flashpoint?"

The woman answered with studied calm. "Five hours forty-seven minutes, sir, plus or minus."

That was more than eight chimes. More than eight and a half. Taya suppressed a moan, barely. She didn't know how she was going to endure the wait.

"Very good." Commander Kennon sounded merely brisk, not at all worried. "All right, boys and girls. Let's maintain course and velocity, shall we, not to mention an attitude of tranquil but mindful vigilance. Seconds, take the boards. Firsts, take a break; four hours off, if you please. Not you, Keith; sorry, I think we'd better have your ear on the comm."

"Yes, sir," agreed Lieutenant Maxson.

Esaias said, his tone neutral, "And you, sir?"

"I might take a break in a little while," Commander Kennon said absently. "Go get something to eat, Esaias, and you can bring me a sandwich or something."

Taya shut her eyes, reviewing vocabulary to help herself feel calmer. She felt she had a great heap of words jumbled in her head. And there were still so many she didn't know. An unending number, and some must be not only useful, but important ... after a moment, she opened her eyes again and looked up at Esaias.

"Mimic? Option? Tranquil? Mindful? Vigilance?" she whispered to Esaias.

He started to answer, but Lieutenant Lockwood, on his feet and heading for the room with the food and couches, said curtly, "Commander Keay has things to do, Taya, and explaining that kind of random vocabulary is not the best use of anyone's time. Come along and I'll set you up with another module."

"Yes," Taya agreed, jumping to her feet. That was a *lot* better than just sitting here waiting—and he would know which words she most needed to know.

Commander Kennon glanced at them both. "Take a break yourself, Samuel. That's an order. I want you bright eyed and bushy tailed and back on Ops in four hours."

"Sir," Lieutenant Lockwood acknowledged. "It'll just take a minute to set her up." He took Taya's arm in a hard, unfriendly grip, but she was glad to work with him and didn't mind that.

It took nearly a chime to set up the module. Lieutenant Lockwood didn't try to take her back to the room she had been given first. That was too far from the bridge. There was a place here, three connected rooms, not as comfortable or peaceful as the Aanuku contemplation garden on *Nkaastu*, but probably meant to serve much the same purpose. Food was laid out inside a table with a glass top, mostly sandwiches stuffed with all kinds of things and wrapped up individually. You slid the top back to get the food out. Lieutenant Lockwood pushed Taya toward a chair, tossed her a sandwich, and sat down with a handheld console, pulling up whatever module he had designed to come next and making rapid adjustments to it while she ate the sandwich and tried not to get in anyone's way.

Sun Grigson patted her shoulder and brought her coffee, the unpleasant bitter medicinal beverage. Taya accepted it. Sun also looked over Lieutenant Lockwood's shoulder, but she didn't comment, only went through to another room where there were places to lie down.

"Here," Lieutenant Lockwood said at last, setting the console in front of her. "Get this in your head. Pay attention to the syntax, Taya, your verbs make you sound like an idiot. I need to get a couple hours sleep, so if you run into trouble, you write down your questions for me, understand? Don't just ask somebody. You're getting some pretty crappy definitions that way."

"Yes," Taya agreed meekly, and began to work through the module. He had added something new this time: a set of exercises that made her put the words into sentences, with a symbol that flashed *idiot* in red whenever she made a mistake with a verb. That was very, very helpful. Naturally he'd set up something so helpful in a way that was supposed to make her feel stupid. She laughed when she realized how he'd set it up. She was tired and scared, that was why she laughed, but it *was* funny.

He had not included some words that had puzzled her. He had not included *clarinet* or *tranquil* or *bushy-tailed,* but he had included *mimic* and *options.* Mimic, imitate, impersonate, deceive.

He had also added *options, choices, possibilities, opportunities, decisions*. But that list graded into a different kind of word, much less nice: *Ruse. Subterfuge. Lie.* Those words didn't make her laugh. Each one felt like a slap. By the time she got that far, Lieutenant Lockwood was asleep in one of the adjoining rooms. Taya did not write down any questions. She did not have any questions about the module. All the things he had put in it were clear.

She wrote, *I am not telling lies. I do not know enough to want to tell lies. I want to rescue Kaamharaa and I want your people to help us and I want us to help your people. None of that is a lie. What is the word for the opposite of telling lies? What is the word for someone who will not believe truth?* She checked those sentences over very carefully, making sure the syntax was correct, especially the verbs. By the time she was finished writing that, it was time to go back to the bridge and sit very quietly in the back. Commander Kennon was there again, or still there. He paid no attention to her. Commander Keay nodded to her. Taya nodded to him in the same way, sat down, and listened carefully to people talking. When no one was speaking, she rehearsed what she had learned and practiced framing sentences in her mind, and most of all just waited. The slide showed in the forward display now. So did the mothership guarding it.

After a tenth-chime or so, Lieutenant Lockwood came back onto the bridge. He gave Taya a frowning look. Something was different in his expression despite the frown, but she couldn't tell what. Maybe he was not as angry, or maybe he was angrier; she couldn't tell. He only looked at her for a hundredth of a chime. Then he went to his station and the other person there moved aside and took the other chair at that place. Taya decided she didn't care what he thought and looked instead at the screen.

The slide was growing bigger and more distinct. The mothership occupied a place so near the slide that at this distance the images in the display almost overlapped. Every single saucer coming from the ring went to the mothership first. Maybe some went through the slide after that; Taya wasn't sure. But none went through the slide without going to the mothership first.

That seemed very unfortunate.

Vengeful was, of course, following the same path as the saucers: directly toward the mothership. They had to, because they were pretending to be a saucer. Taya had no idea how closely Commander Kennon meant to approach the mothership before he ordered *Vengeful* to turn instead toward the slide, or what he intended to do if—as seemed likely—this change of course drew attention. Or attack.

"Ee tee ay seventeen minutes," Annette reported. She had been offering such information with increasing frequency as they drew closer to the mothership.

"Weapons First, you'll supervise targeting," Commander Kennon said quietly. "Weapons Second, set up two nukes. You'll drop the first the instant we hit the flashpoint, and the second when we're partway through. We'll hope that's enough to destabilize the flashpoint at least long enough for us to get well away."

Everyone murmured agreement.

Commander Kennon gave a little nod and asked, "Signals First, what are you picking up now?"

While Taya tried to look up *nukes,* Lieutenant Maxson said, his gaze abstracted, "The calls overlap too much to sort out which ship is making which call. But the mothership is definitely sending out plenty of signals: two or three different variants, I think. There are different little runs of notes at the ends of a lot of the individual songs."

"Can you copy some of that? Do you think it might be advisable to try it?"

"I think so, sir. It sure sounds to me like the songs produced by the saucers sort of fit into spaces left by the mothership's song, if you see what I mean. As far as I can tell, nothing's running silent except us. I can broadcast something, but I *am* worried about singing the wrong song—I think we've been smart to stay quiet—" he broke off, wincing, as a much louder and more resonant whistle broke across them. "Uh, I think we're being hailed, sir."

Taya raised a diffident hand. "One song much more than others."

"Quiet!" hissed Lieutenant Lockwood.

But Commander Kennon waved him off and nodded to Taya. "You have a suggestion, Kha Taya?"

Taya nodded. "I think most common song, you know, chimes like—" she tapped out the peculiarly patternless sequence of chimes on the arm of her chair. "I hear that a lot. Maybe many ships song."

"Yeah, she's right," Lieutenant Maxson agreed, looking at her with obvious surprise. "Sixty-nine percent of the saucers are singing at least part of that particular song. That's the one I've copied; the mothership produces that one, too. Everyone seems to." Lieutenant Maxson looked at Commander Kennon. "It's a total wild-ass guess no matter what we do, commander—"

Commander Kennon raised a finger and said calmly, "Signals First, if you would kindly prepare to play back a short sequence of the suggested song and then produce static; let's see if we can delay just a bit longer and then pretend we have laryngitis."

Taya did not know what *laryngitis* was, but she thought she got nearly all the rest of that. *Pretend* had been one of Lieutenant Lockwood's unfriendly words.

Commander Kennon went on, "Commander Keay, if you will suggest your people stand by. Weapons, stand by, please. Nav, on my signal, please be prepared to run for the flashpoint. Weapons

Second, stand ready. Ops, I would be thrilled if we managed to recapture any surviving shrikes before we hit the flashpoint, but that cannot be a priority. Commander Keay, I regret I must ask you—"

Esaias said flatly, "None of our people will be taken prisoner, sir; absolutely not."

"Nor can we allow *Vengeful* to be boarded."

"We won't be," agreed Esaias. "Depend on it." He turned back to his own console.

That loud yuannkuu whistling scream broke across *Vengeful* once more. This time it seemed to be aimed directly at *Vengeful*; the whole ship seemed to ring with the threat of it. Taya gripped the arms of her chair. She couldn't take her gaze off the forward screen, where the stylized icon of the mothership loomed, taking on greater definition as *Vengeful* came closer and closer ...

"Wait for it, wait for it," Commander Kennon told Lieutenant Maxson. "They're not shooting at us, let's just see how long we can draw this out. Nav, I want us right up in their face before we drop the shrikes; then come about as hard as she can handle. Ops, tell me all the redundant gravitics are optimal."

A quiet, competent murmur of acknowledgement and answer all across the bridge.

"Song change!" Taya warned sharply, not even fully aware that the uut signals had altered until she had already cried out her warning. But it *had*, it *had* changed, part of the song was suddenly a little slower, part faster—

"Permission to answer!" said Lieutenant Maxson, which seemed a terrible waste of time, surely he should just *do* it—

"Answer!" agreed Commander Kennon, sharp now, nothing relaxed or casual about his manner any longer. "Everyone else, stand by!"

Lieutenant Maxson was already moving, sending a fragmentary bit of song out into space, claiming what they all fervently prayed might seem a convincing false identity: *one of you, one of you, one of you*. Or Taya, at least, prayed to all the beloved gods that was what *Vengeful* was saying. *Vengeful's* speakers moaned with a rippling, whistling cry: an answer none of them could possibly understand.

Annette said tensely, "Four minutes, closing."

"Let's just see if we can't get a little closer," the commander murmured. "At two minutes, give us a mark, please, Nav First."

"Saucers taking attack formation," Sun Grigson warned, highlighting a nearby cluster of eight saucers. "Standing by."

"They've stopped singing!" Keith said urgently.

Taya had a sinking feeling they'd picked the wrong fragment of song to play back, but there was nothing they could do to fix that now.

Commander Kennon said briskly, "Shrikes away, singlepods away; fire at will, Weapons. All Weapons boards, fire at will."

Twelve Disks; fourteen. Seventeen, the formation dividing and dividing again, five and five and seven. Suddenly multiplying Blades, more Blades than Disks, swarming from the mothership.

"Nine seconds to firing range," Sun said calmly.

Vengeful jolted; jolted again. Taya was grateful for the safety webbing of her seat. She stared wide-eyed at the swirl of uut fighters in the display, each red spark tagged with identifying symbols. Disks slid over and around one another, Blades slicing more directly forward. Light washed through the display as they engaged. *Vengeful* shuddered, taking damage. The display pivoted, this time not wholly without a sense of motion, and Lieutenant Lockwood said curtly, "First gravitics down, second gravitics up, let's try not to do that again."

"Ee tee ay to flashpoint, six minutes five," Annette reported.

Three of the Disks disappeared in washes of light, and two Blades. *Vengeful* shivered and stuttered sideways so that Taya clutched the arms of her chair.

"Second gravitics down, third up," snapped Lieutenant Lockwood. "We can do that exactly once more, but *let's not.*"

Genee at Signals Two raised her hand. "Two singlepods through the flashpoint, five destroyed; one shrike finalizing kami run, three destroyed."

Lieutenant Maxson raised his hand. "We've got another formation coming up fast, on screen now."

Nine Disks this time, Taya saw, and seven Blades. And most of the first several formations were pursuing, lots of them between *Vengeful* and the flashpoint.

Commander Kennon was keeping half an eye on the display, but most of his attention was on his own boards. "Shrike kamikaze, four seconds," he said calmly. "Brace, people." Light bloomed in the display almost before he'd pronounced the last word, bright enough to be uncomfortable even in the muted display. This time when Taya covered her eyes, it wasn't out of terror, but pain-filled reflex.

"Mothership's showing damage, can't see how bad, definitely not destroyed, might be disabled," Lieutenant Maxson reported rapidly. "Enemy formations intact—damn it, Sun, can't you do something about that?"

Sun Grigson's hands were flicking across her boards with deceptive languor. "Always so damn impatient—"

Lieutenant Lockwood said curtly, "Two more singlepods through the flashpoint; none of the others have a prayer of making it."

"All remaining singlepods switching to kamikaze mode," Esaias Keay stated.

"Flashpoint ee tee ay one minute twelve," announced Annette.

Commander Kennon asked softly, "Weapons First?"

"Damn lot of Enemy fighters, sir, I'll do my best—"

"Got another formation!" Lieutenant Maxson cut in. "Sorry, Sun! Seven and nine; and another behind that; the damn mothership's still in the fight—"

Taya stared at the display, losing track of the rapid speech all around her. There were so many Enemy fighters! Formations of uut fighters swirled and darted, closing in, Disks slashing in and around in their intricate, coordinated dance; Blades cutting in before and around the Disks, drawing *Vengeful's* fire—she realized suddenly that *Vengeful's* people weren't targeting the Disks the way they should, they were letting the Blades draw too much of their attention, they weren't looking past the mad swirling flight of the uut fighters to find the heart-Disks. Taya couldn't believe it, but she was right, she knew she was right. She hit the release for the safety webbing, jumped to her feet, ran forward, and pointed urgently at one Disk in the display. "Sun!" she cried. "Heart-Disk, here! This, here!"

"Get that idiot girl out of the way!" snapped Lieutenant Lockwood, then surged out of his seat, seized her arm himself, and thrust her back into her chair. But Sun Grigson coolly touched her boards, and though *Vengeful* shuddered and trembled, that one specific Disk dissolved into a burst of white light and disappeared. And in the resulting moment of confusion, as the rest of the uut fighters lost cohesion, before they could recover the pattern of their attack, *Vengeful* gained the one long stretched instant it needed to leap into the peculiar inside-out space of the flashpoint, leaving the terrible swarming uut fighters and the damaged mothership and the glimmering ruby ribbon of uut habitats and stations far, far behind.

The man at Weapons Second called out, "Nuclear flash, that's a go! Second flash, go!"

And *Vengeful* twisted back rightside-out, and thank the beloved gods, *Vengeful* poured itself back into normal space—

– except *Vengeful* was at once staggering under renewed attack. The computers threw a lot of red icons up into the displays, too many, surely that was too many even though Taya didn't see any motherships, but there were a *lot* of uut fighters. *Vengeful* shuddered, and Lieutenant Lockwood snapped, "Third gravitics down, fourth up, firecontrol says they aren't close to getting any redundancy back."

He didn't sound afraid, only annoyed, but he'd said they could do that only one more time and now they had, and the attack wasn't stopping. Taya decided, she knew, they were all going to die. Though she looked everywhere, at all the displays, she couldn't see *Nkaastu* anywhere. Vengeful wasn't going to get away, they were all going to die, *she* was going to die and *she would never know* what had happened to Kaamharaa, or Daamon, or *anyone.* So many people, everyone she loved, might have died already or they might die later, Kaamharaa might be dead or he might still be a prisoner somewhere else, trapped, helpless, alone, and she would *never know.*

18

"*Sepuuk*," Tsumon announced, highlighting the Kaoluun full-fighter. She picked out others among the battlegroup: "*Taraaot, Yehnna.* There are three battlegroups here. *Sepuuk* is senior and holds authority. We have provided them with our latest records. *Sepuuk* declares they will cover us as we withdraw. We are to take the fastest possible course for Hanaa. These battlegroups will interdict every slide between this system and Hanaa."

Kuotaan lifted a hand to show she had heard this. She consulted with Tuutka with a glance. Then both captain and secondary captain turned their heads to look at Daamon. He stood with both hands resting on the round head of his cane, his attention divided among the display, the console, and the foreign captain, but he returned this look with a little lift of his own chin—acknowledgment rather than agreement. He had not and could not resume battlecommand because they were not actually in a battle. If they managed to get out of this system without engaging the uut, there would be no need for the battlecrew to take their stations. This seemed likely. If they dropped their darkmask now, and put everything they had to acceleration, they'd have a chimes-long head start over most of those uut fighters down by the slide. Plus the full-fighters of these three battlegroups could handle anything that got in their way.

On the first hand, it made perfect sense to run. It really did. He couldn't sensibly argue otherwise. They'd gotten Kaamharaa back, plus reputation enough to cover Aanuku's losses—that would matter to a matriline. No question about it: that captured Blade, nearly intact, was more than enough to add a shiny accent all by itself. The worldbreaker they'd scooped up with that Blade constituted a second coup, and the remains of the uut mechanism a third. No question but that the Aanuku matriarchs would support *Nkaastu* and Kuotaan and Daamon himself—so far.

Unless they risked everything they'd gained on a wild throw of all the forsaken dice in the universe and lost it all. Not a single matriarch would stand behind them if that happened. Kaamharaa certainly would, maybe pulling in the far-flung network of other uturun reputationists. But not the matriarchs.

Daamon was considering arguing anyway. Not on sensible grounds.

"We cannot doubt the battlegroup's ability to cover our retreat," Kuotaan stated.

She hadn't needed to say it out loud. Daamon counted sixty-three full-fighters out there, and a good many half-fighters in support. *Of course* they could cover *Nkaastu's* retreat. He had no doubt of that. The appearance of uut and then *Vengeful* in Hanaa's system had obviously rallied both Kaoluun and Aanuku and probably every other matriline with significant interests on the near edge of familiar space.

Daamon said, "That's true, Tsaa Kuotaan. Retreating through Aam and interdicting the slides there will, of course, require us to abandon Gerstner's people. Every ship in their battlegroup will be torn apart by the uut." Everyone here knew that. They'd all heard the man ask for help. They'd all seen the recordings. They all knew those people had been holding, might still be holding. Daamon wasn't going to allow anyone to pretend they didn't know that. He added, just as deliberately, "*Vengeful* saved Hanaa. They probably saved the settlements at Aam too."

"This is true," Kuotaan said, her tone thoughtful. "However, we cannot think of any *practical* argument against *Sepuuk's* order to retreat. Battlecommander Siiv u Kaoluun and Captain Tnakaa u Kaoluun have surely made time to view our recordings. They must know of those people besieged in that system." She paused. Then she added, "Those people are very distant cousins. They do not belong to the Ka' Taand."

Daamon tipped his chin up again. He knew, as though he'd stood on *Sepuuk's* bridge himself while the Kaoluun matriarchs gave the orders, that *Sepuuk* had been told to assess the situation, observe the uut presence, and decide whether to retreat, abandon the near edge, and interdict every known slide. Obviously the uut swarms here and in nearby systems had made that decision simple. There wasn't an nturun matriarch anywhere in the Ka' Taand who would argue that they should risk their own ships, three whole battlegroups, to try to rescue strangers rather than pull back and defend their own people. Because that was what nturun did. They defended, and they always defended their own families before anything else.

Siiv u Kaoluun had apparently accepted the order to retreat. Of course he had. He hadn't personally met any of the cousins, nor seen their battlegroup surrounded and besieged in that juncture system.

Daamon was vividly conscious of Captain Gerstner standing near at hand. The tension radiating from the man could practically have powered *Nkaastu*. Kaamharaa had undoubtedly communicated the order to retreat. Daamon could feel the other man's dismay. He said out loud, "On the first hand, obviously we don't want to leave familiar space vulnerable to great numbers of uut. Obviously we should interdict everything between this system and Hanaa rather than risk our heart-stars. On the second hand, we certainly don't have the standing to argue with *Sepuuk*. On the *third* hand, these cousins of ours-and-yours possess these very powerful ships, much more powerful than anything we know how to build—"

"Wait, wait, priority, look!" Saraa exclaimed. Everyone was suddenly talking over one another and pointing.

The display had unexpectedly flared into confusion down near the uut slide. The computers sorted signals and updated the display as fast as they could, but even so, at first Daamon could tell only that the swarm of uut fighters, which had begun to sort itself into attack formations to pursue the battlegroup, had suddenly become confused.

Then a lavender power signature bloomed in the display down near the uut slide, rapidly shading toward blue as the computers recognized *Vengeful.* The slide itself brightened from the ordinary grayed-gold toward gold-white, signifying that someone had set off destabilizing munitions within the slide—thank all the beloved gods for that—but *Vengeful* suddenly trailed a lavender glitter of debris. Hard to tell how much damage the ship might have suffered, either from battle, or from running hard without time to make repairs, or from the powerful bombs it had dropped—attempts to destabilize a slide were never precisely safe.

Before and all around *Vengeful*, uut Blades and Disks were sorting themselves out into battle order.

"The lag is nearly a quarter chime; we're nearly a quarter chime behindhand," Suumat reminded them all. She was right: whatever had happened to *Vengeful* had *been* happening, and they were only seeing it now.

Captain Gerstner came close and gripped Daamon's arm. He didn't speak. The strength of his urgent grip spoke for him. Daamon glanced at him, acknowledging his dismay, but beckoning for Tuutka to take the man back to his place and keep him out of the way. Gerstner did not argue; he flinched slightly when the secondary captain took his arm, but he let Daamon go and backed up. That did not mean his dismay was any less. Daamon was fairly thoroughly dismayed himself. Getting *Vengeful* back was excellent. Watching it torn to pieces before their eyes ... it was insupportable.

"Tough situation they've got down there," Genru observed, his voice almost neutral. "Few too many uut left on this side of the slide, but look, they're handling themselves pretty well for being so outnumbered. Or, I mean, they were a quarter-chime ago."

Paaol smacked his console with the flat of his hand. "Come on, Daamon! Let's at least run in and see if there's something left to rescue! For sure there won't be if we hold here! I bet we can break them out if we go right now, but who knows how long they'll ride the chance?"

"*Sepuuk's* reiterating its orders," Saraa informed them. Her tone and sideways glance at Daamon made it clear she didn't think he was likely to care. "Paaol's right, but I don't think *Nkaastu* alone will be able to get *Vengeful* out of that nasty hole it's fallen into. You think *Sepuuk* will bring its battlegroup in after us if we go get *Vengeful?*"

Daamon returned her look. "I think ... I think this is the wrong time to leave their decision to chance. I think ... Gen, I'll take communications for a moment." Genru tilted his head, puzzled, but Saraa's gaze sharpened suddenly. She'd always been quick.

So had Tsumon, who borrowed Saraa's romance-adventure novels when she was bored. "Nda Daamon, we would not protest," she began. "But that is a device for fiction, not for real battle—"

Paaol got it then and leaned over to smack the turun's lower shoulder. "Shut up, Tsumon! Brilliant, Daamon!" He was grinning fiercely. "I've always wanted to try this."

"Wait," began Genru, catching on at last. "Daamon, that's *Siiv u Kaoluun* ..."

Daamon ignored them all. He pulled all priority communication functions to his console, then looked at Kuotaan, whose opinion was the only one that mattered now. For a long breath, she held his gaze with her one good eye.

Kuotaan u Aanuku, like Tsumon, read uman romance-adventure fiction. And she had always been decisive. And forward-thinking. And bold, with a clear eye for advantage and alliance. That was why Kaamharaa was on her ship.

And she had been right here for everything, same as Daamon had been.

After no more than a hundredth chime, Kuotaan tapped their shared console, settling the functions into battlemode. "We had tentatively accepted the offer of alliance made by your-and-our cousins," she said firmly. "We consider the potential advantage to be gained from that alliance worth considerable potential risk, and we also consider that our reputation would hardly be burnished by abandoning your-and-our cousins—and we trust our battlecommander. But we do not wish to risk this suggestion unless *Sepuuk* and this battlegroup agree to support us."

Daamon opened a hand in acceptance of her resolution, offered a brief and wordless prayer to all the beloved gods, took a breath, opened a channel, and said, exactly like the hero in a thousand epics, "*Sepuuk,* as the battlecommander best informed in this system and this action, I invoke priority overrule, claim temporary seniority, and take command of all armed ships here present."

A wordless sputter from someone aboard *Sepuuk* made it abundantly clear that someone, probably everyone, on Siiv's battlecrew had also read those stories. Daamon said briskly, almost word for word from the novels, "My name is Daamon sepu Kaamharaa. I am battlecommander of Aanuku half-fighter tradeship *Nkaastu*. All battlegroups in the region will immediately bend their efforts toward rescuing that uman ship. I set Kaamharaa's reputation behind this command, my own reputation, and the reputation of Tsaa Kuotaan u Aanuku."

"Yeah, you know, I'm not sure this is going to go over real well," muttered Genru.

Paaol was barely managing to contain his delight. "Are you *joking?* This is *great!*"

Daamon waved them both quiet, cut off communications from *Sepuuk* before anyone could frame a cogent protest—or worse, a flat denial—sent Saraa a course that would take them straight toward *Vengeful* and ordered Paaol, "Start figuring firing priorities and solutions."

"We shall be forceful, if Sepuuk and this entire battlegroup do not rapidly accede," Kuotaan rumbled. "Kha Saraa, please inform us if *Sepuuk* offers the least argument or declines to follow *Nkaastu.*"

"They're not arguing," Genru said, sounding a little surprised. "They're following our lead. They really are!"

Saraa added, "They're only going to be a heartbeat behind us. I estimate *Nkaastu* will engage with the nearest uut fighters in ... zero point six chime-down. Sepuuk's battlegroup should follow us into firing range no more than zero point one zero after that, assuming they follow us at all. Which I guess they actually will." She glanced at Daamon. "So far, they don't seem to have a lot to say."

She meant that after the battle this would change. Daamon said drily, "I'm sure they'll have a few comments, so let's not rob them of the chance to say it by getting ourselves killed beforehand. Gen, track those battlegroups and sing out quick if anything looks like it might turn dicey in that direction. Keep updating *Vengeful* too; if we're too late, let's find that out earlier rather than later, yes? Saraa, options, please."

Saraa sent a handful of possible courses traced across the display, from highly self-protective to extremely daring.

Paaol highlighted one on—of course—the daring side of the spectrum. "I like this one."

Saraa picked out another. "This one offers more chances to disengage."

"It's not nearly as good for covering *Vengeful*—"

"*We* don't have to cover *Vengeful*; that handy battlegroup will do that for us—"

Genru cut her off. "Priority, no, we do have to cover *Vengeful*. Best I can tell, it's lost a lot of defensive capability all along the near flank. It's turning to keep that side away from uut weapons. It won't be able to keep that up long once the uut realize it's vulnerable."

Once Genru had pointed out *Vengeful's* weakness, it was obvious. Daamon selected an option close to Paaol's choice and sent it to the whole battlegroup.

If Siiv u Kaoluun brought his battlegroup into the fight, disengaging wouldn't be a problem. If he didn't, well ... disengaging wouldn't actually help, given the number of uut fighters they'd be facing. But Daamon could hardly imagine Siiv changing his mind now.

"Zero point four one chime-down," Saraa said calmly.

Daamon nodded, though she wasn't looking at him. He said, "Gerstner!"

The foreign captain jerked and turned. His eyes had narrowed; his mouth was hard set—dismayed at the circumstances that rendered him merely a passenger aboard *Nkaastu* when he could plainly see his own ship in peril. Daamon could well imagine how he felt. Time to give him something useful to do.

"Tuutka, kindly assist Gerstner. I'm mirroring our display to Kaamharaa and feeding Kaamharaa's signal to the console nearest you. Kaamharaa, please ascertain how many uut fighters *Vengeful* is reasonably able to engage. Inform Gerstner that *Vengeful* is damaged along the near flank and find out how *Nkaastu* and our associated battlegroup can best deploy our efforts given that fact."

Tuutka stamped her front feet aggressively, plainly pleased to take an active role in this engagement. The secondary captain rarely took action on the bridge, only provided consultation and support and stepped in should some calamity befall the primary captain. Regardless of her reluctance to accept alliance with the cousins, she was obviously delighted to be asked.

Daamon pushed Captain Gerstner physically toward Tuutka and left them to it, himself turning back to the course options Saraa had refined ... her first choice seemed to be a raking course that would take them straight through a dense formation of Disks and frighteningly near a handful of Blades. If they survived long enough, they would wind up tucked against *Vengeful's* damaged flank. He gave Saraa a look.

She shrugged, flashing a grin his way. "I know! That's for if we expect covering fire from the battlegroup. I've mirrored it to *Sepuuk*—zero point one five two before we have to decide—"

Daamon nodded. "Tentatively, yes, so get set to carry out that maneuver on your mark. Paaol?"

"Working on it, got half-solutions, I'll get it, Daamon. It'll take some tight flying, but we'll get it. Figure we'll be adding a glory accent to Kaamharaa's reputation?"

Daamon couldn't help but laugh. "Could be, could be, but let's keep our minds on the moment."

Genru shook his head. "You and your sep' brother are crazy. I figure if we survive this, you can start leaping off cliffs to see if the children's tales are true and clouds really are made of ndao petals, and I'll stand below and watch."

Kuotaan rumbled quietly, "We have prepared three drones with updated reports, all commanded to run dark and quiet until they enter close orbit around Aam. We urge their release."

"Most sensible; altogether an excellent precaution," agreed Daamon. "They must be released on divergent trajectories, lest one or another come to the attention of our enemies. Of course each drone must be willing to divulge its full reports to any turun ship, whether it should be Aanuku or Kaoluun or any other."

Kuotaan waved away the need for this injunction with two of her hands, most of her attention on finishing the downloads. "Indeed, indeed, this need not be said. We do not wish to permit free download by nturun of rival matrilines, but we are setting the full download so that it may be triggered by uman khand of any matriline or polity." She gestured to Tsumon, who launched the finished drones: one, two, three little coughing stutters as Nkaastu's gravitics adjusted for the kick of each launch.

Tuutka broke in, "Nda Daamon, not merely the flank, Gerrstner believes his ship is deficient along the full length of the near side and urgently desires *Nkaastu* to deploy our strength so as to prevent further damage. Tsuumat Kaamharaa believes Gerrstner warns of impending gravitics failure if *Vengeful* takes further damage amidships on that side."

"Paaol," Daamon said, rapidly figuring *Nkaastu's* options.

"Got it, got it," Paaol muttered. "Maybe."

The suggested maneuvers seemed optimistic to Daamon, who shunted them to Saraa and ordered, "Work with *Sepuuk*, get us something better." Saraa nodded briskly. Daamon left her to it.

"*Vengeful* retains considerable aggressive capability and should be able to extend a reasonable degree of protection to anyone within a certain radius," put in Tuutka. "Thus Tsuumat Kaamharaa indicates his understanding of Tsaa Gerrstner's answer to your query, Nda Daamon, but directions and distances remain regrettably opaque at this moment."

"Thank you, Tsaaku Tuutka. Not too narrow a radius, we'll hope." Daamon looked at Gerstner, who gazed back, sober and restrained. The foreign captain spoke, quick phrases that sounded nearly familiar, yet were not comprehensible. But Daamon didn't have to understand the words to hear the urgency in the other man's voice. He tipped his chin up, hoping to convey reassurance. In the display, the narrow shape of *Vengeful* rolled awkwardly to keep its wounded side clear of the most aggressive uut Blades. The only factor that had saved *Vengeful* so far was that uut were too close to the uman ship for their missiles to engage their insystem drives, and so automatic defenses were still fast enough to keep up with uut attacks.

Paaol said sharply, "I've got solutions for three heart-Disks, but two're long-term and taking the other one will put us in place to protect *Vengeful* at the cost of sending us straight into the fangs of a whole formation. Nda Siiv had better come through, but look, you can see the battlegroup's coming in now. Figure zero point zero two."

Daamon signaled approval and held his breath. Zero point zero one ... and Paaol whooped as *Nkaastu* fired on two Blades, then scooted past them practically into the teeth of a Disk. The Disk dissolved into glitter as the computers engaged preset firing solutions, and *Nkaastu* was past and ... yes, heading right into extreme peril as a formation of nine Disks and seven Blades closed around them.

Saraa whirled *Nkaastu* around and tucked them into place against *Vengeful's* near side; Paaol expended nearly their entire remaining supply of munitions in less than a hundredth of a chime; and Genru fed a handful of fairly pessimistic options to Daamon's console, from one that assumed *Sepuuk's* battlegroup abandoned them utterly to one that assumed an even worse scenario where the battlegroup fired on *Vengeful*. Daamon gave Gen a look.

Genru just shrugged. "I like to be prepared. If the battlegroup follows your orders, there's no problem, so I'm thinking of other possibilities."

He didn't say a word, just shunted all Gen's options to one side in case he actually needed one of them later and tried to keep some idea of how the whole battlespace was progressing. The uut had figured out *Vengeful's* weakness and were coming hard; pretty soon their aggressiveness would overwhelm *Nkaastu's* best efforts—

—and eleven turun full-fighters raked past, so close they'd practically be visible to the naked eye. Suddenly the uut were no longer a problem.

Paaol said, his tone envious, "Eleven's not even half a full-strength battlegroup. Did you see how easy they made that look?"

"Right. Easy," Saraa agreed. Genru said nothing, but sighed in relief and leaned back against Suumat, who settled one of her lower hands on his shoulder and pressed gently in reassurance and relief. Near Genru, Captain Gerstner let out his breath, shook his head, and looked at Daamon.

Daamon met Gerstner's eyes. What he saw, what he knew the other commander saw as well, was that if *Sepuuk's* battlegroup had delayed even another tenth-chime, *Nkaastu* and *Vengeful* would most likely have been destroyed together. Paaol, so gifted at battle, knew that too. But Paaol didn't worry about it. It hadn't happened, so to him the risk had never truly existed. Sometimes Daamon envied his near-brother's insouciance.

19

Taya had honestly believed nothing would ever frighten her again after that terrifying slow journey practically right up to the uut ring, and then the even more terrifying flight back out to the slide and the scramble to get past the mothership. She'd really thought they would be safe once they made it through the slide. Somehow that made everything seem worse when it turned out they weren't.

Then it got *even worse,* because it definitely hadn't occurred to her that *Nkaastu* would after all turn out to have waited for them, and would dive right back into battle to protect *Vengeful* the moment they saw the cousins' ship was damaged.

She had been so, so certain that she was going to see *Nkaastu* destroyed, and that *Vengeful* would follow immediately afterward.

Then it turned out, right at the last moment, that a whole turun battlegroup had followed *Nkaastu* into that rescue. She was so bad at reading *Vengeful's* displays that she hadn't even realized the turun ships were *there,* and then all of a sudden everything was over, people were leaning back in their chairs and shaking out their hands, and Taya was still trying to figure out what had happened, but obviously the battle was over.

She was so relieved and happy when she realized about the battlegroup, she nearly cried. She told herself very, *very* firmly that she was safe, they were all safe. It was hard to believe.

Commander Kennon said in his mild, relaxed way, "Well, boys and girls, I see our new neighbors decided to stroll over with a welcome-to-the-neighborhood gift. Looks like *Kaastu* made it. And returned the favor we did her, so that was nice of her. Ops, how are our gravitics looking?"

Lieutenant Lockwood looked up, blew out a breath, and sat back. "Fourth array's holding, more or less. I really don't want to calculate how close it came to not holding. Firecontrol says they'll have the first array back up in twenty minutes." He hesitated, glanced at Taya with a frown, and finally shrugged. *"Nkaastu* saved our bacon. But we should still figure firing solutions, sir. We don't know the rest of them." His voice tightened. "We shouldn't fool ourselves into thinking we can guess what aliens might do."

"That's—" Commander Kennon began.

"Turun, not *aliens,*" Taya protested, indignant at Lieutenant Lockwood's tone. "They help! You want go back, fight Enemy all alone?"

Lieutenant Lockwood didn't even look at her. "For friendly ships, most of those are standing back at a pretty suggestive distance, sir. If their weapons are similar to ours, that's just the right distance they could use their missiles effectively."

"As I was saying," Commander Kennon said sharply. "That's a quite reasonable precaution. Weapons One, calculate firing solutions. We won't expect to *use* those solutions, Taya; sit down. Signals One, let's send a pulse to *Kaastu*. Signals Two, keep an eye on all those other ... turun ships."

Taya wondered what other word the commander had almost pronounced there, instead of *turun*. *Alien*, snapped out in the same angry tone Lieutenant Lockwood had used?

"Commander Keay, assemble a short detail of your marines," Commander Kennon finished. "We may either have guests here or send a party somewhere away, and either way we'll need an escort."

Esaias acknowledged and murmured private commands to his people.

"Pulse, sir," Lieutenant Maxson said suddenly. "Two pulses. I expect *Kaastu* wants to chat, but so does somebody else. The signal's the same; there's no problem with interpretation. On screen?"

Taya jumped out of her chair and bounced on her toes, too nervous and excited to sit still.

Commander Kennon nodded to Keith. "Yes, indeed, Signals, split the screen and let's see who's calling. Weapons, attend to business, if you please; whatever these people have to say, let's not get distracted."

"Yes, *sir,*" Sun acknowledged, her attention strictly on her console.

Taya leaned forward as images built themselves slowly and separately on the left and right sides of *Vengeful's* flat display. The images on the right cleared first: a sweep of color, mostly blue and gold enamels rather than the greens and ambers and browns and turquoise of *Nkaastu*. The black-threaded purple of the emergency lights flared in warning overhead. *High* overhead; this was a substantially larger bridge than on *Nkaastu,* with four times as many battlecrew and twice as many turun as *Nkaastu*. Some of the uman people shared stations with turun partners, but more stood by permanently lowered consoles they didn't share with anybody.

The battlecommander was a thin, intense man with uncommonly pale coloring: skin hardly darker than peeled ndao nuts and hair almost as bright a gold as the fruit, though going white in streaks. Not a young man, this battlecommander; not just the white in his hair but the lines on his face spoke of age and authority and grim experience. His eyes were pale-colored too, and narrowed as he swept a summing look across *Vengeful's* bridge; narrowed again as he took in Taya's presence, and then turned a considering look on Commander Kennon.

His nturun captain was old, too, well into the powerful and imposing turun middle age; a big nturun, grey rather than the more ordinary dark red-brown. Dapples gleamed dark and light down the captain's flanks, and she had striking light yellow eyes. Kaoluun for sure, and Taya definitely had a guess as to what ship that might be. A pale-colored man like that next to a gray nturun definitely stood out. But then a man like that and an nturun like that *would* stand out, no matter their coloring.

Taking a quick step forward, Taya said quickly, "Battlecommander, we are *so* grateful for your support. Captain, I'm sure *Vengeful* will acknowledge their debt to your ship and your matriline." She was *sure* Commander Kennon would acknowledge it when she had a moment to explain. "I'm Taya sep' Kaamharaa, allied with the half-fighter tradeship *Nkaastu* and with Aanuku." She went on, pronouncing the titles and names carefully. "This is Commander Reese Kennon, who is a secondary captain of the uman ship *Vengeful*."

She wished she could list the accomplishments and reputation for this foreigner and explain the honors *Vengeful* had won, but since she hadn't thought ahead enough to ask, she didn't know them. She added firmly instead, "Commander Kennon is most courageous and tgehst and I am sure he and his people will prove good and trustworthy allies, if the Ka' Taand is wise enough to ask for alliance."

The uman battlecommander consulted with his captain with a glance. When she tipped her chin up, he looked straight at Taya. "Kha Taya, I am Siiv u Kaoluun sepu Upuonnu. I am blessed to serve with Tsaa Tnakaa u Kaoluun as her battlecommander."

Taya nodded eagerly. "Oh, yes, I thought so! My full-brother admires you so much, Nda Siiv! He's studied all your actions."

The corner of Siiv's mouth twitched up. "Indeed," he said politely. "I imagine your full-brother is Daamon sep' Kaamharaa? I have recently become slightly acquainted with your extremely presumptuous full-brother, Kha Taya. He proved most adamant regarding the importance of rescuing ... *Vengeful*."

"Oh, well, I'm sure he had to be, Nda Siiv! *Nkaastu* is allied with *Vengeful*—" she hoped that wasn't overstating the truth—"and also I think Aanuku and Tsuumat Kaamharaa are allied with

Vengeful. I *hope* Kaamharaa. You don't actually know—my brother didn't tell you anything about Kaamharaa or Captain Gerstner?" She pronounced the foreign name as carefully and correctly as she could, and was aware of the sharpening attention of everyone around her on *Vengeful's* bridge. And they had all been paying attention to her already. She held her breath.

"I regret your full-brother's attention appeared to be entirely occupied by the immediate exigencies of battle, Kha Taya. Now that we find ourselves with a moment of leisure, Tnakaa u Kaoluun and I personally and all my Ndand, will, I believe, be most interested in becoming acquainted with your brother in person. And with others." His gaze went past her to examine the foreign bridge and all the foreign cousins. "You are able to speak to these people?"

"Yes, Nda Siiv!" declared Taya. She turned quickly to Commander Kennon, who raised an eyebrow at her in an expression that was actually just the same in his people as hers. She grinned at him, too happy to be intimidated. Except she had to translate properly for Nda Siiv and make them understand each other: that was an important job. She stood up straight and tried to look serious and grown up and not like a child. "Commander Kennon, sir, this person Siiv u Kaoluun is very important battlecommander for whole Ka' Taand. Famous captain Tsaa Tnakaa u Kaoluun, very famous ship *Sepuuk,* lot important people." She hoped he understood how urgently the good opinion of *Sepuuk* mattered. He was listening, at least.

Lieutenant Maxson interrupted. "We've got the other signal clear," he said quietly, received a nod, and an image of *Nkaastu's* bridge built itself on the left side of the screen.

Daamon was there, he was right there, he was *perfectly all right.* Better still, *Captain Gerstner* stood beside him. He looked tired, and his shoulder was supported by a sling of medicinal webbing, but he seemed to be mostly all right. So he *had* been on that Blade! Only she couldn't guess whether Kaamharaa had *also* been rescued. She threw Daamon an intense look: *Tell me!*

"He's fine, we got them both," Daamon told her, very quickly, before anyone else said anything, and Taya grabbed the back of her chair because she was so relieved she felt light-headed.

A sharp murmur of reaction had gone across *Vengeful's* bridge, and Commander Kennon came forward a step and was speaking, and Taya had to listen carefully and translate and couldn't take time to ask about Kaamharaa.

"Sir," Commander Kennon said to his primary captain, "We look forward to welcoming you back aboard. We certainly do."

Captain Gerstner didn't seem to be a demonstrative person, but he was smiling now. "I look forward to that myself. I have to admit to some doubts in that direction from time to time. Including right at the end. Flew a little wide there for a while, didn't you, Reese?"

"Bold in action, resolute in duty," Commander Kennon said in a bland tone. "You know how it is." He looked at Daamon, started to speak, hesitated, and glanced at Taya. "If you will kindly ask your people to arrange for our captain's return immediately."

Daamon must have guessed what Commander Kennon said, or else he just came to the same conclusion on his own, because he said without waiting for her translation, "Taya, please inform the secondary captain that *Nkaastu* will send a transport at once. I'm sure Captain Gerstner is eager to return to his ship, and you to return to us here. Only we must be quick; Captain Gerstner emphasizes the importance of haste in returning to rescue his people in the other system."

"Nda Daamon sepu Kaamharaa, I think," said Nda Siiv, reserved and not particularly friendly.

Taya saw her brother's eyes widen. He plainly hadn't realized this was a three-way link, or that Siiv u Kaoluun had already been speaking to *Vengeful.*

"Signals," Commander Kennon murmured, lifting a finger, and Lieutenant Maxson did something at his station.

Daamon blinked and then nodded, glancing from side to side in a way that made Taya guess his display had also now divided so that he was able to see both *Vengeful's* bridge and *Sepuuk's*. He suddenly seemed to be holding himself a bit stiffly, which might be his leg, but Taya guessed meant he was nervous and trying not to show it. But he didn't sound nervous at all when he said, "Nda Siiv, I regret that imperative necessity still exists. My awareness of the situation remains unique and I must continue to invoke overrule. The moment the exchange of personnel has been effected, we—*Nkaastu* and your entire battlegroup—must immediately accompany our cousins' full-fighter *Vengeful* in an urgent attempt to recover the situation now faced by its battlegroup."

"You—" Taya stopped short, because asking incredulously, *You invoked priority overrule, like in a* story? *Really?* might not help.

"Such a broad action is not remotely within the scope of the guidance provided by Kaoluun," Siiv u Kaoluun said, his tone utterly neutral. "Let me just mention that priority overrule is a device of *fiction*. I imagine details as small and trivial as that may have escaped your notice, given the urgency you evidently perceive, Nda Daamon."

Daamon answered, "This is the time to pull it out of fiction and make it real. Please pass the necessary orders to your battlegroup, Nda Siiv." He blanked *Nkaastu* out of the display, obviously intending to avoid argument.

Nda Siiv's unshakeable calm made him very hard to read. His light-colored eyes, almost as colorless as water, were more disconcerting than Taya had expected. He dropped his gaze to his own console, then looked up again, straight at Taya, and raised an eyebrow.

"I'm sure he's right," Taya said quickly. "I'm sure he knows what to do! You won't refuse, will you, Nda Siiv?"

"Possibly not," Siiv said politely. "I'm considering the matter."

"These people are our cousins and our allies, so we have to help them," Taya pointed out. "It's not right to let the uut destroy their battlegroup, especially because they have a lot of very powerful ships and they fight the uut. We should help them because it's the right thing to do, but also because they can help us. You should have *seen* the uut through that slide! More uut than there are blades of grass in Gaatuu's savannahs, more than there are stars in the sky!" She turned sharply and switched to English. "Commander Kennon, sir, say *Vengeful* ally with *Nkaastu*. Say!"

"That seems undeniable," Commander Kennon said drily. "I certainly wouldn't try to deny it. Yes, we're allies, Taya."

Lieutenant Lockwood said suddenly, speaking directly to Siiv, "Nda Siiv, not only *Vengeful* ally with *Nkaastu*. Your people, our people, we are everyone allies, big allies. This is very important."

He had spoken in Uom. Taya was amazed. Then less amazed: she had known he was learning Uom, even though he didn't like it, didn't like her, didn't like the turun. She said in English, not trusting what he said, "Is true, this?"

"It had better be," he snapped, caught himself, and said stiffly, "Commander, I'm telling these people we want a broad alliance between their people and ours. It might be a good idea for you to agree, pending the captain's approval, but right now, sir, immediately. They're arguing *right now* over whether to help Aleph. Taya and her people on *Nkaastu* want to; they're trying to persuade these other people. I'm not wrong about this, sir."

"Lieutenant Lockwood not wrong," Taya agreed at once. "Is very best say as he says."

Commander Kennon nodded. "Say anything you have to: the politicians can fight it out later. Lieutenant, given the opportunity, I trust you'll let Falconer know this was your advice."

"Yes, sir, absolutely."

"We're picking up *Kaastu's* shuttle now," someone else said.

Commander Kennon nodded. "Get down to the ship bay," he told Taya. "Commander Keay, detail a man to see her safe to the bay and onto that shuttle."

Taya nodded vigorously and started to go toward the doorway.

But Lieutenant Lockwood interrupted them both. "No, sir, with your permission. She stays here. I need her, sir. She's better with English than I am in that damned alien gabble." He was frowning, completely annoyed, but he went on, still speaking to the commander. "We can't afford misunderstandings. Plus she can apparently pick the brain out of the swarm, which is a nice bonus, but that's not as important as her own brain. She's quick, she's human enough, she's transparently honest, and she needs to stay on *Vengeful* until we get through this. She knows it. She'll tell that brother of hers the same thing, and that damned alien she's so fond of. Go on, ask her, she understands what I just said."

Taya didn't wait to be asked. She dropped back into the chair, pulled the webbing firmly across her lap, and said, "Yes, is true. Lieutenant Lockwood rude. But still is all true. I stay here. This important."

"*Is* rude. *Will* stay here," he corrected impatiently. "This *is* important. Damn it, Taya, get the verbs right, it's all *be* verbs, you got them in the second module."

Taya rolled her eyes. But she said, emphasizing the verbs, "I *will stay* here and I *will talk* to everyone. Lieutenant Lockwood *is* right. Only I tell Daamon so he know—knows—I will stay here."

"Sounds like it's settled," Commander Kennon said drily. "I'm certainly glad you two work together so smoothly. Signals, get

Kaastu back. Taya, please tell whoever needs to hear it that, pending Captain Gerstner's approval, I, at least, will argue for a broad alliance. If we can pull Task Force Aleph out of the fire, then these important people of yours will have *very* important people with whom to discuss the matter. Emphasize that, please. There are *very important people*, politically influential people, with Aleph—if they're still alive. Ops, where the hell is the captain?"

"In the tube, sir," someone said.

"Politically influential means very important for a lot of people, like the matriarchs in a clan," Lieutenant Lockwood told Taya.

Taya hadn't realized he had learned terms like *matriarch*. She only dimly remembered explaining something about clans and matrilines. But she nodded. Turning to face the display, she said, "Tsaa Tnakaa u Kaoluun, the secondary captain of *Vengeful* says there are very important people, like the matriarchs of important clans, with the battlegroup that's in so much trouble." She looked from the turun captain to the battlecommander. "Nda Siiv, my brother would never do something as crazy as claim priority overrule for real unless it was truly important!"

"One certainly hopes not," Siiv agreed, still very dry.

"This is very—" but she stopped as Captain Gerstner strode onto the bridge, swept one comprehensive look around, and said with no preliminary greeting, "I have the bridge, Exec, and what in God's name did you do to our gravitics?" He looked exactly as Taya remembered: forceful, decisive, and not entirely friendly.

"You have the bridge, sir. Running battle with a trillion Enemy fighters, dodged a little too slowly, sorry about that, the first array should be back up in fourteen minutes." Commander Kennon had stepped back and to the side, yielding the central place to his captain. "We're apparently conducting diplomatic negotiations at this very moment over whether to take a stab at breaking Aleph out of that swarm while there's still a chance of saving something. I just declared we're in favor of that, sir. Lockwood and, ah, Kha Taya, are managing those negotiations."

Captain Gerstner gave Taya a curt nod. "Kha Taya, your Kaamharaa is fine. A little banged up, but fine. He saved my life, I saved his life, we had an exciting day, but here we are. How much English do you understand?"

"Enough I happy I hear this!" she told him. "Thank you, Captain!" She added, pointedly, speaking to Siiv and everyone on *Sepuuk* in Uom, "The uut took Kaamharaa and Tsaa Gerstner, but they allied and got away. *Nkaastu* rescued them, *Vengeful* put itself between all the uut in the whole universe and *Nkaastu.*" Switching back to English, she added urgently, speaking to Lockwood, "Send log to *Sepuuk*, let see how many Enemy!"

Lieutenant Lockwood had provided a rapid, low-voiced translation a beat behind her and added, crisply, "We should do that, sir."

"I second the motion. It's impressive as hell," Commander Kennon added. "Niven ring, absolutely terrifying." He didn't sound in the least terrified.

The captain gave a sharp nod. "Signals, send it." Then he looked straight at the screen, gave a little bow, and said, with creditable pronunciation of the names and titles, "Nda Siiv, Tsaa Tnakaa, good to meet you. I hope to hell you're planning to be helpful." Without pausing, he turned to his own people and went on, "Lockwood, you're off Ops, liaise with Kha Taya and the turun and do what you can to encourage helpfulness. Promise whatever you have to, but it would be good if I can stand behind whatever you promise without getting court martialed. Signals, we'll let them look over our shoulder, but we're not going to sit here and chat. Nav, get us moving. I want to get through the outer flashpoint as quickly as possible. Exec, tell me what we've got."

Taya sat back in her chair and looked at Lieutenant Lockwood, who stood up, letting another person take over his console, and came to drop into a seat next to her. He told her, "Deliberately telling lies is *deceptive.* That's an adjective with the same root as *deceive*. Another word for the same thing is *dishonest.* The opposite adjective is *honest.* I'm sure you noticed the prefix that reverses the meaning. Someone who's honest but wrong is a *sincere fool.* The adjective for someone who won't believe the truth is *suspicious.* Someone who won't quit being suspicious even when handed plenty of evidence he's wrong is a *stubborn fool.*"

"That fair," Taya allowed. "You both kinds fool."

"Exactly. Tell me what I should say to get that battlegroup to help us."

Taya knew, or thought she knew, what he was asking. She said firmly, "Tell true things, not lies. No good alliance build on dishonest."

"Don't use an adjective where you need a noun, and pay attention to the verbs. It *is* impossible *to build* a solid alliance on lies. Repeat that."

Taya repeated it, in exactly the same firm tone as her first statement.

"For once we agree," Lockwood told her, still without the hint of a smile. "I'm logging your advice. Now tell me what I should say to get that damned battlegroup out there to help our people."

This time Taya nodded. "Yes," she said. "I will say. We will *both* say, honest words, not deceptive. You log that."

A curt nod. "I intend to."

He meant it. Taya thought he did. He would also, she was sure, make her say everything exactly right before he put her words into *Vengeful's* log. She thought maybe she was starting to like him after all.

20

"You certainly had an exciting time," Gerstner observed, flicking off the highlights version of the log that Reese Kennon had rapidly spliced together and shot over to the command station. "A Niven ring. Did not see that coming." He glanced up.

"Might've been their home system," Reese agreed. "I hope to God it was their home system. You saw how widely spaced those habitats are. Even so, I'd guess that's thousands of times more living area in that one system than we've got in the whole Imperial Republic. Maybe tens of thousands."

Gerstner nodded. He didn't want to think the Enemy had built up like that in more than one solar system. That would not be good. "Good job destabilizing that flashpoint. I expect they've got others." No one would have centered so much of their civilization in a system with only one usable flashpoint. Or who knew, but *probably* the Enemy had multiple flashpoints in that system, leading God knew where. It was still extremely helpful that Reese had managed to spark that particular Enemy flashpoint to violent fury as he got *Vengeful* out of there. If God was good, that flashpoint would stay impassible for centuries, if not millennia.

One never knew, of course.

The time it had taken to get from the destabilized flashpoint back out to the outer-system flashpoints had been painful, but at least it provided time to review the log, which was fine, and get redundancy back for gravitics, which had been essential. They could have used another ten hours or so to pull *Vengeful* as close to spec as possible without a full powerdown and shipyard rebuild. Even so, Gerstner couldn't help but be glad the waiting was just about over.

He said, in his best neutral tone, "You took *Vengeful* into that system absolutely blind."

This was not approval. Reese knew that. He said blandly, "Devils were driving, sir."

"You were a complete damned idiot. For which I am personally tremendously grateful." Still not actually approval.

Reese shrugged. "I thought of scooting off to hide, hopefully a little more effectively, though since the Enemy found us while we were fully shielded, that might've proved iffy. I could have waited for everything to calm down. Eventually, once everyone but us was dead and the Enemy got tired of picking through the bones, we could have snuck off home with our tail between our legs to explain to Admiralty and probably the Emperor himself how we managed to contact a weird, blended human-alien civilization for about five minutes, lose our captain, and hide while our entire task force was cut to shreds. Then I thought what the hell, might as well pick option B instead. I wanted a look through that flashpoint anyway, and here we are, with a report that'll set absolutely everybody back home way back on their heels. They've got guts. You were right about that."

He meant the turun. Gerstner followed this abrupt segue without effort and nodded. "They do."

"You were also right about wanting to hook these people into an alliance. And about wanting to do it as fast as possible. Offhand, I'd say I was right to commit to helping *Kaastu* with their wildly optimistic rescue scheme, though of course you may disagree, sir. I grant, it was also ridiculously stupid. I logged it as my personal decision."

"I noticed that."

"A short career, but a brilliant one."

Gerstner gave him a look. "You decided you'd either be so extremely lucky a board of inquiry would forgive your idiocy, or too dead to care."

"Pretty much, sir. Taking the ridiculously stupid option gave this turun task force time to catch up to us and primed *Kaastu* to get their buddies to help us, a bit of extreme luck that should help a board reach a more pleasant verdict." He paused. Then he asked, "You think the whole lot of them will stay with us all the way?"

That was a very sober question, not a hint of humor about it. Gerstner said, "In twenty minutes, we'll find out."

Vengeful was still at battle stations—Gerstner had kept the ship at a continual yellow alert since he'd returned—but even at *Vengeful's* current acceleration, it had taken hours to get back to the flashpoint that led toward Aleph. Now they were counting down the minutes to the point at which every ship would have to commit to going through that flashpoint, or else change their minds. Then they'd find out whether they had allies or not. A couple turun ships had already peeled off and headed for that world of theirs, Aam. Either the rest of their turun task force would accompany *Vengeful* or they'd turn aside and run home, leaving *Vengeful* to figure out what they could possibly do on their own, which would be nothing. Probably Gerstner would just have to hide for a good long time while the Enemy picked Aleph's bones, hope no Enemy mothership broke *Vengeful's* shielding a second time, and wait for a chance to sneak for home with their tail between their legs.

Gerstner didn't like that idea any more than Reese did, but this wretched situation could still force that decision.

Third possibility, the turun would fire on *Vengeful* and take her to Aam by force.

Reese had come up with that scenario; one of a bunch he'd logged while he was brainstorming as many possibilities as he could come up with. Gerstner didn't think that was very likely. But tactically, he had to admit, it would make sense. If the turun had definitely decided to turn their backs on Aleph, they might still want to get their hands on a human-built dreadnought. Those fighters of theirs weren't bad, from the glimpse he'd gotten so far, but there wasn't a single ship out there that was remotely a match for a dreadnought one-on-one. But neither could *Vengeful* fight sixty-odd turun ships, if they decided they wanted to take her home to their engineers. If they tried, Gerstner wasn't certain he would be willing to fire on them, even in self-defense.

Reese knew all this, obviously. He'd taken on the job of sorting out tactical options for all three possibilities. The options were terrible for every possibility that didn't involve a real honest-to-God alliance plus a serious rescue attempt. But Reese didn't go through all those options now. He said, "That girl thinks they'll stick with us."

"Then they probably will. She knows them a hell of a lot better than we do."

"She's a little innocent who believes the best of everyone. Or that's Lockwood's opinion, even though he thinks she's probably a spy."

"Lockwood's a cynic."

"Not so much, sir, or he'd be arguing she's a deliberate spy, not an innocent one. Either way, if we have enough luck, I guess we'll be handing her over to Marchetta. Or Falconer."

From anyone else, that would be a sincere comment. From Reese Kennon, it was deliberate provocation. Gerstner glanced over at the girl, sitting next to Lockwood, both of them out of the way. The girl looked about as dangerous as a kitten. She had her head bent over a handheld desk. Working her way through yet another language module, this one—Gerstner had checked—emphasizing political terms and political organization. He doubted she was a spy, but the distinction between *spy* and *innocent kid who's learning more than we want her to know* was likely to get a bit blurred. Any board of inquiry would probably think so, anyway.

Samuel Lockwood sat beside her, his long legs stretched out, frowning over another desk. He didn't look like he was enjoying his side of the language lessons. He looked put-upon and thoroughly irritated. On the other hand, he could have moved over to the other side of the bridge, but there he was, working side by side with the girl, feeding everything they put together into a brand-new translator algorithm as fast as he could. Damn useful man, and apparently just about as flexible as he needed to be.

Gerstner said, "We get through this in decent shape, we'll send her back to *Kaastu*. If the commodore—or Falconer, or Modhwadiya, for that matter—wants her, they can ask her nicely to visit. That's my decision, which I'll log, Exec."

Having found out what he wanted to know, Reese just nodded. "Sir," he acknowledged. He added, "No objection."

"Glad to hear it. Sixteen minutes. If it comes to it, we'll get the singlepods away. The whole lot of them. Keay's in a singlepod himself, yes?"

"Yes, sir, as of half an hour ago. A bit uncomfortable, making your way all the way back to the Shallows in a singlepod."

"If it comes to that, anybody with sense'll be damned grateful to put up with that discomfort."

"I expect that's true." Reese paused. Then he asked, lowering his voice, uncharacteristically cautious, "May I ask what happened on that saucer? Did you actually get a look at the Enemy?"

Gerstner looked at him sharply. Then, blowing out a breath, he shook his head. "I'll send you a copy of the report, provided I get a chance to write one up. But ... maybe. A glimpse. I'm not actually sure what I saw. I think the big snakelike thing Kaamharaa battered to pieces was a mechanism. But there was something else, something different. Smaller. Looked like an animal to me. A little like a silverpede. That could have been an Enemy. I honestly don't know."

"A silverpede," Reese said thoughtfully.

"I think it was kind of shaped like that. Built flat and low. Lots of appendages, had that kind of look to me. Segmented. Silverpede, centipede, something like that, that's the impression I got."

"A bit of a nightmare image there, sir."

"Definitely a weird image." Gerstner shook his head. "It was certainly a hell of a weird ship, Reese, I'll say that."

"You flew that arrowpoint."

"Barely, and damned lucky to manage it at all." The memory seemed almost like a nightmare rather than anything that had actually happened. He said, "Pure chance I figured out some of the controls were heat sensitive. I'd never have thought of that except the lights were so peculiar, I started thinking maybe the Enemy doesn't see the same part of the spectrum we do, and then what parts of the spectrum could they see? I couldn't do anything with ultraviolet, but maybe infrared. Plus for a while I thought maybe some of the controls might respond to breath, and that's oxygen, carbon dioxide, water—and heat."

Reese raised his eyebrows. "I'd never have thought of that."

"Desperation is the mother of thinking outside the box, Exec."

"Does sound that way. I'll look forward to that report." Reese took a lighter tone. "I bet you'll have a *fine* time with the lab boys, sir. They'll want to pick every detail out of your brain. Hypnotics up, down, and sideways, I expect. For days. Weeks."

Gerstner was resignedly sure his executive officer was right about that. But, all things considered, he'd be damned grateful to put up with the discomfort. He didn't respond, only stood up, took a deliberately relaxed stance, and looked over the bridge stations. Everything orderly, everything squared away, firsts at their boards. Except for Samuel Lockwood, who had glanced up and was now showing Taya how to attach the handheld desk to the safety harness, just in case.

Keeping his voice calm and assured, Gerstner said, "All right, people. We'll be heading back to see about Aleph in fifteen minutes. The turun will come with us or they won't. If they do, then we'll see about pulling Aleph out of the fire *and* out of the frying pan, do a lot of Enemy extermination, and dump all our dilemmas in Marchetta's lap." He said all that in a casual, of-course tone, as though victory were a foregone conclusion. Then he went on. "If the turun don't come with us, we'll reassess. We'll likely find Enemy fighters and maybe a mothership in our way before we get through to G67, especially if they've figured out the turun are upset with them, so let's be prepared. I will frankly be embarrassed if we lose three tiers of gravitics again, so let's look lively. Whatever's waiting for us, I want to know about them before they know about us. Signals, you've got *Kaastu* and *Sepuuk* picked out of the herd?"

"Sir," murmured Lieutenant Maxson.

"Pulse *Sepuuk*. Taya, talk to *Sepuuk* and confirm we're definitely going to have allies when we cut into G67. If we're not, I want to know about it now, not at the last minute. Lieutenant Lockwood, assist Taya."

Lockwood flicked a salute his way, and the girl promised earnestly, "Yes, Captain. *Sepuuk* very much ally. I mean, *Sepuuk* *is* very much *our* ally. All battlegroup is our ally." She looked at Lockwood. "Are?"

"One group, is," he told her. "Lots of *tolt-kaarha* are. *Tolt-kaarhand?"*

"Tolt-kaarhand, yes, plural are." Taya agreed.

"Sounds like you're both doing fine," Gerstner said, halfway amused despite everything. "I certainly hope you're right. Signals, give Kha Taya an open channel to *Kaastu* and *Sepuuk*. Lockwood, make sure she knows how to toggle between channels, and you flip those channels off if you see a need for that. Plus this might be a fine time to explain *hope* if you haven't got to it yet. Once you've confirmed *Sepuuk* intends to go through to G67 with us, pulse *Kaastu* and have them confirm it on their end." Gerstner didn't trust the people on *Sepuuk*. He trusted Kaamharaa's people a lot more. Especially since the girl he had right here on his bridge was, apparently, Daamon's baby sister. He didn't believe for a minute either Daamon or Kaamharaa would deliberately betray her. He didn't believe they'd betray him, either. Gerstner glanced at the command readouts. "Twelve minutes. Go to red alert."

A technicality, at this point.

Lieutenant Maxson raised a hand. "Enemy fighters, sir. I'm getting something between twenty and thirty, could be more if they're stacked up deep. I'm not getting a mothership so far, but we're still pretty far out."

Gerstner nodded. They'd expected some number of Enemy fighters on this side of the flashpoint. Those fighters probably didn't know they were going to get a dreadnought and a bunch of turun fighters down on top of them. Or maybe they did; dangerous to assume the Enemy was ignorant just because that'd be convenient.

"Signals, relay our scans to *Kaastu* and *Sepuuk*." They had no idea of the relative scanning capability of those turun fighters; *Sepuuk* was bigger and better armed than *Kaastu* and might have all sorts of bells and whistles, but if *Vengeful's* scans were better, might be a good plan to let their allies know what they were seeing. "Taya, tell them we're going through first. I want *Kaastu* tucked up with us, not going through on her own and getting hammered. Everyone else behind us. Get a confirmation. Ops, tell me if the turun task force begins any kind of maneuver."

"Yes, sir. They are, sir. They're spreading out. I think they've spotted the Enemy and I think they're planning to engage. I can't tell if they're planning to let us flash first." That was Genee Khadaya, who routinely took second at every station except Nav.

She meant the turun task force either planned to engage the Enemy or really, really wanted *Vengeful* to think they did.

"Weapons, run continual firing solutions for every damn thing over ten inches long within scanning range. Assume we're all going straight in against the Enemy until proven otherwise."

Assuming they did that, they should have no trouble getting through. It still looked like close to thirty Enemy fighters, mostly saucers. It also looked like the turun task force intended to take them all on, exactly as though *Vengeful* weren't present. Gerstner added, "It'll be damn embarrassing if we don't fire a single shot. Our allies shouldn't have to do *all* the heavy lifting. Let's just see about that formation at eleven low, shall we? Exec, handle that."

Reese stepped up smoothly, leaving Gerstner to keep an eye on the broader situation. The executive officer said with almost no pause, "Weapons First, Weapons Second, possibly bracketing fire around the specified formation might make it a just a little easier for our neighbors to sweep the rest of this trash off their porch, do you think?"

As Sun Grigson and Doug Bateman coordinated their fire to isolate the specified set of Enemy saucers, Gerstner raised an eyebrow at Reese. *Where do you get these metaphors?*

Reese's expression, perfectly sober, didn't alter at all. But the tilt of his head was like a smile, and his little nod as two of the quick little turun fighters whipped through the suddenly open gap in the Enemy formation and carved up a handful of saucers beyond carried more than a trace of satisfaction.

Gerstner, paying more attention to the turun ships than the Enemy, let out a slow, covert breath. He could see no sign at all that *Sepuuk's* task force intended to do anything but what they were supposed to do—anything but what they'd said they'd do. He said, "Weapons First, disregard the remaining Enemy in this system and sit on the computers. I want covering fire the second we clear the flashpoint and solutions before any Enemy ships in G67 know what hit 'em. Flash in ... three minutes seventeen."

Bateman, at Weapons Second, raised a hand. "We may shave a few seconds off that, sir, if we slide *Vengeful* between those two groups of turun ships at six high. We'd need to take out those three arrowpoints that've got behind them."

Gerstner confirmed this with a glance. "Nav First, plot that. Weapons Second, take the shot when it presents itself. Signals Second, keep an eye on *Kaastu.* I want her under our weapons every second." He was fairly certain that *Kaastu* was about the weakest ship they had on their side, and since she was also the only turun ship he really trusted, he was damned if he was going to let anything happen to her. Fortunately she seemed to have the sense to stick close to *Vengeful.* He'd already seen she had a good hand on Nav; she'd stick tight unless something exciting happened.

That wouldn't be here. There weren't enough Enemy fighters to fill a bathtub here. That'd be the *other* side of the flashpoint.

"Where's *Sepuuk* got to, Ops?" Gerstner asked. And then, as Genee Khadaya wordlessly lit the turun ship up on the screens, "All right. That looks fine. Keep an eye on her and sing out if she looks like she might get into trouble. *Kaastu's* our best buddy, but *Sepuuk's* second in line."

As far as he could judge, *Sepuuk* was bigger, faster, and significantly better armed than *Kaastu*; and Gerstner figured it was safe to assume she'd been out on the front lines more than a time or two, but that didn't mean she was invulnerable and Gerstner did not want to see that ship hard hit. He was fairly certain *Sepuuk's* human commander was something like a commodore. God knew what that made the turun officers on that ship, except important.

Vengeful, with Kaastu tight against her belly and half a dozen turun ships right on her tail, hit the flashpoint. The inside-out warping feeling rippled through the flash, and they came out the other side, with undirected covering fire crackling through space everywhere in front of them.

That ended. "Clear, clear," Grigson sang out. The G67 system was *anything* but clear, but space directly around the flashpoint was clear enough because that was the whole point of flashing through behind a whole lot of unaimed covering fire. Sun Grigson was already targeting and firing on the handful of Enemy arrowpoints that had survived near the flashpoint. If there had been saucers interdicting the flashpoint, they'd already been shredded.

Lights lit up red at command: damage reports, but nothing serious. That hadn't been the Enemy; that had been their own weapons. They'd overflown the last few seconds of their covering fire, which was what happened when you laid it down before you were all the way out of the flash. After one quick glance, Gerstner ignored those reports. Nothing crucial; Ops would handle it. More important was the report from Signals.

"Clear, clear," Genee called. "Still all lovely and clear. *Nkaastu's* with us, right and tight; turun ships are flashing now, we are clear, nothing in range at this moment."

Maxson added, "Building images as fast as we can, it's going to take a minute to sort this out—" A huge smear of red. A white latticework. No details yet, but Gerstner didn't need details to know what he was looking at: Aleph's defensive network was still holding, and a whoooole lot of Enemy were still besieging the task force.

"Could be a hell of a lot worse," he said out loud.

It could have been far, far worse. Nothing irretrievable had happened, yet. The task force was still holding, still game, still standing off the enemy. There was a decent chance they could actually pull this off.

21

"Lots of uut out there, but *nothing* left in range," Saraa reported, her voice tense but steady. "For now I'm keeping us tight in *Vengeful's* shadow. Navigation's fine, no damage to navigation—"

"Did you see what they did?" Paaol demanded, unnecessarily. "They fired every energy weapon they've got, all at once, *before* they cleared the slide! Why didn't *I* ever think of that?"

"Because *Nkaastu's* a half-fighter tradeship and you're not an idiot," Genru told him, not glancing away from his own console. "I'm not sure about the second point. We'd overfly our own fire and how would that help? Even tucked down like this, we took some damage from *their* fire."

"We *need* better shielding forward—"

"If we live through this, take it up with the Ndaand and let them argue with the matriarchs. Daamon, repair teams report we're not getting port forward weapons back in time to do anything with them."

Daamon tipped his chin up in acknowledgment. Losing some weapons capacity to *Vengeful's* own fire wasn't ideal, but on the other hand, there wasn't a single uut fighter anywhere in range, so on balance the cousins' unexpected tactic had been a brilliant choice. Now they knew why Gerstner had demanded point for his own ship; no single full-fighter could have cleared space around that slide the way *Vengeful* had done it.

Now the combined battlegroup was spreading out, putting *Vengeful* more in the center. Which was Daamon's order. It was both intensely reassuring and deeply terrifying that *Sepuuk's* entire combined battlegroup had taken that order. But they had. That would last no longer than Siiv allowed; everyone knew that.

Daamon had ordered that not because *Vengeful* particularly needed protection—Daamon was perfectly willing to let *Vengeful* protect the rest of them—but because losing *Vengeful* now might constitute a very specific sort of disaster. Provided this rescue attempt actually worked, they would need Gerstner to explain everything to his own people. And Taya, who was also on that ship, another reason Daamon did not have any intention of letting anything happen to *Vengeful* if he could possibly avoid it.

He said, "We'll let the full-fighters take the point and the edge. Saraa, keep us tight inside *Vengeful's* shadow. Gen, it'd be nice to have an estimate of what we're facing."

"Working on it, working on it." Genru shunted the majority of his console's functions to Suumat and focused on building up a clear display of this system. Blue and blue and brighter blue, surrounding *Nkaastu's* blue-green icon, tucked up close to *Vengeful*, now a heavily blue-toned lavender. Much farther away, rippling sheets of color as the computers tried to sort out what sensors were telling them. Genru nudged the parameters defining the display, and suddenly fiery curtains of red and white blazed around a solid lavender core. A lot of that would still be estimation, and the trapped uman battlegroup was far enough from the slide they were significantly lagged. Almost two tenth-chimes. If that battlegroup had been holding two tenth-chimes ago, surely they were still holding now.

One dire scenario down. No shortage of dire scenarios that might still play out. The red-and-white in the display was far too bright.

Paaol leaned forward, gripping his console, as the computers solidified their interpretation and the display brightened, and brightened again. "Forsaken lot of uut, do you remember quite that many, cause I don't think I remember quite that many, Daamon—"

"*Taraaot's* moving," Genru interrupted him, meaning that whole unit of the combined battlegroup.

They certainly were, very decisively. "They're putting a lodgment around the slide," Daamon said. That was a fine idea. He'd have ordered it himself if he'd thought of it. A lodgment meant Siiv intended to hold this slide for a retreat, and planning a retreat meant he was willing to order an attack. That was good. That was *excellent*. He'd half expected Siiv to take one look at the mess in this system and order a retreat. He said, "Look sharp, Saraa, I expect *Vengeful's* going to move—"

"Priority," Saraa interrupted. "*Vengeful* signals she's moving, and we're going with her. I've told her our top accel and she says she'll keep to that, she won't let herself outrun us."

She'd barely got the last word out before *Vengeful*, and *Nkaastu* with her, swept into a sharp curving turn, getting clear of the slide. Of course there was no sense of motion; the whole universe seemed to stream past the still point that was *Nkaastu*. A double handful of fighters from *Sepuuk's* subgroup held positions around *Vengeful*, covering the uman ship against any threat. The rest of the battlegroup opened up like a flower around them, flares of color and bursts of glitter as they engaged the small handful of incoming uut ships to keep the area right around the slide clear. That was easy right now. It wouldn't stay that way.

"Got to keep maneuvers tight," Paaol said. "Not used to working with a big group like this." He was trying to sound blasé, but the blazing eagerness hidden underneath came through clearly. He was ranging everything in sight, and before anybody else had sorted out their options, he'd already scattered a handful of missiles that immediately engaged their insystem drives and slashed away to distract an uut formation that was threatening *Taraaot's* battlegroup. If Daamon had had time to think it out, he'd have ordered just what Paaol had already done, because if *Taraaot's* effort to hold a lodgment failed, then they'd *all* be trapped in this system, unable to get out if everything fell straight into the hands of the forsaken gods. If that happened—for an instant he imagined running for the empty reaches of the system: no idea where any other slides might be found or where they might lead, no way out, no way back ... it didn't bear thinking about.

Red and white icons swarmed around the lavender ships of Gerstner's battlegroup like flocks of gaour around a weakened and staggering nehaaot, eating it alive one bite at a time. He had never before thought of uut as being like gaour. But there were so many Disks and Blades surrounding the uman ships, the image came forcefully to mind. Like nehaaot, the uman ships seemed practically untouchable when closed up in a tight herd. He could see how they covered one another with interlocking fields of fire; they were plainly designed for that purpose. He could see how their missile defenses detonated uut munitions at a safe distance while their confounders deflected energy weapons that might otherwise have ripped through their gravitic shields.

Like nehaaot, eventually they would be weakened too much to hold. On a turun ship, the first system to fail would be the gravitics, unless they ran out of hardware defenses first. Either would mean immediate death. He wished he could believe that uman ships like those might not have such weak points, but that seemed unlikely.

Paaol's teeth were showing in a tight, aggressive grin. "Forsaken shame *Vengeful* didn't shut down the slide into the uut ring-system a little faster, keep all these gods-be-forsaken uut locked up in their own forsaken system."

Daamon nodded. The images *Vengeful* had shared, the immense ribbon of uut structures and worldlets and ships, had been horrifying, but this looked nearly as hopeless. The uut they'd seen here the first time had been plenty, but not so many a big battlegroup couldn't have done something useful. This ... this was something else. *Nkaastu,* with *Vengeful,* was coming in toward the uman formation, riding some distance from the main area of battle.

But quite a lot of the uut fighters had peeled away to investigate this new challenge, and *Sepuuk's* battlegroup was forming up defensively because there just did not seem any good way to take the offense. Daamon couldn't see how a half-fighter tradeship could do much to help, even if he was willing to take *Nkaastu* straight down into the maelstrom. If he did something that stupid, *Nkaastu* would probably last about a hundredth chime.

"*Sepuuk's* sending a ping," Genru announced.

Daamon had very little doubt what Siiv sep' Upuonnu intended to say. He ordered, "Delay our response to *Sepuuk*. Ping *Vengeful*."

Kuotaan rumbled wordlessly to show she wished to speak. When Daamon gestured permission, she said, "Tnakaa u Kaoluun is decidedly aggressive, but she is not a fool. Aggression is a fine quality in a full-fighter captain, but I think she will be reluctant to permit Siiv sepu Upuonnu to take his battlegroup against so many uut fighters where there is no possibility of a good outcome, in a system that has no importance to the Kaoluun matriline or clan. The decision will belong to the battlecommander, but he is also not a fool and there is nothing here that matters to the Ka' Taand. He will listen to Tnakaa if she protests. In her place, I would protest."

"In Siiv's place, I'd listen," Daamon admitted. "I wouldn't have any choice."

"Signal from *Vengeful*," Genru said, and threw the signal into the display without waiting for Daamon to give the order.

Taya, tense and unhappy, looked at him from the foreign bridge. She said, "Daamon, Captain Gerstner says he won't retreat, but he understands if you feel you have to. He says he'd put me on a transport and send me back, he says they could hold the uut away long enough, but I don't want to do that! I don't know what he thinks *Vengeful* can do all by itself! Everyone here would die! Isn't there something you can do?"

Behind her, Gerstner met Daamon's eyes in the screen. His people looked completely cold and unmoved, as though they didn't care how he responded to this suggestion. Daamon didn't believe that for an instant.

"*Sepuuk's* moving," Paaol broke in. "I can tell you exactly what Siiv's got in mind, but I bet you don't need me to explain it to you." He sent Daamon a mirror of his console, *Sepuuk's* battlegroup closing in around *Nkaastu* and *Vengeful*.

"They want to force *Vengeful* back through the slide," Daamon said, unnecessarily. The merest glance at that formation made that clear. Siiv was arranging the ships of his battlegroup between the incoming uut and *Vengeful*. They weren't going to fire on the cousins' ship; he could see that. They'd shield *Vengeful*, taking losses themselves, until shame at what his defiance cost his allies drove Gerstner to yield and run for the slide. It might work—and it was a tactic that wouldn't risk damaging a ship Siiv obviously did not want to harm—but Daamon didn't like to think of the cost. He couldn't imagine how Siiv felt about such a tactic.

No, actually, he could imagine it all too clearly.

"They're just going to let the uman battlegroup get eaten by the uut," Paaol said. "Not very public-spirited of them."

Saraa snorted, meaning Paaol never cared about public spirit unless he wanted to.

"They don't see much choice," Daamon said. He didn't either, unfortunately. If he asserted priority overrule now, Siiv would probably shoot *Nkaastu* out of space in sheer exasperation. Daamon wouldn't blame him. He said, "Taya, ask Captain Gerstner, do *they* see anything possible to do here? If there's nothing to gain, will they kindly yield before he forces Siiv to lose ships protecting *Vengeful?* Tell him if there's nothing he can do, he has to retreat. Can you explain that?"

"Yes," Taya said, very simply. She was pale, but she tipped her chin up.

Daamon hoped she could, but he didn't intend to count on it. He said, "Suumat, if you would be so kind, please confer with Kaamharaa and ask him to say the same thing to Captain Gerstner. If it comes to the worst, I very much want to persuade Captain Gerstner to withdraw with us, not throw his ship away for no possible benefit. Please request Kaamharaa develop some persuasive arguments for that contingency."

Kuotaan rumbled agreement and permission, and Suumat signaled Kaamharaa and began to explain the request.

Genru said, "*Sepuuk's* signaling again. I bet they're getting pretty impatient, Daamon."

He bet they were. "Go ahead and answer—"

"Daamon, wait, priority, look here," Paaol interrupted. He highlighted a pink icon way, way over on the other side of the blaze of lavender. Then he changed its color to deep crimson. He surrounded it with a faint ruby-colored cloud to show the range of probable locations it occupied, because they were still lagged enough they couldn't pin down that ship's precise location. The cloud was enormous. The icon itself ... beyond huge. Not an ordinary mothership. Daamon was briefly startled to discover he had started to think of any uut mothership as *ordinary*, but this one was so much bigger ... he mirrored Paaol's calculations on his own console and drew a breath. That thing was three times the size of a mothership. Four times, maybe. The forsaken thing was nearly as big as a small *worldlet*.

"Not a mothership at all," Saraa muttered. "That's a *fathership*."

Daamon said, "Mirror that to *Vengeful*. Taya, please point out to Captain Gerstner that we can't possibly fight that—"

"It's *singing*," Taya interrupted him. She was on her feet now, too excited to sit still, talking to everybody at once, gesturing broadly as she spoke. She was speaking both Uom and English, switching back and forth fast. Now she said, "Lieutenant Maxson says it's singing, and the uut fighters around it are singing back, but not exactly the same song. I don't know what—" The man with her said something in the fast, choppy uman language, and Taya said at once, "Oh! We think those are calls that say who's part of their battlegroup or their clan. We think *all* the uut here could belong to that one big fathership. We think—" she hesitated, listening to the rapid give and take among the cousins. Lieutenant Lockwood said something, and Captain Gerstner said something, and there was rapid give-and-take on that foreign bridge.

Then Gerstner stood up, stepped forward, and pointed straight at Daamon. He said, "Daamon." Then he spoke to Taya, forcefully. Every word was completely incomprehensible. Except one. He said Kaamharaa's name. Twice. Urgently. Lockwood said something else, rapid, every word precise and unemotional.

Taya exclaimed, "A Blade! He says our Blade, *his* Blade, Kaamharaa's Blade."

Kaamharaa broke in, booming with enthusiasm from Suumat's console display. "Daamon! Out of all this clamorous tumult, we have an unexpected asset! An uut Blade, as whole and undamaged as may be! Putting this to use is my friend Gerrstter's desire! He wishes to turn it against our enemy!"

"Yes!" said Taya. She listened to something else Lockwood said. Then she said, speaking quickly, "Daamon, they send little fighters out loaded with huge bombs. They—the battlecrew of the little fighters, they run their ship directly into a mothership, and blow them up. That's how they fight motherships. Daamon, that's horrible, but what they mean is, arrowpoints—I mean Blades—they're the ones that carry worldkillers, Daamon!"

Kuotaan said, "We assume such an act adds a vivid high note to the reputation of the battlecrew across all the public boards. But we are thoroughly dismayed, however effective this tactic may prove."

Daamon patted her lower shoulder. He could not have agreed more. His first appalled thought was that surely *drones* would be far superior for that kind of suicidal tactic. Nevertheless, he could understand that uman judgment might be more effective than drone algorithms—though if the cousins couldn't *see* the heart-Disks—but perhaps their uman perception was still useful, even crucial in some way, for them to strike accurately at these giant uut motherships.

Regardless, he saw now what the uman captain had in mind. "Captain Gerstner believes this giant fathership may be vulnerable to such a tactic? That's why you think the song matters. If the fathership believes our Blade is one of its own ... if it will let it inside ... is this the plan our ally proposes?"

"I think so!" Taya agreed. "I'll make sure, but—it's awful, Daamon, but—"

"It's not awful! It's great! Oh, I *love* this!" Paaol was grinning fiercely. "Turn their own Blade against them! Stab it right up inside the fathership and set off their own worldkiller." He mimed a huge explosion. "It's a *great* idea!"

Genru made a skeptical noise.

"No, look, Gen, you know a good pilot could pull it off! It'll work! Besides, if it doesn't, we'll never break those uman ships free of the uut pin. We've *got* to try this thing with the Blade!"

"If it could actually work ..." Daamon touched his console, making the view leap to focus more tightly on the dark crimson icon of the fathership. He called up the engineers' report on the uut bomb they'd found in the Blade, skimming it quickly and frowning. Then, looking up again, he studied Gerstner, standing tense on *Vengeful's* distant bridge. The man was glaring at him, not angry, but intent. He certainly did not look like he was ready to give up. Probably he had his head crammed with useful information about uut weaponry and simply could not communicate that information, not now, not when it mattered most. Daamon asked, "Is there a particular spot for which we might aim? Taya?"

Almost before Taya could translate, the uman captain adjusted *Vengeful's* display and a spot of darkness appeared on the icon that represented the fathership. He looked straight at Daamon. "Here," he said, one of the few cant words he knew Daamon understood. "Here."

Saraa said briskly, "I agree with Paaol. Running the Blade right up into the fathership, if we've got a real idea where to stick in the Blade, that's brilliant. I think we should try it. I'm running calculations for that kind of move, and I think a pilot could ball up in an emergency bubble, get out right before the Blade sinks home, so that's one problem we might be able to sort out. But can we get the fathership to cooperate? And can we fly that Blade well enough, even if it's willing to let it come close?" She raised her eyebrows at Paaol.

Paaol waved a hand. "I've studied Taam's reports, I've been all over that Blade, I nearly went *blind* tracing the circuits of those weird uut controls, we know how to get that Blade working now—the controls are sensitive to temperature and sometimes pressure and we think maybe electrical currents, but we've got it worked out well enough, we really do—Taam's already thrown together a couple little gizmos that'll trigger guidance. I can fly that thing, Daamon, I really can—"

His partner Aanhk thumped her foot down hard, making a deeply skeptical sound. "No," she declared, the full negative, *absolutely not.*

"No, I know, but really, we do! Daamon, we can do this!" He stared urgently at Daamon. "I've got to fly the Blade! You have to let me fly it!"

"Paaol, no," Aanhk said again. She boomed once in distress and added, "After we have become used to our crazy uman partner? And what of your mate? Will you leave Nkan lonely? Uman suffer so when their mates die."

Paaol hit her on the shoulder, none too gently. "Not your business to get between me and Nkan, Aanhk! I'll get out ahead of the blast, but if I don't, *what* a way to go. *Look* out there! Somebody's got to do it and I'm by *far* the best choice." He turned back to Daamon, "Listen, no matter *how* the dice fall out, I'll get the Blade into that fathership. I'll do my best to ball up and get out right before it sinks into its target, I promise I'll try, but we *can't* come all this way and then just quit! I can do this, I'm willing to do it—I *want* to do it!"

Saraa began, "You're a weapons man, not a battle navigator. Daamon, I think I'd be a much better choice to ride that Blade—"

"No way!" Paaol cried. "You haven't studied the controls, and you don't want it, don't try to tell me you do! Daamon! Think of the glory accent for sep' Kaamharaa! You can't let an u Aanuku woman take that away from us! Come on, Daamon!"

Daamon hesitated. That mad certainty of Paaol's ... Daamon couldn't deny it would be a huge asset. Except that he knew once Paaol took charge of that Blade, he would almost certainly forget Nkan and Kaamharaa and Aanhk and everyone who loved him and ride the Blade straight to the fathership's heart just to make sure it delivered a killing blow.

Saraa would never do such a thing impulsively. She wouldn't be carried away by the heat of battle. But she would do it coldly, to make sure the blow didn't go awry at the last moment, if she decided it was necessary.

Yet the payoff was potentially huge, so immense he could not refuse to let one or the other take the attempt.

"Daamon!" cried Paaol, all but vibrating with eagerness. "You've *got* to let me do this! Saraa's a navigator, not a weapons expert. I've got the *right* to take this!"

He wasn't wrong. The autonomy laws were there to prevent turun overprotectiveness from stifling uman choice, but look at the autonomy laws from the right angle and ... Paaol wasn't wrong.

Daamon said, "Gen, signal the engineers to get the Blade ready to launch, let's get ourselves set to be fast off the mark if we do this. *If*," he emphasized. "Tsaa Kuotaan, kindly request engineering staff to confirm that an uman pilot would indeed be able to fly that Blade and deploy this uut explosive device. We shall wish to enable remote detonation if at all possible. We'll need an emergency bubble tacked into place—we'll need to confirm the Blade is atmospherically tight, remembering the damage we did cracking it open in the first place."

"Yes," Kuotaan rumbled, because everything here was definitely a battle decision. But her tone was far from eager. "Daamon, we by no means wish to send one of our people into this dire danger. One of our *uman* people! We cannot approve!"

"Autonomy," Daamon reminded her, and she stamped one foot down hard, angry and upset, but not arguing because she knew he was right.

"The captain's right. This whole idea's insane," Gen said, not at all happy with any of this, but he opened a channel to the engineering staff.

Daamon acknowledged all this with one economical gesture, but he only asked, "Taya, you honestly think we can mimic the uut song well enough to make this work, yes?" The idea was getting madder and madder. Yet also more and more compelling. "Didn't you say, when *Vengeful* tried that before, it *didn't* work? And that was when you'd had *chimes* to listen to the uut—"

"Yes, but I think I know what we did wrong! I think we played the mothership's part—I think we said *We are you* when we should have been singing *Back to you*. Give us a chance to listen to that fathership and the Blades near it and I bet Kaamharaa and I—and Lieutenant Maxson, and Lieutenant Lockwood—I bet we'll be able to sort out the right song to play. You know we have to try! Or we came all this way for nothing and all our cousins over there will die knowing we couldn't help them! They've even seen us now, you know they have to have realized we came to help them. We can't just *leave* and let them all be torn to pieces. We can't, Daamon!"

"*Sepuuk* just ranged us!" Genru snapped. "That was no gods-forsaken *ping*."

That was Siiv sepu Upuonnu running completely out of patience. Daamon didn't believe Siiv would fire on *Nkaastu* no matter how exasperated he got, but he said, "Right, yes, fine, accept their signal—"

"The uut take prisoners." Kaamharaa's voice rumbled from the speakers. "Truly, Daamon, we cannot leave your-and-our cousins to be taken in that way. The experience was unspeakable. Daamon, I do not wish to risk Paaol, I do not wish that at all, but nevertheless, I will object strenuously to any decision that leaves your-and-our cousins to that fate."

Daamon said steadily, "Saraa, please set up a course toward the fathership and get us moving. Mirror that to *Vengeful*. And *Sepuuk*. Mirror it to everyone. Taya, immediately send us a recording of whatever uut song might cause that fathership to allow our Blade to approach, but I also want anything you can give me that might make them hesitate to destroy a bubble." Daamon met Gerstner's eyes in the display. The foreign captain returned his gaze with a direct, urgent, wordless demand, completely interpretable despite the lack of a common language. Daamon tipped his chin up in deliberate reassurance.

Sepuuk's bridge built itself in the display, which divided to show both *Vengeful's* bridge and *Sepuuk's* on one side, the uut fathership on the right. Siiv stood with his hands clasped behind his back, his expression calm. Daamon wasn't fooled: Siiv was most definitely a man all out of patience. He started to say something, explain about the fathership and the Blade.

"Priority, priority!" snapped Genru, cutting everyone else off. "We have a rock on the way." He threw it into the display, a swirling formation of uut way out and gone in the reaches of the system, blazing bright white as Gen lit it up. It was a rock, definitely, and moving with a direction and velocity no rock could possibly have acquired by chance.

"A rock!" Taya said, and something in English, fast and urgent. Everyone on all three ships' bridges bent hurriedly over their consoles.

"How lagged is the signal?" Daamon demanded.

Genru answered, "Not *nearly* as lagged as we'd like, I can tell you that, and the lag is decreasing fast. That rock's moving way above any natural vee and still accelerating; it's definitely fitted out with an insystem drive. It's coming in like a yuannkuu falls on its prey and it's aimed straight at our cousins. They can buy a little time, but maneuvering that kind of formation, they're like a pregnant giisuaa caught in quicksand, but that rock'll practically turn on a toe tip. There's no way they can dodge, Daamon."

Daamon signed grim agreement. "Our cousins can't make it to the flashpoint either." It wasn't quite a question.

Genru, equally grim, shook his head. "They can try, but they can't go through without breaking formation and obviously if they do that too soon they'd be cut to pieces—too late, that forsaken rock will smash through them anyway—and I don't think there's enough time between *too early* and *too late* for anybody to thread that needle. Daamon, I'm sorry, I should have picked it up sooner, but it looks like we've got less than a chime before that rock comes through."

Any of them should have picked it up sooner. They had all been distracted. And now this rock might smash all their choices down to nothing.

On *Vengeful's* bridge, Gerstner snapped something.

Gensu said tensely, "Yeah, the uman formation's trying to maneuver, but like I said, pregnant giisuaa, quicksand, it's hopeless—there aren't enough favorable dice in the universe to get our cousins out of that trap."

"Unless we help them!" Paaol cried. *"We're* the ruling dice in this hand! Daamon, come *on!"*

Daamon took one breath. Then another. Then he said, to Kuotaan but really to all of them, "If we strike the fathership fast enough and sharply enough, our cousins' ships may be able to scatter out of that formation before the rock arrives. This idea about using our captured Blade is the only thing I can think of that might have a chance. I know everyone here is aware that uman people are not properly prevented from taking risks. But I acknowledge that time now is so constrained, I hardly know whether I may ask the Aanuku matriline to support me in this endeavor."

They should have withdrawn from the bridge for such a consultation. There should be a space of calm in which to prepare and sip tsuaeh while they both got their thoughts in order. He didn't have to point out that there was no time for any of that.

"Nda Daamon, we understand," Kuotaan told him formally, "Of course Aanuku is satisfied to set our reputation in your hands. We are most dismayed by the suggested tactic, but we acknowledge autonomy applies. Paaol is battlecrew and has the right to take this risk if you and he agree. Paaol, please, we ask you to take *all possible care.*"

Paaol laughed. "Tsaa Kuotaan, listen, this will work! It's too beautiful not to work!"

"Paaol—"

"Daamon, this'll be fine, it'll be great, I'll get clear, and even if I don't, it'll be *marvelous,* Daamon, don't *worry.*"

All his focus was on sharp and brilliant victory, not a shred left for the cost. *Daamon* was the one who had to count the cost for Paaol. For them all. He glanced at Saraa. She met his eyes, lips tight. She knew as well as he did that nothing could substitute for that brilliant enthusiasm.

Daamon made his decision. "You've got this, Paaol. Get to the Blade, help the engineers get it set up. Run!"

His near-brother whooped and bolted from the bridge.

Gone. That fast. He might survive. Putting that improbability out of his mind, Daamon leaned against Kuotaan, drawing calm from her stability. He said, "Nda Siiv, Battlecommander, we've got an idea that might yet yield success, but no time to discuss it—"

"Nda Daamon," Siiv said coolly, "there are limits to my tolerance. I am about to hit them."

Daamon was sure he was. He held the other man's steady gaze. "There's no time to discuss this," he repeated. "We'll send the plan to you in a burst, and then it's up to you." He cleared *Sepuuk* out of the display and told Saraa, "Have *Yehnna's* battlegroup interdict *Vengeful*, we can't have that ship destroyed now, so tell them they must not allow uut near it. *Sepuuk's* own battlegroup will escort us. I want a course that'll take us as close to that fathership as we can get before we throw the Blade at it. Aanhk, I'll take weapons control, but your experience looking over Paaol's shoulder may prove valuable, so I'll mirror my console to yours and ask you to oversee my firing solutions. Please also priority any solution of your own that presents itself to you. Don't hesitate."

Siiv would either spend effort and lives to support *Nkaastu* and *Vengeful* or he would not; there was no time left to worry about it. Genru had mapped out his intuition of which uut fighters would present the first and greatest danger to *Nkaastu* as they moved to carry out their plan; he mirrored his calculations to Daamon's console.

"Suumat?" Daamon asked, having no time to check the calculations himself.

"Perilous, but the math appears sound—"

"Send that to *Vengeful* and *Sepuuk*. Genru, get *Nkaastu* on that course and set those solutions up as priorities for targeting. Saraa, you'll have to adapt our course as conditions evolve."

"Certainly." Saraa was concentrating fiercely on her own console. "I don't have time to package up the burst for *Sepuuk*. Tsumon?"

"By all means," rumbled Kuotaan.

Daamon gave her a grateful nod. "Tsumon, please see to that, thank you."

Whatever consternation Daamon's orders might have created across the system, and he could well imagine, when *Nkaastu* took a sharp course toward the fathership, *Sepuuk* led its own battlegroup in to protect them.

Sepuuk had already lost a half-handful of its fighters. They lost another full-fighter as he watched, to the concerted attack of five Disks and a Blade; the full-fighter covered *Nkaastu* and paid for its bravery, blue light blooming in the display. Daamon winced.

It would get worse, until or unless Paaol pulled off this crazy mission. He would do it if he possibly could, if anyone could.

The Blade slashed away from *Nkaastu*. Saraa pretended to fire on it, pretended it was really an enemy, and after a heartbeat *Sepuuk* did the same, which for a moment looked terrifyingly real. But then *Sepuuk* turned its fire against a real uut formation, and Paaol's Blade was still there, running fast and straight for the fathership.

Then it was too far away for any of them to help it. Whatever happened to that Blade now, no one could do anything to help. Daamon tried to set that worry aside. "Gen, Saraa, take a look at this course; how do you like it?" and shunted the one he had in mind to their consoles.

Saraa said appreciatively, "Ooh, nice."

"Dangerously tight," was Genru's assessment.

Saraa gave a quick, cool smile. "Yeah, but it'll definitely fix the uut's attention on us and get them looking away from our Blade. Siiv won't be very happy with Daamon, though."

If *Sepuuk* didn't bend its full attention to protecting *Nkaastu*, they'd never make it through the course he'd set—it was a course that took them right into the teeth of nineteen Disks and twelve Blades. If *Nkaastu* couldn't depend on *Sepuuk's* battlegroup for cover, that course would be nothing but suicidal. But it would certainly distract a lot of uut.

"Take that course," he told Genru. "Reverse at this point *here* and then, Saraa, get us out of the way as fast as we can move."

He left that to her and ran different calculations, estimating the best maneuvers the uman formation might manage, the likely speed with which the computers driving that rock would adjust. He came up with approximately zero point six five until that rock slammed though the uman formation. Might be a little better margin than that. On the other hand, might be a little less. Daamon didn't count it down out loud, not wanting to hear the numbers actually spoken. There was just so little time, and still so much that could go wrong.

In the first moments after *Nkaastu* moved into its feint, it looked very much as though Siiv u Kaoluun and his whole battlegroup might pull away, leaving *Nkaastu* to die. It turned out that Siiv was merely sending a division of his battlegroup to assist *Taraaot* in the essential task of holding the lodgment around the slide. Blue-glimmering icons swept around the slide, scattering aggressive white Blades, targeting the red Disks that centered the uut formations. Colors bloomed and faded in the display; glitter spread around the gray-gold of the slide.

But the other full-fighters whirled like leaves in the wind and spread out around *Nkaastu*.

"Get us back to *Vengeful*," Daamon told Saraa. Once they were tucked in with the uman ship, Siiv's battlegroup could protect them both together. That would be easier for everybody, especially since *Vengeful* was quite handily protecting itself, firing past battlegroup ships to take out one and another Disk in nearby formations. Someone on *Vengeful* was finally prioritizing heart-Disks, which made a huge difference. Daamon suspected that was his sister.

He looked for heart-Disks himself, and, as they were just barely close enough, began to highlight those in the display and mirror that to *Vengeful*.

Yes, the uman ship certainly had tremendous range and power. The heart-Disk he'd shown them bloomed into light, followed, as the uut formation stuttered, by a good two handfuls of the other Disks as *Sepuuk* and the rest of the full-fighters engaged. Then they were through, tucking themselves tight into *Vengeful's* shadow. Safe. Safe-ish. For at least a scattered handful of moments.

He looked for Paaol's Blade, but he had lost it in the confusion. At almost that moment, Saraa found it. She gave it a brilliant orange-and-blue outline in the display, but it was so near the fathership now that despite the contrasting colors, it was practically invisible in the crimson glow.

Nothing he could do about that now. He glanced at his console. "Saraa, I've got zero point four seven for our Blade. What have you got for the rock?"

"Zero point five eight."

Right down to the edge. The rock was coming fast. Faster all the time: still accelerating. Uut icons surrounded that rock, spatters red as blood across the emptiness. Those were Disks, ready with confounders to turn aside missiles aimed that way. They'd swarm any fighter that tried to get close enough to use energy weapons.

The lavender uman ships hadn't shifted out of their protective lattice. They couldn't move. Not yet. Not surrounded as they were. Not unless the intensity of the uut attack was broken.

Zero point three four.

Daamon blinked as he realized that *Vengeful* was moving. In the display, Gerstner gave brief, quiet-voiced orders to his people and then looked up to meet Daamon's gaze before speaking to Taya. Before she even nodded, before Saraa traced out *Vengeful's* new course, Daamon was already setting *Nkaastu* to follow. He was exasperated with himself.

Of course *Vengeful* was moving. Of course *Nkaastu* ought to be moving. If the trick with the Blade worked, they'd need to be in position to support the uman ships that would immediately scatter. He said sharply, "Taya! Has *Vengeful* warned their people of what we're attempting to do? They have to be ready. Even if this works exactly right, they'll have only a tiny chink out of time to escape that rock. Hardly more than half a tenth-chime. They'll have to be ready to move fast, engage hard while the uut are still disoriented—" he *hoped* the uut would be disoriented; the loss of that enormous ship *ought* to be disorienting. Dismaying, at least.

"He says he's warned them, Daamon. I think he says so."

Daamon nodded, tensely watching the displays. The giant uut fathership filled a third of the divided screen now, crimson dark as old blood, immense as a dying star. A single Blade against that ... it seemed impossible, no matter how powerful the munitions fitted into it.

Sepuuk was bringing its battlegroup in toward the defensive formation of uman ships, ready to support them if they could only make a chance. Uut fighters were thicker here. They were staying just out of range of the umans' superior energy weapons, throwing missiles, waiting for the uman ships to run out of countermeasures, ready to claw down any ships that broke away from the herd.

Zero point one eight. Zero point one seven.

"We will all do well," Kuotaan rumbled in her softest voice, the tone turun used to soothe children.

Daamon wished he could be soothed. He tipped his chin up in a deliberately calm response. Zero point one five ...

On *Vengeful's* bridge, Taya said urgently, "Paaol's Blade is singing! I think it's nearly reached the fathership and I don't *think* anybody's fired on it." She said something else in English, probably repeating that. Someone on that bridge provided the sound for *Nkaastu's* general speakers, and the fathership's song as well.

It was the first time Daamon had heard the uut signals his sister called *singing,* and he found the sound chillingly alien. It was a little like the rapid trill of tayaeh, but ... not the same. There was something there that wasn't in the call of any animal. He studied the best estimates the computers could provide. His sister was right. The uut weren't firing on the Blade. Slashing through the last little distance, that Blade was moving at nearly its top possible vee. At that speed, Paaol wouldn't have much time to ball up in his bubble and get clear.

"Point zero eight chime-down," Genru said quietly, and Daamon nodded. In the display, the vivid orange-and-blue Blade disappeared, *Nkaastu* losing track of it against the far more powerful signature of the fathership.

For a long moment, Daamon thought nothing had happened, or was happening, or would happen. He couldn't take his eyes off the display. But there was nothing. Only the immense crimson fathership like a red sun amid the swarm of smaller uut craft.

Then the display dimmed, and dimmed further, almost to black, protecting vulnerable eyes from an actinic bloom of light, a bloom that grew and grew, exactly as though the giant icon truly had been a red giant star and was now exploding into a nova.

For a long time, for well over a tenth-chime, it was impossible to see anything. *Nkaastu's* sensors were all blinded, and only chance and the vastness of space protected them from smashing into another ship. The computers plotted the likely position of every nearby ship based on its last known position and course, and *Nkaastu* didn't hit anything, and eventually the displays cleared and began updating.

Everything had changed. The immense spreading crimson smear must be what was left of the fathership; the red and white of uut fighters had turned into a haze because the computers were still sorting out the actual positions of those ships. Nothing seemed to be nearby, which was a blessing. Stuttering lines of lavender meant the computers were extrapolating possible courses for the uman ships, which had scattered violently, probably while they were blind, unless their sensors were much better than *Nkaastu's* in dealing with sudden extremely massive explosions. Right now the computers seemed to have guessed that their formation had broken all at once and in every direction, like a shattering taka seedhead. That seemed likely. Daamon couldn't tell yet whether they'd all gotten clear, whether they'd all survived the aftermath of the explosion. He hoped uman ships were built to withstand substantial collisions; unlike *Nkaastu*, they couldn't have avoided hitting uut fighters.

The rock, blazing white in the display, had slammed through the location where the uman formation had been. The computers had no problem painting that into the display; its course and vee had been entirely predictable. At least the computers weren't throwing the lavender glitter of debris from destroyed uman ships into the display. Yet.

Suumat, without comment or official notice, bent over the low-set console, helping sort out the signals. Slowly lavender icons began to clarify, surrounded by the smaller white and red icons of uut Blades and Disks. But though a lot of the uut were attacking, they were not coordinating their attacks. And out there among them, threading through their confusion and cutting them to pieces, driving them into the deadly fields of fire from the uman ships, came the bright vivid blue of the ships of the battlegroup, their courses slashing around and past the fire of the lavender ships.

The nearest icon, blue-lavender, was *Vengeful*. They had not left *Nkaastu* alone. That ship held its course and relative position, efficiently destroying any uut that dared approach.

Emergency bubbles were so tiny, difficult to find. Even so, Daamon couldn't help but look. But there was nothing orange-and-blue in the display.

22

"Well, Captain," Marchetta said without preamble when at last Gerstner handed *Vengeful* over to Reese Kennon, came aboard *Inexorable,* and reported to the commodore's personal office. Both Viceroy Modhwadiya and Witness Falconer were present, which was not in the least surprising, though slightly inhibiting. Nevertheless, Marchetta's eyes crinkled at the corners, though his mouth was stern.

He rose to shake hands, swept Gerstner with a comprehensive glance, and observed, "Your report made for exciting reading. You look good for a man seized by the Enemy. You've had an even more eventful couple of days than the rest of us, fortunately. We'll certainly want to hear every detail about your time aboard the saucer. Before we go on to more urgent matters, your log indicates that you actually saw an Enemy? And, even more remarkable, stole and flew an arrowpoint! I predict you're going to be an extremely popular dinner guest for years, if Fleet's research personnel ever let you out of their grasp." He smiled at Gerstner's expression, which must not have been entirely blank. But he only added, "Tell us about that, please."

Gerstner nodded, taking a moment partly to gather his thoughts and partly just to assess the three men in front of him.

Marchetta was a straightforward man, mostly. Formidably intelligent, formidably competent, not easily knocked off balance. That was all good. Tired, at the moment. His uniform was impeccable, every silver button and the single silver clip of his rank freshly polished, gleaming against the otherwise unrelieved black. But despite his light tone, he was not a young man, and the past couple of relentlessly desperate days had left their mark.

Viceroy Modhwadiya wore an understated civilian outfit in the style of Hemadri, in brown and tawny gold; his eyes were lively and expressive despite his obvious weariness. Everyone knew Gopaal Modhwadiya, Viceroy of Kaman, was on the Emperor's very short list of possible successors. Modhwadiya had the right experience, the right kind of family, the right connections, and enough personal energy and charisma to light up a failing star. No doubt Modhwadiya was also an ambitious man, though it didn't show. He was about Gerstner's age, with the short, plump build and the round face common to people from Hemadri. He looked affable and energetic and completely unaffected by anything that had happened. He would also have gone over *Vengeful's* log with keen attention. What he thought of recent events was not obvious.

Ronsard Falconer was a taller man, bigger, his size accented by the severe lines of his Haven-style clothing. He was far more reserved. Certainly no one would have described him as expressive. Gerstner knew almost nothing about him. He didn't even know where Falconer was from or whether he was planet- or station-born. Though he wasn't from Terabithia; Gerstner would have taken any odds on that. You didn't have to meet many Terabithians before you learned to recognize them.

Falconer was also about Gerstner's own age, but he had no public record at all, so far as Gerstner knew. Loyal to the Emperor rather than any political party, that was the idea of an Imperial Witness. Aligned closely enough with Elliston to declare preliminary rulings on the Emperor's behalf, Falconer was here to evaluate Viceroy Modhwadiya and Commodore Marchetta and the whole task force. Now he'd be evaluating the crazy situation they'd gotten themselves into. His opinion mattered, possibly more than anyone else's.

Gerstner was just as glad it was Marchetta's job rather than his to deal with both men. As long as the Commodore made the right decisions, of course. And got the other two to make the right decisions as well.

He said, "Getting that arrowpoint moving was sheer luck. I could hardly even see the controls. They don't respond to touch, at least not human touch, but it turns out they do respond to warmth—body heat. Or I think that's what the controls I got working responded to. I didn't play around with much once I got the arrowpoint moving."

Marchetta nodded. "Enough of a miracle right there."

"Exactly. A whole string of miracles," Gerstner agreed. "The turun engineers figured out more later, fortunately, or their man wouldn't have been able to take the mother of all kami runs." He caught that moment of near-informality and brought himself firmly back to the topic at hand. "I'm sorry to say that I didn't get a particularly good look at anything aboard the saucer, sir. The lighting system ..." He shrugged. "At the time, it seemed insane. Mostly dark, then sudden whips of light slashing past, way too bright. Looking back on that, it still seems insane, but I'm wondering now if maybe nothing on that saucer actually sees in the visible light spectrum. Maybe they see mostly in the ultraviolet or something, so the lights I saw were just part of what they see, or maybe even a side effect of Enemy tech. Like waste heat, sir. If something saw in the infrared, they might see waste heat generated by our equipment and think it meant something."

"That's an interesting suggestion, Captain," Marchetta said thoughtfully. "You thought of that after realizing the controls respond to warmth?"

"Yes, sir. Not right then."

"You were probably a little distracted at the time. Please append that speculation to your log. But you did get a visual impression of an Enemy?"

Gerstner opened a hand, shrugging. "I saw something. I don't know. It could have been an Enemy. But the thing I saw just didn't seem big enough. A little like a silverpede, sir, but a good deal smaller, not much more than knee high. Pretty long, granted, maybe four feet or so. Tentacles, though, so that's suggestive."

Falconer broke in. "Jointed appendages *and* tentacles?"

Gerstner turned to face the Witness, nodding. He hadn't though of that oddity, but now that Falconer pointed it out, that combination did seem odd, though he didn't know a lot about comparative animal anatomy. "Yes, sir," he said. "Little jointed legs, maybe with claws—tiny claws—but definitely tentacles on and behind the head."

"That seems peculiar. You did have the impression it was a biological creature, not a mechanism."

Another good question. Gerstner had thought about that. "It could have been some kind of construct, but it looked biological to me. The big thing Kaamharaa battered to pieces was definitely a mechanism, no biological parts; I'm sure you saw that detail in my report, and if the turun don't want to turn all the bits over to us, I expect they'd probably let our engineers look over their shoulders at them. Or," he added, a little drily, "Perhaps that's the wrong expression."

Marchetta smiled. "We'll certainly want to hear every detail, but let's move on for the present. Please tell us about the turun."

Gerstner was just as pleased to change the subject. He definitely wanted to explain the turun, if he could. He glanced at Falconer, but the Witness sat back, gesturing permission for him to comply with that change of subject. Nodding, Gerstner said, "I imagine you got a decent look at *Kaastu* when we popped into and out of G67 a couple days ago."

The commodore signed agreement. "We did, yes. That was a surprising incident in several ways. I won't say we precisely expected to see you again, with or without company, but it was nice to have a whisper of hope. You brought us more than a whisper, thankfully. Sit down, Captain, and tell us all about it."

Gerstner sat down. Everyone sat down. They were in the commodore's briefing room, which had decent chairs arranged around an oval table and a generous amount of space devoted to screens. He folded his hands on the table, cleared his throat and said with considerable restraint, "The turun are big, sir."

Commodore Marchetta smiled a little. "The recordings from *Vengeful's* ship bay were remarkable. A bit unorthodox, your taking a first contact situation on yourself rather than delegating to your Exec."

"Yes, sir. We had a lot of important decisions to make. Commander Kennon was perfectly capable of picking up the bag if I left him holding it."

"As you did, of course, in the event. Allow me to commend you on your ability to ... make friends and influence people."

Gerstner said honestly, "It could accurately be described as a mad scramble from one frying pan and fire to another, sir. I don't deserve much credit for the outcome. I think the commander of *Kaastu* deserves most of the credit. And my crew, and his. And Kaamharaa."

"That particularly large turun who was abducted along with you. Yes. A most impressive individual. If you could summarize your opinion of the, ah, turun in one or two sentences right now, that would be excellent. I know that may be something of a challenge," the commodore added.

A truly brief summary was indeed difficult. Gerstner kept his gaze on Marchetta's face rather than looking at the other two men. He said carefully, "I believe the human-turun civilization we have encountered could prove a considerable and perhaps decisive asset to the Imperial Republic. I'm fairly certain we could prove a considerable and possibly decisive asset to the human-turun civilization here as well. I believe it would be best to make sure we get a chance to try out an alliance."

Commodore Marchetta nodded thoughtfully. "Please expand on that a little, Captain."

That request was a good sign. Gerstner had picked out just the details he most wanted to add to this interview, on the record, in front of these men. He kept his tone carefully matter of fact. "Yes, sir. One detail you may have picked out of my report, and Commander Kennon's, is that the human people in this foreign civilization are able to pick out the brain of a swarm. They do it by eye, apparently. It's not automated. They just do it, somehow. Fast, too."

"You're certain of that." Marchetta didn't sound doubtful. He, like Gerstner, probably wanted to get this on the record.

"Yes, sir," Gerstner said. "I saw them do it—so did you, sir, during that very brief episode when *Vengeful* and *Kaastu* flashed into G67 and out again. I'm sure someone picked up the details. Take a good look at those recordings and you'll see *Kaastu* take out three saucers. Very specifically three, no hesitation, no wrong guesses. Then, in this most recent engagement and previously, Kha Taya marked out the brains of various swarms for the Weapons personnel aboard *Vengeful*. That was logged. You can review that any time you wish."

"We certainly will," Marchetta agreed. "I acknowledge, that skill would be immensely beneficial to Fleet. Very well. And on their side?"

"I think that's obvious, sir. Their real fighters aren't bad, but they've got nothing that can touch our dreadnoughts."

A thoughtful nod. "That does give us a strong negotiating position. And it's certainly reassuring to know that. Very well." He glanced at the other two men.

Taking that invitation, Viceroy Modhwadiya leaned forward, brought the closest screen to life, and called up one still image of Kaamharaa. The image showed the turun right after he had stepped down from the transport onto the deck of *Vengeful's* ship bay. "This was a most interesting decision, Captain. A very bold decision, bringing this person onto your ship," the viceroy observed. "Though, as events demonstrated, not actually over-bold. A remarkable species, and evidently inclined to be well-disposed toward humans."

"Possibly," said Falconer, his tone neutral. He called up the rough starmaps drawn by Sun Grigson and Kaamharaa's Taya, the flashpoint threads weaving their contorted, Escherian pathways between and among the systems without regard for the actual distance or direction from any star system to any other. Taya's map didn't exactly follow normal conventions, but anyone could see the flashpoint web tied her eleven stars tightly together.

Indicating the latter, Falconer went on. "Eleven stars to our seven. This is not a small polity. I do wonder how large a proportion of the citizens are human."

"Yes, sir," Gerstner agreed. He'd already taken time for a quick look at the log entries Grigson and Lockwood had put together, so he'd seen those images before. He wasn't a bit surprised the Witness called them up now. "We don't know that yet. We know almost nothing about them. But we do know they broke Aleph out of a dire trap, that they took losses to do that, and that in a fight, they aim their weapons at the Enemy. That seems like a good start."

Falconer looked at him. Gerster didn't flinch. He gazed back, steady and level.

"There could certainly have been worse beginnings," the Witness conceded.

Viceroy Modhwadiya said in a mild tone, "It seems quite remarkable to me that these turun evidently persuaded or allowed a lost human colony to merge into their civilization. You agree that this description seems appropriate to your observations, Captain? 'Merge' seems to you a reasonable term? Does it seem a complete merger? *Does* an independent human colony remain somewhere in turun space?"

"I have no idea, my lord. Lieutenant Lockwood might be able to answer that question. I understand he's worked extensively with Kha Taya sepu Kaamharaa on the languages. I will note that the title kha seems to be applied equally to human and alien crewpeople, and of course you notice that the family name indicates that Taya is a member of Kaamharaa's family."

"Certainly suggestive," Falconer said. "Lieutenant Lockwood suggests that an alternate meaning of that locution could be, for example, *possession.*"

Gerstner stopped himself, barely, from saying, *Of course he does.* He said instead, "Yes, sir, I suppose that's possible. However, during my stay on *Kaastu*, that's not the feeling I got at all. The humans I met seemed to consider themselves Kaamharaa's family."

Falconer didn't argue. He only said, his tone neutral, "Perhaps they do. Lockwood informs me that he hadn't yet had an opportunity to approach questions regarding human independence within turun families or the broader turun polity. That's understandable, as conversations regarding battlefield maneuvers were obviously somewhat more urgent at the time. But it is unfortunate. It would certainly be a good question to explore in the near future. I agree that your personal impressions may provide important evidence for the peculiar social arrangements that may exist among these ... people. Please comment on your observations in that regard."

Gerstner nodded. "Yes, sir. They share not merely the same ship, but the same living quarters. I stayed with Kaamharaa's household, which also included the human commander of *Kaastu*, but no other turun, so far as I could tell. Of course, I was only there briefly. I can tell you that both humans and turun eat the same foods, with the same utensils, at the same table. The captain of *Kaastu*, Kuotaan u Aanuku, shared the same name with a human woman I met, Saraa u Aanuku. I think family names might matter a good deal."

Modhwadiya said thoughtfully, "How very intriguing. How very encouraging."

"Unless we build too many of our expectations onto a sense of familiarity that proves false," said Falconer. "The actual captain of that ship is a turun. Correct, Captain?"

"I think so, sir," Gerstner agreed. "It was a little difficult to determine that. The turun might have been a co-captain. It seemed to me that both turun and human officers had to agree to cooperate with *Vengeful* and rescue Aleph in order for the effort to be undertaken. I think Nda Daamon was in command during military action. That may not be exactly correct, but that's how it seemed to me."

"For which we must all be grateful, evidently," said Falconer. "Your impression is that this was not an autocratic decision?"

"That's correct, sir. I believe the human commander was not the final authority aboard *Kaastu*, but he seemed to have authority over the other turun ships that turned up. I can't be certain. I can about manage *yes* and *no* and *please* and *thank you*. Samuel Lockwood can do a good deal better than that, I believe."

"He has become somewhat capable in the alien language, yes. I'm told the human woman, Taya, may be rather useful in working out the details of the turun language. Lockwood tells me she's gifted. But profoundly influenced by alien mores, one gathers." Falconer touched the commodore's screen, advancing the image to one of *Kaastu's* bridge, humans and turun paired at every station, including the command dais. "Cooperation certainly seems important for these ... diverse personnel. But one doesn't like to assume too much understanding. These people don't speak English at all?"

"Yes, sir. Or rather, no. Just a word here and there, as far as I could tell. Everyone speaks the turun language. Kaamharaa seemed to know a little more English than any of the humans."

"I certainly look forward to learning more about the peculiar history that has produced this singular arrangement," murmured the viceroy. "Captain, Commodore Marchetta and Witness Falconer and I have discussed this extraordinary situation at some length. We find ourselves in agreement on two points. We've agreed that Task Force Aleph should return to Haven and there communicate to Fleet, to the legislature, and most of all to the Emperor the results of our ... eventful investigations of this region. We've also agreed that someone must make a formal diplomatic approach to the turun without delay. Commodore Marchetta will undertake the former. Witness Falconer and I will detach ourselves from the task force for purposes of the latter." He paused.

Gerstner was fairly certain he could see where this was going. He thought the viceroy was correct, on both counts. He said, "With the commodore's permission, my lord, I would be glad to put *Vengeful* at your service for that purpose."

Commodore Marchetta made a little *Of course* gesture, and Viceroy Modhwadiya smiled. "Captain Gerstner, I would be delighted to accept your ship's escort. Thank you. Witness Falconer and I will both, however, request permission to stay aboard *Nkaastu* for ... well. For whatever interval seems reasonable to all parties involved, shall we say, if *Nkaastu* can be spared from her ordinary duties." He pronounced the difficult alien name without difficulty. He'd practiced that, Gerstner assumed.

Falconer merely looked dour, but Modhwadiya was smiling at Gerstner's surprise. "I believe," he said gently, "that the only way to become acquainted with strangers is to allow yourself to know them. And allow yourself to be known."

"Within reason," said Falconer.

"Indeed. Within reason. Thus I will make this request. I would consider it a favor if you would put in a good word for us with your friend Kaamharaa."

Gerstner glanced from one man to the other. He cleared his throat. "I will, of course. I'll warn you, if I may, my lord, that standing next to a turun is not the same as looking at an image on-screen. You're going to find the turun ... awe-inspiringly big. Especially Kaamharaa."

Falconer made no comment, but the corner of his mouth crooked up.

"I look forward to being awed by your friend Kaamharaa," Viceroy Modhwadiya said serenely.

He said that now. He had no idea. Neither of them did. Gerstner controlled an impulse to smile. Thinking of their first sight of Kaamharaa *was* entertaining. But, unfortunately, fraught.

"You've done an excellent job handling this contact, Captain Gerstner," Falconer said unexpectedly brisk. "But we have to meet them sometime. Certainly I do, in order to represent them accurately to the Emperor."

It was true. It was undeniably true. It was reassuring both these men seemed to grasp that. Even if they were moving faster than Gerstner had expected.

23

Nkaastu's bridge seemed very quiet and ... not *lonely,* precisely. But ... empty, somehow.

It was amazing how big a hole, and how crushingly *empty* a hole, one man could leave behind. But Paaol's absence left a hole that seemed as big as an uturun. Paaol had always filled up more space than seemed reasonable for an uman.

Paaol was dead. They were certain of it now, which was possibly better than not being *entirely* certain. He'd never even had a remote detonator at all. The knowledge of that horrified Daamon, though he suspected it hadn't daunted Paaol. He could easily imagine his near-brother giving himself to the flame-pure commitment of launching without any way back.

The engineers just hadn't had time to fit the uut fission bomb with any kind of remote. Or the truth was, Paaol hadn't let them take time. He'd had his eye on the count, the same as Daamon. He'd known how slender a slice of time lay between his Blade and system-wide disaster.

Paaol ... Paaol had been just the kind of man to make a wide and wild choice; to forget all the bonds of family and discard his future and ride their captured Blade on a straight, unwavering course that stabbed the giant uut ship to the heart. He had dreamed of glory, not children. His family had loved that in him, and feared for him, and trusted Daamon to keep his near-brother's dreams leashed. Nkan had loved that in him; loved his brilliance and his fire.

Now she held only ashes. Daamon couldn't comfort her. His hands were filled with ashes too. He had known when he let Paaol go that there was every chance his near-brother would not come back.

Daamon had watched the recording of that final moment; the moment when the great crimson star of the uut ship bloomed into a great cloud of light. The computers had to enhance the view; it had been too violent a destruction for uman eyes to safely witness. But no degree of enhancement could let Daamon perceive Paaol's blade at the moment it cut into the giant uut ship. It had been too small, too far away, its power signature too dim. Once he found himself at leisure on the bridge, chimes after everything had ended, he watched the enhanced recording over and over, trying to find that moment. He had sent the rest of the battlecrew away; he had stepped down from command himself; he had let his mind go blank because now there was no more need for him to make hard decisions. And he had watched that recording until Kuotaan finally used her captain's mark to seal it away under her most private code and beckoned him to join her in the adjoining Aanuku apartment.

"He never meant to survive," he told her, once they were more nearly private. This time Kuotaan had not brought him to the Aanuku contemplation garden, but had turned the other way, into a quiet room, small by turun standards, with its own console and tank display. This way they could both keep an eye on surrounding space and the movements of their allies—their presumed allies—without having to be actually present on the bridge.

The uman ships were in the process of withdrawing; all except *Vengeful*. Their course would take them to another near-star slide, and after that ... a good number of juncture systems, Daamon had gathered; and then at last their own familiar space. No doubt their own families and lines and allies and officials would find their report of recent events most riveting.

Daamon wished them all good fortune and the blessings of the beloved gods on their journey. But he could not help but feel the beloved gods were very far away from *Nkaastu*, just at this moment.

Tuutka joined them, too, murmuring wordlessly in the lowest possible tone, barely audible to uman people. Her sympathy was both subtle and profound and required nothing at all from

Daamon. Unlike uman, turun did not try to find words to fit such a time.

Sinking down to sit on one of the cushions, he said, "He always meant to ride that Blade all the way in. I should have seen it. How did I miss it?"

"We did see it," Kuotaan told him gently. "Your words to us were correct. Your sep' brother had the right to take the risk and make the choice. We knew it, and so we let him go. This deepens our grief. But not all sorrow is evil, and our grief does not mean we were wrong. Nor does your grief suggest that your decisions were in error. We believe you were correct to decide as you did decide." Tuutka, still rumbling softly, handed Daamon a cup of tsuaeh laced with laon brandy, pressing his shoulder comfortingly with another of her hands.

Daamon took the cup and sank down to sit on the cushion placed here for uman comfort. "He deserves a note in Aanuku records."

"He shall have one," agreed Kuotaan. We shall record his name as Paaol sepu Kaamharaa u Aanuku. We shall ask Tsuumat Kaamharaa for permission to write his name so, and of course we shall pay the honor-fee to Guuan, as his nearest matrilineal line, in order to acquire the right to list him among our own. We shall ask Tsuumat Kaamharaa to write his name in that way when he hangs the accent in the tree."

After a moment, Daamon tipped his chin up and drank off the brandy-laced tsuaeh like medicine.

"These cousins of yours-and-ours," Tuutka said. The change in subject meant that she considered the other subject satisfactorily concluded. Or, at least ... concluded.

Daamon hesitated. But then he opened one hand to show he accepted the change of subject, set his empty cup down and opened his other hand to show he was willing and able to listen.

Kuotaan blinked her one eye, slowly. She prepared another cup of tsuaeh, this one sweeter and without the brandy, handing it to him across the low table. "These cousins have departed. *Vengeful* remains. We are pleased. As it was *Nkaastu* and *Vengeful* at the beginning, so it is again now that we have come to the end. Or the end of the beginning," she amended. "This argues a proper sensibility. Yet these cousins of yours-and-ours request that we permit officials of theirs to guest aboard our ship. We have no objection. We believe they have requested to guest with sep' Kaamharaa. We have no objection to this either, but we suggest, we strongly suggest, that they also request the status of guests with Aanuku."

"Yes," said Daamon, acknowledging this. "I'll see to it that this is communicated to them, and I'll indicate that they would do best to accept Aanuku's hospitality as well as Kaamharaa's." That was easy enough. He waited to see what else she would say.

Tuutka said, "We wish to meet these persons ourselves. We have some hope that we will be able to indicate our belief that these are persons of discretion, good judgment, and above all nhaanu. We look forward to gaining a reasonable familiarity with both officials before we come to Aam and find ourselves in a position to introduce them to a wider acquaintance."

Nhaanu, the nturun quality of giving a little to get along, was not always considered as widespread among uman people as might be desirable. Daamon had to admit that it would probably be a useful quality under the circumstances. Daamon took a deep breath, let it out, and sipped the hot tsuaeh, feeling his mind clear as he began to think of wider concerns. He said, "If Taya hasn't yet explained concepts of that kind, I will suggest she do so before we come to Aam."

"Good, good." Kuotaan could see that he was becoming more settled within the present moment, no longer so drowned by the immediate past. She reached across the table to grip his arm gently in sympathy and approval, then let go and settled her weight. "We feel no urgent need to rush toward Aam. We might, by taking a more leisurely pace, find ourselves with opportunity to become better acquainted with these persons. And they with us, of course. We believe this must be their purpose in placing themselves within *Nkaastu* rather than reserving their office upon *Vengeful*. Moreover, we suspect—we *strongly* suspect—that Tnakaa u Kaoluun will be better pleased if she and her close allies come to Ta' Aam well before we do. Certainly well before your-and-our cousins. Indeed, a secondary captain of *Sepuuk*, speaking for Tnakaa u Kaoluun, has quite recently communicated this preference to us."

Daamon nodded. He understood. This would give Kaoluun time to sort out the complicated changes that were going to suddenly re-weave the network of alliances and understandings among the gathered captains and battlecommanders and the matrilines represented by the officials of the Suund who might be on hand. Ordinarily Kuotaan would have wanted to arrive in good time to position Aanuku advantageously among the rest, but Daamon supposed they could all be confident Aanuku had already sent at least one senior matriarch to make certain of their line's position. And none of this was properly the concern of a battlecommander anyway.

Besides, she was right that *Nkaastu* and *Vengeful* and the officials sent by the cousins would all alike surely benefit from a quiet, leisurely journey from this place to Ta' Aam. Provided no further disaster or crisis intervened. Daamon sighed. At least if the greater part of the battlegroup went ahead, they should ensure *Nkaastu* did not run up on a great number of unexpected uut fighters. "Indeed, Tsaa Kuotaan, we agree. Unless *Vengeful* presses for greater haste, I see no need for hurried flight."

"Good," said Kuotaan. "Then we urge you to rest, Nda Daamon. However, before you retire, we must ask you to accept a communication from Siiv u Kaoluun sepu Upuonnu. We feel we must inform you that Nda Siiv has requested such communication twice in the past chime."

Daamon could not quite restrain a flinch. Everyone had been too busy in the aftermath of battle, and then as the cousins put themselves in order and began their withdrawal. But of course Siiv u Kaoluun would require an accounting.

Kuotaan said gently, "We have put him off twice, Daamon, but we suspect he may soon become moderately impatient. And we cannot easily put off Tnakaa u Kaoluun."

"Yes," Daamon said. "Yes. Of course, Tsaa Kuotaan. Shall I withdraw, or ..." he looked around the small room, understanding that Kuotaan had brought him here with this in mind. "If I may borrow this chamber for a few moments," he finished.

"Of course, Nda Daamon." Kuotaan regarded him shrewdly, her one eye seeing more than most nturun perceived with two. She said in her slow, calm way, "Aanuku asks that you style yourself Daamon u Aanuku sep' Kaamharaa. We hope you do not find this suggestion out of order or presumptuous."

Daamon looked at Tuutka. The secondary captain said, "Nda Daamon, we approve. We consider this appropriate."

He nodded. Offering him the name of their line was the clearest possible way of showing that Kuotaan herself, and all of Aanuku behind her, supported everything he had done, during these mad, intense days. For a long moment, Daamon could find no answer. Then he said, "Thank you. I'm honored to accept. Sepu Kaamharaa will be grateful for Aanuku's definitive support. Kaamharaa will certainly approve the appellation."

"Good," said Kuotaan. "Good. Then by all means, Nda Daamon, communicate with Nda Siiv, that he may complete his business with you, and thus *Sepuuk* may be freed to depart." She began the awkward process of heaving herself to her feet, signaling him with a flick of one hand that he need not rise. "This chamber is yours as long as pleases you," she added, meaning she suspected that Daamon might need some time to recover from the coming interview. "You should feel no need for haste."

Daamon nodded, unable to think of anything more to say. He waited for Kuotaan and Tuutka to withdraw. Then he poured himself another cup of hot tsuaeh and drank it one astringent sip at a time. Finally he set the cup down, carefully, with a little click of porcelain against wood.

Then, getting to his feet, he reached out and touched the console.

***

"Danaa u Kaoluun sep' Upuonnu, *Sepuuk,*" said an uman voice, answering his ping, and as the visuals built themselves in the display, a woman old enough to be Daamon's mother looked him up and down from her place on *Sepuuk's* generous bridge. She said, without needing to ask his name, "Ah, yes. Daamon sep' Kaamharaa. Nda Siiv has been waiting for your communication." There was a sting in that, though her tone did not change.

Daamon cleared his throat. "Also u Aanuku. Just recently," he added, to make it clear he didn't take her omission as a slight.

The woman no doubt guessed just how recent the addition actually was. "Indeed. I will make a note. One moment. I will transfer your signal to Nda Siiv's private quarters."

Daamon accepted the transfer without a word, and as the new image formed in the room's small display, braced himself with his cane, straightening respectfully.

Siiv was also on his feet when the image cleared again. He was just lowering his hand from signaling acceptance of *Nkaastu's* signal. His private room was plain to the point of austerity, with no furnishing save the most minimal table in front of the console. Not even any potted plants. Nothing to soften appearances or distract the eye.

Even if Daamon hadn't watched every record of Siiv u Kaoluun's actions, hadn't watched and re-watched every interview ever recorded with the Ka' Taand's first and still most famous battlecommander, Daamon would still have recognized this man just from his air of implacable, unassailable authority.

The lines beside Siiv's mouth suggested both long-controlled anger and relentless patience. His deep-set eyes were so light a gray as to be almost colorless. His hair was long, pale gold, streaked with near-white, and caught back in a enameled clip of Kaoluun blue. His expression as he considered Daamon was unreadable.

Daamon was all too certain of his mood. For a long, fraught moment, he could think of absolutely nothing to say.

"Daamon u Aanuku sep' Kaamharaa," Siiv said in a quiet voice. "You're a younger man than I expected. Public records contain almost nothing about you; not even your age. I've had ample time to peruse them while I waited for you to return my call."

Daamon said, "I apologize, Nda Siiv." Then he waited for the rest.

"You had a great deal to see to, of course, with emissaries of our ... cousins ... choosing *Nkaastu* for a guesting residence."

There was nothing to say to that. Daamon nodded, and waited.

Siiv said, in the same quiet, polite tone, "I wouldn't have thought a young man such as yourself, battlecommander of a half-fighter tradeship such as the estimable *Nkaastu*, would have the sheer conceit to declare incontestable understanding of not one but two battlespaces. Invoking a rule that, so far as I am aware, does not exist other than as a convenient plot element for a number of adventure stories that regrettably stretch the actual rules of combat out of all recognition."

Yes, that was about what Daamon had expected. He cleared his throat. "Any rule does exist so long as battlecrews recognize and follow it under conditions of actual combat, Nda Siiv."

"Well." Siiv might have smiled, just a little. "Plainly you are correct. Let's say, due to your actions, the rule may now have become half-real. Defend those actions, Nda Daamon."

Daamon took a breath. He hadn't intended to present his case right now, at this moment. Nor directly to this man. But here they were. He said, "On the first hand, we on *Nkaastu* were better acquainted with the prevailing circumstances than the captains or battlecommanders of any other ships. Our perspective was complete and unique at that time. On the second hand, we had the captain of *Vengeful* actually aboard our ship, witness to all our actions and all our possible failures to act. On the third hand, as the situation continued, we became acquainted with tactics that seemed potentially useful—that did in fact prove useful—and again our perspective at that moment was complete and unique." He finished, deliberately, "On the fourth hand, our cousins' space obviously connects to ours. We've met them now. No matter what else may happen, no matter how the dice roll across the table, we'll meet them again eventually—there are always new slides being discovered. If we couldn't have saved *Vengeful* or if we couldn't have rescued their battlegroup, that would have been one thing. If we had refused to try, that would have been something else. Our actions at that moment seemed likely to echo well beyond the moment into the near future, possibly into the far future." Daamon took a breath and added, "I and *Nkaastu*—and our cousins—are deeply in your debt, Nda Siiv. We are grateful you regarded our ... our advice, under the extreme and possibly unique circumstances we faced."

"Your *orders,"* Siiv said softly, using the singular *you* that put the blame, or credit, precisely where it belonged.

"My orders, then." Since the senior battlecommander wasn't going to allow Daamon to soften what he'd done, he went on, "Which were correct and appropriate given the extreme, unique circumstances. I would argue that before the Ndand. I'll argue that on my own behalf, not on behalf of Aanuku and Kaamharaa."

A pause. Finally Siiv said, "You are making your case to me, not to the Ndand."

"Yes," said Daamon. "Persuasively, I hope. The Ndand will decide whatever you tell them they should decide."

Siiv sighed, a long breath, and met Daamon's eyes in the display. "Given the admittedly remarkable circumstances surrounding your recent actions, I thought it best to accede to your invocation of a near-imaginary rule. Now that our actions are complete, that was clearly a correct decision. Your decision was therefore also correct, however presumptuous. Arrogance is not necessarily a fault in a battlecommander. I will point that out to the Ndand."

Daamon tried not to show the depth of his relief. "Thank you, Nda Siiv."

"When we reach Ta' Aam, it's possible—not certain, but possible—that Upuonnu and Kaoluun may consider alliance with Kaamharaa and Aanuku. That might make your necessary justifications of ..." a slight turn of one hand and a significant pause took in, by implication, not only Daamon and *Nkaastu* and *Vengeful* but everything to do with the foreigners, and all the complications that accompanied them. "All this, somewhat easier, when you present your case to the senior battlecommanders of the Ndand and then, I expect, to the Suund. Neither of which body, contrary to occasional perceptions otherwise, will necessarily agree with my suggestions, or those of Kaoluun. I agree we do carry some influence."

"I—we, all of us—would be very glad of your support, Nda Siiv."

Siiv nodded. "I, however, will want to talk to you *before* you make any sort of presentation to the Ndand. I, and Upuonnu. There is no time now. But the moment *Nkaastu* arrives at Ta' Aam, we shall expect your signal. *Before* you speak to anyone else."

Daamon bowed in acknowledgment. "I will certainly comply with this expectation, Nda Siiv." Then he asked cautiously, "But Upuonnu. In person? You're sure."

A thin smile answered him. "Upuonnu is far too experienced, and his field of expertise too different, for him to feel that Kaamharaa is a rival. I assure you, he definitely wants to talk to you. As do I. We will probably also ask you to arrange a meeting with the ... shall I say *battlecommander?* Is that the correct term?"

"Not precisely, I think. Our cousins appear to blend the role of captain with that of battlecommander. And they seem to recognize a different sort of commander for closer combat, or perhaps for a different kind of combat. Their Commander Keay appears to be the one who oversees the small craft that sometimes ..." he had trouble framing it, even to himself. "That, in extremity, run munitions against motherships."

"A terrible but fortunately effective tactic," Siiv said frankly. "We shall discuss this as well. These sounds Kha Paaol caused your captured Blade to produce ... I gather your Kaamharaa's expertise in linguistics has proved useful to you in multiple ways." He paused, then added softly, "I am sorry for the loss of Kha Paaol. He was also sep' Kaamharaa, yes? Your brother to some degree."

Daamon, wordless, managed another nod.

Siiv inclined his head in return. "It is the custom for a battlegroup leader to hang personal glory accents for each of those who have been lost. This is not a comfort, precisely. But we remember their names. I commend the custom to you." He paused. "How is it you are battlecommander of a half-fighter tradeship rather than a full-fighter? Is that because of your leg?"

That was certainly blunt. Daamon tried not to sound defensive, though his grip tightened on the head of his cane as he made certain he stood straight. "No. No, that's healed well enough. You probably know I was on a full-fighter once. At the far edge. After the destruction of Nguaa, the running battle that followed, the difficult retreat, I found a half-fighter tradeship seemed more ... more inviting. My ambition did not extend to battlecommand of a full-fighter. At the time Kaamharaa allied with Aanuku, the matriline had also withdrawn from the far edge. At the time, Aanuku possessed primarily half-fighters and half-fighter tradeships to support its primary tradeships. Even now, Aanuku possesses few full-fighters."

Siiv shrugged, clearly meaning, *Well, that will change.* He said, "We shall discuss the matter. But I imagine Kaoluun may decide to support Aanuku, if Aanuku wishes to re-establish itself within the Ka' Taand as a matriline in possession of a substantial full-fighter contingent. I'm confident the Ndand would support your taking battlecommand of such a ship. However, I certainly acknowledge that your half-fighter tradeship has represented us all quite creditably to our cousins. This may well prove fortunate for us all. It's clear the Suund, despite its occasional short-sightedness and inertia, may soon be compelled to accommodate a wider universe than hitherto. The broader Ka' Taand will, I'm sure, extend itself with reasonable grace to encompass these ... cousins." He gave Daamon a long look. "Upuonnu and I shall see that it does. And you and Kaamharaa. And Kaoluun and Aanuku."

Daamon had little doubt that the Ka' Taand would become anything Siiv u Kaoluun sep' Upuonnu wanted, if Siiv put his mind to making it happen. He said, "I'll look forward to introducing you and Tsuumat Upuonnu and Tsaa Tnakaa to Captain Gerstner."

This was true. And he suspected that after that, the Ka' Taand and all familiar space would never be the same.

Epilogue

Nharutsuukaa uul, ka' sem kuannaas uul. When traveling far from home, it's best to have faith in the goodwill of strangers. Taya had recited that aphorism to herself when she'd first left Kaamharaa's household to spend her year-and-a-half at Guuan, as sepu children always spent time at a matrilineal clanhouse. She'd remembered it again when she'd been stranded on the cousins' ship by herself. It had been good advice both those times. She thought of it now because she could see, very clearly, that Lieutenant Samuel Lockwood did not know the aphorism and didn't trust anything on *Nkaastu*. He was afraid. She saw that at once, though he was trying not to show it. He was afraid because he was among strangers and he was afraid because those strangers were turun.

She might have been offended. But she understood too well how it felt to go among strangers. After everything that had happened, she was willing to be patient and not be offended.

Lieutenant Lockwood might not like turun, but he was the first off the transport. He stepped down onto the decking, his expression neutral but his jaw set, and looked around. *Nkaastu's* transport bay was tiny compared to *Vengeful's* huge ship bay. There were only five transports in the bay now, none very large, so the bay was not crowded and it was easy to see everything. One of the transports was silver with the Guuan sigil in red, one was a soft sunrise gold-pink with the Kaoluun sigil in black and light blue, and the others were Aanuku green and gold. Of course, one side of the bay was open to space, protected from depressurization by the gravitics airshield, but the colors of the murals on the other five walls complemented the colors of the transports. Lieutenant Lockwood glanced quickly at all this, but his gaze lingered on the turun, not the murals. Tuutka and Aanhk stood close, about three strides from the transport. Plainly he thought that was too close.

Tsaa Kuotaan had not come herself to greet her guests. That would not have been appropriate because it would have suggested she intended to speak to these important people *for* Aanuku, with the authority of a matriarch. Secondary Captain Tuutka u Aanuku had come instead. Since she was a secondary captain, she could speak for herself and for *Nkaastu* without implying anything broader. Tuutka had brought Aanhk with her because nturun didn't like to do anything alone—well, almost nothing—and because poor Aanhk was grieving for Paaol and it was better to give her something else to think about. The two of them stood side by side, their upper arms folded across their upper torsos. Aanhk had one of her lower arms around Taya's shoulders because they both found that comforting. Paaol had been Aanhk's partner for a long time, and of course he had been sep' Kaamharaa and therefore Taya's near-brother.

Lieutenant Lockwood looked at how Aanhk touched Taya and his jaw tightened. Taya saw that. She pretended not to. She patted Aanhk's arm, moved a step away from her, and came forward to say in English, "Lieutenant, welcome! This is good. You are Aanuku's guests and Kaamharaa's guests. Everyone is glad you come here."

He met her eyes. After a very small pause, he nodded jerkily and said, "We're glad to be here, Kha Taya." This was obviously not true, but he turned and added crisply, "Sir, it's fine. But the turun have sent someone with Kha Taya to meet us."

Another man appeared in the door of the transport. Taller. Older, but not very old. Light-colored skin, more like an uman person from Kaoluun, but his face was different, the way the cousins just looked a little bit different. His hair was dark. He was not wearing black, but gray and blue. His clothing was still plain and boring, but at least not black. He stepped down to the deck, looked deliberately around, nodded to Tuutka and Aanhk and then to Taya, and stepped to the side.

Taya knew who he was; Lieutenant Lockwood had explained all this. This man's name was Ronsard Falconer and he was something called an Imperial Witness. He was a very important person. He represented someone else called Emperor Elliston. An emperor was very important, more important than any matriarch. Taya was not sure how much more important, but a lot, like someone responsible not just for a matriline, not just for a clan of related matrilines, but for a lot of clans together. Sort of like someone responsible for ruling the whole Ka' Taand. That was *very* important.

She bowed as politely as she could. "Witness Falconer, good you come."

He looked at her and smiled and said, "Kha Taya, thank you. I'm happy to be here." If he was afraid of the turun, she couldn't tell.

The next person was Sun Grigson. That was nice. Taya smiled and said, "Sun! Welcome! Good you come!" and Sun smiled back and said, "I was glad to come," a little more carefully than necessary. She looked at the nturun and smiled again, not afraid, so that was also good.

Then the last person stepped out of the transport. This was a man older than Witness Falconer, his hair more gray than black. He had browner skin than the others, more like Guuan and Aanuku people. Though he looked around quickly just like everyone else, he also looked completely comfortable. This was Viceroy Modhwadiya, just as important as an Imperial Witness, but in a different way. A viceroy was responsible for all the clans and matrilines—families—on a world or a system, like a secondary emperor.

This man did not seem to feel his own importance at all. He smiled at everyone and said in Uom, "Thank you for your welcome, Kha Taya." Then he said to Tuutka and Aanhk, still in Uom,

"Thank you for your welcome." Then he went on in English, "Kha Taya, please introduce us to these people, if you would be so kind."

"You speak Uom a little!" Taya was delighted. "Everyone will be happy you learn this."

"Very little," he said in English, smiling. "Only very little."

"Still very good!" Lieutenant Lockwood had explained carefully how to make introductions properly, the best and most formal way to address everyone. He'd made her practice saying the titles and names until she could do it exactly right. Since this was obviously important to the cousins, she had explained just as carefully the right ways to address people on *Nkaastu*.

Turning to the turun, she offered a small bow and said, "Tsaaku Tuutka, Secondary Captain, this is Viceroy Modhwadiya, and this is Imperial Witness Falconer and this is Lieutenant Lockwood and Lieutenant Grigson, who helped me learn English." Then she turned back to the uman—human—people and switched to English, "Viceroy, Witness, this is Tsaaku Tuutka u Aanuku, secondary captain of *Nkaastu*, and Kha Aanhk, a person of the bridge crew."

Tuutka rumbled, a sound that meant she was well disposed to Aanuku's guests. Lieutenant Lockwood's mouth tightened. Tuutka pretended not to notice. She said carefully in English, "Good you come." Her pronunciation wasn't bad, though she drew out the vowels a little. She went on in Uom, "You are our guests and Tsuumat Kaamharaa's guests. Tsuumat Kaamharaa has kindly offered space within his household for all our guests. He expects you momentarily; we will escort you ourselves to his household. We wish you to be comfortable here. You may speak to us if anything makes you uncomfortable."

Taya would have been tempted to add, *Other than the presence of turun, which you're going to have to get used to.* Tuutka was much too polite to say something like that.

"A moment, please," Viceroy Modhwadiya requested, after Taya had translated this. He ducked back into the transport, then came out again a moment later.

He had brought a gift for *Nkaastu,* a wonderful gift, a beautiful little tree with dark green leaves and leathery yellow fruits. The tree was about as tall as Taya, set into a ceramic pot as wide around as she could reach; he brought it out on a float pallet. He presented this to Tuutka, not to Taya, bowing very slightly as he presented the gift.

"Kha Taya, please explain this is from Earth," he said, but he did not look at her, only at Tuutka. "The human homeworld. It's one of the few kinds of trees we have from the human homeworld. It's called a *lemon*. The trees do well on ships. Sauces and sweets are made from the fruit; it's the custom to serve something with lemon on all important occasions. It's our hope the turun and human people of the Ka' Taand will also enjoy this fruit."

Taya translated all this, one sentence at a time. It was a splendid gift; the viceroy could hardly have chosen better if he'd asked her—which he hadn't, and that was interesting. He'd been clever on his own.

Tuutka boomed with pleasure—Lieutenant Lockwood swayed backward, but didn't actually step back. Tuutka picked the tree up by the pot with her two lower hands, stroking a glossy leaf with the tip of a finger of an upper hand. "Wonderful!" She boomed again. "How very generous and appropriate! Aanuku is most delighted with this gift. We will cherish this individual tree, which we will bring to our foremost line house and install in a place of honor. Aanuku will profit greatly from its propagation. A tree from the uman homeworld, now lost! Fruit of ceremonial importance! Everyone in the entire Ka' Taand will desire this beautiful and important species! We are very pleased." She handed the little tree to Aanhk, who took it, also rumbling with approval, stroking one of the fruits with the tip of a finger.

"Everyone will like," Taya assured the Viceroy. If Viceroy Modhwadiya had deliberately set out to choose something that would guarantee all of Aanuku was immediately well-disposed, he couldn't have done better. She didn't know how to explain how good a choice this tree was as a gift, so she said as warmly as she could, "Tsaaku Tuutka is very pleased. Aanuku will be very, very pleased. This is *very* good! Everyone will like very, very much. Matriarchs of Aanuku will like very, very much."

"Very good is *excellent*," Lieutenant Lockwood told her. *"Like very, very much* is *love*, which is a complicated word, Taya, remind me to explain it later, but that is one of the meanings. The matriarchs will be *delighted*."

Sun frowned at him, displeased he would correct her right now. But Taya didn't mind at all. She was glad he wasn't too afraid to correct her. She smiled at him. "Good, yes. This is very excellent. Everyone will be delighted—Aanuku will be *very* delighted. Thank you very much, Viceroy. This is an excellent gift. Very good you choose this."

Viceroy Modhwadiya bowed, smiling.

Witness Falconer cleared his throat and offered something else: a little crystalline stick thing and a small, flat box. "Another gift. A library of historic human literature. Do you understand *library?* Samuel, if you would be so kind?"

Lieutenant Lockwood explained, "A library is a collection of written and visual media. In this case, literature. Stories."

She didn't know that word, there were too many words for this gift she didn't understand.

He saw that, of course, and thought for a moment. "A story is something like a detailed log of things that happened, told as if someone were there or someone were watching. These are called stories, plural, story, singular. A collection of stories is called a library. This library is mostly history, stories of events that happened in the past; also historical and contemporary—that is, present-day—fiction, stories of events that didn't happen, meant to entertain. Witness Falconer offers this library so that you, your people, can learn about the history of our kind—humankind—about our history and how we used to live and how we live now. Many of these stories were written—made, created—before the Enemy attacked Earth. Witness Falconer also offers a reader in case your technology is too different to read the stories in this library."

Taya listened to all this in growing delight. She realized she was staring at him and looked away, but found herself staring at Witness Falconer instead. She started to take the library stick, touched it with one fingertip, jerked her hand back and folded her hands behind her back. She said, careful of her verbs, "*Please* give this gift to Tsuumat Kaamharaa. To his hand. Beautiful tree is for Aanuku, but this library is for Kaamharaa! He will be very, very delighted with this gift. This is very, very excellent." Unable to contain herself, she bounced on her toes and turned to Tuutka. "This gift is *perfect!* Tsaaku Tuutka, this is many stories, uman stories from the uman homeworld! Aanuku will surely not object if this wonderful gift is given directly to Kaamharaa!"

Tuutka rumbled with pleasure. "We will speak with Kuotaan, but we hardly feel anyone will object. We certainly approve. This is exactly a gift for Tsuumat Kaamharaa: precisely in his area of expertise. Our ally will gain great reputation from this gift, to his benefit and ours."

Taya bounced again and spun back to Witness Falconer. "Yes, give to Kaamharaa! When you give this to him, you should say, *Suurakaau taruuk tsumaa*. This is, ah, this say to him, gift for him, for him to share with all people, for him to gain tsumaa ...

importance. Tsumaa is very good for uturun, very important, uturun not have—do not have matriline, need this kind of importance. Kaamharaa has good tsumaa now, but this give him much more." She would *have* to find out how to say reputation. "He will be very, very delighted by this gift. He will make something like this for you." She would help. She would put in all her favorite romance-adventures written by uman and all her favorite finance-adventures written by nturun.

Witness Falconer smiled. "That's exactly what I'd like most. *Suurakaau taruuk tsumaa*. Is that right?"

It was not exactly right, but Lieutenant Lockwood corrected his pronunciation—he seemed as ready to correct everyone else as he was to correct her, which amused Taya very much. Witness Falconer had particular difficulty with the ts- prefix. Some Uom prefixes, ts- and nk- and tk- and nt- and others like that, were hard for many humans who weren't used to them.

Sun added in a murmur, "*Uturun* means male turun, my lord. The big ones. Don't be misled by their features; it can be a bit hard to tell, but the really big ones are males, all the smaller ones, like these two, are *nturun*—females."

Sun couldn't quite manage the *nt-* prefix at the beginning of the word, but she came close. Taya nodded approval. "Good, yes. Nturun." She exaggerated the sound a little bit. "Yes, nturun are female, like we say uman woman. Human. Uturun are male, like human man. Uturun are only big males. Little young males are a different word. Ehturun. Like little young human males are ehman."

Lieutenant Lockwood started to tell her what the English word was, but Viceroy Modhwadiya smiled at her and spoke before he could. "Boys," he told her. "In English, young male humans are *boys*. In Gujarati, a boy is *chōkarō*. A girl—a young female human—is *chōkarī*."

Taya stared at him, both charmed and dismayed. "Oh! You speak a different language, too? Besides English? Should I learn that also?"

Lieutenant Lockwood made a scornful sound. "Probably take you all of a week."

The corner of Witness Falconer's mouth folded up a little, and Sun grinned. The viceroy said warmly, "If you wish. It isn't necessary, but Gujarati is the most important language of Kaman. My world. A very beautiful world." He smiled at her. "If you become an ambassador for your people, you may indeed wish to learn this beautiful language, which is widely spoken in the Imperial Republic. Perhaps Lieutenant Lockwood will explain what an ambassador is when he has a moment. He would be happy to teach you Gujarati."

Lockwood snorted.

Taya grinned at him, "Lieutenant Lockwood is very good teacher. I mean, *a* very good teacher."

He snorted again, but she decided he was actually amused. "Come," she said to them all, gesturing to show them which door. "I show—I *will* show you where we go. We will go to Tsuumat Kaamharaa's household." She had to say the last word in Uom since she didn't know the English word. She caught Lieutenant Lockwood's eye and added, "Place where family live. Sepu Kaamharaa. Other place for family on Gaatuu. Gaatuu is world. Best world, turun homeworld. I am girl there—*chōkarī.*"

Lieutenant Lockwood said, "House, household, home, residence. Remember your articles, Kha Taya, and your verb tenses."

She corrected herself. "Gaatuu is *the* best world. It is *the* turun homeworld. I *was a girl* there." Then she added, "The big sepu—home—is there. But the small home is here. Tsuumat

Kaamharaa welcomes human guests. Aanuku also welcomes guests. I show everyone."

They were going to Aam first, maybe only to Aam. No doubt there would be lots of meetings and lots of discussions. For days, probably. Lots of days. A Gaatuu month, she wouldn't be surprised. It would be *so* tedious. At least she would have time to practice her English and teach Kaamharaa's guests more Uom.

All the rest of the human ships were going back to their home space. That was very appropriate. At the beginning, it had been *Nkaastu* and *Vengeful*, so now it was right that *Vengeful* would continue on with *Nkaastu* even though all the other ships of the cousins went back to their own heart-stars to explain everything to their own Suund.

As far as Taya could tell, Viceroy Modhwadiya liked everything he saw as they walked from the bay to Kaamharaa's apartment. He liked the beads in the doorways and the murals on the walls and the big mosaic when they cut through the central foyer. The mosaic seemed to Taya to show maybe a tree, maybe a ndao or a lemon tree. That would be very good luck, so she paused to admire the mosaic and point out the shape that could be a tree so they would all see it. Viceroy Modhwadiya was very interested in that.

There were other nturun in the foyer, other uman too, who all paused and turned and looked with great curiosity at *Nkaastu's* guests. The viceroy looked back at them with just as much curiosity and goodwill as he gazed at everything else. One and then another nturun approached to touch his hair or shoulder or arm, friendly little pats that he did not seem to mind, though Taya would have warned the nturun not to do that if she'd thought ahead. Even Sun stepped back from that kind of touch. Lieutenant Lockwood actually stepped between Witness Falconer and the first nturun who looked like she might try to touch him.

"Touching is not polite, we observe," Tuutka decided, and rumbled a curt negative that made everyone who had moved toward their guests move away again.

Witness Falconer had shown no fear at all, but Lieutenant Lockwood relaxed a little, visibly, when every nturun backed up a step or two. Taya wanted to say, *Nturun like to touch, there's nothing impolite about it, you should be friendlier.* But she thought she would ask privately about this. She would ask Sun, who wouldn't be offended by questions about manners. And if she didn't understand Sun's answers, she would ask Lieutenant Lockwood. In fact, she would just ask them both, separately. They were so different, maybe they would think different things, and that could tell her something too.

"Sepu Kaamharaa is this way," she told her companions, gesturing. "Tsaaku Tuutka and Kha Aanhk will leave us here. Not correct nturun go to sepu Kaamharaa." She repeated this in Uom so the nturun would understand the humans knew what she had said, and Tuutka and Aanhk rumbled and bowed. Tuutka said "We assure our guests of our goodwill. They should inform us if they are uncomfortable." She added, "We shall have to consider gifts to return. A ndao is perhaps too obvious."

"A ndao, a library, and something else," said Aanhk, speaking for the first time. "A mosaic. A mosaic would be appropriate."

"Entirely appropriate," Tuutka agreed, rumbling in approval. "An excellent notion. We shall discuss this broadly, but we have no doubt everyone will approve."

It *was* a good idea. If the beloved gods did not already know about the cousins, making them aware would be good for everyone. Taya patted Aanhk's lower shoulder in appreciation and said to the human people, "It is a little far still. We not—do not have those moving ... places where you walk? But it is not *very* far."

"We will all enjoy seeing more of your interesting and beautiful ship, Kha Taya," murmured Viceroy Modhwadiya. He sounded like he meant it.

"Good, Viceroy, I will take you by a beautiful way." She added, "Turun will not say *viceroy*. Even Kaamharaa not say that word. Mouth is not right for some sounds. I think maybe more like *vokerroyeh*. Not very close! Please do not feel offend." She glanced apologetically at Witness Falconer. "*Witness* is also hard. I think more like *Ehtanneh*. The *s* sound is hard for turun when it comes at the end of a word."

"No one could possibly be offended," Witness Falconer said gravely. "We understand the difficulty."

Taya nodded, relieved. Titles were so important to the cousins; she hadn't been sure that would be all right. She was glad she'd had a chance to explain the problem and that everyone was willing to be agreeable.

Viceroy Modhwadiya put in, "I am certain we shall find some mutually acceptable solution. My name is Gopaal Chinmaya Modhwadiya. Perhaps some part of that will be more practically useful."

Taya repeated this carefully. She especially liked the feel of the *dhw* in her mouth. "Gopaal is not hard," she observed. She guessed at how turun would say his full name: "Gopaal Chehnmaya Mohtyaadiya."

"Perfectly acceptable," the viceroy agreed, undisturbed by this pronunciation. "Any part of that or all of it."

Witness Falconer did not say that it would be acceptable for turun to call him by his name. Lieutenant Lockwood said, "We'll work on titles, Taya."

"Yes," she agreed. "Here." She felt a little nervous now that they were so close. "We go this way. This—these—are the places people live, all here and here."

Everyone, even Witness Falconer, looked with interest at the widening corridors with the changing patterns of their murals and of the floor coverings underfoot. After a tenth chime or so, Taya hurried forward so she would be in front of the little group, and touched the outer door to Kaamharaa's quarters, sending in the whistle that would tell him they were here and he should be prepared to welcome his new guests.

Who hopefully would not be too afraid of him. She said to all four of her companions, careful of her verbs, "Tsuumat Kaamharaa comes to greet you. You are our cousins and our allies and our friends, and he is happy you come here. I do not want offend, but I say now fast, all uturun like uman people! No uturun dangerous to human people. Kaamharaa especially like any uman person who give—gives—him library! He is big, but is nothing to fear, yes? Kaamharaa will learn the names of your stars and teach you the names of our stars, until there is between us no foreign sky."

Witness Falconer almost smiled, Taya thought, though Lieutenant Lockwood did not. Sun Grigson looked at Viceroy Modhwadiya. He was the one who answered, with a firm little nod. "That is, I think, exactly what we desire."

Then the door slid open. Kaamharaa himself was right there to greet his guests.

Lieutenant Lockwood took a step back, realized it, and made himself stop with an obvious effort. Witness Falconer only straightened his shoulders, though his eyes widened just perceptibly. Sun blinked, took a slightly ragged breath and stood still.

The viceroy had been looking at Taya. He turned now and looked up at Kaamharaa. And up, and up. His eyes widened. Then he smiled and said, perfectly correct, "Tsuumat Kaamharaa."

"Welcome!" boomed Kaamharaa, flinging all his arms wide in enthusiastic greeting.

But still, though everyone else, even Witness Falconer, flinched, Viceroy Modhwadiya did not. He bowed politely and stepped forward. He was a brave man, Taya decided. She liked him. She was sure Kaamharaa would like him, too. They would all be allies and friends. She was certain of it. Even the people who were frightened at first. They would be friends, and everything would be well.

Endnotes

I'm happy you've read my first (published) foray into science fiction! I hope you enjoyed it. It's something of a departure for me, but perhaps not as much as it may seem. I've spent my share of time designing alien species and alien societies; this is just the first time readers have had a chance to see the result.

I enjoyed the Little Fuzzy stories quite a bit when I was a kid, particularly Ardath Mayhar's *Golden Dreams*, from the Fuzzy point of view. Perhaps it's obvious that those stories were the inspiration for the backstory here, except, of course, in reverse. Here, the failing human colony was human, and the civilization that rescued the descendants of those colonists were ... not.

There's plenty of room in this story-universe to go both forward and backward. I have a fairly clear notion where Captain Gerstner, Kaamharaa, Daamon, and Taya might go next; I have some ideas about the political situations that are going to occur in the Imperial Republic and the Ka' Taand; I have some ideas about who, and what, the uut are and why they are so aggressive. I'm not sure how to solve the problem they represent, but no doubt something useful will occur to me when I write that story.

Or I might back up and tell the prequel story, concerning the turun explorer and his discovery of that lost human colony.

But first I've got various other SF worlds to explore. For a preview of a completely different character, a completely different situation, and a completely different universe, turn the page.

INVICTUS: CAPTIVE

1

Every soldier knew there were endless ways to die. Every Ubez of every line and any description, soldier or not, knew there were far worse fates than death.

Syova stood in a relaxed pose, his hands at his sides, idly calculating odds as he gazed through the transparent hull of his emergency pod toward the Elysian destroyer currently sifting through the distant wreckage of their station and his ship. At the moment, he was inclined to set the odds of death much higher than those of any worse fate. Elysian scanning technology was quite good, so the probability of dying from a pulse burst to the head was probably marginally higher than the probability of dying of radiation poisoning. As emergency pods enjoyed a fair supply of air, both of those possibilities seemed substantially more likely than death from asphyxiation. One never knew exactly how long a pod's air would last, of course, which made the calculation somewhat unreliable. Still, he'd call it roughly point two, point one eight, and point zero six.

A fate worse than death ... he'd probably pegged the probability of that about right, at something close to point zero two. The senior command staff of that Elysian ship out there wouldn't subject an Ubez prisoner to anything worse than an ordinary interrogation followed by a brisk execution, no matter how suspicious his presence in this vicinity. He knew every dossier of every senior officer on that ship forward and backward, and he was thoroughly confident in that judgment.

Unfortunately, the probability that they would turn him over to Elysian Admiralty was more difficult to calculate. If that happened, the odds of a fate worse than death would go sharply upward.

The more urgent question right now was whether the burst of radiation that had masked his pod's signal from his own people would fade quickly enough that the Elysian ship would pick it up. If they did, they would certainly collect him. They would undoubtedly want to know *all about* the incident that had left their station derelict and drifting, scattering all this debris through a broad region of space practically next door to the new Karesheshavin slipway.

Syova was perfectly willing to tell them absolutely everything he knew about it, which ought to make any reasonably competent interrogation survivable. He put high odds on better than reasonable competence. If the Elys in that ship killed him, it wouldn't be by accident.

He studied the slow course of the Elys ship. Impossible to tell yet whether they'd picked up his signal. In astronomical terms, that ship was close enough to touch. In absolute terms, it was much too far away for them to pick him up visually despite the flashwork on the outside of his pod's hull. If the radiation masking his pod's signal hadn't faded enough, then eventually they'd decide they'd seen enough and off they'd go. That would narrow his choices to either radiation poisoning or suffocation. Unless he tired of waiting and cracked the pod. He wasn't yet prepared to calculate odds for that.

Nothing to do but wait. Wait, and try to decide whether the Elys ship might have turned a little, might have begun an approach. He had been watching that ship for ... he checked the time, one of the few link functions available given the severely truncated linkspace available within an emergency pod. Three hours, forty-three minutes and nine seconds. The probability the Elysians would continue to poke through the debris of their destroyed station for as much as another hour, oh, call it point three or so. If they didn't pick up his signal before that, well. They'd have things to do, places to go. Once they decided there were no survivors, they'd drop a signal packet and a buoy and off they'd ... that ship *was* turning. Syova realized he was holding his breath and deliberately began to breathe, slowly and deeply, getting the unhelpful surge of adrenalin under control. This was not a fight-or-flight situation. Definitely not. He already knew how he wanted to play this, and neither of those were options.

For the next nineteen minutes, Syova watched the Elysian ship turn from a slowly moving occultation against the backdrop of stars into an enormous, powerful, Empire-class destroyer. Blocky letters blazed white across the nearly unrelieved black of the hull, unreadable from this angle, but he didn't need to read those letters to know that ship's name. His pod had picked up her signature hours ago. Every Ubezhishche soldier knew this ship—certainly every S line soldier of his modification. *Invictus*.

Syova had hardly been able to believe the sheer luck of that happenstance when he'd realized. Though, yes, *Invictus* was a perfectly reasonable choice to task with exploring beyond the Karesheshavin slipway. Even so.

He was holding his breath again. He exhaled, deliberately, and began a meditation exercise to get his heart rate under control.

The ship certainly *loomed* when she finally slid past his emergency pod. And past, and past, and yes, there was the bay lock, open and glowing with light. Syova's pod began to move toward that lock. He had felt nothing, no jolt at all: someone had a very neat hand with the tractors. Here was the edge of the lock. And in, with a praiseworthy transition from his pod's internal gravity to that of *Invictus*: the changeover had been almost imperceptible. The slightest thump as his pod settled to the floor of the bay, and Syova found himself looking through the transparent hull directly into the face of the tactical officer of *Invictus*, Commander Chatham, whom Syova immediately recognized from his dossier images.

Of course it would be the tactical officer. The captain herself would hardly concern herself with the interrogation of an Ubez survivor of ... whatever had happened here. They wouldn't have any idea. But they would certainly be inclined to blame him for it. Interrogation might change that. Or maybe not, hard to say.

The commander was, Syova saw, a smaller man than he had seemed in images; small even for an Elys. Probably a good thirty-five or forty centimeters shorter and at least sixty or seventy kilos lighter than Syova. But he certainly didn't seem in the least intimidated. Nor should he. Fifty-six years old; tactical officer on one ship or another for twenty-nine of those years, Captain Ila's tactical officer for twelve; experienced, intelligent, accomplished. Chatham didn't have either the connections or the political reliability score necessary for promotion to independent command. That did not make him any less formidable. Nevertheless, Syova immediately felt more comfortable just for the sense of familiarity the recognition gave him.

Commander Chatham was supported by eight marines: a full team. Unlike the commander, the marines were armored up and looking at Syova through the sights of their weapons. Clearly, Chatham was starting off with the assumption that Syova's people were to blame for whatever had happened. Syova had known that would be the assumption. Of course it would.

Elys marines were tough enough, in their own way. Dedicated, generally. Courageous, almost always. Obviously not physically a match for an Ubez soldier, but if Syova seemed even remotely aggressive when this pod opened, eight marines could certainly put him down. He might be able to kill Chatham before he died, possibly some of the marines, but they could do it, no question.

That calculation was automatic, but not relevant. Fighting—offering any resistance at all—would be utterly pointless. He met Chatham's level gaze. Then he held up his hands, shoulder-high, palms turned forward, and dropped to his knees. Only then did he trigger the pod to open. He held perfectly still as the layers of transparent composite unsealed and folded back.

The commander's eyes had widened just perceptibly. Ubezhishche never knelt to Elysians. Never. But the gesture was reasonably safe for an Ubez of Syova's line and modification, and it had certainly made the commander stop and reassess, exactly as Syova had intended. After about half a second, Chatham gave Syova a little nod, acknowledging his surrender. "Lie face down," he ordered. His tenor voice was quiet. "Hands behind your head. Lace your fingers. Cross your ankles. Are you armed? Other than the standard arsenal."

Syova complied with every order immediately. "I have no weapons except those inbuilt," he answered. Obey every command, answer every question. Complete cooperation. That was the only reasonable strategy now.

One marine approached and moved Syova's hands behind his back, cuffed him, and locked the cuffs together with his forearms tightly overlapped from wrist to elbow. His bad shoulder felt the strain immediately. Syova had expected that. He relaxed, accepting the discomfort, setting it aside.

After the wrist cuffs, the marine pulled off each of Syova's boots in turn and closed cuffs on his ankles, setting those to act as hobbles. At that point, every Elys marine abruptly shifted from a possible target to nearly unassailable. Syova knew of exactly one Ubez soldier who might have managed to take out some number of Elysian marines, maybe the whole team, even from this bad a position. He was not that soldier.

Deep, smooth breaths. Calm. Accept everything. Protest nothing. No tension. No resistance.

The marine searched him with professional thoroughness. "Clean, sir, as far as I can tell," the marine reported at last. "Except for the usual arsenal, as you say, and I think we've got that pretty well locked down."

"Any unexpected new designs?" Commander Chatham asked Syova. "Darts under your tongue? A bomb in your belly?"

"No, Commander," Syova answered, not looking up. Not moving at all. Uncomfortable not to be able to see Chatham, read his responses; keep an eye on the marines and *their* responses. But he stayed exactly where he was, face against the decking, completely still.

"We'll do a full scan."

"Yes, Commander. You'll find nothing. I am not a combatant. This was not a military action. At least, not from *our* point of view."

Chatham didn't ask any of the obvious questions. He asked instead, "Radiation exposure?"

Syova tried not to react visibly, but he was deeply relieved. If the Elys had intended to put him to death immediately following interrogation, Chatham probably would not have bothered asking that question. "Approximately five hundred thirty rem, Commander."

"You Ubez can last quite a while with that kind of dose. You're S line, obviously. Three days, four? More than that?"

Ah. That question was much less reassuring. Syova answered, "S line third modification. The damage will be irreversibly lethal after approximately one hundred thirty hours, but it will be seriously debilitating much earlier. I took the primary burst of radiation twenty-seven hours ago. I will probably be too weakened to permit useful interrogation after another twenty-four to thirty-six hours."

"Understood. On your feet."

Syova flexed his back and legs, came smoothly to his feet, then answered the commander's ironic gesture of invitation and moved forward. The hobbles had been set for an extremely restrictive range of motion—about twenty centimeters. That was awkward. Syova let tension and impatience flow away, accepted the restriction as a meditative exercise, and considered, in the back of his mind, the sort of move he might use, even bound as he was, to take out ... probably no more than one marine, before the others shot him to pieces. Ridiculously pointless. The calculation was automatic despite its uselessness.

They took him to Medical. This was a cold, stark place, all bright lights and shining steel. Elysians treated Medical as an adjunct of science, and they thought science cold and hard. Syova much preferred the reassuring warmth his own people considered appropriate for medical facilities.

Scans first, right down to the component atoms, probably. The main scanner was above a wide, slightly raised dais. Syova stood in the center of the dais, concentrating on projecting complete harmlessness. That wasn't easy for an S line Ubez, who could not be disarmed without being dismembered. Pulse weapons in his forearms, dartcaster built into his left hand, microfilament blade into his right. That was all standard. No miniature dartcaster under the tongue: that was an assassin's modification, not a soldier's, regardless of what the serials showed. No bomb in the belly: that was for operatives at the highest level; anyone whose final duty in case of capture was to avoid interrogation.

Other weapons might have been built into his clothing. Nothing was, as their scans must have shown, but they cut every stitch off him anyway—a reasonable precaution given the situation. They would quite reasonably suspect new developments in miniaturized and disguised weaponry. Syova stood perfectly still, not wishing to risk any slip of the microfilament scalpel.

Then they gave him a large orange pill. The pill was extremely welcome, implying that the Elys did after all intend for him to survive long enough that the radiation poisoning might become inconvenient for them. The medical officer in charge, an older man with a calmly interested manner, put the pill in Syova's mouth himself and then, to his surprise, held a cup of water for him. After swallowing the pill, Syova met the man's eyes and departed from his policy of strategic silence far enough to say, "Thank you, Doctor."

The medical officer raised his eyebrows, nodded and said, "We do take an oath, you know, young man. Ubezhishche aren't specifically excluded." He added, speaking to Commander Chatham, "Five more doses, one every twelve hours. That could be overkill for an Ubez, but on the other hand I don't want him collapsing in two weeks because oops, not enough healthy bone marrow left to fill a teaspoon. I'd like to see him again in ten days or so if that's practical."

The commander didn't offer an opinion on whether Syova might still be alive in ten days. He merely told Syova, "This way."

An annex of the main Medical facility: small, private, secure. Blank consoles, narrow counters. Several chairs. One was plain metal, heavy, bolted to the decking. At Chatham's gesture, Syova lowered himself into that chair. The metal was cold against his bare skin. His cuffs locked to the chair, and that was that. The marines filed out, and no wonder. Naked, cuffed, and locked down tight, Syova was completely helpless. He was not going to be able to offer the slightest resistance to anything the Elys did.

They had given him an anti-radiation pill. Syova fixed his mind on that. With his arms still locked behind his back, it was difficult to sit up straight. He made the necessary effort, though it put additional strain on his bad shoulder. Dismissing the discomfort from his attention, he began to take deep, slow breaths, deliberately bringing down his heart rate. *Accept everything. Endure anything.*

He made sure his tone was calm and level. "I'll willingly answer any questions you ask, Commander. You don't need to use drugs, but if you choose to do so, Verity is safest, especially in combination with atropine. MemStim will immediately trigger my interrogation block even if you don't ask a single question. Disinhibit is not as certainly lethal, but is generally more dangerous for my modification than Verity."

Commander Chatham didn't sit down. He leaned a hip against the edge of the nearest counter, his arms folded over his chest, regarding Syova with close attention. "You're willing to volunteer that information?"

"I'd like to survive this interrogation. You obviously believe that my people deliberately destroyed your station and that I'm a hostile combatant. That's reasonable given everything you've seen so far, but your suspicions, though justifiable, are mistaken. I'm a specialist assigned to an exploratory task force. I'm quite willing to answer any questions you may have. There's nothing I have a duty to reserve."

This was true. Syova didn't want to share certain personal details, but this interrogation shouldn't move in that direction—and if it did, personal information shouldn't trigger the inbuilt block. Probably. Verity was survivable, as a rule. Calm was important. Slow breaths. Settle the nerves. He could do this. He could absolutely do this. He had nothing to hide. Nothing that mattered to anyone but him. There was *definitely not the slightest need* for the resistance to trigger. He absolutely believed that. Conviction on that point was extremely helpful for an S line Ubez facing drug-assisted interrogation.

Chatham turned his head as the doctor came in. "Dr. Hale?"

"Yep, Verity's always my first choice for S line," the doctor said, his tone bland. "Atropine's not a bad suggestion either." He shook out the blanket he was carrying and draped it over Syova, tucking it behind his shoulders to keep it in place. "Chilly in here," he added in response to the commander's raised eyebrow. "There, young man, how's that?"

"Much better," Syova answered truthfully. "Thank you, Doctor. That's very kind of you."

An easy nod, and Dr. Hale said to Chatham, "Not that Verity's exactly safe. Safe-ish, let's say. One never quite knows what might trigger cardiac events in these sorts of situations. That's what makes drug-assisted interrogation so exciting for us all. As a favor to me, please try just asking nicely to start with, Commander."

Commander Chatham gave the doctor a look.

"Fine, whatever. I can probably keep the reaction from being fatal. At first, anyway. It'd be better to avoid letting him arrest a whole bunch of times in quick succession. Three or four's about your limit?" the doctor added, speaking to Syova. "When you're not suffering from radiation poisoning?"

"Yes, Doctor, that's most likely correct. I've never tested the limit personally."

"Ideally you won't test it today either. I'm sure the commander'll try to avoid pushing you that far. You're all right," Dr. Hale added, laying a hand on Syova's shoulder, a firm, friendly pressure. "You're going to be fine. I'm going to take care of you. Relax."

Syova hadn't realized the doctor's air of friendly authority felt familiar until that moment. Hale must have worked with plenty of Ubez before; he had clearly learned how to trigger important trust responses. Syova was more than willing to allow himself to respond. He needed to be as relaxed as possible; if the Elys decided they couldn't question him, the odds of a quick execution would go way, way up.

Not a good thought. He needed to *relax*. He breathed out, let the tension go, drew in a slow, deep breath. Nothing to hide.

Nothing to hold back. No duty required silence. That was absolutely true.

***

Or, you know, maybe it's not *absolutely* true. Preorder the Invictus duology and find out!

Invictus: Captive, forthcoming September 2023

Invictus: Crisis, forthcoming October 2023

Other Works by Rachel Neumeier

Urban Fantasy:

The Black Dog Series

BLACK DOG
BLACK DOG SHORT STORIES I
PURE MAGIC
BLACK DOG SHORT STORIES II
BLACK DOG SHORT STORIES I & II (Collection)
SHADOW TWIN
BLACK DOG SHORT STORIES III
COPPER MOUNTAIN
BLACK DOG SHORT STORIES IV
BLACK DOG SHORT STORIES III & IV (Collection)
SILVER CIRCLE (forthcoming)

High Fantasy

THE CITY IN THE LAKE
THE KEEPER OF THE MIST
THE WHITE ROAD OF THE MOON
THE MOUNTAIN OF KEPT MEMORY
WINTER OF ICE AND IRON

The Floating Islands duology

THE FLOATING ISLANDS
THE SPHERE OF THE WINDS

The Griffin Mage trilogy:

LORD OF THE CHANGING WINDS
LAND OF THE BURNING SANDS
LAW OF THE BROKEN EARTH

The House of Shadows duology

HOUSE OF SHADOWS
DOOR INTO LIGHT

The Death's Lady series

THE YEAR'S MIDNIGHT
OF ABSENSE, DARKNESS
AS SHADOW, A LIGHT
SHINES NOW, AND HERETOFORE

The Tuyo series

TUYO
NIKOLES
TARASHANA
KERAUNANI
SUELEN
TANO
TASMAKAT
TUYO World Companion (forthcoming)

Adult SF
NO FOREIGN SKY

The Invictus duology

INVICTUS: CAPTIVE (forthcoming)
INVICTUS: CRISIS (forthcoming)

Collections
BEYOND THE DREAMS WE KNOW

www.ingramcontent.com/pod-product-compliance
Lightning Source LLC
LaVergne TN
LVHW090557191125
825958LV00011B/27
* 9 7 9 8 2 2 4 1 4 0 1 6 9 *